SHELTER ME

BY JULIETTE FAY

Shelter Me

SHELTER ME

JULIETTE FAY

AVON

An Imprint of HarperCollins*Publishers*

SHELTER ME. Copyright © 2009 by Juliette Fay. All rights reserved. Printed in the United States of America. No part of this book may be used or reproduced in any manner whatsoever without written permission except in the case of brief quotations embodied in critical articles and reviews. For information address HarperCollins Publishers, 10 East 53rd Street, New York, NY 10022.

FIRST AVON PAPERBACK EDITION PUBLISHED 2009.

Designed by Justin Dodd

ISBN-13: 978-1-60751-733-7

For Tom, with great love

ACKNOWLEDGMENTS

THREE WOMEN HELPED ME grow this novel from its seedling days, reading it as I wrote it and handed it to them in chunks that sometimes ended mid-scene. Alison Bullock, a talented author, taught me many things, including that if I am going to break the rules, I should know what the rules are. Her collegial generosity was boundless. Megan Lucier put up with me taking more than my share of airtime to discuss this book during our weekly walks. Her edits often ended with highly motivating remarks such as, "GIVE ME MORE, NOW!" Catherine Toro-McCue, who has known me the longest, was the most surprised at the odd and sometimes bizarre inner workings of my imagination. She also came up with the most interesting questions.

Emi Battaglia, Ruth Sullivan and Liz Welch offered good advice and were generous with their contacts, even without knowing me well. Their willingness to give an unknown novice a leg up was very encouraging. Dan Greenwood, a contractor friend, gave me a tutorial on porch building. All factual details are to his credit; anything that sounds like faulty construction is my mistake. Amanda Demersky was my respiratory therapist reference and gave me excellent words like "tachypneic" to work with.

Jih-ho Donovan put me in touch with her sister, Mih-ho Cha, who gave me some very fortuitous advice in sending me to Theresa Park of the Park Literary Group. I think of Theresa not only as my Fairy God-Agent, but now also as a friend. No new author could ask for a better guide through the strange wonderland of the publishing industry.

Executive Editor Lucia Macro has been wonderful to work with. Enthusiastic and responsive, she was spectacular at figuring out what was missing. It's a better story thanks to her.

My father, John Dacey, a prolific nonfiction writer, read the finished product and gave it the thumbs-up, as did my friend Anne Kuppinger. Anne and my brother-in-law Paul Allen became delightfully, almost compulsively, involved in trying to come up with a good title for this story. Paul sang me songs over the cell phone on occasion.

Kristen and Keiji Iwai, my sister and brother-in-law, gave me the benefit of their vast professional knowledge by coaching me on photographic suggestions for the book cover.

I also received invaluable help with publicity, not to mention rock-solid confidence in my eventual success, from my great friend Julia Tanen.

My children, Brianna, Liam, Nicholas and Quinn, received somewhat less than all of my attention and mental energy during the writing of this book. Nevertheless, they were wonderfully enthusiastic about it. Their interest and pride in my line of work is an unexpected bonus, and highly motivating (especially that dreaded question, "What page are you on?").

Tom Fay, a man of great honor and kindness, has nonetheless harassed me mercilessly to write something—anything—throughout our eighteen years of marriage. It is to him, to his faith in me, and to his willingness to take the kids to Chuck E. Cheese whenever I needed a few extra hours, that this book is lovingly dedicated.

SHELTER ME

1

TUESDAY, APRIL 24

Today wasn't so bad. Carly seems to have made friends with the bottle finally. When my milk stopped she went on a hunger strike, pushed formula away like it was vinegar. Then she'd only take it from Aunt Jude, of all people. Never thought I'd be so happy to see her on a daily basis. But now even I'm allowed to feed her. Time marches on, I guess.

This isn't working.

Father Jake is now officially in the deep end without a life-guard.

THURSDAY, APRIL 26

Dylan's pretending to play Monopoly. He just likes rolling the dice. I'm not allowed to play because I ruin it; he says he can't think what rules he wants to have when I'm watching. I know how he feels. I can't think what rules I want to have when I'm around, either.

Not sure why I'm trying this again. (See, Aunt Jude? Occasionally I do try.) Options seem to be dwindling since I jumped ship on the grief group she found on the Internet, Googling her way to my happiness. But, please, it was worse than bad. That facilitator was so annoying. Her lipstick was orange, her shoes were pointy, and she looked like an upscale elf. That constant sympathetic nod she did made me want to throw my drippy tissue wads at her. Add six or eight people wailing in self-pity, and you might as well crack open the Chex Mix, because hey— it's a party!

I might tell Father Jake not to come anymore. Pretty much a waste of time, though I suppose it's good cover. After the grief group didn't work out, I figured Aunt Jude was planning an intervention. But all I got were visits from the boy priest, Father Listener.

He's the one who came up with this journaling idea, which is gimmicky and hideously '70s. (What's his next idea—a mood ring and a shag haircut?) If he had handed me one of those cheesy blank books with teacups or inspirational sayings on it, I would have dug out Robby's blowtorch and lit it up on the hood of that boring gray sedan Father drives.

Actually I would have just given it to Dylan with a box of Magic Markers. "Grief" makes you sound so melodramatic.

JANIE CLOSED THE 89-CENT black-and-white-speckled composition notebook. It reminded her of one she'd had in third grade for the purpose of practicing her cursive writing. She would sit at Aunt Jude's kitchen table after school, gripping the pen as if it might get away from her and do some certain but unspecified damage. All those loops and slanty lines. So messy and complicated compared to the clear clean strokes of the printing she had been used to.

The doorbell rang, jolting Janie from her memory. She tucked the notebook in the cabinet above the refrigerator and forced herself to face the intrusion, hoping it wasn't another pity offering of quiche or lasagna or baked fucking ham. Friends and neighbors had stopped coming by, sensing, she knew, that their company was all but unbearable to her. It was just too hard to answer that stupid question over and over. "How are you?" She could barely keep herself from saying, *Still shitty, thanks for asking. Care for some ham? God knows I can't eat it.*

The man who now stood at the door carried nothing but a smudged manila folder. He scratched his fingers through the caramel-colored hair over a recently healed scar on his forearm. "Hi," he said, squinting into the room's relative dimness, the faint lines around his eyes clustering against each other. "Rob around?"

"No," said Janie.

"Uh, well, can you give him this?" He held out the folder. "I told him I couldn't start 'til summer, but then another job got postponed, so I'll start here next week. Permit's already pulled." He checked his watch, the crystal so scratched it must have been hard for him to see the face. "I'll pick those up tomorrow. If he wants to call me, the number's there."

The man waited for a response, which was not forthcoming. Janie stared back at him for a second, then glanced away. "Okay," he said, his lips flattening into a confused smile. He walked quickly to his truck. When he opened the driver's side door, Jane saw "Malinowski Custom Design, Inc." written in curling maroon script on the door panel. "Pelham, Mass." was in smaller type below it.

He's from here, she thought. Not that it mattered.

"Who was that?" Dylan asked, the little metal Monopoly dog bounding around the board.

"Some guy," said Janie, and tossed the manila folder on the stairs.

THURSDAY NIGHT

It's my screened porch. Maybe a birthday present? Where on earth did he get the money—already paid for half of it. Already signed a contract with that Malinucci guy. He said he didn't need a new car, even though the Subaru was twelve years old. Said he'd ask for a raise at the bank if I wanted to hold off going back to work at the hospital. Robby, goddammit. I don't want the stupid porch now.

SHELLY MICHELMAN BANGED ON the front door, opened it a face-width, and yelled "Hey!"

"It's open," Janie called from the back of the house. This was not very far. It was a small house, a Cape, the modern version of a Colonial style that had been built with zeal throughout the Boston suburbs in the 1930s and '40s. The front door opened directly into the living room. To the right was the kitchen, just big enough to hold a round butcher-block table and four chairs. The painted white cabinets, and counters devoid of all but the most necessary small appliances, kept it from feeling claustrophobic. A staircase divided the living room from the kitchen and led up to two bedrooms on the second floor, their ceilings slanting down toward eaves on the front and back of the house. Janie was in the tiny office behind the living room rummaging through bank statements.

"I know it's open," said Shelly, her heels clicking authoritatively on the muddy green manufactured tiles. "I opened it. What are you up to? What's that? Good God, this room's a mess."

Janie found Shelly's relentlessness exhausting, but Janie found most people exhausting these days. "I don't even know," she said.

"*Pfff,*" said Shelly with a flick of her hand. "For a man who worked at a bank, you'd think he'd have kept his files better. Look at this, these dates are all mixed up. What are you in here for, anyway?"

"This guy came by yesterday . . . Malineski or something. I guess Robby hired him to build a screened porch on the front of the house."

"*Ohhhhh,*" said Shelly, uncharacteristically still for a moment. "Tug."

"Pardon me?" Janie said, irritated.

"The builder. He did my renovation, remember? Very clean. You never have to clean up after him. Well, you know you have to vacuum all the time when you're under construction, but other

than that, I mean. No little slivers of wood or bent nails. No cigarette butts under your rhododendrons. You cannot *believe* what
builders will do to your landscaping."

"Shelly . . ." Janie wondered how it was that this woman, the
next-door neighbor with whom she had managed a strictly wave-
from-the-driveway relationship for the better part of six years,
was suddenly in her house all the time now, issuing orders like
the commander of a ship taking on water.

Shelly tapped the back of her index finger delicately under her
nose. "Robby asked me for his number last fall. I think it was supposed to be a surprise."

Janie felt the familiar tingling in her gums and the tightening
of her throat. "You think maybe this was something you could
have mentioned?" Janie told herself to calm down, take a breath.
But that never worked these days. "You know, now that he's
DEAD?"

Shelly gave her a mildly apologetic nod. "I definitely would
have, bub. You know, if I hadn't been distracted with coordinating all those meals people were bringing and driving Dylan to
preschool and all."

Janie's laugh served to help her exhale. "God, you're such a
bitch."

"Don't I know it," said Shelly. She leaned closer and bared her
teeth. "Spinach for breakfast. Any stragglers?" Janie inspected
the big too-white teeth and shook her head.

"I have two houses to show, Pelham Heights," Shelly said. Pelham Heights was a wealthy neighborhood on the north side of
town. "Then I'm back to deal with this disaster. Just get the bank
statements in order. That's chronological, not alphabetical or as-
trological, or however the hell they're organized now." She tapped
her mochaccino-colored plastic nails on the only clear spot on the
desk. "Get them all straightened out and put them in a pile right
here. Then have a cup of coffee and take the baby out in the backyard. It's a beautiful day, for godsake."

Janie stared at the pile of bank statements. *Goddamn him*, she thought, as her eyes began to ache.

Shelly patted Janie's disheveled black curls with her perfectly manicured hand. "Have the coffee first," she said. Then she clacked back through the living room and slammed the front door.

Friday, April 27

It's sunny. She loves that old airplane swing of Dylan's. The soft brim of her hat flaps up and down as she goes back and forth. She laughs and laughs.

Wish I could.

At eleven o'clock, Janie heard the unimpressive hum of Father Jake's car in the driveway, the careful latching of the car door, the muted squeak of what she knew were rubber-soled black shoes coming up the asphalt. Those shoes. So him. Not sneakers, no, that would be too casual, almost disrespectful. But they weren't the standard-issue black leather shoes the previous pastor had worn. They were youthful, yet somber. So him.

Janie made sure to be at the door before he gave two light raps with the front of his knuckles, a sound that made her want to open the door just to slam it at him. Not one, not three, always two infuriating raps.

"Hi," he said, as if the way she whipped the door open and declined to look at him was how all parishioners greeted him. She strode toward the kitchen, and he followed. "Baby asleep?" he asked.

No, she's out weed whacking the yard, she thought. *She's always asleep when you come, and you always ask me the same dumb question.* "It's her naptime," Janie replied, running water into the teakettle and landing it hard on a stove burner. She put an empty mug before him as he sat at the kitchen table.

"Thanks," he said, and pulled a small packet out of his pants pocket. Black jeans, not slacks. Janie pinched the back of her hand under the table to keep from rolling her eyes. Out of the packet came a teabag, a further expression, Janie sneered inwardly, of his utter lack of impact. When he left, there was no indication that he'd ever been there. You weren't even short a teabag.

He stayed for an hour. At noon, as he always did on Fridays, he rose from the round butcher-block kitchen table that Robby had assembled from a kit, placed the dead teabag in the trash, and put the mug in the sink. By the time his somber black sport shoes were squeaking back down the driveway, Janie could not remember one detail of their conversation. Not that she tried.

A LITTLE PAST NOON, Shelly returned peeling a grapefruit, its pale yellow skin a perfect match for the brighter streaks in Shelly's short, perky hairdo. Strangely, it also matched the silk shell she wore under the tailored beige suit. Was this purposeful? Knowing Shelly, as Janie had come to do in the three and a half months since Robby's death, it was a definite possibility. The woman's attention to detail was maddening.

After they'd pinpointed the payment Robby had made to the builder and determined that Janie could, in fact, afford the porch, Shelly announced, "I'm going out to Amherst tonight."

"When will you be back?" asked Janie, hating the faint tremor of panic that rippled through her.

"Sunday. Pammy's got a play."

"She's in a play?"

"No, she's on the sound crew. I'll be sitting in the audience watching *other* people's children perform a play called *Beth and Dawn and the Metaphysicality of Cheese*." Shelly flicked the underside of her nose and shook her head. "As you know, I wouldn't eat cheese to secure peace in the Middle East. I think the last time I had cheese I was wearing a training bra. What a stupid invention. Like boobs need training. Like they would act up if you didn't teach them to behave. Anyway, I'll be having a cocktail or three before the curtain goes up."

Janie had to smile despite herself. "Are you staying with her?"

"In the dorm? Are you insane? Do you have any idea what those dorms smell like? No, the minute Pammy got accepted to college I dug up an adorable little bed and breakfast. Arts and Crafts style, set back from the street, exposed wood beams. Very quaint, very Berkshires, but without the . . . you know . . . nature."

AT 12:52, JANIE STOOD outside Dylan's preschool classroom holding Carly, who was chewing noisily on a pink pacifier. The previous week Janie had taken her for a long-overdue checkup at the pediatrician's office. It was one of those group practices where you might get your actual pediatrician, the one you chose with such anxious care when you were still pregnant and naive. Or you might not. You might get the one who was just a little rough when putting your baby on the scale. Or the one who was not nearly as funny and endearing as he thought he was. *Or,* thought Janie, *you might sit in the waiting room with six or seven other mother-child pairs, in various states of impatience and snot coverage, while Dr. Whoever-Is-Next-on-the-List lights up a cigarette and checks the personal ads.*

Janie had not been late to pick Dylan up the day of the doctor visit, mainly because she had driven like a teenaged boy exiting a high school parking lot on a Friday afternoon. But she was the second-to-last mother to arrive at his classroom door, by which time he was clutching his teacher's hand and chewing madly on the dangling strap of his backpack. He lunged toward Janie, forgetting to release the viselike grip on his teacher, yanking her forward so that she banged her shin on the sand table.

Today Janie was first in line, as she had been every day except Tuesday, when she was third. On Tuesday, Dylan had said, "Why are you late? Did you go to the doctor again?"

"I'm not late, Dylan. I'm just not first," she'd told him. "Third has to be okay, too. Even last has to be okay every once in a while." *I'm doing the best I can,* she wanted to say. *That I get here at all is a minor miracle some days*. She wanted to remind him that Shelly and Aunt Jude had been taking him to and from preschool until fairly recently. Even her cousin Cormac had left the bakery to swing him home a couple of times. She wanted him to be impressed with third and ecstatic about first. He had merely chewed his backpack strap and asked if they had any marshmallows at home. Which they did not.

Today, Friday, Janie was first again. She stood quietly while the mothers behind her chatted and exchanged things: tips on good roller-skate sales, recently released G-rated movies, cruise vacations. Borrowed baby clothes, forgotten lunch boxes, money for group teacher gifts. News about the upcoming tax hike, candidates for school committee, another unsolved burglary in the neighboring town of Natick. There was a whole Mommy Marketplace happening in the hallway, and if Janie were first in line, it was not considered rude to have her back turned to it. Or not that rude, anyway.

". . . That's nothing!" she heard a woman behind her say. "Barry loaded them into the car on Saturday. Brought not one blessed thing—not so much as a baby wipe. He's always complaining that it takes me too long to round up all that stuff they don't really need."

The other mothers murmured their solidarity, "Mmmhmm . . . Oh, yeah . . . Been there . . ."

"They get back a few hours later," the mother of Barry's children continued. "They're sunburned, covered in bug bites, the two-year-old has a massive load leaking out of his diaper, the five-year-old has dried blood on his leg from scraping his knee, and lunch was a half-eaten bag of barbecued potato chips they found on a park bench."

There was a short burst of laughter, which was then oddly curtailed, as if the humor had gone out of it suddenly. *They're looking at me,* thought Janie. The pity was palpable. Moments of silence followed. *I am the joy killer. My life is a cautionary tale.*

When the classroom door opened and Dylan came out, he needed to rummage around in his cubby for what seemed like decades. This gave a mother, whose name Janie no longer knew, a chance to approach. She was wearing tight black biking shorts and a neon orange polyester tank top. Her knife-straight blond hair evidenced a slight dampness around the bangs, but she wasn't actually sweaty. Her figure was gallingly perfect, no remnant puckers across her midsection, where babies had once rolled and punched from the inside; no breasts drooping from months of expansion and contraction as they ballooned up with milk, only to be sucked flat on an almost hourly basis.

"Would Dylan like to come over and play with Keane today?" Biking Mommy ventured. "Or, maybe if today isn't good, some time next week? Or, you know, any time you need a break . . . ?"

"Uhh," said Janie, briefly wondering whether Keane was a boy or a girl. Dylan's arms slipped around one of her thighs as he hid behind her, pressing his nose into the small of her back. "We're hanging close to home these days. But thanks."

"Okay, well, whenever he's ready," said Biking Mommy, inching backward toward the safety of her own child's cubby.

And your little dog, too, thought Janie.

AT 1:30, DYLAN LIKED to watch *Clifford the Big Red Dog* on PBS. *What a world, that Birdwell Island,* thought Janie, as the theme song rang out from the living room. There was "diversity" but no real cultural tension. There was one not-too-nice girl and her not-too-nice dog, but she always came around in the end. Everyone was, in a word, happy.

"I can't play right now, guys," said John Ritter, the voice of Clifford. "Emily Elizabeth told me not to get dirty before the party."

Janie couldn't watch *Clifford.* John Ritter's voice was one of the many things that was guaranteed to make her sob. John Ritter had died unexpectedly several years before, in his mid-fifties. He'd had a heart attack on his daughter's fifth birthday. These were facts, and Janie had known them before Robby's death, when they had seemed distantly sad. Now they seemed emblematic of her life. Life in the real world, not terminally happy Birdwell Island. Janie lived in fear of the day that Dylan found out Clifford was actually a dead guy like his dad.

When the doorbell rang, Janie was sitting on the back of the toilet tank in the dark with a hand towel over her face to keep tears from dripping onto her T-shirt and betraying her to Dylan. Or whoever. She knew that Dylan would not open the front door. He would continue to sit six feet away from the small TV in the corner of the living room, legs crisscrossed in front of him, head tilted back, mouth slightly open. He wouldn't even hear the damned doorbell.

Possibly it was Aunt Jude, Janie's mother's only sister. Unmarried, retired, and childless, Aunt Jude had found a way to absorb, unbidden, whatever part of motherhood Janie's own mother seemed to neglect. Where Mum was quiet and, at times, distant, Aunt Jude was never at a loss for words. Or syrup of ipecac.

If it were Aunt Jude at the door, Janie knew she would ring a second time, and a third. Then she might very well assume that Janie had fallen into a diabetic coma (though she was not diabetic) and the children had drunk bleach, and Aunt Jude would have to heft her sizable bottom through a window and force-feed them all syrup of ipecac to induce vomiting. She carried ipecac in her white vinyl purse at all times. It was her antidote of choice, suitable for any occasion.

Janie ran one end of the hand towel under cold water and pressed it against her eyes and cheeks; with the dry end, she patted her face. She tossed it into the hamper and stepped into the lighted hallway.

"Door," droned Dylan, eyes still captive to the screen.

It was the contractor, wanting to know if Robby had gone over the papers. Dylan blinked and shifted his gaze to his mother.

"They look fine," said Janie, glancing at Dylan. If he hadn't been sitting there, having broken free of his Clifford-induced trance, Janie would have been able to continue with her "Robby's not here" tactic. It was not a lie. In fact, nothing could be truer. He was completely not there. This she knew to the core of her being, every minute of the day, in every possible way that mattered. Robby, who was so very much there for so many years, no longer was.

But Dylan did not understand the utter verity of this simple fact. Even a very mature four-year-old would be confused about the permanence of death, the book had said. Janie had only read a few pages, but she had retained that one thing: kids don't really get it. They have to talk about it—Janie tried but found it excruciating—and they have to see for themselves that it really is true over time. Her instinct was to shelter his boy-sized heart from the enormity of this loss. But evidently her instincts were wrong. For this one reason, and for the fact that Janie was sure she was failing Dylan in so many other important ways, she made herself say it out loud.

"My husband died in January, but I checked the papers myself, and everything seems in order." Actually it was Shelly who had reviewed the contract; Janie had merely stared at the plans until the lines blurred before her eyes. Knowing that Robby had dreamed up this porch, that he had meant to surprise her with it, compelled her toward it as if she were caught in a riptide.

The contractor's face fell. "Oh God, I . . . ," he muttered. "I had no idea." He shook his head slightly, as if this might dislodge an appropriate response. "You're sure you want to . . . ? I mean, it's okay if you don't—"

"I'm sure," she lied, and tried to move the conversation up and out of the tar pit of her revelation. "So, how long's this thing going to take?"

"What?" he said. "Um . . . what?"

Janie enunciated, "How long will it take you to build the porch?" *You think this is hard for YOU?* she thought, the rage monster snorting himself awake inside her. *You didn't even know the guy.*

"Oh yeah . . ." He scratched the red scar on his arm and tried to focus. "Well, lemme think . . ."

Jesus H. Christ, it's a porch, not the Louvre, she silently retorted. Rage monster rattled his chain.

"First we gotta . . . you know, dig the footings . . ." He saw her recross her arms, tighten her chin. "Six weeks," he said. "Starting Monday."

"A porch?" said Dylan, as Malinowski's truck pulled out of the driveway and the *Clifford* credits rolled. "Daddy likes that porch, you know the one we saw that time we went to that lady's house that time? It had that . . . that . . . that thing around and around up high?"

"A ceiling fan. Yeah, Daddy liked that."

"Are we going to have a ceiling fan?"

"I think so."

"Good. Daddy will like that."

FRIDAY NIGHT

Cormac, good cousin that he is, came by at 5:30, right when I was starting to slide into my pre-six-o'clock stupor. There are a lot of bad times of the day. I used to think the worst was right when I woke up, that moment before I realized I was alone. Not just alone, but you know, Alone. I think I'm getting better at that one, though. I think I'm starting to handle it.

Now six is the worst. Six is when he would be walking in the door from work, when I would be handing him the baby and saying "Tag, you're it" with a big sigh, and he would smile and kiss me and squeeze the baby. And Dylan would come barreling in and hang on the back of his belt until his pants were halfway down his nice, tight butt. And he would swing around, back and forth, saying, "Where's Dylan, where is that little bear?" and Dylan would howl with the satisfaction at having stumped him again.

Six still completely sucks. I am not getting better at it.
Cormac got me laughing, though. Some crack about Uncle
Charlie. Wish I could remember it now.

Janie stopped writing, pushing herself into a memory from her childhood. She hungered for moments like this, when her brain let itself be distracted with events that had occurred before the day her life had come to a grinding, colorless halt.

She remembered being young, fourteen or so. She and her twin brother, Mike, were up on the counters in this very kitchen, their feet dangling down, banging occasionally into the lower cabinets. Mike was working the cabinet door by his head, opening and closing it, studying the hinge as if it held a proof for the string theory. As usual, he barely heard the conversation, much less contributed. Cormac was sprawled in one of the kitchen chairs, not the chairs that were here now, but ones that had eventually become so irreparably battered that Janie had given them to Uncle Charlie, her mother's only brother, to take to the dump.

Janie had asked Cormac why he had such a thing about his father. He had said it was because Uncle Charlie named him Cormac, Irish for Charles. It was proof that he had had a son for one reason and one reason only—spare parts. "And believe me," Cormac had said, "he needs 'em."

The three of them had laughed at this, made funnier because Cormac and his father did look so much alike—huge, beefy Irishmen with thick black hair and pale blue eyes. Uncle Charlie was always so proud of his size, as if it were a personal accomplishment instead of a genetic outcome. Cormac would do impressions of him, like "Well, at six foot five and 254 pounds, I don't feel I need any help doing my taxes."

Cormac figured out how to keep all his own parts, though, Janie mused. He did whatever Uncle Charlie thought was unmanly. He took ceramics instead of wood shop. Janie couldn't imagine those huge fingers making anything smaller than a watering trough, but he wasn't too bad. She still had a little mug-pot-bowl thing he had made her.

Freshman year in high school Cormac refused to join the football team and played tennis instead. He gleefully reported that you could have heard Uncle Charlie screaming and carrying on in the next county: "No one in the entire history of this family has ever hit a goddamned ball with a goddamned racket of any kind, and I'll be goddamned if any son of mine is gonna start! I swear to Jesus, if I see you in a pair of little white shorts, I'm not gonna be responsible for my actions!"

Cormac started playing tennis on the sneak, and as big and strong as he was, he had a serve that blew the briefs off any other kid his age. He started winning tournaments and getting his name in the paper. Uncle Charlie didn't know whether to blow a gasket or congratulate him. Then Cormac was named team captain, and Uncle Charlie started going to all the matches and yelling at the judges. It drove Cormac so crazy, he threatened to take up figure skating. He told Janie and Mike, "Pop's so steamed, I'm thinking of joining the friggin Ice Capades!"

Janie could see Cormac so clearly—the self-satisfied grin, the long, muscular legs splayed out across the kitchen floor. But the chair was wrong. The chair she saw now was one of a set that Robby had ordered from a do-it-yourself catalogue and came in parts. Janie wished she'd kept just one of those old chairs. It was from before, an inducer of memories. She picked up the pen and finished the journal entry.

Thank God for Cormac at 5:30 with his box of day-olds from the bakery. Thank God for a six o'clock that doesn't completely suck.

2

ᓭᕀ

MONDAY MORNING JANIE WOKE to the sound of torrential rain.
And something else. A kind of splatting sound. She un-
wound herself from the stranglehold she had on Robby's pillow
and sat up. "What is that?" she said to the pillow. "Weird house
sounds—that's your job."

But they were all her jobs now. The hunting, the gathering,
repair and maintenance of the shelter. The division of labor, discussed and renegotiated countless times over seven years of marriage, had become meaningless in one blown stop sign.

Janie lay back down and tried to reclaim unconsciousness, but
the odd sound jabbed at her until she sat up again and flung the
covers off the bed. Marshaling her self-control, she reined in the
temptation to stomp her feet, and tiptoed to the landing at the top
of the stairs. She peeked into the kids' room. Dylan was on his
side, his face buried in his stuffed bunny's floppy gray ears. The
baby slept on her back, her arms thrown back by the sides of her
head, as if she were preparing to dive.

Downstairs, Janie opened the front door to find tiny waterfalls
leaping from the roof above her and splattering onto the front
step. Clogged gutters. It was April, after all, and the gutters had
waited patiently for Robby to clear the dead sticks and leaves that
winter storms had thrown into them, as he did every spring. Except this one. Janie closed the door and made a pot of coffee.

Monday, April 30
Fucking gutters. Fucking rain.

On Thursday the rain stopped and the yard glistened radioactive green, a color so strong and loud Janie thought she might fall in and never be found. She gave the grass a good hard cut, wielding the mower like a small cannon. The baby rode in a backpack slung across Janie's shoulders, squawking at squirrels, clapping at cars, and finally falling asleep to the little engine's grinding drone.

The contractor had not shown up on Monday, or any other day that week, nor had he called to say he wasn't coming. It wasn't until Thursday morning that Janie had remembered he was supposed to come at all, and the thought instantly infuriated her. The nerve, after all. She had weathered his surprise attack, with all those papers, asking for her dead husband. And she had honored the deal they had cut behind her back, though it would have been easy to say, *Sorry, little change of plans. Your deal's with a dead guy, not with me.*

She had kept up her side of the bargain, though it wasn't even her bargain, and he had left her at the altar of her porchless house, the egotistical son of a bitch. She fed her fury as she laid waste to the ankle-high grass, imagining a confrontation so full of threats and recriminations that it might actually have come to blows, had the yard not unexpectedly surrendered, fully mown.

Hopped up on her own anger, Janie was in no mood to stop. She wasn't finished with him yet, and since she was, of course, winning the imaginary fight, she was anxious for the final showdown. She put the sleeping baby in her crib and cranked up the volume on the baby monitor. Then she hauled a ladder out from the garage and climbed up onto the roof to attack the gutters.

Sliding her hands into Robby's sweat-stiff work gloves threw cold water on the hypothetical skirmish. She thought of Robby's long, gentle fingers, the way they stroked a keyboard the same way they stroked her skin. She realized with horror that there was no record of him at the piano, no video footage that she could show the children of how beautifully their father had played. Dylan would soon forget, and the baby would have no memory of it at all.

She crawled over the peak of the roof onto the back side to hide from passing cars. She sat on the hot gray shingles and wrapped her arms around herself, the work gloves resting gently on her sides. *Sorry I never thought to videotape you at the piano,* she thought, and her throat tightened into a painful rope. *But I remember it, if that helps.*

After a while the breeze blew refugee drips from an overhanging branch onto her face. She crawled down to the gutter and started throwing handfuls of wet leaves and muck onto her freshly mown back lawn. She heard the creak of metal and wondered momentarily what she would do if the ladder blew down. If she jumped, would she sprain an ankle? Or would she merely feel like an idiot for stranding herself on top of her own house?

"Hello?" called a man's voice. Malinowski the contractor appeared over the roof peak. With the sun lighting him from behind, his thinning auburn hair looked almost orange. "Gutters," he nodded seeing the muddied gloves. "Just did my own."

"Nice of you to show," she said.

"Are you a lefty or a righty?" asked Malinowski, as he squatted and hobbled toward her.

"What? Righty."

"Give me this one then." He pointed to her left hand. She looked down at Robby's glove, smeared with muck. Malinowski held out his hand for it. Confused, she slipped the glove off and gave it to him. He dug into the gutter, lobbing a massive handful directly onto her pile below.

"You're making a mess of your lawn like this. Better to put something down there to throw it into."

Janie picked up a handful and winged some muck out across the yard. "You could have called, at least," she said, trying to ramp up to the satisfaction of her earlier fury.

"We don't call," he said.

"We who?"

"Contractors. We don't call. It's in the handbook."

"What handbook? There was no handbook . . ."

"No, the Contractor Handbook. They give it to you at Contractor School. It's says, 'Don't call. Especially if you SAY you're gonna call, don't. And if you have to call, wait a couple days.'" He dropped another glob onto the pile below. "We take an oath. Sort of like the Hippocratic Oath doctors take, except without the 'Do no harm' part."

"What?" Janie demanded, her face pinched in irritation. Then a slow grin bloomed on Malinowski's face, and she understood the joke. She rolled her eyes and shook her head, trying not to smile. "Then why are you here?"

"Well, listen," he said, scooping and dropping a little faster. "When I saw it was going to rain all week, I started this kitchen rehab over in Weston. That way the footing holes aren't full of water when the town inspector comes out."

"It only rained for three days, not all week," said Janie.

"It's going to start up again tomorrow, and I can't afford to lose a week of work for a porch. No offense." He kept moving and scooping, and Janie had to crawl after him to hear what he was saying. "So, I'm going to start here in about a month. Probably around the first of June." He took off the glove and handed it to her. "There, the whole back side is done. I'll put a piece of plastic down in the front yard for you." A hint of a smile crossed his face. "Aim your muck at that."

THURSDAY, MAY 3

That porch guy came by today to tell me he's NOT going to start work like he said he would, not for another month. At least the gutters are clear.

Aunt Jude brought dinner over. Franks and beans, even though it's not Saturday, the "official" franks and beans day. A package of generic hot dogs, a can of Boston baked beans, and a bag of Tater Tots. Gotta be the most highly processed foods known to man, with nary a vegetable in sight. Oh, excuse me, Aunt Jude is of the opinion the Tater Tots are a vegetable—they're potatoes, aren't they? Sort of, I told her. If you squint.

Carly adores her. I think it's all the colors. The dye job makes it seem like her head's on fire, and the lipstick looks like the fire engine's on its way to put her out. Then there's that baby blue eye shadow she orders online to match the color of her eyes. What with all the big shiny jewelry, Carly probably thinks Aunt Jude is a toy.

Dylan was happier than a pig in slop. Would've eaten the whole pile of Tater Tots himself if Aunt Jude didn't grab some. I'll admit I may have had a few, too. Dylan wasn't so big on the hot dog, however, until Auntie Nutrition slathered it with a spoonful of honey! She's completely losing it! She never would have done that when we were kids.

One time, when we went out for one of our Saturday morning breakfasts while Mum was working at the dress shop, there was a little smidge of honey left on the table from the previous meal. Mike stuck his tongue out and licked at it. She went wacky, telling him he could get botulism and die, and how her sister couldn't afford a funeral. I, of course, had to take her on about this, and we got into a fight about how much money Mum might or might not have.

We always got under each other's skin, Aunt Jude and me. Neither of us is what the other hoped for. Even now, with everything, she's on me, pecking at me to do this, try that. Go to this grief group I found for you. Talk to the priest, Father No-Actual-Life-Experience. My policy is to take as little of her advice as possible, while doing just enough to keep her off my back. I realize now it's exactly how Mum handled her.

So, I put the kids to bed, I stretch and yawn, but she sits her butt down on my couch and doesn't leave. Finally she tells me one of her friends she volunteers with down at the soup kitchen *has a son who just got divorced. At first I wasn't sure what she was getting at, so I made little sympathy noises, hoping that would satisfy her and she would go home.*

She tells me way too much information (as usual) about how he owns his own business, and how I must have heard of it, Walking on Sunshine Carpet Cleaners? With that funny jingle on the radio? Apparently he has kids, but they're grown. She made a big point of how he married young.

I'm yawning and checking my watch, but she keeps going. Then she says, "So?" with her eyebrows way up high. With all that reddish-brown pencil on her eyebrows, her face turns into the Joker from Batman.

Can you believe it? She's trying to get me to date! I put a stop to that little fantasy quick as a lightning strike. Still, she gives me her special performance of the "You're an Attractive Woman/At Thirty-eight You're Not Getting Any Younger" Medley. So then, of course, there was a fight. I told her I wasn't going to date, EVER, and she said think of the children, they need a father, and I said it's my business not hers, and she said she's older and knows a few things. On and on. She and her shiny white purse left in a huff. So predictable and too boring for words.

I'm going to bed.

Janie slept fitfully, dreaming that her feet were cold and wet. In the dream she looked down to find the rugs swimming in soap-suds. At about 4:00 a.m. Carly began to wail for no reason that Janie could determine, so she brought her into bed and tried to go back to sleep. The baby's chubby fists flailed around mercilessly. Finally they both drifted off. Shortly thereafter, Janie woke to find Dylan and Nubby the Balding Bunny hovering over her face.

"I'm tired," said Dylan, as if this were the only explanation necessary. He climbed in and burrowed into Janie's armpit. She lay there, held hostage by her dozing children until she was certain she could extricate herself without waking them. She went downstairs and made a full pot of coffee. It was going to be a high-caffeine-index day.

The rain did return, just as the contractor had said it would. What he hadn't mentioned was that the temperature would shoot upward, and the air would feel hot and squishy. The coffee made Janie sweat.

At 8:45 she went back upstairs to wake Dylan. His teacher, Miss Marla, gave parents her Disappointed Look if children were dropped off after 9:30, when free play was over and circle time began. Circle time was serious business for Miss Marla, and interruptions disappointed her. Miss Marla appeared to be in her late thirties, and Janie guessed that her social life was not going well. It was hard to know, however, which might have come first: chronic disappointment or lackluster dates.

Dylan was groggy and uncooperative, and screeched when Janie tried to get him upright. This woke Carly, who bellowed until Janie let Dylan slide to the floor so she could pick the baby up. The two crying, sagging children grated on Janie's exhausted, overcaffeinated nerves, and she yelled, "Stop it!"

Carly howled even louder, her furious screams stuttering like toy machine gun fire. Dylan went silent, covering his ears with his palms and looking up at Janie in fear.

"Sorry," Janie sighed, shushing the baby and slumping onto the floor next to him. "Sorry, sorry, sorry. But you have to get UP, Dylan. We just have to keep MOVING."

They threw on clothes, tossed down breakfast, raced to school, and skidded into the classroom just as Miss Marla was calling the children for circle time. Dylan's relieved smile, the way he squeezed Janie and whispered, "You will pick me up?" decimated her. He was such a trooper, after all, and she felt so mean these days, with no end in sight.

Every so often, time passed at a normal pace. An hour took an hour; an afternoon lasted just about an afternoon. But more often than not, days were long. Slogging through the puddles and humidity on their way back to the house, Janie knew the day would be endless. This was confirmed when she walked into the kitchen and saw Dylan's lunch box sitting on the counter, an item he would panic over if it weren't in his cubby by 11:35.

"Damn, damn, dammit!" Janie yelled, sending the grouchy baby in her arms into fits. Knowing Carly would scream until she got a little diversion, Janie spent the next half hour on the living room floor, piling up towers of blocks for her to bash down over and over again. Janie was just thinking she had done sufficient penance for her bad temper, and was about to end the block bashing so she could deliver the lunch and be back for Father Teabag by eleven o'clock, when the phone rang.

"Janie, it's Mum."

"Hi!" said Janie. "Where are you?"

"I'm home. Just got in from school. Glory be to God, but it's a rowdy group this year."

"Well, summer's coming, you'll be out soon," said Janie, throwing the blocks into a pink plastic basket and sliding it over to the designated toy corner.

"Oh, I'm looking forward to that, let me tell you," said her mother. "How are my babies?"

"Missing their Gram. Have you got a flight yet?"

"Not yet."

"Mum, it's May," said Janie, stunned by her mother's lack of attention to this task. Noreen Dwyer was nothing if not responsible. *Dutiful* was the word Janie had often thought described her best. She was never the last one to pick up her kids from school. She always volunteered to send in cupcakes for the Valentine's Day parties and never forgot a conference or field trip. She was the sole provider for two children and she took this seriously. Dutifully.

But Janie always sensed somehow that her mother was only biding her time, waiting to sprout wings. Noreen had the heart of a traveler; itineraries were her own personal poetry. She would have knit a bridge to Europe if only it would have held.

"Well, I'm not going back right away," said Noreen. "Marcella—you know, the earth sciences teacher?—she asked me to spend some time with her family near Napoli, so I thought I'd wait on booking a flight to the States."

Neither spoke for a moment. The silence was tempered only by the standard overseas call static, a sound that often reminded Janie of lapping water. She could almost hear the vast ocean, exposed to every kind of weather, that separated her from her mother.

"Naples?" Janie said finally. "You're staying?"

"Just until August, Janie. I'll be back for August."

The call ended quickly. Janie had to get the lunch box to Dylan, and Noreen had to answer her door. *Her Italian door,* thought Janie. *In Italy.*

The wind and rain had picked up. Janie got soaked as she ran holding Carly under her coat to the preschool entrance from the only available parking space on the far side of the lot. She dropped off the lunch box and dashed back to the car. As they neared the house again, Janie saw that Father Considerate had pulled into her single-lane driveway. If she pulled in behind him, she would have to move the car later so he could get out. He was just walking up to the front door of the house, and she rolled down her window to call to him to pull his car out so she could get in first. But a quick glance in the rearview informed her that Carly had dozed off, and the sound of her mother screaming out the car window was certain to wake the surly baby. Figuring she had provided more than enough provocation for Carly's temper that morning, Janie parked on the street.

"Hi," said Father Jake.

"Right," said Janie, attempting to shelter the sleeping, rain-spattered baby as she fumbled for her keys.

"Can I take her?" he offered, holding out his hands, water dripping down his wire-frame glasses.

Janie snorted at him, twisted the key in the door, and lurched into the house. She dropped her purse and trod up the stairs to put the baby in her crib, her sneakers squeaking with water. When she came down to the kitchen, Father Jake had already filled the teakettle and set it on a burner. He was sitting at the table, Robby's table, waiting with a quiet, understanding sort of patience that made Janie want to break things.

She sat down heavily into a chair across from him and proceeded to take off her wet shoes and socks. "So, Father," she said flatly, without looking at him. "How's it going up at the rectory?"

"Fine," he said. "The roof's got some leaks that apparently never bothered Father Lambrosini. But that's what buckets are for, I guess."

The teakettle began to sing, a hissing screech that went right up Janie's spine. She stared at him, unmoving.

"Should I . . . ?" he asked, tentatively.

"Make yourself at home, by all means."

He moved the kettle to a cool burner and the sound deflated. Janie watched him pull his teabag from his pocket and carefully pour the scalding water, and her skin began to itch as if she were having an allergic reaction. When the hot water hit, Father Jake's mug threw an aroma into the air that smelled to Janie like a combination of orange and cloves and dirt.

"How old *are* you?" she demanded.

"Thirty-eight. How old are you?"

"You are *not*. You are not thirty-eight."

"No?" he said, pleasantly.

"Did my Aunt Jude tell you to say that?"

"No. She told me to say a lot of things, but not that." He leaned against the counter, sipped his tea, and pushed a clump of brown hair off his forehead. He had the standard man's haircut, but longer. Waves of hair rested on the curls of his ears.

"Oh, I have no doubt she has a whole script for you every time you show up." Janie pitched the wet shoes toward the front door and slumped back down in her chair.

"Why would me being thirty-eight matter?"

"Because you don't even look like an adult. And you sure as hell don't look as old as me . . ."

He took another sip, and set the mug gently on the counter. "So. How's it going here?"

"Kinda sucky," she said. "But thanks for your concern."

"What's up?"

"What's up?" she replied, her ice blue eyes widening in incredulity. "What's up?" Janie shook her head, raising her hands as if to surrender. "Look. Father. I know this is all . . . I know you're not . . . I mean, thanks for coming and everything . . . but this just isn't working."

"Oh?" he said. "Well, how could we make it work better? What would help?"

"Nothing," she said. "It's just not . . . you don't . . . You can't possibly understand this."

"So explain it to me."

"That's the whole point," she said, putting her bare damp feet up on one of the chairs. "I can't. First of all, you're not married, maybe never even dated, for all I know. Marriage is like this . . . well, anyway, mine was like this huge surprise. I never knew I could ever be . . . you know, loved . . . like that. I never thought it would happen, that I would feel so . . . I mean, not like we never fought or anything. But even that was just . . ."

"I know what it's like to feel loved," he said, his expression darkening slightly.

"Yeah, okay, your parents loved you. Great. But it's not like that. It's like nothing you've ever experienced. I thought this was it. *He* was *It*. And I was never going to have to . . ." The ache behind her eyes, the constricting of her throat, infuriated her. She pointed an incriminating finger up at him. "You live alone. You'll *always* live alone. That's what you *chose*."

Father Jake looked at her thoughtfully, surprisingly unscathed by this assessment. "Are there any other reasons?" he asked.

Janie wanted to hit him. She needed to silence him, to deliver a blow so fatal he would never return. "The other reason," she said. And she almost smiled, her tone matching his. "The other reason is that I *see* you. Father Friendly, Pastor Perfect. Everyone likes you, but no one can say exactly why. You glide through Mass and church suppers leaving everyone feeling pleased. They don't realize that they haven't affected you in any way. The main reason, Father, that this little arrangement is a sham is because you're just as locked up as I am. You have a secret life of misery just like me."

He didn't move. His face remained relaxed and thoughtful. He looked down at his somber black sport shoes, then placed his mug courteously in the sink. "We'll talk next week," he said, and only his rapid, shallow breathing belied him. A direct hit.

It took about twenty minutes of sitting in the silent house, with the rain slapping the shingles, for Janie to start feeling badly. And sorry. Self-disgust grew in her like a blush that wouldn't subside. She tried to recapture the righteous rage that had made her feel justified—even obligated—to knock him down a peg. *No sale,* said her conscience.

When she couldn't rationalize it away, she tried to stop thinking about it altogether. She busied herself with tidying the house. She spoke for a few extra moments with Dylan's teacher when she went to pick him up. Uncle Charlie came by to get her trash to take to the dump. She made him stay for coffee, and thawed one of the many banana breads that neighbors had delivered in prior months. She called Shelly and asked detailed questions about her daughter's play.

Yet Father Jake, the mild-mannered boy-priest, bland, bespectacled, and benign, loomed large in her brain. The sickening feeling of having bullied a weakling would not leave her, and the longer it lingered the more she began to sense the truth and weight of her words. The more she began to wonder what his "misery" might be. By 2:00 a.m., she was talking to Robby about it, explaining, rationalizing, confessing. In her mind, he remained very, very disappointed in her.

WHEN SHE GOT UP the next morning, Janie knew what she had to do. First she dropped the kids off at Aunt Jude's for their usual Saturday visit. Then she went to the bakery. She prayed that her cousin Cormac would not be there, but of course he was. *The guy's going to be buried with flour in his hair and frosting under his nails,* she thought.

"Hey, what's up?" he said too casually. Janie knew he was checking her for signs of deterioration.

"Hey, nothing," she said, searching for something nonchalant to say. Cormac's girlfriend of the moment was a safe subject, a nonsubject, really. She was a tall, attractive former blonde who had tried to perk up her now flat tan hair with an overabundance of honey-colored highlights. She wore "outfits," even to work at the bakery.

"How's Barbie?" said Janie. *Casual right back atcha.*

"It's Barb, you snob."

"Yeah, well, I'll believe that when I see her in flat shoes."

Cormac laughed a real laugh, and Janie felt okay for a minute. "She thinks she's too short," Cormac confided, still chuckling.

"Compared to what? You, ya buffalo?"

"Hey, that's bison to you, chickie."

This patter went on for a few minutes, and then Cormac went in for the kill. "So, what's up?"

"Nothing much," Janie said, perusing the huge glass display case. "What've you got for cakes?" There were at least ten different kinds, from basic to exotic, elegantly plain to elaborately decorated.

Cormac's face went motionless for a second too long. "For who?"

He knows, thought Janie. *No details, not why, but he gets the gist.* She made one last-ditch effort. "None o' your beeswax, nosey," and she shoved him. There was something intensely satisfying about shoving such a big man. And Cormac knew it. He staggered back a step, letting her feel powerful for a moment. Then he shoved her back, not hard, but enough to throw her off balance, enough to make her feel that she was a worthy opponent. Which she was, but not physically.

"How bad was it?" he asked as he shoved.

"Bad enough." Shove.

"Who?" Shove.

Janie groaned and shook her head.

"Come on," he threw a huge, floury arm around her. "Tell ol' cousin Cormac what you did to warrant Pology Cake." After she told him, all he said was, "Wow." Then she knew he was worried about her, even more than before.

"He provoked me," she insisted.

"Still . . ." he said, and squinted at her. "I think you gotta go homemade on this one, chickie."

"Come on, Cormac," she whined. "It's not like I ran over his cat. Besides, I don't have time."

"Boo-hoo. Make time."

"I'll owe you big."

"You already owe me big. Besides, you're the founding mother of Pology Cake. You know how it works. It has to be a sacrifice."

"He doesn't know that," she said.

"Father Jake's a smart guy, he'll figure it out."

Janie sighed, bested. "Any thoughts?"

"Hmmm," said Cormac, unwittingly scratching flour into the stubble on his chin. "Something sweet, but not gooey . . ." He went on for a while in recipe rapture, finally deciding on some ginger concoction the name of which Janie couldn't even pronounce.

She slunk home and reviewed the ingredients he had written out for her on the back of an order sheet. She was missing a few and finally decided she didn't even agree with his prescription.

It wasn't the type of cake that mattered, anyway. What mattered was the sacrifice—that the transgressor offered a symbol of his or her remorse in a form that best suited the injured party. And since she was the patron sinner of Pology Cake, Janie followed her own counsel and went with lemon cream cake. She thought Father Jake might be a lemon kind of guy.

As she measured the flour, her thoughts drifted to the inception of Pology Cake. She remembered the incident, of course, but it went back farther than that. It really began because she and Mike were so completely different. Janie was the chatty, smart-alecky one, Mike was the silent, speedy one. She back-talked Mum to death; he just took off.

But more than that, Mike had always been a little odd—too easily overwhelmed, shy to the point of reclusive. He was often unable to attend to the simplest tasks, yet mysteriously able to create complex works of art in the sanctuary of his room. An enigma even to his twin.

Perhaps it was because of this lack of true understanding that Janie and Mike nurtured little commonalities to get along. Foremost was the currency of food. They had an elaborate scale of which Halloween candies equaled other things. Like two Tootsie Rolls was fair trade for an extra turn on their only pair of roller skates. Choosing the TV show cost a full-sized Snickers bar—not the mini kind. Food restored the balance of power, which had always been tipped decidedly in Janie's favor.

For Cormac's tenth birthday, his mother, Aunt Brigid, told him that he could have any kind of cake he wanted. So Cormac, the original envelope pusher, thought about it for a solid week. When he placed his order, Aunt Brigid stared at him with her mouth open for a few seconds, and muttered, "You gotta be kidding me . . ." Then she narrowed her eyes at him and said, "Fine."

It was ten layers. She built and decorated it to look like the Prudential Center tower in downtown Boston, as requested. It was colossal, an edible engineering masterpiece. Uncle Charlie had helped her to steady it with a series of upright chopsticks hidden inside. And there Janie and Mike were, two eight-year-olds sitting with all those big-boy friends of Cormac's, being served slices of cake bigger than their heads.

The moment was perfect, until Mike got a little frosting on his fingers. Janie saw it coming and wanted to scream, "Don't!" But, of course, he did. He stopped Aunt Brigid from sawing up the cake and asked her for an extra napkin. Then, with maddening fastidiousness, he scrubbed each finger. Even in his adulthood, sticky hands were still cause for panic.

Janie was mortified by his prissiness, especially in front of Cormac's friends. She was ashamed of him, and not for the first time. So she huffed, "God, Mike, don't be such a girl."

Mike stopped mid-wipe. The big boys snickered and sneered at him, happy to have a new target for their insatiable taste for teasing. And Cormac, a forkful of cake inches from his open mouth, gave her a look of withering disgust. Mike was to be protected, not shot down from within family ranks. This was understood. The shame that washed over her was oceanic. Her first thought was to run home, but that would have called even more attention to the gaffe. So, she did the only thing she could think of that might set things right. She slid her as-yet-untouched cake over to Mike.

"Hey, she doesn't want her cake? I'll have it!" yelled clueless Dougie Shaw.

"Shut up," growled Cormac. "It's apology cake."

"Pology Cake?" said Dougie. "I thought it was a Pru cake."

They all laughed and punched each other and shouted "You idiot!" and "Duh, Dougie!"

And Pology Cake was born.

SATURDAY, MAY 5

Had to drop off a cake at the rectory for Father Jake. He wasn't there so I left it in the front hall with a note that it was from me. It was lemon with butter-cream glaze. Sweet but not gooey. Self-effacing without being overly self-denigrating. It says I was right, but I had no right to say so.

I hope Father Jake speaks Baked-good-ese.

On Monday morning, after taking Dylan to preschool, Janie drove by the church. *Expecting to see what?* she thought. *The flag at half-mast?* Father Jake stood on the shady side of the rectory, garden hose in hand, watering flowers. Janie hung a hard right into the church parking lot, wheels letting out an aggravated squeal. She parked in the shade, prayed for the courage to be meek, and got out.

"I didn't know you were a gardener," she said, trying to sound offhanded.

"I'm not," he said. A question floated behind his standard issue smile. "These are Father Lambrosini's. When he retired and I got assigned here, he asked me to take care of them." He watered one of the rose bushes a little too long and a muddy puddle formed. "Unfortunately, he never left any instructions. So I just water them and hope they don't die."

Janie stared at the roses as if her next line were written on the leaves. Finally, she said simply, "I'm sorry." His smile relaxed and he nodded. The relief she felt was extraordinary.

"Thanks for the cake," he said, and aimed the spray at another plant. "It's delicious."

"You don't have to say that," Janie sank onto a wrought iron bench by the little plot of roses. "I bake like you garden, just trying not to kill anyone."

He released the handle on the hose and the relentless spray ceased. The bobbing blooms slowly regained their regal composure. He sat down on the bench next to her. "Where's the baby?"

"Asleep." She pointed to the car, parked in the deep shade of a leafy maple tree. The humidity had broken and a cool breeze passed over them.

"What you said the other day," he said, studying his hands, "it wasn't totally unjustified."

Don't, she thought. *Please. It's the first peace I've had since you left on Friday. Let's just enjoy it.*

"Nobody's caught me like that in a long time," he continued.

Oh, God, she realized, *he's going to tell me. And I made him do it. I baited him and now he feels he's got to answer. Please, please don't tell me.*

"My family was kind of . . . what do they call it now? Dysfunctional? Such a tidy term for something so messy." His lips flattened into a thin smile. "My mother was an alcoholic and my father was . . ." He squinted at the rectory walls, as if to assess their height. "He was sick."

"I'm sorry," said Janie. "What did he have?"

A mirthless snort burst out of him, and he said, "Cancer of the soul."

Janie's thoughts spun out like tops, as she considered the possibilities of this revelation. Her own defenseless children came to mind, and the knot in her stomach tightened.

He glanced quickly over at her. "Boy," he said, shaking his head. "That was way too much information. Now it's my turn to apologize . . ."

"No, I asked for it."

"You didn't. You only realized that I have a dark corner in my heart, too."

"And used it against you."

"You lashed out, and I happened to be in reach. I know how rage feels, trust me." He stood and stretched, as if waking from a long sleep. "Hey," he said with a gentle smile. "Want some cake?"

3

THURSDAY, MAY 31

Dylan's been doing this weird thing. On the way to the library last week, I looked in the rearview mirror and he had his swim goggles on. They must have been left in the car the last time we went to the pool. Which was when, exactly? Can't even remember. He took them off when we went into the library, but put them on again when we got back in the car. I asked him to bring them in the house so they don't get lost, and he didn't say anything, so I assumed he would.

Actually I forgot the whole thing as soon as we got home because Shelly came over to tell me she'd sold one of the Pelham Heights houses and was ordering Thai food to celebrate. It was Friday, so it was okay for her to eat something other than a red pepper or a pomegranate or other single form of vegetation for dinner. I said great, but Dylan won't eat Thai, so I'll just make him some pasta. She got a bee in her Neiman Marcus bloomers because "the whole idea of ordering out is that you DON'T HAVE TO COOK." Not like she ever cooks. I don't think she even owns a pan.

So I said, okay, how about pizza? But she doesn't eat white flour, and she thinks she might be allergic to tomato-based products, and cheese is simply unthinkable. It was like I was asking her to eat asphalt. I think Shelly is frightened of food. But we

ordered, and I gave Dylan Pad Thai, which he would not eat until I dabbed it with honey! Thank you so very much, Aunt Jude.
When he goes into insulin shock someday I hope she's there with
her ipecac so she can give herself a nice, big dose.

Yesterday, when we were driving to that gas station with
the free car wash, there he was with the goggles again. I said,
"Hey, Diver Dan, how come you're wearing those?" He looked
out the window and said, "I just like to."

Fair enough, I thought. What's the harm? So, now I'm
starting to get used to seeing him sitting back there, perched on
his booster seat with those big green goggles, looking like some
sort of frog prince with curly black hair.

Friday, June 1

It's June first and that porch builder isn't here. Probably in
Acapulco with my money.

Father Jake came by today on his teabag tour. I wonder
how many other lost souls and life wrecks he visits. That could
be a lot of tea.

He said he thinks I'm depressed, qualifying it with, "though,
I'm not a therapist." I made a dumb joke about him playing
one on TV, and he laughed. I have to admit I appreciate his
patience with my sarcasm at his expense. Maybe he's tougher
than he looks. Two months of Friday visits and he still isn't
sick of me. At least he doesn't let it show.

Today, he told me he doesn't hear me talking about anything
good in my life. He thinks the pain is starting to overwhelm
me. I said I can handle it. Plus, good things do happen. I just
don't always mention them. When I told him a kind of amazing thing happened today, his whole face changed. He looked so
hopeful. I was glad it was something good enough.

I told him the baby let me stroke her hand. He said, "Really" with that kind of neutral tone that means I have no clue
what you're getting at but keep talking anyway.

When I used to nurse Carly, she would open up her hand and let me stroke it. I would start at the base of her palm and just stroke upward so that my fingertips ended up sort of tickling her little thumb and fingers. The inside of a baby's hand is the most amazing thing. Warm and soft and silky. Not one thing in this world compares. When she opened her palm and stretched out her fingers, she was letting me into her little world.

But, when Robby died I just shut down. My milk stopped and she had to go on bottles, and she wouldn't even let me feed her at first. Then, she would let me give her a bottle, but she kept her fists clenched, as if she didn't want to expose them to pain. Lately, though, little by little, she's been straightening out her hand, and today she held it out, just out in the air, not to me, or anything. And when I touched it, her fingers closed at first, but then she opened them again. She never looked at me. She just drank her bottle and stared off past my shoulder like she always does. But, she let me stroke her palm. I was so happy for that moment, when life seemed normal again and we were together, not strangers wandering around alone on some airless planet, but me the mommy, her the baby. I was so grateful.

I didn't think Father Jake got it at first, how big that was to me, because he didn't react right away. Then he said, "You know, I bet something like that happens every day." I gave him my best too-bored-to-be-annoyed look, and he said not something that big, obviously. But maybe something smaller might happen. And if I looked for it, I would see it, and maybe that would help. He suggested I write down one little miracle every day.

Actually, I thought the idea was sort of simplistic and Oprah-ish, but tonight after the kids went to bed, I realized that I wanted to write it down, anyway. I probably won't have another baby, now that Robby's gone, and when she's big I'll

*want to remember that sensation of touching her hand, of con-
necting with her in such a mommy-baby kind of way. So, I
suppose for today, anyway, I'll take his advice and write down
my little miracle. If something happens tomorrow, I'll think
about that then.*

THE SECOND WEEK OF June turned scorching hot, as if to taunt the
palefaced and those without central air. The drastic change made
Janie feel weak and sweaty. It was only minimally satisfying to see
the other preschool mothers looking damp and blotchy, too. "You
will pick me up?" asked Dylan, the goggle-shaped rings around
his eyes still noticeable. Miss Marla had given Janie a look of concern when she'd first seen them, but Janie had just shrugged and
busied herself with putting his Clifford the Big Red Dog lunch
box in Miss Marla's designated lunch box basket.

When she returned home, the white truck with MALINOWSKI
CUSTOM DESIGN, INC. on the door was parked in front of the house.
The contractor was standing in the yard staring up at the roof. Janie
struggled out of the car, Carly in one arm and a grocery bag on
the other. Malinowski came toward her, took the bag, and set it on
the front step. "What's her name," he asked, nodding at the baby.

"Carly," said Janie. "And you're . . . Augustus?"

"I go by Tug," he said. "I only use my given name for contracts.
And elderly clients. For some reason, a guy in his forties named
Augustus makes them feel like the world might not be going to
hell in a handbasket, after all."

Standing in the blazing-hot yard with a drip of sweat running
down her cleavage, Janie didn't feel like smiling, but her mouth
curled up of its own accord. "Why not Gus?" she asked.

"My father was Gus. Also Gus was one of the mice in *Cinder-
ella*. The stupid one." Malinowski squinted back up at her roof
and ran a hand through his sparse auburn hair. "When I was a
kid, some of my friends used to call me Mal, but I wasn't too big
on that."

"Why not?"

He glanced over at her, his dark eyes seeming almost black as the pupils dilated. "It means 'bad.'" He looked away, then down at his scar-faced watch and said, "Okay, I gotta go. I'll be here tomorrow with a backhoe. You have a little boy, right? About four or five years old? Keep him home from school. He'll love it."

"HEY, GUESS WHAT," JANIE said to Dylan at bedtime.

"What?" said Dylan, tucking the mangy ears of his stuffed bunny under his chin.

"You're not going to school tomorrow. A guy is coming with a big backhoe to dig in our yard."

Dylan looked dismayed. "Dig holes? Is that okay? Will he do trouble?"

"No, it's not trouble," said Janie. "I want him to. He's digging holes so he can build us a porch. With a ceiling fan. It's good."

"But . . . I don't know." Dylan rubbed a formerly white bunny ear across his cheek. "A backhoe?"

"A big one. And you don't have to get ready for school, so you can sleep as late as you want. We can all sleep until we're ready to get up."

At 5:42 the next morning, Dylan was ready to get up. "Mom?" he whispered, hovering over Janie. When she didn't respond he delicately pulled up one of her eyelids. "Mom? Where's the backhoe?"

Janie took him into bed with her and mumbled, "It's too early. Go back to sleep."

And it seemed as if he would, until he asked quietly in her ear, "Mom? What's the guy's name?"

"Tug."

"Tug? Like a tugboat?"

"Yeah, now please, Dylan, it's too early."

He was still, and Janie dozed and dreamed she was riding a red bike with Carly in the baby backpack and Dylan on the handlebars. She had forgotten to put helmets on them and it was dark.

"Mom? Is that guy Tug a good driver?"

Janie groaned, wondering how she could have been so stupid as to tell Dylan about the damned backhoe. But there was no going back, as she had learned all too well in the past four months. Actually five months today, now that it was the fourteenth of June. You never got a do-over, especially for the stuff that really mattered.

They got up. Janie made coffee. Dylan made a shelter out of couch pillows for two plastic ducks, a goat, a brontosaurus, and a stuffed monkey. The barnyard animals and the dinosaur got along very well. They could share. The monkey was a problem, and was eventually evicted from the compound for "doing trouble."

Tug Malinowski and his backhoe did not arrive until 2:15 that afternoon, by which time Dylan himself had had several bouts of "doing trouble" in between periods of standing sentry at the living room window, asking "Is that the Tugboat guy?" every time a car passed.

When Tug's truck finally pulled up in front of the house with a flatbed trailer hitched to the back, Dylan ran out the front door. Janie had to pull Carly out of her highchair still smeared with strained peas and scramble after him, afraid he would run into the street. When she got outside, Dylan was nowhere in sight, and Malinowski was beginning to unchain the small backhoe from the flatbed.

"Dylan!" screamed Janie. The contractor's head popped up from behind the backhoe. "Don't move that thing!" she ordered him. "I can't find my little boy!"

"Here I am, Mom!" called Dylan, grinning from the passenger window of the truck. "This is SO COOL!"

"Dylan, get out of there!" she hurried toward him, the baby bouncing on her hip. The boy's face fell and his chin began to tremble.

"I told him to," said Malinowski, coming from around the back of the flatbed.

"The Tugboat guy said to!" said Dylan, his hazel eyes wide.

"He shouldn't be in there—it's not safe," Janie admonished. "He could push some button, turn something on, God knows what—"

"The keys are in my pocket, the emergency brake is on, and there are blocks behind the tires," said Malinowski. "I just wanted him out of the way of the heavy machinery."

"You don't tell someone else's kid to get in your truck," said Janie, pointing at him, the baby clutched in her other arm. "I'm his mother. I decide whose vehicle he can get in, not you, not some guy I barely know."

"Well, then, you need to watch him, because he was ready to climb right onto the flatbed." Malinowski put his hands in his pockets and stood staring back at her.

"Don't you tell me . . ." sputtered Janie, narrowing her eyes at him. "Don't you dare tell me . . . You know what? Let's just call off the whole thing. This was HIS idea, I just . . . I was just trying to . . ."

"Hey," said Malinowski, those unblinking dark eyes taking her in. He was motionless, except for the rise and fall of his chest. Then he said, "You're right. I should have waited until you came out. He's your boy. You get to decide."

Hot air surged in and out of her lungs, and she wanted to keep yelling at him, point her finger at him, fire him. But it was over. He had yielded, though he had managed to do so without sounding like he'd actually conceded anything. Janie had to pull her haywire emotions back into some semblance of control. She looked up at Dylan, his little hands gripping the edge of the truck window, and she let out her breath. "You scared me."

"Sorry, Mom," he said. "Sorry big as a monkey."

Janie, Dylan, and Carly sat on the front step and watched Malinowski maneuver the small backhoe off the flatbed and up the driveway. The thing made sensationally loud grinding noises, like some menacing yellow rust-speckled beast. Malinowski nodded to them and Dylan waved back, giddy and pulsing with excitement. "This is so cool," he whispered several times. "Wait till Keane hears."

Huge chunks of mossy lawn came up in the backhoe's gaping maw and were dumped into a neat pile on the edge of the yard. *Less grass to mow,* thought Janie, *but more house to clean.*

"He's too hot," announced Dylan, rising from the step. "I'm going to get him a drink." He returned with his favorite Clifford sippy cup. Janie could see something dark at the bottom of it.

"What is that?" she asked.

"Chocolate milk." He moved a few steps toward the backhoe with the cup held out in front of him like a chalice. "It was a tiny bit messy," he murmured, "but I licked up the puddle. The counter's all clean again."

Malinowski turned off the motor, wiped his sweaty face on the shoulder of his T-shirt and hopped down from the machine. "What's this?" he asked with a smile for Dylan. He took the cup and sucked on the sippy top. "Chocolate milk! How'd you know it's my favorite?"

Dylan's grin was so wide it almost toppled him over. He ran back to Janie and hid his face in her lap. Malinowski took the top off and swallowed the rest in one long impressive gulp, Adam's apple bobbing in his thick neck. When he handed back the cup, he caught Janie's eye, pointed at Dylan, and cocked a thumb at the backhoe.

She could see that his deference to her was purposeful. He was humoring her, as people tended to these days, and she didn't enjoy feeling like an oddity for whom others had to make allowances. That was her brother Mike's role, not hers. But it was tiring to wonder at people's motives all the time, and Malinowski hadn't actually done anything wrong, other than present her with a decision she didn't feel like making. She glanced toward the backhoe, as if it were the source of her concern, not the man standing in front of her. *He seems okay,* she thought. *And I'll be right here watching.*

"Dylan," she murmured into the curly black hair. "Mr. Malinowski says you can have a ride." Dylan's head popped up, a look of amazement just short of horror on his face.

"Is it okay if he calls me Tug?" Malinowski asked Janie.

"Tug says you can help him for a few minutes," she said to Dylan. "Go get your bike helmet."

"Why?" he asked.

"In case you fall."

Dylan gave Malinowski an assessing look.

"I won't let you fall, buddy," Malinowski answered the look. "But do as your mother says."

A squeal came out of Dylan that Janie realized she hadn't heard in many months. "Get the . . . get the . . . get the . . ." he stammered at her.

"Camera?" she guessed.

"Yes!"

So Janie took pictures of Dylan sitting on Tug's lap, waving, moving the levers, face as open as a meadow under his lizard-themed bike helmet. Dylan wanted Carly to have her picture taken on the backhoe, too.

"She's too little," said Janie.

"I can hold her! I can hold her so tight!" offered Dylan.

"Not this time," she said, realizing her blunder: Dylan might think there would be a next time.

"But she will feel sad!" he insisted. "She will want *my* pictures."

Janie knew that it was no use to try and explain to Dylan that eight-month-old Carly would not only not care about having her own picture, she would have no idea. Yet Dylan's ever-expanding and sometimes inconvenient sense of fairness would prevent Janie from using the argument that they could hide his pictures from Carly. It was a can of worms. A can among many.

Without seeming even to look at Janie, Tug cocked his head to one side, in a bring-her-up-here sort of gesture. Janie snorted and squinted into the street. She knew he meant to be helpful, yet it irritated her to no end that he wanted her to reverse herself. Yes, he seemed to say, Carly could, in fact, come up here and have her picture taken. It was easy. It was safe. Janie was just overprotective. Except, of course, when she was being underprotective, like when she let Dylan out of the house without her. The lack of confidence Janie felt in the still-unfamiliar land of single parenthood made others' apparent assessments of her barely tolerable. Everything was so full of worms these days.

While Janie weighed feeling incompetent against being countermanded, Dylan piped up again. "Hey! Maybe he—" he looked at Malinowski, "maybe you—maybe he could hold Carly. His muscles are very, very STRONG!"

Janie took a deep breath. *Worms everywhere,* she thought, as she stood up with the baby. She handed Carly to Malinowski with a brief but meaningful glance meant to imply a warning for the baby's care, and another warning about her sole sovereignty over her children. Whether he received it or not, Malinowski answered with his now-familiar dark unblinkingness. He wrapped his muscular, scarred arm around Carly, tightened his grip on Dylan, and smiled for the picture.

"Great," said Janie, and "Thanks," as she retrieved the baby. "Dylan, I think it might be time for Mr. Malinowski . . . Tug . . . to get some work done."

"I gotta get this thing back, buddy," Malinowski said to the boy in his grasp. "But, you can still watch if you want to."

Dylan did watch from the kitchen window for the better part of the afternoon. He only left his post once to bring Malinowski more chocolate milk and a small baggie of Cheerios. The contractor consumed them in seconds with the sincere yet casual kind of gratitude to which small boys aspire.

The footings dug, Malinowski told Janie he'd be back when the building inspector came out to check the holes. Then he wordlessly loaded the backhoe onto the flatbed. He tooted twice and threw an arm out the window of the truck as he pulled away.

"BYE!" screamed Dylan, his whole body wagging like a dog's tail. "BYE, TUG!"

WHEN FATHER JAKE CAME on Friday, Janie was impatient with his tea preparations and his small talk. "What did you do with all your rage?" she asked him, a non-response to his polite inquiry about the holes in the yard.

He didn't say anything for a few seconds. He dunked his teabag in and out of the hot water, in and out. Then he set it on the spoon and carefully wrapped the string around, as if he were binding sticks of dynamite. "I went to a therapist, but mostly I prayed."

Like that would help, thought Janie.

"You don't pray much," Jake ventured, "or attend Mass regularly, I take it."

Janie and Robby had been taking Dylan to church, sometimes as often as once a month, she told him, "But, that's not what you mean by 'regularly.' It certainly isn't what my Aunt Jude means, I can promise you that."

"What about when you were growing up?" he asked.

She told him her mother had taken her and Mike every Sunday. They sat with her mother's brother and sister, Aunt Jude and Uncle Charlie, and with Charlie's wife, Aunt Brigid, and son, Cormac. Aunt Jude insisted they sit over on the left side because she liked to be near the music. Cormac made it fun. He would do something, just one little thing every Sunday that would get them laughing, clutching back the sound in their quivering chests to avoid being scolded. For instance, he would go to Communion, take a sip of wine, and then, catching their eyes, he would smack his lips.

One time, he pointed out to Janie and Mike how people tend to contract their butt muscles when they kneel. After that, he could just tip his head toward someone and whisper "contracting." Sure enough, there would be somebody's buttocks gripping a skirt or a pair of pants like a hand.

Janie told Father Jake all this, secretly hoping he'd be horrified. But instead laughter burst out of him that kindled the color in his face and made the ghostlike quality recede. It was easier, then, not to hate everything he said. "Okay," she pressed him, "other than prayer and therapy, how did you deal?"

"That's like saying, 'Other than hats and scarves, how do you keep your head warm?' You can use whatever you like. Or you can just stay inside when it's cold. But assuming you want to go outside and you want to use something convenient and effective, it's hard to beat a hat or a scarf."

"But those hats don't fit me. They're tight and itchy and smelly, and they piss me off even more than I already am, which is no small accomplishment."

He rubbed his thumb and forefinger over his eyebrows for a moment, considering this.

"I know I'm a pain in the ass," she offered. It was true, wasn't it? She was the lead weight that everyone else had to carry around.

"Jane, you are not a pain in the ass," he sighed. "You have no idea of the people I talk to." There was an edge to his voice she hadn't heard before, a whiff of exasperation that, like his laughter, was somehow reassuring in its normalcy.

Who does he talk to? she wondered. Aunt Jude sprang to her mind, and she felt a fleeting pity for Father Jake. *I hope I'm a little bit interesting, in addition to being a pain in his ass. Which I most certainly am.*

He thought for a moment more, rubbing at his eyebrows again, as if his intention were to remove them. "I think you need exercise," he said.

"Exercise?" This was the best he could do? And how would she accomplish it, even if she wanted to? Leave the kids home to fend for themselves? Janie could just see herself, jogging with

Jesus, weight-lifting her worries away. She picked at a scab on her arm and said, "I don't think so."

Father Jake continued talking, rattling on about taking walks, and how she might collect something along the way, something that catches her eye, like a rock in an interesting formation or a brightly colored leaf. Janie didn't pay any attention.

He knows I'm not going to do it.

FRIDAY, JUNE 15

Father Jake just left. He's such an odd, quiet little person. Not little, really—he's average size. Average everything, I guess. Except for the hair—he's got a ton of that. It's just that sense you get that he's about thirteen years old at a school dance and trying to blend in with the bleachers. His hiding makes him small.

I don't like knowing about his father. Not that I know anything, really. But I guess I know enough to keep me from torturing him too much when he comes over now. I feel for him and I don't want to. I can barely stand to feel my own feelings, let alone anyone else's.

He drank his tea and asked his tentative little questions and made his silly suggestions. I got bored, or maybe impatient. He just goes on like nothing happened. Like I didn't attack him, and he didn't tell me what he told me. He doesn't really listen. He just goes on. He's a Go On-er.

AT FIVE O'CLOCK THAT night, Janie was hungry. And by the crabby, whiney behavior of her children, she knew that they were probably hungry, too. But it was just too hard. Meal planning seemed unfathomable, like space travel or extreme sports.

So when Aunt Jude rolled in at 5:10 with two boxes of frozen pizza (one plain and the other mushroom and olive) and salad-in-a-bag (Caesar) and a package of Fig Newtons (fat free), Janie felt like crying. In fact, she did excuse herself while Aunt Jude was fussing with the salad packets, and went into the bathroom to sit on the back of the toilet tank and sob silently into a hand towel. *Crying over frozen pizza,* she chided herself. *Get a grip.*

When she returned, Carly was in her highchair wrangling pieces of a fat-free Newton with her tiny thumb and forefinger and triumphantly placing them in her mouth. Janie knew that an eight-month-old—a toothless one at that—probably shouldn't be eating something that chewy. And she had tried to keep the baby off sweets so that she wouldn't balk at vegetables. Dylan hadn't had refined sugar until his first birthday cake. But Carly looked so happy. And Janie was just too tired from crying. She sat down in the seat next to Carly's highchair to watch for signs of choking.

Once Aunt Jude had put the pizzas into the oven and tossed the bag of salad, she shifted her attention to Janie. Or more precisely to Janie's shoulders. Aunt Jude had recently developed a habit of sliding up behind Janie and setting her gnarled, ring-heavy hands to massaging Janie's neck and upper back in a surprisingly gentle manner. Janie relaxed under these ministrations despite herself.

"Guess what?" whispered Aunt Jude.

"Huh," Janie grunted in response. She aimed her half-lidded eyes at the figgy baby.

"I won that raffle they did for a fund-raiser at Table of Plenty."

"Good," said Janie. Somewhere in her foggy brain she remembered that Table of Plenty was the soup kitchen where her aunt volunteered. She had no recollection whatsoever of any raffle.

"Well, I didn't win the grand prize, you know, that sunset dinner cruise for four on Boston Harbor. I was really hoping for that, because I was thinking you and I and Auntie Brigie and Uncle Charlie could go, and maybe we'd meet some interesting people because I think they seat you at tables of ten, so there'd be six others with us. I heard the food isn't that good, but there's lots of it."

"Okay," said Janie, telling herself that if she happened to doze off, Aunt Jude would see the baby choke, and Aunt Jude's scream-ing would wake her.

"But I didn't win it," Aunt Jude said with a sigh. "I should've bought more tickets. But I did win something pretty good. For you."

"Thanks," said Janie, now in a half dream about being on a boat and eating pizza and choking.

"Remember how I took that self-defense course after I got my bag snatched when I went to the Isabella Stewart Gardner Mu-seum with the group from the Pelham Senior Center?"

"Hmm?" said Janie, pulling herself back from the unpleasant boat ride.

"That was just a two-hour course on self-protection they did at the Senior Center. I set that up, you know. I didn't want any of the other ladies to go through what I went through. So I just went online and found Experiential Safety. Well, I didn't find it right away of course. I had to surf around awhile. That word 'experi-ential' can get you into some pretty risqué sites, let me tell you. Even 'safety' can get a little dicey . . . But then there it was, the perfect solution. So Arturo, he's the new director at Experiential Safety because the old director left to go to acupuncture school. Arturo set up that class for the ladies at the Senior Center. I think a couple of the men took it, too. Ralph and Sol, and Art, I think. No, maybe Art didn't come. Or did he? I can't remember now if Art was there. He's so quiet, you barely know if he's with you or not."

Aunt Jude stopped to check the pizza and plunked down into a chair, which served to rouse Janie from her stupor. "Oh, okay," said Janie, attempting to seem as if she'd been listening.

Aunt Jude continued. "So when they decided to do a raffle to raise money, I called up Arturo, because he was so friendly and helpful. Such a nice man. He's Argentinian. No, now wait, I think he's Perunian . . . Perunian? Is that right?"

"Yup," mumbled Janie, combing her black curls onto the back of her head with her fingers. What was this about prunes? She let the hair fall back onto her shoulders.

"Well, didn't he give me a whole Experiential Safety class for the raffle! A whole class! That's from nine in the morning to five in the afternoon. You can bring your lunch and eat in the classroom, but not on the mats, I don't think, because that could be messy. Or there are some very reasonable restaurants nearby. There's a Pirate's Hideaway, you know the one with the nets over the order counter and a gangplank by the restrooms? They have those in Rhode Island, too, because Auntie Brigie and I took a trip to Newport once, just for the day. It's kind of a long ride, though, so I wouldn't recommend it. Not with the little ones, anyway. So, guess what? You're going!"

"To Newport?"

"No, to the class! So you won't have to be so scared around here at night, when the house makes all those strange noises. You can protect the babies." Aunt Jude got up to check the pizza again. "You know they still haven't caught that cat burglar, the one that broke into those houses in Natick. Right in the middle of the night, he did it, with everyone just snoozing away. Pelham could be his next target." She sucked air in through her pursed lips. "I shudder to think!"

"Whoa, hold on," said Janie, finally realizing something had transpired that involved her. "I don't want to go to any class. You have to stop this."

"Stop what?" Aunt Jude closed the oven. She stood there with the oven mitts held up, as if she were about to perform surgery on a fire-breathing dragon.

"Stop signing me up for things. I don't want to go to classes or grief groups or harbor cruises or any other crazy thing you find online. The Internet is not the solution to all of life's problems!"

Aunt Jude tossed the oven mitts on the counter. "You're just hungry."

Janie blew an agitated huff. "So? Even if I stuffed myself with frozen pizza, and ate every friggin' Fig Newton on the planet, I still would NOT GO TO ANY CLASSES."

"Jane Elizabeth Dwyer LaMarche—"

"And don't start using all my names, because that does not work with me—"

"Your mother would be so ashamed to hear you speak like—"

"YOUR SISTER is in ITALY. In EUROPE. A whole OCEAN away. She came home for ONE WEEK when Robby died. ONE . . . GODDAMNED . . ." Janie clenched her teeth on the ache in her jaw, willing herself, commanding herself not to shed one single drop.

"Yes, well," Aunt Jude shook her head, opened her mouth to say something, shook her head again. She put the mitts back on and took the pizza out. One side of the mushroom and olive was almost black. "Noreen's the sensitive one," she said finally.

"SENSITIVE, MY ASS!" yelled Janie. Reeling away from Aunt Jude she caught sight of Carly sitting in her highchair. The corners of her little mouth were turned down into her trembling chin. Her eyes filled and overflowed onto the reddened cheeks, but no sound came from her. Janie burst into tears and put her hands over her face.

"There, now," she heard Aunt Jude say, lifting Carly from her seat. "There, there, now." Holding the baby in one loose-skinned arm, Aunt Jude put her other arm around Janie. Carly reached out to grab a handful of Janie's black hair. Ashamed of herself, Janie could not reach back.

THE NEXT EVENING, SATURDAY, Cormac stopped by with a bag of muffins.

"Ah," said Janie. "The Pelham swat team has arrived."

"Available for crises of all varieties, chickie," he said, and gave her a hug that lasted a second or two longer than usual. "Aunt Jude came by the bakery for soda bread this afternoon."

"Give you an earful, did she?" Janie closed the front door and followed him into her kitchen.

"Well," he said, reaching for the blue flowered plate on top of the kitchen cabinet. "Yeah. You know her." He took pineapple coconut muffins from the bag and arranged them on the plate. The last muffin, pistachio, he handed to Janie. She poured him a glass of orange juice and they sat down.

"I'm alright, you know," she said. "It's only her that makes me flip out. She's been capable of that my whole life, not just since Robby died."

"Nah, I know." His massive fingers delicately pulled the top off a muffin and returned the bottom to the serving plate. "I was just thinking about your mom."

Janie rolled her eyes.

"No," he said, "just that it's weird, her staying in Italy. I mean, I know she loves that job at the American School there. But, you know. It's summer." The entire muffin top went into his mouth.

"She can do what she likes." Janie picked a pistachio, still in its shell, off the top of the muffin. A year ago she had convinced him not to put green food color in the pistachio muffins, telling him it was old-fashioned, like dressing boys in blue and girls in pink. He solved the muffin's ensuing identity crisis by placing a whole pistachio on each one, like a flag announcing its country of origin.

"She should be here," he said.

"Well, she's not." Janie rolled the pistachio between her fingers. "I'm thirty-eight years old. She's no longer responsible for my mental state. And, honestly, I don't even know that I'd want her here."

"Come on."

"She'd be watching me like a hawk, worrying, fussing, sewing things like her life depended on it."

Cormac finished off his juice and dissected another muffin. "Hell of a stitcher, that one," he said. "Still, it'd be nice to have the company."

Janie shrugged and nibbled a piece of her muffin.

Cormac licked a crumb from the corner of his mouth. "You thinking about going back to work any time soon? Not like I'm pushing or anything," he said. "But maybe a little outside contact might be a good thing. People to talk to."

"People with respiratory problems aren't usually too chatty," she said.

"You know what I mean. At the hospital. Co-workers, janitorial staff . . . flower delivery people . . . pushy family members . . ."

He meant well, but the very thought made her stomach clench. "I can't even imagine getting dressed in work clothes, much less actually getting out the door. Besides what would I do with the kids?" She took another bite of her muffin. "You change the recipe on these?" she asked.

"Not really," Cormac replied, his mouth full of muffin top.

"You did too." Janie took a bigger bite. "It's sweeter."

"We just added a little brown sugar. Not that much. I can't believe you can even taste it."

"We?" said Janie. "What's 'we'? There is no 'we' at Cormac's Confectionary. There is only Cormac. Or was that the royal 'we'? As in 'We are not amused.'" She affected a British accent.

"One of the employees suggested it, and I decided to give it a try," he said, though the color was rising on his large cheekbones.

"Cormac McGrath, you have made a career out of never doing what anyone wanted you to do, so don't give me *that* load of bull. Who, exactly, suggested it?"

"Can't remember."

"Let me see if I can jog your memory. Unnaturally tall, thin, and busty? Comes complete with oven mitts and matching flour sack? Yes, it's Bakery Barbie, now available at a toy store near you!"

Cormac grinned, but didn't let out the big laugh Janie expected. "She's nice, you know," he said.

"Oh, I'm just teasing," said Janie, covering her surprise and an odd twinge of jealousy. Cormac took advice from Janie only rarely, and virtually never from anyone else. He'd had a lot of girl-friends in his forty years. A few had been serious; one had even enthralled him to the point that he followed her to Oregon and lived with her for a year. But then he came back. Janie suspected him of being too happy for marriage. He never seemed to need anything or anyone in his life that he didn't already have.

"So what about that self-defense course?" asked Cormac.

"Oh, please!" said Janie. "What are you? Aunt Jude's min-ion?"

"If I were Aunt Jude's minion, I'd have horns coming out of my head and a spiked tail. I know it's hard to believe, but from time to time I just happen to agree with her."

"Why, for godsake? It's not like I live in some bad neighbor-hood in Boston. I don't even *go* to Boston very often. I just sit here in boring old Pelham, where the biggest crime is throwing recy-clables in with the garbage."

"Read the police log in the paper. Stuff happens."

"Oh yeah. I could get my mailbox bashed in by a Red Bull–crazed lacrosse player. You've been giving Dougie Shaw too many free cupcakes."

"Hey, Officer Dougie may not exactly be Starsky or Hutch, but he knows about all kinds of crazy crap that goes on."

"Like?"

"Like those break-ins in Natick. And he says there's a whole lot more wife beating than anybody knows about."

Janie looked away. "I think I'm safe on that score."

"Oh, shit," said Cormac. He reached out his hand, speckled with tiny oven-burn scars, and patted her pale arm. "Chickie, I'm sorry."

She gave him a weak smile, "You're forgiven if you lay off the self-defense course."

He leaned toward her and whispered, "No chance."

TUESDAY, JUNE 19

Shelly came by this afternoon, all excited about a nibble on that other Pelham Heights house. The one she sold a couple of weeks ago was what she calls "A Big-Girl House." Women who wear good jewelry to the gym and whose parties are never potlucks. This one is even bigger, the grandest house she's ever listed, she says. Must cost a couple million. I don't want it to sell. Not sure why. I guess I don't want her to turn into a Big Girl and get a house to match.

She was all over me about the stupid self-defense course. I shouldn't have even mentioned it, except I thought she would be on my side. She's always on my side about everything else, which is weird when you think about it. I'm probably wrong a lot.

Anyway, she kept saying, "I'm a Real Estate Agent," as if this might actually INCREASE her credibility. She says there was an attempted break-in up in Pelham Heights, but the guy ran when the alarm went off. Then she peppered me with all the robberies and scams and near misses she's heard of in her fifty-three years. Shelly would consider it an assault if someone accidentally bumped her with their grocery cart and put a run in her twenty-dollar stockings.

I told her I don't need to worry about intruders. Anyone stupid enough to sneak up on my house in the middle of the night is going to break his ankle in one of the many gaping holes in my front yard—all thanks to her good friend the contractor, Mr. Dig-and-Disappear.

After she left, I took the kids to Town Beach for the first time since last fall. Just couldn't stand to be in the house anymore. I forgot how big Lake Pequot is. It's big. And windy. I know the water's probably full of goose poop, but there's something about the place that makes you feel almost healthy. It calmed me down from Shelly's suburban tales of evil and woe.

Dylan was busy digging a hole for a family of twigs he collected and Carly was sleepy, so I lay down on the blanket with her. She kept looking and looking at me. I had to close my eyes to get her to settle down and doze off. When I opened my eyes I saw what seemed like teeny, tiny fireworks hovering above the sand. Then my eyes focused and it was just a swarm of little bugs with the sun glinting off them. It wasn't a miracle or anything, but for a moment or two it was pretty entertaining.

4

WHEN FATHER JAKE ARRIVED that Friday he looked dramatically different. Actually, the difference was rather minor, but it made him seem like another person—his twin, perhaps, who was pinch-hitting while the ghostly priest haunted some other woebegone soul. He had on the same black jeans and black shirt he wore every day of his life, as far as Janie knew. But in place of the somber black sport shoes, there were tan low-cut hiking boots. And because the weather had turned cooler, he was wearing a brown chamois shirt over the black cotton button down. Strangest of all, the little white insert in his collar was gone. It was as if Johnny Cash had made a side trip to L. L. Bean.

"Everything okay?" asked Janie.

"What—you mean this?" he asked, holding up a large glass jar with a white screw-top. Distracted by his new persona, Janie hadn't even noticed what he was carrying. "We had a thank-you brunch for all the church volunteers," he explained. "This had fruit cup in it. I saved it for you."

"Thanks," she said, baffled.

"You're welcome." He set the jar on the counter in the kitchen. Carly was sitting in her highchair, aiming her tiny thumb and forefinger at a sprinkling of Cheerios on her tray. "She's up," said Father Jake. "That's perfect."

"For . . . ?" asked Janie.

"For a hike. I thought we could walk over to Jansen Woods."

"Well, that's a nice idea but it's her nap time."

"You have one of those baby backpacks, right? Would she sleep in that?"

She'd pass out like a drunken sailor, thought Janie. "I guess, but we wouldn't get very far. Jansen Woods is half a mile from here. You have to be back by noon."

"Why?" he asked.

"I don't know. You just always leave at noon."

"Well, it won't matter if I'm back later. Do you have sneakers or something?"

Of course she did. There was nothing at all keeping Janie from taking a walk, other than the fact that she didn't want to. She didn't even know why she didn't want to—it was a beautiful, clear, cool day. She and Robby had spent many days just like this one hiking in New Hampshire or Vermont before they'd had kids. She loved to hike. But not now.

Nevertheless there she was, trudging up her shady street. Carly was strapped into the carrier on her back, the wide pink brim of the baby's hat flopping with each reluctant step Janie took. Father Jake commented on various things around them: a squad of bicycles in a neighbor's yard, the height of an evergreen, the lack of fences. "How do you like your neighbors?" he asked.

"Well, I don't know everyone," she said. "Some keep to themselves. But most are nice. A few are still here from when I was a kid growing up in the neighborhood. When Robby died they sent an unbelievable amount of food. Kind of funny because I'd never had less of an appetite in my life, and suddenly I was up to my armpits in casseroles and banana bread."

Father Jake nodded and strode silently for a few minutes. "You know, I was thinking," he said quietly. "That's one of the worst things about being homeless. I mean, other than being without shelter. No neighbors. No one to notice when your life takes an unexpected turn. No one to bake banana bread."

"So you're saying I should be glad."

"Glad?"

"That though I'm a widow, pushing forty, with two small children, at least I have a roof over my head." She felt Carly slump slowly forward against her back, the little dozing body collapsing by degrees. "Of course, if I were homeless, I suppose I could be glad that I wasn't also blind. Or lame. Or cursed with the heartbreak of psoriasis."

Father Jake smiled at her. "You always make things funny."

"By that you mean I'm a sarcastic smart-ass."

"By that I mean you're funny. I wish I had that gift. I imagine it helps."

Janie stopped and put her hands on her hips. It took Father Jake a step or two to realize she wasn't moving forward anymore. He turned toward her and waited.

"You know," she said quietly so as not to disturb the sleeping baby, "you'd have a little more credibility if you weren't so unflinchingly nice." His eyebrows shot up. Janie continued, "I've been a total bitch to you, and you keep acting like visiting me is somehow pleasant."

He squinted at her, nodded slightly, looked away. Then he met her gaze. "I guess both things are true. You have been a total bitch to me. You're antagonistic and snide and a terrible listener."

Janie stepped back, stunned.

"You're also . . ." he searched for the word, "oddly likable, underneath all the sarcasm. And," he rubbed his thumb and forefinger over his eyebrows. "And you bagged me doing my . . . what did you call it . . . ? My Father Friendly impression." He chuckled then and shook his head. "I *am* unflinchingly nice, and it's a kick to be around someone who challenges me to be more than that."

Janie turned slowly and began to walk again. The baby was now snoring gently against her shoulder blade, the weight propelling her forward. "Where's your collar?" she asked as Father Jake fell into step with her.

"In my pocket. I got the feeling it annoyed you."

They turned right at the end of her street, down a less-frequented road; this dead-ended at a path that climbed gradually up a hill. Father Jake matched her pace, neither slow nor fast, and she began to feel her limbs warm up. Not a surging, angry heat, the kind that had become so familiar in the past five months. More of a steady warmth that poured through her like hot honey. "So, I'm a terrible listener," she said.

"Either that or you misunderstand me on purpose. I haven't decided which, yet."

"Probably a little of both."

"Probably."

THE VIEW FROM THE top of Jansen's Hill was obscured by the oaks and evergreens that had moved in since the Jansen family had given up and let the farmland revert to forest in the 1930s. But hikers still got the sense that they had ascended to a satisfying height when they sat on a fallen tree-trunk and smelled the oxygen-rich air.

"Hey," said Janie. "Can I ask you something?"

"Sure."

"Do you see your parents very often?"

"No," said Father Jake. He inhaled deeply and let the air in his chest out slowly, carefully. "Last I knew, my father was the deputy chief of police in Hamilton, Bermuda."

"Jesus!" Janie whispered, immediately regretting her choice of expletives.

"Yeah," he snorted. "Miserable bastard."

"Your mom's there, too?"

"No. He left her years ago. I'm not really sure where she is." He was completely still for a moment, then he blinked. "Where are your parents?"

"My mother lives in Italy. She teaches Home Ec at the American School in Turin."

"Even during the summer?"

"Nope. She's off now. Visiting a friend in Naples. Noreen Dwyer spends every cent she earns on travel. She'd rather board a plane than eat."

"Oh," he said, watching her.

"My parents split when we were little, and my father took off. I have a feeling my Uncle Charlie, my mom's brother, made the options clear: you either step up to the plate or you get traded to Siberia."

"And you have a brother?"

"Mike, my twin. He's in Flagstaff, Arizona. He's a sculptor."

Two crows flew screeching across the treetops and landed in a nearby hemlock. The birds sat quietly on separate branches, as if their prior outbursts had been embarrassing lapses in otherwise decorous behavior.

"And you have Jude," said Father Jake.

"Like a bad rash," replied Janie.

The priest chuckled and shook his head.

THEY BOTH SEEMED TO know when it was time to go, and rose simultaneously from their separate spots on the huge log. As they descended the trail Father Jake mentioned, "I'm going over to that soup kitchen, Table of Plenty, to help serve dinner tonight. I guess that's what got me thinking about homelessness."

"Don't tell me," said Janie, her quadriceps burning as she worked not to jostle the sleeping baby on her back. "Aunt Jude roped you in."

"She's definitely blessed with determination," he said diplomatically.

"If she told you to work on me about that stupid self-defense course," she said "you can save your breath. I'm not doing it."

"I'm not going to work on you."

"But you think I should do it."

"I don't think you'll get anything out of it if you don't want to be there."

"She did tell you about it, then," said Janie.

Father Jake smiled to himself and glanced at Janie. He looked for a split second like he might roll his eyes, but he never did. "A lot of those women at Table of Plenty have been assaulted at some point in their lives. Jude's probably heard some pretty grisly tales."

"I'm sure she has. And if I slept behind the Dumpster at Stop & Shop on a regular basis, self-defense would be high on my list, too. But I don't. Which is why it's so annoying that everyone's on me about it."

"Who's everyone?"

"Well, Aunt Jude, of course. And my neighbor Shelly. Also, my cousin Cormac, who stopped by last weekend to ply me with muffins."

"So all the people who've done the most to support you through this terrible time are asking you to do something that helps them sleep better at night."

"Exactly—it's not for me, it's for them. They just don't want to have to worry about me."

He stopped and waited.

"Shit," she whispered, the sudden realization of her utter self-absorption causing her to slump in defeat. "Sometimes I just can't stand myself."

They continued on. When they got back to Janie's house, Father Jake pulled a rock speckled green with lichen out of his pocket. He placed it in the empty fruit cup jar on the kitchen counter.

"What is that?" she asked.

"Something for your jar."

"Why that?"

"I don't know," he said. "I just liked it."

WHEN JANIE WOKE UP Sunday morning she felt frantic and didn't know why. She dearly wanted to go back to sleep and wake up the next day, but reminded herself this was not an option when you have two kids and you're the only grown-up in the house. Also, it was just generally not a good idea. *I guess everyone wants to spend the day in bed sometimes*, she told herself, *but when you feel half dead to begin with, it's an urge you really ought to fight.*

Dylan was feeling low, too. The first thing he said to her as he climbed into her big Robby-less bed was, "The sky is white." She didn't fully understand until he made her look out the window. Sure enough. White. Not a speck of blue, but also not gray. It wasn't sunny, but it didn't look like rain, either. It was as if the sky had stayed in bed.

And they had no plans. No one to see, nowhere to go. Well, Dylan had some ideas. As they collected Carly, went downstairs and started breakfast, he suggested that Disneyworld, snowboarding, or a volcano would work for him. Finally Janie offered up Paint 'N' Plaster Zone, with the cheesy plaster figures that you buy for about a 9,000 percent markup and coat in acrylic paint, which ends up on your clothes no matter how completely you've covered yourself with one of their overused, underwashed aprons. She was feeling pretty selfless when she suggested that one.

Dylan wasn't interested. "What does everybody else do?"

Damned if I know, thought Janie.

"What does Auntie Jude do?" he pressed.

Janie took a big slurp of coffee, requiring fortification at the mere thought of her aunt. She had more or less decided to do the self-defense course, but couldn't stand the idea of admitting it, feeling sure that Aunt Jude would be openly and annoyingly proud of herself.

"She goes to church," Janie told Dylan, never thinking that this would interest him.

"What kind of donuts will they have?"

Janie told him they don't have donuts, they have Eucharist, which he's not allowed to have because he's not old enough. He insisted that he was, too, old enough, and did the U-Triskets have

chocolate frosting and rainbow sprinkles, because that's his favorite kind. This got her laughing. All she could think of was
some old joke about an ad for "Eucharist Lite—I Can't Believe It's
Not Jesus!"

Dylan was not amused. She offered to take them out for donuts
(such was the level of her desperation). But by then he had it in
his head that church was the place for him. She told him they
had to dress nicely and sit quietly for a long time, which he was
absolutely certain he could do. He went to his room and returned
wearing his very best Hawaiian shirt, the one with gyrating hula
dancers on it; a yellow clip-on bunny tie from last Easter; red and
blue shorts that said "Go Patriots!" courtesy of Uncle Charlie; and
his cowboy boots.

The earnestness of the attempt combined with the adorable
absurdity of the outfit undid her, and she agreed to take him to
church. Then she hid in the bathroom and cried, because Robby
would have laughed so hard and been so proud and loved him so
much, and Dylan would never again see how happy he made his
father. But she would see it over and over in her mind until the
day she died.

She took a shower and ran the water just a few degrees shy of
scalding to help her stop weeping. When Dylan saw her dressed in
gray slacks and a tan blouse he pronounced her not nearly fancy
enough, and insisted she wear the macaroni-and-plastic-bead
necklace he had made for her at preschool. He thought Carly was
okay in a pink ballerina dress, especially after he accessorized her
with neon green sunglasses he got at a birthday party. He put his
swim goggles on in the car, and refused to take them off when
they got to the church parking lot. Finally, they compromised by
having him wear them around his neck instead of over his eyes.

Our Lord is having himself one heck of a laugh today, thought
Janie, searching the pews for Aunt Jude.

They found Aunt Jude at her usual post, standing sentry
(kneeling sentry might have been more accurate) in a pew by the

pianist. The expressions that passed over Aunt Jude's face when she saw them troop in were worth whatever lecture Janie knew awaited her. First it was shock that Janie and the kids had shown up at all, then bliss that they were paying a long-overdue visit to God. Then it was pride that evidently she'd gotten through to Janie. Then it was horror at what they were wearing.

By the time she got to horror, Dylan was hugging her, suffocating himself against her spongy stomach, and Carly was reaching out to grab the shiny, jingling necklaces. Janie knew that, despite the explaining Aunt Jude would have to do to her church lady friends after Mass, she was in bliss.

It was strange for Janie to see Father Jake processing up the aisle in his Mass attire: the white robe and multicolored stole around his neck. He saw her as he walked solemnly by, she was sure of it, but there wasn't even a hint of recognition. *The opposite of Aunt Jude,* thought Janie. *Pastor Perfect.*

Janie didn't have much of an opportunity to focus on the Mass, spending a good deal of time trying to keep Carly from strangling Aunt Jude with her own necklaces or chewing on the hymnals, which she preferred over the baggie of Cheerios Janie had brought. Most of them ended up on the floor, anyway. Then there were a couple of "emergency" trips to the bathroom with Dylan—he just wanted to check out the church basement and the crying room full of squirmy babies and their weary parents. Janie suggested that maybe the three of them should sit in the crying room instead of the pew, but he wasn't having any of that baby stuff.

Accompanying Janie in line for Communion, Dylan refused to believe that the host would have no frosting. "Maybe just whipped cream," he said in a loud whisper. When the Eucharistic minister gave Janie her wafer, Dylan grabbed it from her hand to inspect. "You can't eat this!" he yelled. "It's a Bingo chip!"

We are definitely going to get thrown out of here, thought Janie.

When Mass ended, they found themselves trapped in a stream of people heading for the basement instead of freedom. Aunt Jude told Dylan he'd been such a good boy, did he want a donut? Then Janie understood Dylan's confusion. It was a little social thing she had always bypassed: coffee and donuts after Mass. Dylan must have remembered from some long-ago time when Aunt Jude had taken him, Janie realized. And sure enough, there were ones with chocolate frosting and rainbow sprinkles.

"Janie, dear, how are you?" murmured a raspy voice as Janie reached to secure a plain donut for Carly. It was Mrs. Northup, an old friend of her mother's.

Still shitty, was the response in Janie's head, but she said, "We're doing better."

"Oh, isn't that good to hear," said Mrs. Northup, relieved, as she turned to another older woman who had asked her a question.

Yes, thought Janie. *It's a lie, but it's a good one. For you, anyway.*

Dylan ate his donut like he was auditioning for a donut ad. His whole body grinned in ecstasy, and by the time Janie had had her fill of smiling bravely at all of Aunt Jude's friends, he'd had three. Janie pretended not to notice. At least they had killed the morning. She could be thankful for that

Sunday, June 24

We went to Mass today, of all places, dressed like gypsies. Dylan was our stylist. It was pretty much a fiasco, but we made it through to donut time, which is all Dylan was really after to begin with, so I guess it ended okay.

It was weird to see Father Jake in his Mass gear, all serious up on the altar. He acted like he didn't know me, at least until he came down to the basement afterward. He'd gotten rid of the white robe, and I saw him smiling and telling little jokes with the older folks who were basking in the knowledge that the parish priest knows them personally. Little do they know there's nothing personal about it. I watched to see the guy who

told me I was a bitch, and called his father a "miserable bas-
tard." Nowhere to be found.

When his crowd of admirers had gotten their fill, he came
over to us. Aunt Jude got all twittery, like he was some sort of
religious rock star and we had backstage passes. He admired
Dylan's outfit, especially the goggles, and Dylan offered to let
him try them on. Father Jake politely declined. He doesn't need
them. He's already got a built-in set that keeps everyone from
seeing him too clearly.

"Hello, Jane," he said to me.

"Hello, Jake," I said back. I'm not sure why I left off the
"Father" part. Maybe I just wanted to shock him a little, see if
he was even in there. And suddenly there he was, the real guy,
not the body double he uses 99 percent of the time. Just for a
moment I could see him. Miraculous.

THE NEXT DAY, MONDAY, was Miss Marla's End of the School Year
Family Breakfast. Janie dreaded it. It meant acting normal and saying, "I'm fine, how are you?" when she knew—and *they* knew—it
wasn't true. It involved small talk, a skill she seemed to have lost
along with her gregarious husband. It required cappuccino coffee
cake.

The Confectionary was always busy in the morning, and Janie
had wanted to pick it up the day before. But Cormac would ask
what it was for, and he did not approve of day-old bakery items
at festive occasions except under the direst of circumstances. So
there she was, in line behind a short man with an expensive suit
and way too much product in his hair. The dull shine of the mousse
or gel or whatever kind of personal lubricant he used made Janie
want to dab him with a napkin.

"I'll have two, no three of those," the guy rapid-fired at Cormac. "And about six of those crescent-looking jobs, and what are
those? Crullers? Yeah, about five of those, and, I don't know, like
ten of those little sprinkly things down there—"

He looked up to see Cormac with his huge hands planted firmly on top of the display case, and stopped his barrage. Cormac gave him a bored stare and said, "You want fries with that?"

The coffee-sipping regulars at the counter along the windows nudged each other and guffawed. One of the middle-aged baker women called from the kitchen, "Be nice to the customers, Cormaaaaaac!"

To his credit, the short well-dressed, well-oiled man laughed. Cormac decided to fill his order and threw in a free small coffee, too. Janie was next, and told him what she needed.

"Good choice, chickie," Cormac murmured as he handed her the box. "Nothing like caffeine-spiked baked goods to pump you up for a challenge."

At school, Miss Marla looked less disappointed than usual. In fact, she looked downright enthusiastic. Janie speculated that, in addition to being understandably glad for the summer break, she seemed particularly interested in one of the fathers in the classroom.

There were two divorced fathers, Janie seemed to remember, and possibly more had become available since January, when Janie had stopped noticing even things that were specifically brought to her attention. One father was the recipient of more than his share of Miss Marla's glances and purposeful smiles. Around his neck he sported one of those leather strand necklaces with a single shell on it, as if he might be wearing board shorts underneath his business-casual attire, and was going surfing later. He seemed to be standing closer to Miss Marla than was absolutely necessary.

Good for her, thought Janie. But in her brain it played more like *Better her than me.* The thought of any man breaching her personal command module made her skin prickle. Unless it was Robby. But of course it wouldn't be Robby ever again. It had once occurred to Janie that his big, warm Robby-smelling body was now decaying. His skin might already be gone. The thought had filled her with such a dark hopelessness she had banned it. Whenever it surfaced unbidden, she pinched the back of her hand and changed locations. Watching Miss Marla and this father do their subtle little flirting dance evoked a sudden sense of Robby's body now lying in a dank, airless box. Janie clutched Carly a little tighter and told Dylan, "Let's go up in the loft and read a book."

"Can Keane come?" he said. Keane turned out to be a skinny blond boy with a big laugh. They sat on the loft pillows, Janie reading books, and Keane found them all completely hilarious. Dylan didn't think they were that funny, but he liked laughing with Keane.

"Oh, there you are," said a woman whose slight edge of exasperation indicated that she was Keane's mother. Janie almost didn't recognize her without her sporty biking outfit. She wore tan slacks, high-heeled shoes, and a pink silky sleeveless blouse with a large but tasteful beaded necklace. "I have to go to work now, sweetie, but I didn't want to leave without saying good-bye."

"Where does she work?" Dylan asked Keane.

"She does mucus groups," Keane answered.

"*Focus* groups," Keane's mother quickly corrected him. She glanced at Janie, the skin on her neck now matching the pink blouse.

"Oh yeah!" said Keane, with a belly laugh. "*Mucus* means boogers, right?" He turned to Dylan choking with laughter. "MUCUS groups, get it?"

"Does she have to wear a RAINCOAT?" Dylan yelped. The two boys were now rolling in the pillows of the loft, howling with laughter. Carly dove out of Janie's arms and onto her brother, wrapping her little fingers in Dylan's short black curls and pressing her drooly lips against his cheek. This made Dylan scream even louder, which sent Keane into a convulsive hilarity that looked almost painful. "I wet my pants!" he finally shrieked.

"Oh, Keane," his mother said with a slumping sigh. She checked her watch. "I'm late already . . ."

"You go," said Janie, feeling oddly sympathetic toward the mother of the giggling wonder. "I'll get him changed."

"Oh God no," she said quickly. "That's the last thing you need."

"It's just pee," said Janie, pulling Carly off Dylan. *Small potatoes compared to my shipwreck of a life.*

Keane's mother hesitated for a second, gauging whether Janie really meant it, and whether she could actually bring herself to allow the class tragedy to clean up her son's bodily fluids so she could be slightly less late to her new life-eating job and fend off the advances of her sweaty boss for one more day. Janie herded the boys toward the bathroom.

"I really owe you," called Keane's mother.

"It's no big deal," said Janie over her shoulder.

She located Keane's bag of extra clothes. When he'd changed, she put the wet clothes in the bag, intending to leave it in his cubby. They all washed their hands and went back into the classroom. The only parent left was the father with the shell necklace, and he was on his way out.

"'Bye, Dad!" called Keane.

"'Bye, buddy," he said, and wagged his thumb and pinkie in the "hang loose" sign.

Ew! thought Janie. *Check your birth certificate, pal. You're not nineteen.*

She said good-bye to Dylan and Keane and carried Carly out the door. It wasn't until she got to the parking lot that she realized she was still holding the bag of pee-pee pants.

MALINOWSKI'S TRUCK WAS PARKED in front of the house when Janie arrived home. An aging green station wagon with municipal plates was parked beyond his truck. Janie pulled into the driveway and saw Malinowski and a short gray-haired man peering into one of the holes in the yard.

"Hit any ledge?" the older guy was asking.

"Nope," said Malinowski. "Nice and sandy."

"Hi," said Janie as she carried Carly, who was asleep in her bucket car seat, toward the house.

Malinowski gave her a nod, then cocked his head at the older man. "This is Burton Cranston, the building inspector." To Cranston he said simply, "Homeowner."

"Good morning!" Cranston said, hitching his dirty khaki pants up over his gut. "Lovely spot you've got here, nice little place. And who's this now?" He aimed his too-wide grin at the sleeping baby. Janie instinctively pulled the car seat away from him, transferring it to her other arm.

"Her daughter," said Malinowski. "You about ready to sign off?"

"Well," said Cranston, eyeing Janie. "Long as I'm here, probably should take a look around, make sure everything's sound." He went to the kitchen window and banged his hand against the sill. "Might be some rot." He licked his lips. "It's a hot one. Shoulda brought a tonic with me." *Tonic* was an old man's word for soda, Janie knew. He was angling for a drink, and apparently irritating Malinowski, who crossed his arms and kicked the heel of one boot against the toe of the other.

"I should get her into the house," Janie said, and left the two men to their business. After putting Carly in her crib, Janie went down to the kitchen. As annoying as the building inspector was, she figured giving him a drink wasn't much trouble, and it might help smooth the way for her porch. As an afterthought, she poured a glass of ice water for Malinowski, too.

Cranston licked his lips again when he saw her coming, and said, "Now that's just the thing, just what the doctor ordered, yessir!" She gave them each a glass, and Cranston grabbed her hand and swung it back and forth as he took a tiny sip. "Ohhhh," he said. "Aren't you just wonderful. And pretty." He turned to Malinowski, "You ever see eyes like that? White-blue, like . . . like . . . well, I had a bucket that color once. Where *is* that thing?" He slurped another few drops of water and smiled. "If I find it, I'll bring it over here and show it to you."

Malinowski downed the water and handed Janie the glass, furrowing his brows at her and giving his head a barely perceptible shake. He turned to Cranston. "You all set with the holes?"

"They're fine, okay?" said Cranston, suddenly irritable.

"Great. Well, we should head out and let Mrs. LaMarche get back to work. She's very busy."

"Oh?" said Cranston, grinning again at Janie and waiting for an explanation.

Janie nodded. "Guess so."

Cranston pulled a wrinkled card from his back pocket and handed it to her. "Well, if you have any questions about his work, any concerns at all, whatsoever, you just call me. I'll run right down and take a look at it for you as a free service of the town. Okay? Don't forget now. You just call."

"Okay," said Janie. "Thanks."

The two men got into their vehicles and pulled away. A few minutes later, as Janie was putting the glasses in the dishwasher, there was a knock at the front door. It was Malinowski.

"Sorry about Cranston," he said. "The guy's a lech."

"Thanks for moving him along," said Janie.

"Yeah, I didn't think you'd be much in the mood for that."

"Oh," said Janie, the muscles in her neck starting to tense. "You were worried I'd flip out on him. Ruin your chance to pass inspection."

Malinowski stuck his hands in his pockets. "A little." Before Janie could summon sufficient breath to tell him to . . . to go . . . to go somewhere and do something to himself, Malinowski changed the subject. His words came out quickly, as if they had been trapped in his head for too long and now saw their chance to escape. "Your husband, Rob. He seemed like a good guy. How'd he die?"

Janie exhaled. It was a simple question, but before now she'd never had to answer it. Everyone she came in contact with knew exactly how her husband, who was definitely a good guy, had died. She surreptitiously pinched the back of her hand, and said, "He went out for a bike ride. He couldn't find his helmet so he went without it that day. An old guy didn't see the stop sign and hit him."

Malinowski was still. "I'm sorry."

"Thanks."

"Did you ever find the helmet?"

"What?"

"Where was the helmet?"

Janie was caught off guard. No one had ever asked about the stupid helmet. "In the toy bin. Dylan had been playing with it."

"Where is it now?"

"The dump."

"You threw it in the big compactor and crushed it."

She looked away. "Damn straight, I did."

He nodded. "I'll be here tomorrow with the Sonotubes. Now we can finally start this thing."

5

~

FRIDAY, JUNE 29, LATE

Shelly just left. She stayed with the kids while I went to that Experiential Safety course. Aunt Jude didn't tell me it was Friday night in addition to all day Saturday. I put the kids to bed before Shelly got here so she wouldn't be endangered by the necessity of child butt-wiping. This gave her more time to rearrange my book shelves and add ornamental touches to my mantelpiece. Not much of a babysitter, but she's got the home decor thing down.

As I've made clear to everyone who comes within ten feet of me, I did not want to go. Jake and I talked about it on our walk this morning. In his careful way, he suggested that "sarcastic humor might not be well-received." No kidding.

So I went, and I just hated it at first. It was like that grief group! Almost everyone was some kind of wounded creature. When the instructor asked us each to tell why we had signed up, it was a horror show. Two were rape victims, one was an incest survivor, one had been mercilessly teased all her life because of a truly wicked case of acne. An older woman had lost her only child to leukemia, which tanked out her marriage, so she was living alone and scared all the time.

Some weren't so bad. One was a nurse who worked the night shift and was afraid of walking to the parking garage at odd hours. There were two girls who had just graduated high school and their parents had made them come so they would be safe at college. They never left each other's sides. Their mouths dropped open when the others talked. A chocolate pecan pie says they won't be back tomorrow.

Then it was my turn. I had thought I'd go the single parent, alone-at-night route. Nuf said, right? But then these women were just so—what? truthful? serious? bullshitless? There was no bullshit. It was humbling. My prerecorded answer just wasn't going to cut it. I was already choky from their stories, so I just out and told them my husband died in a freak accident five months ago, and I have two small children. And this sound went out from them. It was all of them, but it was one sound, one really low note, half groan, half hum. Unrehearsed, un-planned. And it made me think that this is a sound I've heard before but didn't recognize. I always assumed it was pity, and it made me want to scream. But these random women from every walk of life, having just leaked out a little of their own misery—different flavors from mine, different packaging, dif-ferent brands—they did not feel pity. No. It was something else, something that's always there, like the rumble of the earth's core. It was like the hum of all the world's sorrow.

I don't feel scared, I told them. I don't feel much at all, ex-cept tired. And mad.

At the break, Instructor Debbie said, "This is going to be good for you."

After the break, Debbie introduced Arturo, her guy counter-part. Then they did a lot of talking about "walking defended" and "giving yourself permission to yell." Permission? News to me. But that was the hardest part for a lot of them. We think life is so much better now for women. But apparently we still need permission. The Dark Ages are alive and secretly thriv-ing like a herpes infection among us. You think you're in the twenty-first century and then up pops a sore of subjugation the size of a pepperoni slice in the middle of your face for everyone to see. Dab liberally with permission.

We practiced walking and yelling and a few cute little moves like eye pokes and foot stomps. We grabbed each other's wrists and learned how to twist out of it. It's too much partnering up and touching for me. Debbie said we might have a hard time falling asleep tonight, we might be too wound up. Not me. I'm exhausted.

IN THE DARK, JANIE woke from a dream of floating in fog. The source of her levitation seemed to be a steady hum, flowing like a low-voltage current through the marrow of her bones. She opened her eyes to a creaking, scratching sound and froze in her bed. Even her hair strained to determine the source of the noise. She sat up quickly, certain that someone was walking up the stairs.

"WHO'S THERE?" she boomed, having given herself permission.

The creaking continued.

"Mommy?" said Dylan.

Janie leaped out of bed and lunged to the top of the stairs, prepared to eye-poke the intruder to death. No one was there. She flung herself into Dylan's room, where the noise was louder. Squinting through the darkness, Janie saw the light on the baby monitor flickering erratically, and ripped the plug from the socket. The noise stopped.

"Who yelled?" said Dylan.

"It was just me," said Janie, trying to regulate her breathing as she straightened his tangle of blankets and tucked them around him.

"No," said Dylan. "Who said, 'Who's there?'"

"Me."

"Were you being a giant?"

"Kind of," she said. She kissed him and stroked his cheek with the backs of her fingers. By degrees his muscles undid themselves and he drifted off.

Having slain the mighty monitor, Janie sat on the edge of her bed, waiting for fatigue to topple her over. But her heart continued to pound, apparently unaware that the battle had been won. Knowing sleep was a while off, Janie decided to kill some time by ordering a new baby monitor.

Downstairs in the cluttered office she flicked on the computer and surfed haphazardly through several websites, one offering medical advice on postoperative care of implanted heart monitors, and one hawking very expensive baby clothes. After a while she found a good-enough monitor at a reasonable price with no shipping charges, and clicked Purchase.

Before shutting off the computer, she checked her e-mail. As usual, there were several from Aunt Jude, mostly forwarded messages from her online friends. There was an account of a vision of the Blessed Virgin seen in the boughs of a Douglas fir tree in Washington State; pictures of pets found sleeping in unusual places, including a dishwasher and the basket of a tricycle; and a quiz that would supposedly determine which Sesame Street character you were most like. The only message Aunt Jude had actually written was a reminder not to wear jewelry to the self-defense class. She had made that mistake herself, and her necklaces had gotten all tangled up in her purse. Since Janie only ever wore her wedding ring these days, it wasn't difficult advice to follow. Delete, delete, delete, delete.

One last e-mail was from Father Jake: "I forgot to ask—is Dylan entering kindergarten in the fall? If so, you might want to sign him up for religious education sooner rather than later. It's filling up."

Janie responded: "Not going to KG till next year," and hit Send.

The plans for the porch caught her eye and she picked them up and studied them. Robby's porch. His last gift in a long line of gifts he had given her over the years. She wondered which details had been his ideas. For instance, had he been the one to say, "Build the door diagonally across the corner closest to the driveway," or had that been the contractor's suggestion? She thought of asking Malinowski, but then dismissed it. Too pitiful.

A faint ping from the computer gave notice that an e-mail message had arrived. It was from Father Jake: "Okay, just checking. Hope the course is going well."

Janie replied: "Going okay. Was not sarcastic even once. At least not out loud. What are you doing up?"

In a few minutes, his reply came: "I'm not a very good sleeper. I do a lot of work at night. I like the quiet. How about you?"

"A spastic baby monitor woke me. Think I'll try to catch a few winks before the kids get up. Good night."

A few days later when she checked her e-mail, his response was waiting passively for her: "Good night, Jane."

JANIE AWOKE BLEARY-EYED AND cantankerous to the sound of Carly yelling, "Da! Da! Da!" from her crib. A memory of saying "He wants you" skittered across her mind. *He wants you? Who wants who?* Then it came to her. As a baby, Dylan had learned the "da" sound before he'd learned "ma." If he wanted someone, no matter who it was, he said, "Da!" On early mornings, when he woke them with his demands, she would nudge Robby and say "He wants you. Hear him? He's calling you."

"Okay, I'm coming," she now heard four-year-old Dylan say, and then the sound of his straining to release his sister from captivity. Knowing they would be on her in moments, Janie ground her molars together to keep from crying.

Jesus, Robby, she begged silently, *find the goddamned helmet.*

WHEN AUNT JUDE ARRIVED with a blueberry loaf from Cormac's and a new triple pack of Play-Doh, the children were dressed in clean, not-obviously-mismatched clothes, the beds were made, and Janie was pouring tar-black coffee into a carry mug. Before

Aunt Jude could grill her about the prior evening, Janie kissed
them all, including her fluttery aunt, and ran for the door.

Arriving several minutes early, Janie sat in her car in the
parking lot and sipped the coffee. The cinder block building that
housed Experiential Safety on the second floor was painted stale
blue, a color that attempted to be cheery but fell short. *Like Play-
Doh,* she thought.

Another car pulled in several spots down. Out popped the two
teenagers from Janie's class, wearing sweatshirts and ponytails,
one holding an iced coffee. Suddenly the other grabbed it and took
a big swig. The drink's owner faked a foot stomp and an eye poke,
startling her friend so that the iced coffee flew from her hand. It
fell several feet away, cracking open and pouring itself onto the asphalt as it rolled. The two girls laughed so hard they bumped into
a Mini Cooper parked in front of them, which made them clutch
each other and laugh even harder. Janie watched them struggle
to compose themselves before they opened the door to the building. She waited until the stick-on digital clock on her dashboard
turned to 9:03, then forced herself to exit the vehicle.

Most of the women were already in the classroom, waiting quietly, nervously in the chairs that lined one wall. Instructor Debbie
entered from a door across the room, affixing her light brown hair
into a bun from which strands stuck out at odd angles. "Okay,"
she said to the group. "How'd everyone sleep?"

A few told of unsettling dreams that sounded random and
mildly psychotic to everyone but the teller. One of the rape victims said she couldn't sleep at all. The teenagers were silent. At
the last minute, strictly from boredom, Janie told them about her
brief stint as a giant. The women laughed a few seconds longer
than they normally would have under other circumstances.

From there the training took off. They practiced elbows to the
chest and thrusts to the nose. They rehearsed demanding attention and ordering help. They kicked and poked and punched. Arturo, who had been adjusting a stance here, reviewing a technique

there, left for a bit. He came back covered from head to foot in a bizarre suit apparently made from football pads, well-placed pieces of Styrofoam, and a massive amount of duct tape. On his head was a cross between a football helmet and a beekeeper's hat, the mesh stretched tight, obscuring his face. He was huge and shiny. Janie might have laughed, but she didn't. They were preparing to be attacked.

Each woman got a turn. First was the nurse. She was very good at yelling, but when the attacker grabbed her wrists, she couldn't remember how to twist out and she struggled without purpose against him.

"Tell her what to do!" prompted Instructor Debbie.

"Foot stomp! Knee to the groin!" the classmates called breathlessly.

The nurse's knee flew up and her heel crashed down on the bridge of the attacker's well-protected foot. He released her and grabbed his foot, faking pain. She backed away and he lunged for her.

"Kick! Kick!" yelled the watchers as she landed on the mats. "Kick for your life!" cried one of the rape victims. Women on either side of her instinctively reached out to clasp her hands. "Do it!" they screamed, "Get him!"

The nurse rolled over, propped herself on one side, and swung at him with her foot. The first swipes were ineffectual and only served to push him away momentarily. He kept crawling back toward her in the menacing suit.

"Harder!" the classmates bellowed. "Take him out!"

The nurse's foot began to swing higher, her heel coming down in a hacking motion on his head. The relentless thumping on the padded helmet felt like fireworks in the women's chests. Finally the attacker curled into the fetal position and surrendered. The nurse jumped up and screamed "911!" as they had been instructed, barely getting it out before the group rushed toward her. They hugged her and patted her, a couple of them crying. Janie

was surprised to find herself caught up in the crowd, reaching out
to pat the nurse's shoulder.

One by one, they got their turns, the scenarios changing
slightly each time. The woman with terrible acne yelled "BACK
OFF!" with such intensity that the attacker put his hands up and
walked away.

The older woman whose son had died went limp during her
turn. She just lay on her back and cried. The attacker sat back on
his heels as Debbie crawled up to her and murmured, "Bea, we're
with you. You're not alone. You have to fight back."

"No," whimpered Bea, "I can't."

"You can do it," a few called to her. "Come on, Bea. Just try."

"No," she groaned.

One of the two teenagers, the one who'd grabbed the iced coffee in the parking lot, approached. Surprising everyone, she lay
down on her back next to the older woman.

"Mrs. Benson?" she whispered. "I would personally really
appreciate it if you would make this loser evaporate." And she
closed her eyes.

The attacker surged to life, lunging for the girl who lay prone
on the mat. Mrs. Benson groaned, "No!" and blocked him with
her foot. He fell back, giving Mrs. Benson just enough time to
come to a crouch over the girl, creating a shelter with her aging body. When the attacker lunged again, his mesh-covered face
met with the heel of Mrs. Benson's palm. He fell back again, one
hand to the mesh, the other hand swiping at the girl. Mrs. Benson
grabbed the arm and sunk her teeth into the duct tape.

The women screamed "Go!" and "Yes!" and "Do it!" They
squeezed each other's hands and shoulders; they howled their approval.

Mrs. Benson maneuvered her body to kick him, her foot coming down in an axing motion over his stomach. She continued to
do this even after he had gone into the surrender position. Only
the group calling "911!" cued her to stop. The teenager helped the

older woman get to her feet, and together they called out for the police, the girl throwing her fist into the air like a cheerleader.

Janie found tears leaking down her face, and quickly wiped her eyes and nose on the sleeve of her shirt. It was her turn next, and she screamed and stomped and axed as she'd been taught. But the whole time she was thinking of Bea Benson and her dead son.

JANIE HAD ASSUMED SHE'D have to go out and buy something to eat during the noon break. But Debbie appeared with sandwiches, sodas, chips, and cookies. It was a working lunch, she explained.

"You did great, Janie," said the incest survivor, sitting in the next chair. "You really know how to yell." She took a sip of her diet soda and considered, "I think I should learn to swear more."

"Sometimes it comes in handy, I guess." Janie said. "I'm sorry, I can't remember your name."

"It's Katya." She took another sip. "I'm really enjoying this. Are you?"

"Well," stalled Janie. "It's better than I thought it would be."

"Yeah," said Katya. "I was kind of embarrassed at first. But it's like group therapy, don't you think? All weird in the beginning, and then it gets really inspiring."

"Maybe," nodded Janie. "Chips?"

"No thanks," said Katya, patting her flat stomach. "I'm getting married in seven weeks, and the dress shows every ounce!"

"Everybody got what they need?" called Debbie. "I want to do a little checking in to see how we're doing after your first attack."

"It's not my first attack," said one of the rape victims. There was a silent but palpable gasp as everyone recalled the vicious assault she had tearfully described.

"Oh, I'm sorry—I meant—" stammered Debbie.

"It's okay," replied the woman. "It was definitely my *favorite* attack."

The group smiled in relief. They shared what they were thinking as the attacker came at them, how they felt as they struck
back. The girl with acne said she saw the faces of all the kids
who had taunted her over the years. Another commented on how
much harder it was to watch than to fight.

"The next set of attacks is a little tougher," said Debbie. "Before the attacker was silent. Now he's going to say things."

"Bad things?" asked one of the rape victims.

"Disarming things. Things that keep you from doing what you
need to do."

ARTURO HAD GONE INTO the office and taken off the suit. He came
out and ate with them, complimenting each one on a particular
poke or jab they had delivered. Janie saw this as systematic and
contrived, but then he turned to her. "You did fine in the attack,"
he said, "but your best defensive move is the way you hold yourself. No one's going to mistake you for an easy target. It's clear
you're ready for a fight."

She knew he was sincere.

During the next round, each woman was attacked from a standing position, as before. But this time, Arturo said things from behind the mesh. Taunts, threats, even crazy things, as if he were
on drugs. It heightened the tension, but this time the potential
victims were more prepared with their defense. No one fell apart;
no one needed to stop.

Then they learned "horizontal defense."

"Sometimes attacks happen when we're at our most vulnerable," said Debbie. "Can anyone guess when that is?"

"When I'm with my future in-laws?" said Katya. The group
chuckled.

One of the rape victims mumbled something.

Debbie said, "I don't think everyone heard that, Rhonda."

"When we're asleep," Rhonda replied flatly.

"That's right," said Debbie gently. "When we're feeling safe in our beds, unaware of any intrusion."

The women lay prone on the mats with their eyes closed, imagining waking up with a stranger on top of them. They learned the counterintuitive technique of allowing him to remain there for a few moments without struggling. They waited for the moment when the attacker would need to loosen his grip, when they could then spring into action, focusing their strength and intent on disabling him. Arturo supervised as the women practiced in pairs, taking turns hurling the other off. Janie found it uncomfortable and distasteful to have someone on top of her, even for the few brief moments before she pitched her partner to the mat. For others it was even more disturbing. Rhonda needed to stop several times, and eventually Instructor Debbie became her partner.

When Arturo put the attacker suit back on and stood in the corner of the room, the women couldn't take their eyes off him. They found themselves picking at their cuticles and hunching their shoulders as each waited her turn to be attacked "horizontally."

It went quickly, Janie surmised, because Arturo was too easy on them. Carefully he placed himself on each potential victim and silently waited to be thrown. When they kicked and poked, he pulled into his surrender position too soon, Janie concluded. He let Rhonda disable him in under fifteen seconds.

After practicing a bit more, Debbie announced, "Now we're going to put it all together."

Again the women waited for their turns. But when the attacker got on top of them this time, he was not careful and he was not silent. He snarled nasty, disgusting things at them. He pinned them and made them wait long moments for an opportunity to take action. Debbie crouched close by, watching each woman intently. When it was Rhonda's turn, she inched a little closer.

"Okay, bitch," growled the attacker, "now you're going to get it."

"Wait, Rhonda," whispered Debbie, "wait for your chance."

"I followed you back from that party, 'cause I just knew you wanted it," he sneered.

A breathy, high-pitched keen of terror escaped from Rhonda's lips.

"Don't fade out, Rhonda," breathed Debbie. "You stay right here and get rid of him."

"You want some of this, bitch? You know you can't wait for it." The attacker released one of her arms and reached down toward his waist. The watchers sucked in their breath in horror.

"Go!" said Debbie. "Eye poke!"

"YOU FUCKER!" screamed Rhonda and rammed her clenched fingertips so hard into the mesh-covered face that a tiny hole appeared. The attacker's hand flew to his face and he screamed, flailing to contain her with the other hand.

"NO FUCKING WAY!" howled Rhonda and, pulling a leg up to brace herself, pitched him off her. In an almost graceful, swooping motion she pivoted and sank the heel of her foot into his groin. "YOU—" she slammed her heel again—"CAN'T"— again—"HAVE ME!"—and again. "I'M MINE!" The heel came down more rapidly now, "I'M MINE, YOU MOTHERFUCKER! I'M MINE!"

Debbie had to intervene. As the women swarmed around Rhonda with hugs and congratulations, the attacker rose gingerly and limped toward the office. He needed a little "break."

The only one who hadn't had a turn yet was Katya, the incest victim. When the attacker returned, Katya lay patiently on the mat and waited for him to descend upon her. Once engaged, the attacker started his patter: "You slut," he hissed. "You're a little slut, just like your mother."

"Uh, Debbie?" said, Katya, twisting her head around. "Can I speak to you for a minute?"

The attacker got off Katya, and the two women crossed the room and whispered to each other. Then Debbie motioned the attacker over and whispered to him while Katya went back to lie on the mat with her eyes closed.

"Katya?" said the attacker climbing onto her again. "Muffin, are you awake?"

"Go away, Daddy," she said.

"I love you so much, Muffin. I just love to be close to you."

"Daddy," said Katya, her voice starting to tremble. "Please go back to your own bed."

"But, my bed is so cold, honey," he crooned. "Mommy is so cold and you're so warm. Just like a hot, fresh, gooey muffin."

Katya started to cry. Janie felt as if she might be sick.

"Make him go," whispered Debbie. "He has no right, Katya. Make him go."

"You . . ." Katya breathed. "You have no right, Daddy."

"No right?" said the attacker. "You're my daughter. *My* daughter. You belong to *me*."

"Who do you belong to, Katya?" murmured Debbie.

"Me," choked Katya. "I belong to—"

"Don't speak to your father like that, Muffin." The attacker released his hold on her wrists to stroke her face. "I don't want to have to punish my best girl."

"GO!" screamed Janie, surprising herself. Katya's head snapped toward Janie, momentarily making eye contact. "THAT'S NOT WHAT FATHERS DO!" Janie yelled at her.

Katya heaved the attacker off. He came back at her on his hands and knees and she poked at him with the ball of her foot.

"Kick!" the women screamed. "Stop him!"

"Say it!" yelled Debbie. "Tell him!"

"No more, Daddy," grunted Katya, her kicks picking up speed. She glanced again at Janie over the attacker's shoulder.

"He's no father!" yelled Janie, pointing her finger at Katya. "He's a rapist! MAKE HIM STOP RAPING YOU!"

Katya screamed then, a howl that would shame a banshee. She slammed her heel into his face, forcing him to roll away from her.

She jumped to her feet and kicked him in the ribs. "YOU'RE NO FATHER, DADDY!" she screamed raggedly. "YOU'RE NO EFFING FATHER!"

The attacker surrendered. Katya put her hands to her face and wept. As the women surrounded her, Katya lowered her hands and searched the crowd. She reached for Janie, wrapping her arms around Janie's neck and sobbing into her shoulder.

"Good work, Katya," whispered Janie. "Good effing work!"

6

◆

MONDAY, JULY 2

Malinowski's out there with those big cardboard tubes in the holes, pouring heaping gobs of cement into them. Hopefully the yard will stop looking like it's been attacked by giant gophers sometime soon. I should probably be paying him time and a half for keeping Dylan entertained. School's out and camp doesn't start until next week.

His little friend Keane is coming over. When I called, his mother (whose name is Heidi—doesn't it just figure? All she needs is pigtails and a little Swiss jumper), practically kissed me over the phone. Apparently she took him to work one afternoon last week, and he knocked over the water cooler, among other things.

She had a sense of humor about it, though, which I didn't expect. She said, "The upside is my boss is no longer trying to get me to go out with him." I guess giggling, pants-wetting, hyperactive boys do come in handy sometimes. As human shields in the dating game, if for nothing else.

Oh God, Malinowski is letting Dylan hold the cement hose . . . but he seems to be getting most of it into the tube. He's imitating the cement coming out now, in a pantomime of barfing. Malinowski is laughing.

Every once in a while, for just a second, everything's okay.

———————

WHEN KEANE ARRIVED, HIS mother barely stopped the car long enough for him to get out. "Thank you SO much," she called from the driver's side window. "I can't thank you enough!"

Yeah, you can, thought Janie. *You can actually thank me too much.*

"I'M STARVING!" announced Keane.

Janie said to Malinowski, "Okay if they're out here while I make lunch?" She nodded toward Keane and murmured, "This one's kind of . . . busy."

Malinowski surveyed the blond boy, who was hacking furiously with a stick in a nearby mound of dirt. "I'll trade you for one of whatever you're making," he replied. "Left my cooler home."

Janie came out with a stack of peanut butter and banana sandwiches, a bowl of grapes, cups of chocolate milk, and a box of wipes. She parked the boys on the wide front step and scrubbed the dirt off their hands. Malinowski joined them, sitting on the lower step, his square shoulders the height of the boys heads.

"Hey," Keane said to Dylan, with a mouth still full of peanut butter. "Hey, where's your dad?"

Janie went still, the grape in her hand hovering like a hummingbird in front of her chin. She didn't look at Dylan, but she listened so hard she thought she could almost hear his cells dividing. In her peripheral vision, she saw Malinowski glance over at her.

"Umm . . . ," said Dylan, squinting for a second. "Uh, he's in heaven. He got hit by a car." He pulled the crust off his sandwich and put it on the step. "You should always wear a bike helmet."

"My dad says I don't always have to," said Keane.

"You should," replied Dylan.

"Okay," said Keane. "Want this grape? It's kinda squishy."

"Pretend that's a grape tree over there," said Dylan. "Pretend it eats grapes!"

The boys winged the few remaining grapes toward the tree, widely missing their mark, but hooting like champions nonetheless. They jumped up and began to search for small stones and half-rotted acorns to throw at the tree.

Malinowski piled their napkins and paper plates onto his own. "I think I hear the baby," he said, handing them to her without looking up.

Janie hadn't heard the baby, though the monitor was aimed out the kitchen window, as usual. When she went into the house to check, Carly was still fast asleep. Janie wondered momentarily if Malinowski had purposely given her an excuse to take a moment to collect herself, but dismissed it. How could he know how hard a simple exchange between four-year-olds could hit her?

When she went back to the kitchen to put away the peanut butter and dispose of the banana peels, she heard Malinowski say, "Boys." He didn't yell, or sound alarmed, but his tone was mildly menacing, meant to be taken seriously. She glanced out the kitchen window and saw him aiming a warning look at Dylan and Keane, who were facing each other, frozen in mid-throw.

"What's going on out here?" Janie said as she strode out the door toward them.

On closer examination, each boy was holding a clod of dirt, apparently not for the first time. They were filthy. Janie caught the edge of Malinowski's smile as he turned back to the cylindrical tubes of cement that would hold up their porch.

"Hey," she said to the boys. "This is not a good game, someone could get dirt in their eyes or hit with a stone."

"Sorry!" called Keane immediately, and threw down his dirt. "Sorry Mrs. . . . Mrs. Dylan's Mom!"

Dylan started to laugh. "THAT'S not her name! She's not Mrs. ME!"

"She's Mrs. YOU!" Keane giggled.

"You can call me—" started Janie.

"She's Mrs. YOU CAN CALL ME!" yelled Keane and fell down in the dirt laughing.

"She's Mrs. TELEPHONE!" said Dylan.

Janie rolled her eyes and glanced at Malinowski as the boys lay in the dirt and poked each other with their muddy fingers.

"Who's on first?" he said with a smile.

"What's on second," she answered. "Do you have kids?"

He shook his head. "Nieces. But they're teenagers now, so they've kind of lost their sense of humor temporarily."

"These two think they're Abbott and Costello."

"Boys and dirt," he said. "Instant happiness."

She looked at him, taking in the scar on his right arm as it shifted obediently with the movements of his ropy muscles, and the calm, mildly amused set of his dark eyes. And she could think of not one thing to say. He went back to work. She told the boys to meet her at the swings in the backyard and she would bring them pirate hats.

WHEN KEANE'S MOTHER ARRIVED she looked at him and sighed. "What happened?" she asked Janie.

"Oh they got filthy, playing in the dirt out front and, so I put bathing suits on them and turned the sprinkler on in back. I hope that's okay."

"No, it's fine!" Heidi insisted, running a hand over Keane's clean wet hair. "I just feel bad he made such a mess. Wait, whose clothes are those?"

"They're Keane's, from when he wet his pants at school. I took them home by accident and then washed them, but I forgot to get them back to you."

"It's pretty rare to find Keane cleaner at the end of the day than when he started," Heidi said. "Thank you so much."

"Stop thanking me. How was work?"

Heidi gave a meaningful smile over the boys' heads. "Uneventful."

Janie smiled back and nodded. The boys ran over to inspect the bugs on the grill of Heidi's car.

"Are you . . . I don't mean to be too personal . . . ," said Heidi.

Then don't, thought Janie.

Heidi continued, "Are you thinking about dating at all?"

"No."

Heidi nodded quickly. "It's too soon. Only six months since your husband passed. Way too soon."

"How do you know when my husband passed?"

Heidi gave her an incredulous look and stammered, "Uh . . . Well, we all . . . they told us at school. I just remember Valentine's Day was my turn to send over a meal and that was exactly a month after it happened. I wanted it to be really nice because it was the first month anniversary of his death, and it was Valentine's Day for goodness' sake, and I just felt so . . ."

"Bad for me."

"Well . . . ," said Heidi. "Yeah."

Janie handed her the bag of Keane's muddy clothes. "Sorry I didn't get to wash them."

"Oh God, don't worry about that," she said, snatching the bag. "We'd love to have Dylan over some time. Maybe on a Sunday? Keane's usually with his father on Saturdays."

"Maybe," said Janie. "We have church on Sundays, so it gets kind of busy. We'll see how it goes."

"Oh," said Heidi. "Okay."

When they'd gone, and Dylan had returned from running along the edge of the front yard, waving and yelling to Keane as they drove away, he put his arms around Janie's waist and collapsed against her. "That was so fun," he sighed.

"Keane's pretty entertaining," said Janie, rubbing his small shoulder blades. "Is he nice to you?"

"Yeah," said Dylan. "He's my best friend."

"HEY, I GOT THIS un-freakin'-believable cake that's past the sell-by date. How about if I stop by with some takeout?"

It was 5:45, and Janie's daily downward spiral was halted before impact by a call from her cousin Cormac. For a brief moment,

Janie imagined a balding man floating behind a metal desk in the Cosmic Department of Prayer. He was stamping hers, "Answered." Not that she had actually prayed. But maybe there was a God, and maybe He saw her lying on the living room rug with the baby gnawing on the hem of her T-shirt and the small boy begging her for just one more game of Candy Land, the most heinously annoying game ever invented, and He could tell that dinner was going to be bowls of Rice Krispies for yet another night. And maybe He was feeling merciful.

"Sure, that'd be great." And trying not to sound desperate, she added, "When will you be here?"

"We're at Ricky's Ribs. We already ordered, so about fifteen minutes."

We?

"Cormac's coming!" Janie told Dylan, who was a little confused by her sudden burst of energy. "Ten-second tidy!"

Janie put Carly in her "activity center," a circular seat surrounded by rattles and mirrors and toys. On average, Carly enjoyed "activities" for about twelve minutes before she would scream for release. Janie called out "Ten . . . nine . . . eight . . ." while Dylan scrambled to put away the toys, and she darted into the kitchen to put the breakfast and lunch dishes into the dishwasher. She ran a sponge over the counters and the kitchen table, and dusted up the battalion of Cheerios spread under the chairs.

"Why do we have to clean up so much?" asked Dylan, as she smudged a remnant of cream cheese off his face. "Cormac's not tidy."

Janie thought of Cormac, who would likely show up with chocolate glaze on his white cotton baker's pants and confectioners' sugar on the back of his neck. "No," she answered, "but it's good to do when someone's coming over. We don't want him to think we're messy all the time."

"Or too sad to put our toys away."

Janie looked at him. His T-shirt was too short, she realized. It hiked up above the waistband of his shorts when he moved. How had that happened? How did children keep growing no matter what?

"Mom, the bottom of your shirt's all wet with baby slobber."

The front door opened as Janie slid a clean gray T-shirt over her head and came down the stairs. "Rib guy!" boomed Cormac, setting down two big brown bags.

"Yuck!" yelled Dylan, who ran to sit on one of Cormac's huge, sticky sneakers and wrap his arms around Cormac's tree-trunk of a calf.

"Okay, Chicken-Nugget-and-French-Fry guy! How's that?"

"Sweet!"

Cormac walked over to rescue Carly from her toy-encrusted prison, dragging Dylan along with his foot, and revealing Barb, who had been standing behind him.

"Hi," she gave a little wave to Janie.

"Oh," said Janie. "Hi."

Barb removed her shoes, baby blue canvas espadrilles with four-inch wedge heels, and placed them tidily by the front door. Her toenails were painted hot pink.

"You don't have to take off your shoes," said Janie.

"I always do when I go somewhere after work, otherwise I'd drag flour all over your nice clean house. Plus," she said with a shy grin, "they're killing me."

Janie surveyed the outfit: a thin, pale pink T-shirt with cap sleeves that clung delicately to her breasts; white cotton pants that matched Cormac's, except they were clean and didn't seem to bag around her narrow thighs; and a pink-and-white smiley-face printed belt, which held the pants about a half inch below the hem of the shirt, revealing a flawlessly flat and well-tanned stomach. Her navel was neither innie nor outtie. It lay snuggly in its little cave like a pearl.

It was the scrunchie wrapped around her honey-highlighted hair that made Janie want to spit. Pink smiley faces to match the belt. *Where do they sell this crap?* wondered Janie. *On the sidewalk outside of Wal-mart?*

Cormac gathered up the children and hauled them into the kitchen, and Barb carried in the bags of food, leaving Janie with nothing to hold but her disgust. Cormac tickled and juggled the kids into their seats. After they settled in to eat, Cormac excused himself and headed to the bathroom.

"So . . . ," ventured Barb, holding a rib delicately between her thumb and forefinger. "It must be nice to live in the house you grew up in."

"Uh, it's okay." Janie sank her teeth into the meat, pulling off a large chunk so that she had to suck in the last bit of it.

"Bet the price was right, anyway," Barb joked.

"We paid market value," said Janie still chewing.

"Oh, I didn't mean . . . of course you wanted to be fair to your mother . . ."

"And my brother." Janie reached for a napkin and wiped a spot of grease from her chin.

"Of course." Barb served herself a spoonful of creamed spinach. "Have you changed it much? Redecorating your mother's house could be a little . . . touchy?"

"She couldn't have cared less. She was so happy to get that job in Italy I could have lit the place on fire and she wouldn't have noticed."

Barb chuckled uncertainly.

"Lit what place on fire?" asked Dylan

"Thinking of torching something, chickie?" said Cormac as he strode back into the room and folded his large frame into the wooden chair.

Janie rolled her eyes. "No one's lighting anything on fire, it was just a figure of speech."

"What peach?" asked Dylan.

"You!" said Cormac, with a light poke to Dylan's belly. "You're a peach!"

Dylan giggled and climbed onto Cormac's spacious lap. He slid his chicken nuggets over next to Cormac's pile of ribs and butternut squash. Cormac gave him a greasy kiss on the cheek. These were the moments Janie feared the most: the times when she felt so grateful and so bitter all at once.

"Can I get her?" said Barb. Janie had failed to notice the increasing volume of Carly's irritability.

"Oh. Yeah." Janie stood up, forgetting for a moment why, and then turning toward the cupboards. "She needs a bottle." While her hands completed this task, she contemplated asking Cormac to move in with them and also asking him not to come over anymore. *You're gripless*, she told herself and turned back toward the table, where Cormac held her firstborn, and this woman, Barb, held her baby.

Carly was standing on Barb's thighs and sticking her fingers in Barb's mouth. *Jesus!* thought Janie. *Why do grown-ups think it's a good idea to slobber their nasty germs all over a baby's fingers, knowing they'll go right into the baby's mouth. Would they let someone slobber in* their *mouths?* Then she remembered that that's exactly what French kissing was and shook herself. Cormac grabbed one of her fingers and jiggled it before she could lambaste his girlfriend, Typhoid Mary.

"Hey, did you know Barb's a photographer?" he said with more volume than usual.

"No, I didn't," she replied tightly.

Before Janie realized it, Barb had taken the bottle. "I am not," she said with a little flush that Janie knew was probably completely adorable. "Not until I finish school." Carly assumed a reclined position in Barb's lap, bottle snug in her chubby hands, limp with contentment as she slurped.

"Before she got into the photography program at Mass College of Art, she was a sous chef at Le Roux," Cormac explained.

"I used to call it 'Le Zoo.' The hours were bizarre, and everybody smoked and slept with each other and had crying jags at work. I just couldn't handle it."

"But apparently you're tough enough for the scone business," said Janie.

Cormac and Barb found this hilarious, and when their laughter died down, they glanced at each other and started laughing all over again. Dylan laughed too, his mouth revealing bits of partially masticated French fries. Carly closed her eyes and slurped harder.

Christ, thought Janie and shook her head.

When dinner was over, Cormac put Dylan in the bath and Janie cleared the table. Barb held the sleeping baby in her lap. "This is heaven," she whispered, kissing Carly's silky head. "Janie?"

"Yeah." Janie pitched the takeout boxes into the trash one by one.

"Do you think you would ever let me photograph them? I have this portraiture class and I'm supposed to do a range of ages."

"Oh," said Janie, hating the idea, but not sure why.

"It wouldn't be Olan Mills-y, though. It's supposed to be creative so I might try some things . . . if that was okay with you. Actually it would be great if you would be in some of them."

"Oh . . . I don't . . ." Janie shook her head.

"You're such a matched set, the three of you," Barb pressed her point. "I mean you look alike, but also . . . more than that . . . you just go together."

"Do it," said Cormac, returning to the kitchen with a freshly scrubbed, pajama-clad Dylan. Janie glared at her traitorous cousin. He shrugged. "It's time for new pictures."

JANIE WOKE IN THE middle of the night for no reason. The kids were sleeping soundly; the house was making only its usual repertoire of fifty-year-old house noises. To her knowledge she hadn't been dreaming. Her eyes opened and she was awake.

If Robby were here, she thought. Her fingers could feel his skin, smooth and warm and slightly moist. Living skin. When she was cold, or less than content for any reason, she would press herself against his back for comfort. If she wanted to wake him, she would kiss the spot just between his shoulder blades. For a few moments he wouldn't move, letting her kiss him. Then he would arch slightly, pressing his backside against her, stirring her. It was their signal.

And now her signal went wandering out into nothing, like those alien hunters playing Mozart into space, hoping for a response. Maybe aliens on some distant planet were listening to Mozart, but for Janie there was no receiver. At any rate, there was no response.

Janie got out of bed and went downstairs in the dark, not toward anything really, just away from their bed. She put a load of wet laundry into the dryer, the loping hum of it obscuring her hopelessness. She leafed through two days of mail, most of it junk, some of it bills. There was a postcard from her mother, with a view of Mount Vesuvius, addressed to "Dylan & Carly LaMarche."

"Hello, Little Ones! How are you! I am having a lovely time in Napoli, Italy. It's way, way down the boot from where I live, near the ankle. Someday your mother will bring you to see me and I'll take you all around. I am coming to Pelham next month, and I'll be there for your birthday, Dylan! *A presto!* Love, Gram."

Presto? thought Janie. *Presto would have been a month ago. "Soon" is such a convenient word when you're not the one waiting.* She tossed the postcard back onto the pile of junk mail and wandered into the office. When she flicked on the computer and checked her e-mail, there was a message from Father Jake: "Hello, Jane. I was wondering if we could take our walk a bit earlier on Friday. I need to meet with the Worship Committee Chairperson, and 11:00 a.m. Friday was her best time."

Janie sent back, "Dylan's in between school and camp this week, so a walk wasn't really in the cards, anyway. Maybe we should just skip it."

A few moments later his reply came. "I'd rather not skip it altogether. How about if I come by at 10:00 and we sit in the backyard with the kids?"

Janie tried to picture Father Jake in his darkened rectory, face illuminated only by the indifferent glow of the computer screen. What was he wearing? Pajamas? Probably the kind that come in a set, the top a button-down with a wide collar. Were they black? Plaid? No, maybe white with little black terriers all over them. Maybe the terriers had little red bows around their necks. Janie smiled. Now she wanted to know.

"What are you wearing?" she typed. But just before she hit the Send button, she stopped. *Asking a priest what he's wearing in the middle of the night?* she laughed at herself. *Are you high?* She deleted the sentence and asked instead, "When do you sleep?"

"A couple of hours here or there. I don't seem to need that much," was his reply. "I'd prefer not to skip Friday, if that doesn't conflict with your plans."

Plans. Her plans involved getting from one end of the day to the other. Didn't he know that? He knew that, and yet he acted like he didn't. "Jake, you know I don't have any plans. Your little visits are the most planned thing in my life right now." She hit Send this time, and regretted it. *When are you going to stop being so snotty,* she admonished herself.

"Sounds like I'm pretty important, then," he replied. "I'll make sure to be there at 10:00."

"Sorry," she sent.

"When do *you* sleep?" he asked.

"I try to keep normal hours, but I get up a lot since January."

"Your body's adjusting to sleeping alone."

"How do you know? Maybe this is what I'm like from now on—the ghost of marriage past."

"I just know. So 10:00 on Friday, then?"

"You just know? What the hell does that mean?" she wrote. Her cursor hovered over the Send button. *He won't tell me,* she knew. *At least he won't send it by e-mail so I can forward it to all his parishioners past, present, and future. He's vacant sometimes, but not stupid.* She deleted the lines she had just written and sent instead: "Friday it is. Good night, Jake."

"Good night, Jane."

WEDNESDAY, JULY 4

We set up camp in front of the Confectionary, just like last year. To tell the truth, the whole day was pretty much like last year, excepting the obvious. Cormac stayed open for the parade, Barb by his side, slinging pound cake and half-caf skinny lattes with extra whipped like her life depended on it. Maybe her love life depends on it, who knows.

Aunt Jude, Uncle Charlie, and Aunt Brigid sat in the same thirty-year-old lawn chairs with the green nylon straps, and clapped for every band, float, and baton twirler. Their hands could have been chapped and bleeding by the end, but they seem to take it as their solemn duty to offer encouragement to anyone with a costume.

Dylan loved it, except for the fire engine sirens and the American Revolutionary guys firing off their muskets. He sat in Uncle Charlie's lap clutching those huge catcher's-mitt hands of Charlie's. He pulled them over his ears every time he saw a loud noise coming. Uncle Charlie did his usual running commentary, "And here we have the Middlesex County 4-H Fife and Drum Corps. Now look at those lads in their tricorn hats, Dylan. That's just the way it was in the olden days. Whoops, here comes a fire engine, cover your ears, boy!"

I saw a few people from high school. Melanie Koutzakis took my hand in both of hers and gave me a big "How are you?" with that sympathy look she has where her eyes go all soupy. Boy, she's been perfecting that for the last twenty years. I told her we were doing okay, thanks for asking, and pulled my hand away as soon as her grip loosened.

After the parade, we all went to Town Beach and had a picnic. The aunties sat in their lawn chairs in the shade and quibbled over the ages of their friends' grandchildren. I was sure Barb wouldn't go in the water when I saw her wearing a lime green string bikini. I hated her for a few seconds and then I got bored of that and took Dylan to the dock so he could jump into my arms about four hundred times. Then Barb swam up and he jumped to her.

Later, I heard Cormac tell her she should have brought her camera. From the corner of my eye I could see her shake her head at him and glance over at me. Maybe some day in the distant future I will no longer be the reason for every uncomfortable moment on the planet.

Dylan begged me to stay for the fireworks. I dreaded it. Robby loved fireworks. Of course, the ones at the Esplanade in downtown Boston were his favorite. We used to go early in the morning to get a good spot on the lawn and hang out all day playing cards, reading the paper, and listening to music. We tried it once when Dylan was a baby, but we ran out of diapers, and he was teething and miserable and we never went back after that. So, Robby researched the best suburban fireworks, and we'd go to at least two sets every year. In the nine Fourth of Julys we had together, not one went by without us lying on a blanket somewhere, his arms around me, staring up into the dark, explosions of light booming in our chests. We always had great sex after that. Post-fireworks sex is unbelievable.

I really didn't want to stay. Cormac said he'd bring Dylan home. But I thought I should be with him, knowing that the noise would bother him. And I felt like Robby might almost somehow be there. Like if there were any time or place that Robby would miraculously show up, it would be during fireworks.

Guess what? He didn't. No miracle today.

7

THE NEXT DAY, MALINOWSKI found rot. When he pulled shingles off the side of the house to set the floor joists, there it was, dark and pungent.

"Janie." He said it through the kitchen window as she was setting down a plate of toast. She wondered if she'd ever heard him use her name before. "Something I gotta show you."

She wrapped her blue flannel bathrobe more tightly around her and listened at the bottom of the stairs for a moment. Dylan and Carly were still asleep, exhausted from the late-night festivities. When she came through the front door, he studied her for a moment. "Are you sick?" he asked.

"What?" Her hands went up to her face, searching for what he'd seen. "Oh. No, I just didn't get a good night's sleep."

"Looks like allergies," he said skeptically. "Fireworks keep you up?"

"Kind of. What do you need to show me?"

"See this?" he waved his hammer toward the discolored wood. "It's all rotted out. I can't set the joists against that. It has to be replaced."

"Replaced?" Janie wished he would explain it after she had a second cup of coffee. Or maybe a third.

"Yeah, I have to pull these boards here and put in new ones. At a minimum."

"What's the maximum?"

"Well, if there's rot down at the bottom, there could be more. Especially if the moisture came from above, which it often does. Could be a buckle in the flashing up by the gutters. Or seeping in around this window. I know the plan was to keep the shingles, but you might want to reconsider."

No, thought Janie. *Stick to the plan. Robby's plan. No reconsidering.* "But he wanted . . . it was supposed to be . . ."

Malinowski nodded. "I know."

She tried to make sense of it. Tried even harder not to cry. "You should have told me . . . It's your job to . . ."

He cocked his head to one side. His patience was infuriating. Even so, she couldn't quite make it his fault. He had not created the rot, only discovered it. She sat down on the front step, surrounded by unattached floor joists, and leaned her head against her hand. "Okay, you tell me."

He squatted down near her, his elbows propped on his knees. "If it was my house, I'd pull it," he said quietly.

"How much will it cost?"

"I won't know until I see how far it goes."

She knew there were more questions to ask, but none came to her other than, "Are you good at this?"

He nodded. "I'll take care of it."

"Want some coffee?"

"No thanks," he said. "But I will take a little chocolate milk if you've got any. In one of those sippy cups, so I don't spill? And maybe a baggie of Cheerios?"

She smiled wanly at his joke. "He worships you, you know."

Malinowski grinned. "That's a good boy you've got there. You're lucky."

"I don't always feel so lucky."

"Nobody does."

Apparently Jake drank tea even on really warm days.

"Doesn't that make you hotter?" Janie asked, as they sat on a blanket she had spread out in the backyard. The spot was shaded by a tree that hung over the fence from the front yard. Carly sat with them, surrounded by toys appropriate for a nine-month-old, chewing on the sunscreen bottle. Dylan hung stomach down on a swing toward the back of the yard, orchestrating a pirate attack in the dirt below him.

"The tea?" said Jake. "It should, I guess. But it doesn't." He wore his standard black slacks, but today's black shirt was short sleeved, and the top few buttons were open, no collar in sight.

Janie shook her head. He raised his eyebrows in question.

"How come nothing affects you?" she asked. "You're like made of steel. Or PVC, maybe."

"You know things affect me," he said, his gaze diverted to a leaf in his hand. He twirled the stem between his fingers. "I just don't show it very much. You don't show it that much, either."

"Oh, come on—I'm a walking wreck and everyone who comes within fifty feet of me can tell."

"You think that's true because that's how you feel inside. But it doesn't show nearly as much as you think. To most people you probably seem very stoic. Are you still having trouble sleeping?"

"Yep," she said, and replaced the sunscreen bottle in Carly's hands with an actual toy. Carly threw it down and picked up the bottle. "How long did it take you to 'adjust,' like you mentioned in that e-mail the other night?"

He squinted back down at the leaf. "Six or eight months, I would guess."

"What exactly were you adjusting from?"

For a long moment he didn't answer, and Janie's first instinct was to apologize for asking. But she really wanted to know, so she held her tongue in the faint hope that he would reveal something.

"I don't usually talk about this," he said tentatively.

She strained against the urge to respond. In the silence she could hear Malinowski ripping shingles off the front of the house.

"First of all," he said, "it puts me in a position of vulnerability to gossip."

Janie's wall of reserve broke. "Jake, you know ALL about ME!"

"I know a lot about this episode in your life. But you have to understand something." He looked directly at her, his gray eyes taking on a sudden purposefulness. "We are not friends."

"Excuse me?" was all she could think to say.

"I am a priest. I hear people's innermost struggles and shame all the time. It's my job to listen, to offer reconciliation with God and with oneself, and never to share a single word of it with another living soul. You have no such commitment."

"Well, no, I haven't taken any vows or anything, but do you really think I would subject you to gossip? That's insulting. And I'm not asking you as a *friend*. I'm asking you because you seem to know something about this! Also, frankly, the fact that you may have had a relationship gives you some credibility." She pointed at him. "Being a real guy might actually make you a better priest!"

He twirled the leaf some more. The shingle ripping had stopped, and the quiet seemed to enshroud them. Jake glanced over at her and then back toward the leaf. "I was engaged to be married. We dated in college."

Engaged? Father Solitary? "What happened?"

"I couldn't go through with it. The closer the wedding got, the more uncomfortable I felt." He pressed his lips together momentarily, as if to bite back some remnant shred of shame. "I had no vision of myself as a married man."

"What did you do?"

"Went and talked to an old friend, a mentor really, the parish priest who helped me get into a Catholic boarding school and away from my father. He was going to marry us."

"What did he say?"

"He said that God was in my feelings, telling me to pay attention. He said that if I wasn't ready to embrace married life with my whole heart, it would fail. I would end up hurting her more if I married her than if I backed off."

"So you backed off."

He sighed and shook his head, abandoned the leaf to the grass. "It was terrible. She was such a good person, and I loved her. But I felt sick to my stomach every time we talked about the wedding or being married. I couldn't ignore the signs anymore."

"And you signed up for the priesthood."

"Oh no. Not right away. That was a year or so later. I wasn't that clearheaded. I had given up the one thing I thought I wanted, and for months and months I hadn't a clue as to what to do next."

"You were adjusting."

He shifted on the blanket. "In every way."

"Where is she now?"

"She's married. She was pregnant last I heard, but that was about ten years ago."

"Any regrets?"

"No." He looked at Janie again. "You know the one thing that helped me back then? I prayed for her. Every day, every night, I prayed for her happiness. When I heard she was engaged to a good man, that's when I found peace. That's when I could embrace my own vows."

Janie studied her hands, twisted her wedding ring. "And you never get lonely." She heard him chuckle and she looked up.

"Any priest who says he never gets lonely is a liar. Nothing makes you immune to loneliness. Not God, not marriage, not even sex." For some reason, hearing him say that word out loud made Janie blush, and she busied herself with straightening Carly's sun hat. Jake went on: "But loneliness has a purpose. It makes room for something. It's built to make us reach out. That's not such a bad thing."

"It's not making *me* reach out," she muttered. "It's making me a wretched bitch."

"Loneliness is painful. But suffering is not wrong in and of itself. It's part of the human experience, and in that way, brings us closer to all people."

"Thank you, Pope Jake," she said.

He laughed out loud, a true laugh, she knew, and it lifted her for a moment. "Hey," he said. "I look good in white—and it beats the heck out of all this black!"

On Monday, Pond Pals camp started at the Town Beach. Dylan was worried that it wouldn't be fun and they wouldn't have good snacks and the camp counselors wouldn't be as nice as Miss Marla. But when they arrived, Keane was already there, having been dropped off by his mother the minute the camp opened.

"DYLAN!" he screamed, and turned to the teenager who was helping him put stickers on his name tag. "That's my friend, Dylan LaMarche, and he has big holes in his yard, and he likes pirates. DYLAN, sit next to ME!"

Janie never got a backward glance from Dylan after that, which felt a little strange, but better, she told herself, than having him cling to her and refuse to stay.

When she got home, Shelly was in the yard with Malinowski. She wore an ice blue suit with a large flowered pin on the lapel, which Janie thought was garish, even though she knew it was probably high fashion. The short skirt showcased the length and tautness of Shelly's legs, an advantage she pressed by leaning one high-heeled jet black pump against the front step of the house. At fifty-three Shelly still had it.

"Hey," she called, as Janie walked toward them with Carly on her hip. "I just came over to check up on the project and watch Tug work his magic. I like a little beefcake in the morning, don't you?" She nudged Tug for emphasis. Tug shook his head in mock disapproval and tried to resume the work of replacing boards on the side of Janie's now-naked front wall. "Nothing like the sight of a healthy young man using his muscles," teased Shelly.

"Not so young," he muttered at her.

"What are you, thirty-six, thirty-seven?" demanded Shelly.

"Forty-five next week."

"Well, that explains the thinning hair, but don't you worry about that, that's just a sign of virility. Testosterone flowing full speed. So, Janie," she said as Janie tried to sneak by her and into the house. "What's the deal? I thought we were keeping the rustic look with the shingles and everything. Now I come over and find young Tug, here, ripping things apart. Is that in the budget? I don't seem to recall it being in the contract, so now I'm worried about your finances again."

"It wasn't on a whim, Shelly," Janie retorted. "Of course I wanted to keep the shingles, but it was all rotten under there."

"Says who? Tug, did you tell her there was rot? Because every house has rot. Unless of course you live in the desert, and Massachusetts is not, as we know, the desert. We're at sea level here, for godsake, of course there's rot."

"Stop sounding like you're trying to sell me my own house!" Janie's voice was rising in irritation, and a vague sense of having let Robby down by succumbing to some myth of decay. "There was a lot of rot, okay? A LOT. And if you're telling me not to trust him, you're about two months too late, and I may have to kill you."

"If I don't get to her first," said Tug as he measured another board. He let the measuring tape wind fast into its metal case with a sharp snap.

"Trust him!" Shelly laughed, clearly enjoying herself. "Janie, honey, you've been out of the game too long. You can never trust a man this fine, especially if he can make a buck off you."

"That's enough," warned Tug.

Thank you, thought Janie.

"Oh, alright," said Shelly, deflated. "I'm just kidding, for god-sake. Of course you can trust him. Do you know how much work he has lined up? Probably eighteen months' worth. You don't create that kind of demand by being untrustworthy." She turned on Tug, all business. "So what's this going to cost her? She's a widow with two small mouths to feed, living off the insurance money, which won't last long if you keep tearing her house apart. I don't want her going back to work at that hospital before she has to."

"Shelly, you said I was fine, I could afford it!" Janie could feel the tingle of panic on her skin.

"It won't be that much," said Tug quickly. "Under a grand."

"For all this?" Shelly was skeptical. "Under a grand. You're sure."

"That's what I said." And he started up the circular saw, effectively ending the conversation.

Shelly followed Janie into the kitchen and shut the window to quell the screech of the saw. "Everything okay?" she asked. "Are you happy with his work?"

"It seems fine. I just wish we didn't have to take the shingles off."

"Yeah, that wasn't in his plans," Shelly said, leaning against the counter as Janie cut up avocado pieces for Carly.

"What, now I'm supposed to feel guilty for keeping him from all his eighteen months' worth of work?"

"No, not Tug's plans. Robby's."

Janie tried to shrug it off. "What can I do."

"Nothing," said Shelly, patting her shoulder. "Just play the hand you're dealt."

Janie delivered the little squares of avocado to Carly's high-chair tray and sat down. "What's new? How's Pammy?"

Shelly fingered an avocado remnant off the cutting board and slid it in her mouth. "She moved in with her boyfriend for the summer, did I tell you? Her father went berserk, but I calmed him down by reminding him that he wouldn't have to pay me child support if she wasn't living at home. That perked him right up, the skinflint."

Janie smiled. "You have a real knack for perspective."

"Listen, honey," Shelly said gently. "I came over to tell you about something. I sold that other Pelham Heights house. The jigunzo one with the four-hundred-square-foot master bath."

"Congratulations!" Janie made a valiant attempt at enthusiasm as her stomach clenched.

"Yeah, it's great. The commission equals what I made in the last two years combined, and it wasn't the only house I sold this year."

"You're rich!" Janie smiled, but she could sense the other shoe about to fall.

"Also, I've been seeing someone."

"Dating?"

"Yeah, I didn't make a big deal out of it because I met him through this Internet dating service, and you know how hit or miss those things can be. I didn't want to bother you with it. It was nothing, just e-mailing for months because he lives in Rhode Island, and neither of us wanted to get into a commuter relationship if we didn't really like each other."

"And now you like each other."

Shelly sighed. "He's very sweet. Sweet, sweet man. And handsome. And financially comfortable. The whole package."

"So that's great!" Janie's veneer of vicarious happiness was beginning to crack.

Shelly sighed again. "It's getting serious. And we're tired of driving an hour and forty minutes each way just to go for a movie and dinner. And he lives in a spectacular, architecturally dramatic house on the water."

"You're moving," Janie breathed.

"Yes, sweetie. It's time. I'm just too lonely without my Geoffrey."

"Okay," said Janie, pinching the back of her hand under the table.

"If I could wave my magic wand and take you and the kids with me, it would be perfect, honey. But that wouldn't be right even if I could, would it?"

Janie pinched harder and harder, but the tears came anyway. "We're really going to miss you."

"I'm going to miss you more, I swear. And of course I'll come back to visit. And I expect an invitation to every birthday party and Holy . . . well, whatever it is you Catholics do. And any other time you need me, you just call. An hour and forty minutes isn't so far for a friend, right?"

Janie shook her head and swiped at the relentless rivulets of tears. "When?"

"I'm putting it on the market next week."

"It'll be snapped up right away."

"Maybe yes, maybe no. I'm not exactly a motivated seller, now am I?"

Janie tried to smile but it came off forced and pathetic. Shelly held her in the shelter of her long, thin arms. "It's okay, baby. You can cry to me."

ALL WEEK JANIE FELT as if she were recovering from a bad cold: not sick exactly, but achy and slow. At night she dreamed of scary new neighbors. A particularly awful one included a snarling pet panther and children with fingers that lit on fire at random. When she rose to wander around the house in the dark, attempting to outrun the vestiges of the latest sleep disturbance, she checked her e-mail.

The first night there was an e-mail from Jake, asking if she thought Dylan would like to bring up the basket of money from the collection plates to the altar at the upcoming Sunday Mass. Parishioners seemed to feel more connected to the Mass when children were involved, he explained.

No, she didn't think he'd want to, she replied. Also he was too young.

"Okay," he sent, moments later. "I just thought I'd ask."

They e-mailed back and forth for a while, and she admitted she was upset about Shelly moving. No, not the least bit jealous that Shelly was advancing to a new phase of her life. Well, maybe a little. Since there would never be a new phase to Janie's life. She would be stuck in the current morass of bitterness and seclusion forever.

"I know you have a totally different take on this," she wrote, "because you like your life. But it occurred to me that there's a very good chance that I'll live for another forty or fifty years. And also a very good chance that I'll spend those years alone. Who wants an aging widow with two kids?"

"You are aging—as we all are—but you're not quite aged. You certainly don't look or seem old. And your children are very nice. I think it's likely you'll fall in love again and be very happy. Also, don't assume that forty or fifty years without intimacy is perfectly comfortable for me. I am human."

Janie wrote and deleted several responses. She finally sent, "I thought you liked being a priest."

It was a longer interval than usual before she received, "I do. But every choice has its disadvantages, and I am well aware of the disadvantages of my choice."

After she returned to bed, she thought about Jake and his life's disadvantages more than she expected to. It relaxed her to ponder something other than her own pain, and she drifted quickly into a soft, dreamless sleep.

THE NEXT NIGHT, AWAKENING with her teeth clenched and her feet arched, Janie went straight for the computer. She was surprised to find no benign e-mail from Jake. "Do other four-year-olds ever bring up the money basket?" she sent, initiating the cyber-conversation.

"Sometimes," he quickly replied. "Usually when their parents or older siblings are bringing up the wine and the host, I offer them the job. They like to feel a part of it, and if they drop the basket there's no harm done. Bad dreams have you up again?"

Janie related the latest dream about a family of goat-eating trolls. As she typed, she realized that she'd read Dylan the story of the Billy Goats Gruff at bedtime. "So at least there's an outside source. It's a little comforting to know that my brain didn't come up with that hideousness on its own. Do you ever have nightmares?"

"Not that much anymore."

"How do you handle it?"

"If I can't shake it, I go out for a really hard run."

"In the middle of the night?"

"Sure. It's a great to run when the temperature is cool and the streets are quiet."

"And there's no one to see you."

His return e-mail had only a sideways smile made of a colon and an end parenthesis. ":)"

It occurred to Janie that if they were going to talk like this every night, maybe they should try instant messaging. The response time would be a lot faster. But even if she had instant messaging on her computer, she felt too exhausted to learn how to use it. Besides, there was something good about having to wait. Something good about the world slowing down for one hour a day, with breathing room in between all those words. It didn't make things any clearer, really, just less overwhelming. She wished that, for the time being, anyway, all her relationships came piecemeal.

WHEN JAKE ARRIVED FOR his usual Friday visit, he and Janie had a hard time getting in stride. They bumped into each other twice while hiking up Jansen's Hill. There were long periods of silence and then both would speak at the same time. And most of the way they talked in unnecessary detail about the misty fog that had filtered into the area, the size of Carly's feet, and how exactly Dylan should make his way up the church aisle with the basket of money. After they'd talked over each other for the tenth time, Janie yelled, *"Blah!"* and they both laughed.

"We're used to e-mail," said Jake.

"I can't take the pressure!" said Janie.

"Let's not talk at all for a while," he suggested. So, they sat on the fallen tree-trunk in companionable silence, breathing the vaporized air and feeling their throbbing muscles slowly relax.

"Do you ever run during the day?" she asked finally.

"Almost never," he said. "The parish keeps me too busy. In the old days there would be three or four priests living in the rectory, sharing the duties. Now it's just me rattling around in there, trying to keep on top of everything. Also . . ."

"Also what?"

"People feel a little funny seeing their pastor in running shorts. It's a little too much exposure."

Janie smiled, but the image made more of an impression than she liked. "My brother Mike runs every day," she said. "He needs it like a diabetic needs insulin. Sometimes I worry that he'll sprain his ankle or something and have to stop for a while. He'd go crazy, I think."

Jake looked out into the treetops. "I know how that is. When I was in college I ran every single day, no matter what. Nothing could keep me from it. I did the Boston Marathon all four years, plus a few others, too."

"What about after college?"

"I had a job. I couldn't just take off whenever I wanted. I remember the first time that I couldn't run. I had to work late, and then my future in-laws surprised us with an engagement dinner. When midnight came and I hadn't had my run, I fell apart. I went into the men's room of the restaurant and had a silent fit, locked in a stall so no one would know."

"Why did you run so much?"

"It was just my way of dealing with things—or maybe not dealing with things sometimes. We all have our ways. But I had to come to terms with the fact that I was too dependent on it. I had to develop more coping skills so I wouldn't be caught up short like that again."

"How did you do that?"

"My therapist helped me figure out other things that keep me on an even keel. Reading, prayer, talking to friends. I never was much of a confider. I had to learn to talk about things, even if it was mostly in therapy. I still run, but I don't have to every day."

They were quiet again for a while and then Janie said, "Robby was my way."

Jake nodded and waited for more.

"I'd had boyfriends before, guys I liked, whatever. But Robby was the first guy I really trusted. He got me. He totally got me, and he never flinched no matter what I did or said. And not like he just took it. Ho, no. He could dish it right back. But somehow, no matter what we fought about or how pissed we got, I knew he loved me. After a couple of years we didn't fight so much. I guess we sort of got into a groove—a rut, maybe. But it was a good rut."

Janie got up, needing to cut the emotion with motion. Jake followed her back down the hill as she continued, "I did what girls say they'll never do—lost touch with friends. I didn't try to cut myself off, it just sort of happened. Robby and I were always together, and then the kids came, and we were in our own little pod. I liked getting together with my friends, but I didn't *need* to anymore.

"And if I was pissed at Aunt Jude or worried about the kids or just, you know, *happy* . . . Robby was who I told. He was my home base." A breath caught in her throat, making a little gasping sound. She hoped it seemed like a hiccough, but then she felt his warm hand give a little pat to her shoulder. She stopped, afraid that the tears in her eyes would make her trip, and she didn't want to endanger the sleeping baby on her back. She put her hand on the closest tree to steady herself, a birch, and when they finally continued on, a piece of the smooth white bark peeled off into her palm.

Back at the house, Janie opened the big glass jar that already contained several rocks, pinecones, and a piece of moss, and she laid the birch bark on top.

8

SATURDAY, JULY 14

I took the kids for their regular Saturday morning at Aunt Jude's, and then hit a sale at Baby Gap. Carly is growing like a weed. Apparently formula isn't the growth-stunting, bowel-irritating spackle I once thought it was. At least I don't have to feel so guilty that I couldn't nurse her from three months on.

Auntie was a little funny when I dropped them off, a little more fluttery than usual, but there didn't seem to be anything actually wrong. At least not that she said. At the time. I should have known it was something.

When I got back, she said, "I think I should tell you something. I heard it from Sol's wife. You know Sol."

Who the hell is Sol? I can't keep track of every poor soul she befriends. Anyway, it seems he's the Grand Poobah of the Parish Council. They just got word there's an allegation against Father Lambrosini, the pastor before Jake. Actually it's looking like a bunch of allegations. A bunch of kids, grown-ups now, who say he molested them.

Molested—such a passive word. Like he bothered them. Disturbed them a little. Was insensitive to their need not to be fondled or raped or screwed up for life. I can't stop thinking about Katya, pinned down and defiled by "Daddy."

I remember Father Lambrosini, he seemed like this kindly
older guy. He gave mildly humorous homilies—not hilarious,
but just enough to give you a chuckle or two. The moral of the
story was always that you should come to Mass more often,
and be generous to those second collections for the missions in
Africa or Afghanistan or wherever.
    Good God. I wonder what Jake thinks.

JANIE E-MAILED JAKE AT 2:00 a.m. She checked for his response
about forty times over the next hour, as she intermittently folded
laundry, scrubbed the grout around the bathroom sink, and watered
long-dry plants, the ones that hadn't already followed the light to
plant heaven. Shelly had been the chief waterer, Janie now realized,
and her successful social life was the cause of their demise.

    Then she stretched out on the couch, thinking she would doze
for an hour or so. At 5:45 she awoke with a sharp pain in her arm
from sleeping on it. It felt almost broken, certainly sprained in
some catastrophic way, as she held it across her waist and went to
the computer. E-mail yielded nothing more than a 10 percent cou-
pon for printer cartridges. *Where is he?* she wondered on her way
back upstairs, where she crawled under the covers and passed out
for another hour and a half.

    Dylan's voice saying, "Give Mommy kissies, Carly, she needs
lots of kissies," and the feel of tiny wet lips on her chin woke Janie
from a dark jungle dream where malevolent primates chased her.

    Church had become a given on Sundays since their first cos-
tumed trip to Our Lady, Comforter of the Afflicted Church a
month before. The donuts were, of course, the main attraction,
but Janie knew that Dylan also found the music and candles and
comings and goings of various readers and singers entertaining.
When Father Jake processed in, Dylan never failed to whisper
loudly to Aunt Jude, "We know that guy. He comes to our house
sometimes."

As they got ready for church, Janie wondered if Jake would address the allegations about Father Lambrosini. It might distract people from the Mass, and that wasn't good. She remembered Auntie Brigid growling at Cormac about his distractions when they were kids, as if the distraction police would burst through the huge wooden doors at any minute and drag him away. On the other hand, Jake had a gentle way of addressing a subject without being alarming, so Janie guessed he would reference it in some way. All that therapy had given him a penchant for truth, she figured.

When she pulled into the church parking lot, it was Father Lambrosini's rose garden by the rectory that tipped her off. There were no roses, just mounds of gaping soil from which plants had been extricated, a remnant tangle of roots peeking from each small, volcanic-looking eruption.

As Jake came down the aisle with the candle bearers and lectors, Janie knew for certain he would not say a word about the allegations. He was as locked down as she had ever seen him. He went about conducting the service as he did every Sunday, quiet and deliberate. But there were no benevolent smiles and no color in his cheeks. His ghost twin inhabited his robes, not him.

The first lector, a middle-aged gentleman with a dandruff-speckled suit and a nasal voice, approached the lectern. "A reading from the book of Jeremiah," he intoned officiously.

"Woe to the shepherds who mislead and scatter the flock of my pasture, says the Lord . . . You have scattered my sheep and driven them away. You have not cared for them, but I will take care to punish your evil deeds . . ."

Janie watched Jake as he sat in his ornate chair, displayed on the altar like a caged animal in a zoo, and her heart began to pound. She briefly considered taking the children down to the church basement early. Maybe the donuts were already set out.

There were certainly no donuts up here. It was not going to be a sugar-glazed Mass.

At the appointed time, Jake rose and walked slowly toward the lectern. He proclaimed the Gospel as if he were reading the extended warranty for a refrigerator. Then he said nothing for a moment, the rise and fall of his chest visible even under the heavy robes. His lower lip equivocated, uncertain as to whether it would cooperate.

"Woe to the shepherds," he said finally, his voice strangely even and calm. ' "*Woe*' isn't a word that's used much anymore. It's an old word, not one that most children would recognize. We might translate it today to mean sadness or bad luck, but that would not be sufficient. Woe is so much more.

"It is calamity.

"It is affliction.

"It is suffering without hope.

"Woe to the shepherds who mislead and scatter my flock." Jake paused, and it wasn't clear if he would speak again until he emphasized, "*My* flock. The flock does not belong to the shepherds, it belongs to God. God's flock. God's beloved children. *All of us.*" Jake raised his hand and laid it onto his chest, like a startled bird roused from the comfort of its nest. The hand, now splayed out over the front of his vestments, magnified the heaving of his lungs. "The prophecy here is one of endless," he paused, "hopeless," another pause, "suffering for those leaders who *mis*lead. Whose abuse of power is so egregious it scatters the flock. Our God promises us that such abuse," he inhaled as if there were not enough oxygen in the room, "will be avenged."

Holy Christ, thought Janie. *That's it. That's what his father did.* Again she thought of Katya and "Daddy." But she was pulled abruptly from this image by the sight of Jake wavering momentarily at the lectern. She saw the signs that as a respiratory therapist she'd been trained to notice: nasal flaring and increased use of accessory muscles around the neck. He was mildly tachypneic, straining to pull more oxygen into his lungs. But his lips were not blue, so she guessed it was not a medical issue. It was likely happening in his head, possibly the first signs of a panic attack. She waited to see if it would progress. His mouth opened as if he might say more, and then closed again. He walked quickly back to his seat and sank unsteadily into it. Janie watched as his respiratory rate began to slow into the upper range of normal.

The two lectors sitting in the front row looked at each other. It was the shortest homily Father Jake had ever given. They looked to him for some sign that they should proceed, but as Janie knew, he was there in body only. The dandruff-speckled lector rose and walked tentatively toward the podium, watching for any indication from the pastor that he should change course. No sign evident, he proceeded with the Prayers of the Faithful. "For . . . For Cardinal Sean," he read, "and all Church leaders, that they be mindful of the awesome responsibility of selfless service to others that God has laid upon their shoulders . . . we pray to the Lord . . ."

When the baskets were passed for collection, Janie ushered Dylan to the back of the church. "Can I have some?" asked Dylan, as the cash and envelopes were dumped into a deeper basket for him to carry.

"No. It's for the church," whispered Janie. "So Father Jake can pay the bills."

"Oh," he nodded. "Like Daddy does. Go sit with Auntie Jude now, so you can see me."

From the pew Janie watched Dylan walk solemnly up the aisle behind the teenagers bearing the bread and wine, which they quickly handed off to Father Jake. He placed them on the altar and turned back to take the basket of money.

"Hi," said Dylan with a sheepish smile. Janie could just barely hear him from her place in the second row. "It's for the bills." Jake never made eye contact. It was as if he were retrieving the basket from a conveyor belt. *Holy shit,* thought Janie. Dylan looked confused for a moment, and then galloped back to the pew.

"Good job," whispered Janie.

"Thanks," he said, but he was irritated and began to riffle the pages of a hymnal.

In line for Communion, Janie could hear Jake's declaration to each parishioner as he handed them the host. "Body of Christ," he said woodenly, "Body of Christ."

When it was her turn, he handed her the tasteless wafer and intoned, "Body of Christ," his unseeing gaze aimed somewhere in the area of her chin. She noticed tiny red nick marks on his fingers and palms, and she realized he must have pulled out those rose bushes bare-handed, thorns piercing him with every grasp. She felt so sorry for him then, a strangely foreign sensation, since she hadn't felt sorry for anyone other than herself in a very long time. Instead of answering, "Amen," she found herself mouthing the words, "Come over."

He focused on her then, and she could feel the rage behind his eyes. *Bad idea*, she thought. *Never mind*, and quickly returned to her seat.

After Mass, the church basement crowd was uncharacteristically small. Only a few daring souls, or oblivious ones, braved the small talk and snacks following such an odd Mass. The others seemed to have fled for their lives. Even Aunt Jude didn't stay long, explaining that she had to sort clothing donations at Table of Plenty. Father Jake never came, and no one seemed to expect him. The ladies of the Hospitality Committee implored Janie to take the extra donuts home. While Dylan was busy buckling himself into his booster seat, Janie heaved them into the Dumpster in the parking lot.

As she drove home from Mass, Janie wondered what to do. He was falling apart. Maybe this was more evident to her than to other people. Maybe they just thought he was having a tough day because of the Father Lambrosini news. But she knew. It was bad.

She would e-mail him when she got home. But she was almost certain he wouldn't answer. It was none of her business, really. And as he himself had made perfectly clear, they were not friends. But, still . . . she had this unshakable feeling that it was somehow within her power to divert disaster.

By the time she turned onto her own street, she had decided she would e-mail him anyway. If and when he decided to get back to her, she'd figure out how to help—if that were even possible. Besides, she told herself, he probably went directly from Mass to his car, stopping off in the rectory just long enough to change into his running gear. At this moment, she calculated, he was probably about twenty miles west of here, at the start of a mercifully anonymous marathon run. Good for him.

It wasn't until Janie turned into her own driveway that she saw his car. He was still in it, watching her approach in the rearview mirror. She pulled in behind him and took Carly from her car seat. Dylan scrambled out after.

"Come in," she said to Jake through his driver's side window.

"I shouldn't be here."

"But you are, so come in."

Jake got out and followed them into the house. Janie put Carly down for a nap and sent Dylan into the backyard to play with his dump truck and backhoe in the sandbox. "But the shovels are all lost!" he protested. Janie handed him a serving spoon from the silverware drawer, and he raced out the back door with his new acquisition.

"Tea?" she said to Jake, who sat rigid at the kitchen table.

"I didn't bring any."

"I have plenty." She laid four boxes of various sizes and colors on the table before him. He glanced at them and then looked out the window. Janie picked orange pekoe, thinking it was most like the strange kind he usually brought, and put the rest away.

"I apologize for coming here," he said inertly.

"I invited you." She sat down at the table. "And don't worry. This isn't friendship." He looked at her for the first time since he'd arrived. "You were having trouble breathing," she said. "I'm a respiratory therapist. It's not personal, it's just emergency response."

"Was it that bad?" He rubbed his eyes with his thumb and forefinger. "Shit, I'm going to get reassigned."

Janie's face went wide for a second. She wasn't sure if he meant a reassignment would be forced on him or requested by him, but either way, it sent a tremor of panic through her. "It wasn't bad," she said quickly. "Anyone would understand that you were disturbed by the news. And half of them never listen, anyway, so they probably didn't even notice."

He looked up quickly, and said, "Dylan brought up the basket."

Janie nodded.

"Was he nervous?"

"He was fine," she said. The teakettle began to sing, and she got up to pour the boiling water into his cup. "Do you think the allegations are true?"

Jake let out a long breath, and then banged his fist on the table. "God DAMN him."

"I'll take that as a yes."

"They're true," he snarled. "When nine adults who've never met each other all come up with similar stories about the same person, it's considered very credible. Miserable bastard."

Janie's memory banks flicked back to Jake's description of his own father. "So he definitely molested nine different children."

"At least. If nine came forward, there are twice that many that just don't want to think about it."

"But you're thinking about it."

"Yes, I'm thinking about it!" he yelled. "Good Lord, how can I KEEP myself from thinking about it! It's not enough that I know

exactly—EXACTLY—how each of those people feels. No, it's beyond that! I'm sentenced to sleep and shower and eat my lunch
in the very rooms where it happened!" He slammed his hand on
the table again. "God DAMN it—how can I possibly sleep in a
bed where children have been PHYSICALLY ASSAULTED AND
EMOTIONALLY MUTILATED!".

His rage sent shockwaves through the tiny kitchen, and Janie
had a moment of fear, not so much that he would hurt her as that
she would fail—at what, had yet to be determined. "Maybe you
can't," she said.

"Damn right, I can't! No one in their right mind could—it's
unimaginable!" He expelled a long breath. "Except for me. I can
imagine it in detail." He rubbed his eyes hard, jostling his glasses,
and Janie could tell he was concentrating very hard on not crying.
When he finally lowered his fingers from his face, he wiped them
on his crisp black pants leaving damp marks that soon evaporated. "The press called all morning," he mumbled.

"What did you tell them?"

"I said what those drones at the Archdiocese told me to say: 'I
can't comment because of the ongoing investigation.' After a while
I just stopped answering the phone. Like a coward."

"You can't be mad at yourself for that," she said.

"No? Can't I?" He pushed away the full mug of tea and
turned on her. "Your husband died in a completely avoidable
accident, leaving you alone with two small children. You're
mad all the time. Are you trying to tell me that anger never
doubles back on you?" Before Janie could answer, he continued, "Of course it does. Your anger fills every room you
enter, so how could it not? Despite the fact that you bear no
responsibility whatsoever for this tragedy, your rage is probably aimed at yourself more than anyone. Even your beloved
husband, the guy who could've prevented all this agony by
taking an extra ten seconds to find his goddamned bike helmet!"

Her mouth dropped open and her eyes went wild and she thought she might hit him.

"Holy Mother of God," he whispered. "Forgive me; that was shameful."

"You're a real prick sometimes, you know that?"

"Yes. Absolutely."

She pushed the mug back toward him. "Drink your fucking tea."

HE MEANT TO LEAVE and she wanted him to leave, but after a while, the steam went out of them and he just stayed. They ate lunch. Dylan gave him a tour of the whole house, including Janie's clothes closet. Janie almost stopped them, realizing that there were bras and panties in the hamper that he might see. But she was still just mad enough to derive some private, vindictive little humor out of the prospect of his discomfort.

By midafternoon they were in the backyard eating watermelon. It was the seedless kind, and Dylan complained that there was nothing to spit. He went back to digging with his shiny new spoon, and Janie regretted giving it to him, knowing she was unlikely to get it back without a fight.

"Okay, so where are you going to sleep tonight?" she said to Jake.

He shook his head slowly. "Maybe my car."

"Alright then, where are you going to sleep the next night, because you're going to get caught, and by noon tomorrow the church ladies will be all atwitter." He ripped a divot out of her lawn and began to split each blade of grass into slivers. Janie pressed him to problem solve. "Is there any place in the rectory that's . . . ?"

"Not teeming with child-sized ghosts?" he snorted. "Maybe the front steps."

"Isn't there sort of a reception area right where you walk in? Where we did the paperwork for the kids to be baptized. It's out in the open with a lot of people coming and going."

"An unlikely spot for rape."

"Well, yes."

He pressed the divot with its shredded green blades back into the hole it had come from. "I bought new furniture for that room last year," he muttered. "Everything was so bald and dusty. I thought it should be more welcoming. The Finance Committee was against it, but I told them to move the money from the landscaping budget, and I'd cut the lawn all summer myself." He almost smiled. "It made them feel just ridiculous enough to get off my back."

"I've never seen you cutting the lawn," Janie said.

"And you never will."

IT WAS CLOSING IN on dinnertime when Jake got up to leave. Janie asked him to stay, hoping he'd say no. She was exhausted. His problem was exhausting, and she couldn't make it go away while he was still in view. "Do you want a camping pad in case that couch is uncomfortable?" she asked.

"No, it'll be fine. Thank you, though." He stood at the door with his hand on the knob, not leaving. "Thank you," he repeated. "I didn't know where to go."

"I'm familiar with that one myself," she said.

"It helped."

"I'm glad." She waited, but he still wasn't leaving. "You help me, too," she added.

He smiled and took a full breath. "We don't make it easy, do we?"

"We're prickly," she said with more warmth than she expected.

BY WEDNESDAY, THREE MORE people had come forward with allegations of sexual abuse against Father Lambrosini. Janie was compelled to read the ongoing coverage, though it was really the last thing she wanted to do. However, she felt she should know the latest so that when Jake e-mailed her in the middle of the night, which he had done every night but one since Sunday, he wouldn't have to recount it for her. Reading the paper online was one of the many things she'd stopped doing, along with plant watering and correspondence of any kind, when Robby had died. She found herself becoming current on things that had no meaning to her—school lunch menus, town selectmen's meetings, the ongoing investigation of those burglaries in the neighboring town of Natick. The police had found footprints in a newly loomed shrub bed and had determined it was the work of a lone man wearing size nine sneakers.

The one night that Jake hadn't begun the nightly cyber-conversation, she got worried and e-mailed him. He responded an hour later, when he came in from a run. She imagined all kinds of things in that hour, and it aggravated her. *Like I don't have enough to worry about . . .*

She did, however, have a growing awareness that she gravitated toward this problem, toward the bearer of this misery, more than she would have expected to. More than she wanted to. Partly she felt that it was like passing a bad accident on the highway. You knew you shouldn't slow down to look, and yet somehow you always did. There was some fundamental human relief in seeing the results of bad decision-making, or inadequate response to danger, or sheer misfortune of others. Made you feel lucky by comparison, no matter your own sad story. Shameful, yet human.

There was also an oddly increasing sense of her own influence when talking to Jake. Janie hadn't realized how completely ineffectual she had felt until she began to see that she had some small power to help this unlikely recipient, if only briefly, in the middle of a sleepless night.

The morning temperature was cool for mid-July as Janie sat at her computer, reading about Father Lambrosini's move from the priests' retirement home to the house of an anonymous friend in an anonymous location. As she skimmed the *Boston Globe* article, she simultaneously wondered if she had put a sweatshirt in Dylan's backpack. There was always a breeze at Lake Pequot, no matter how stultified the rest of the town felt, and he might be cold after his swim lesson.

When she heard Tug's truck pull up in front of the house, she looked at the clock—ten minutes to ten. Late for Tug, who was always there by 7:20, which was a little irritating, since she was never dressed by then. Several weeks ago, Shelly had dropped by with three sets of "full-coverage construction pajamas." For all their coverage, they were much prettier than any other pajamas Janie owned. Satin-trimmed cotton in pastel colors that fit perfectly, and yet somehow felt clingy. *Very Shelly,* thought Janie, embarrassed but thankful. *The little snob has never worn ratty pajamas in her life.*

Now wearing a pale blue T-shirt and her oldest pair of jeans, Janie came out on the front step. "Hey," she said. "Need supplies?"

"Nah, I'm stuffed."

Janie blinked a couple of times, trying to make sense of his response. "No, I meant did you need to go get supplies."

"Oh." He began laying two-by-ten boards in pairs across the footings. "No, I'm in good shape." He glanced up from his work suddenly. "Oh, you're asking why I'm late. My nieces took me out for breakfast." He chuckled. "Actually I ended up taking them, since neither of them had any cash on them. What a shock. Then the two of them got into a fight right there in the booth about who owed who money. They wouldn't shut up until I started singing 'Happy Birthday to Me,' and they got embarrassed that their friends might see them with a crazy man. Not that any of their friends were at Carey's Diner at 8:30 in the morning. But you know how things get around." He rolled his eyes.

Janie laughed—a relief after three days of vicarious rage. "It's your birthday?" she said.

"I guess so." He was clearly embarrassed at having brought it up.

"Any plans to celebrate?"

"Nothing big. I got a softball game tonight and we'll probably go to The Pal after." The Palace sat on the shore of Lake Pequot, a house-sized bar that seemed to grow more beloved by Pelhamites the more worn out it got. Every year or so the septic system failed or the taxes backed up or some other garden variety violation was reported, but pals of The Pal always seemed to rally round and bail it out. The general thinking was that if you didn't mind a certain level of stickiness, or a wine list that consisted of "red, white or rosay," The Pal was the place to be.

"I haven't been there in years," said Janie.

"You should come," Tug said, and then added quickly, "sometime. Take Shelly with you. She's something isn't she? I can't believe she's moving after all that work she did . . . I did . . . she hired me to do." He pulled a pencil from behind his ear and began making what appeared to be haphazard lines on a board that he then carried to a pile of lumber on the far side of the lawn.

WHEN JANIE PICKED UP Dylan at Pond Pals, he and Keane had their arms wrapped more or less around each other's shoulders. Because Dylan was an inch or two taller, Keane's hand slipped several times to grasp Dylan's neck. "Keane," he murmured, "you're squeezing me."

"Can we have a playdate?" Keane hollered to Janie as she approached.

"Keane, stop choking me," croaked Dylan as he pried Keane's fingers off him.

Janie studied Dylan for a moment. He was red-faced but smiling and nodding. "Who's picking you up?" she asked Keane.

"My dad, but he's usually last, so just tell the camp counselors to tell him you took me. Sometimes he's first, like really, REALLY first. But this is a last time. This time he's last."

"Uh-huh," said Janie. "Let's see what the counselors say."

The camp director confirmed that Keane's father was often a bit on the early side except when he seemed to be running late, but that they could not hand Keane over without his father's express consent. The discussion of Keane's father's timeliness or lack thereof went on longer than Janie's interest in the topic, and she was just about to tell Keane it would have to be another day, when he screamed, "He's here! That's his car, the kind of gold-colored one!" Keane's father extracted himself from a low-lying sports car and loped toward the camper pickup area.

"Hey, little dude!" he said as he high-fived Keane. He handed a ten-dollar bill to the camp director with a smug grin. "Late fee."

"I'm going to Dylan's!" Keane announced. "He's got construction!"

"Oh," said his father, face falling. "Alright, if that's what you wanna do, that's cool."

"Keane," said Janie, "maybe this isn't the best day. You can come over tomorrow."

"No, today! Please? Please, Dad?"

"It's cool," the father assured Janie. "I didn't have anything teed up for him, anyway."

Is this how you let your marriage go, too? Without any effort? Janie thought, looking at him for a second longer than she should have.

A slim smile emerged on Keane's father's face, and he unclipped the BlackBerry from his belt hook. "Fire off your number and I'll reach out to parlay a pickup."

Ew, thought Janie. *Keep the lingo to yourself. It sounds like a verbally transmitted disease.* "Just pick him up at three." She told him the address and ushered the boys to the car.

Immediate speculation began about what tools Tug was using and how big they were, and how loud they were, and whether he would let them use that really big, loud saw thing . . .

"It's Tug's birthday," mentioned Janie, hoping to turn the conversation away from the potential use of power tools by four-year-olds. Within moments they had planned a party with cake and red juice, the kind with too much sugar that Dylan wasn't allowed except for special occasions. "I don't think we have time to make a cake," Janie warned.

"Let's go to Cormac's!" Dylan sang out like he'd discovered the secret of time travel. Janie sighed. She knew that resisting this kind of boy-powered enthusiasm was going to be a long hard swim against the current, and reluctantly headed for the Confectionary.

"You're getting a birthday cake for your contractor?" said Barb when they barreled in the door, the boys immediately pressing themselves against the glass cases. "He must be pretty good."

"He's perfectly average," replied Janie. "It's just an activity for the kids."

Barb grinned at Carly, wriggling in Janie's arms, and held out her hands. "Can I?"

Death by enthusiasm, thought Janie, and handed over the baby.

"This one . . . no THIS one!" the boys called to each other up and down the cases.

"Where's your smallest cake?" Janie muttered to Barb.

"Wha? . . . Oh, thith one," said Barb, her mouth full of Carly's fingers. Barb's pink fingernails tapped on the top of the nearest case, indicating a tiny white cake with purple frosting flowers.

"No," said Dylan, who had materialized by Janie and was now standing on her sneakers to get a better look. "That's no good."

"It's fine," said Janie. "Box it," she said to Barb, and held out her arms for Carly.

"No, Mom," insisted Dylan. "He will not have a good birthday with that one."

"Dylan, it's fine, he'll love it." *He expects nothing*, she wanted to say. *He's just a guy who works for us. Temporarily. Don't get attached. Don't expect him to stay in your life forever just because you picked the right cake . . .*

"This is good—look at this one!" Dylan was pointing to a massive chocolate cake with artfully broken pieces of dark chocolate protruding jaggedly around the top. It was the most expensive item in the store. Janie wondered how she had gotten in so far over her head with a damned birthday cake. Malinowski wouldn't even care, and Dylan would think they were best friends forever.

"Oooh, Dylan, I'm so sorry, but that one's already sold," said Barb, who was suddenly holding Carly out toward Janie, her little legs dangling over the huge glass case. Janie grabbed Carly just as Barb let go. "Boys, come over here, I have to show you this really special one." She led them to the last case and bent down to point out a small chocolate cake with a checkerboard pattern inscribed in the frosting. "Does he like chocolate?" she asked Dylan.

"It's his favorite."

"This is the most chocolate cake in the whole store, AND it doesn't have any jam filling or nuts!"

"Nuts—gross!" said Keane, his body shuddering in disgust.

Barb boxed the cake, waved off Janie's offer of cash, and told Dylan and Keane to sing "Happy Birthday" extra loud for her. They practiced the whole way home.

By the time Janie pulled into the driveway, the boys were aquiver with anticipation and spilled out of the car as soon as it stopped. Tug was laying dark brown boards across the floor joists.

"Happy Birthday!" they screamed and launched into song, but then realized they were not holding the cake, and dove back into the car to get it. Janie unboxed the cake and walked it toward Malinowski with a boy on either side of her, their fingers sliding into the frosting where they grasped the circular cardboard tray. They sang like it was their own birthdays and candy was raining from the sky. Janie forced a smile, embarrassed by their unbridled enthusiasm and her evident complicity.

Tug played his part, slapping his thigh in surprise and grinning widely. He glanced at Janie, who gave a little shrug and paid all her attention to keeping the cake from falling into the dirt. When they reached him, they lowered the cake onto the boards he had laid out, and Janie went back to the car to get Carly who was shrieking to be included. By the time she returned to the little party, Tug had hacked off pieces of the cake with his jack knife and laid them into the boys' unwashed hands.

"Oh," said Janie, "I was just going in for plates and napkins."

"No need," he said. "Thank you, by the way. This is very . . . it's very nice."

"It was the boys' idea." She looked around at his work. The project seemed to be going slowly. She wondered how he would get it all done in a month. "What's with these boards?" she asked. "I thought the floor was going to be pine."

"No, it was," he said, licking a smudge of chocolate frosting from his lower lip. "But when I got to the lumber distributor, they had this huge order of mahogany that never got picked up. I talked the guy into selling me some for the same price as the pine. Can you believe it?"

No, she couldn't believe it. The plans called for pine. What would possess him to purchase anything else? "It's supposed to be pine," she said.

"Yeah, but . . . mahogany's better. Stronger, nicer looking . . . You don't like it?"

It was beautiful. She could see that. She didn't actually know why Robby had chosen pine, other than maybe to keep the cost down. But it's what he had chosen, and it was how he'd envisioned this porch for her before he'd become unable to envision anything at all. Before he'd lost his sight. And everything else. But not the bike helmet. That had stayed safe at home.

"I can return it," Malinowski offered. "I haven't cut anything yet. I wanted you to see it first."

"Uhh, I just . . . I don't . . . when do I have to decide?"

"Tomorrow? How's that?"

"Okay. I'm sorry. You just surprised me."

"I know," he said. He nodded at the cake. "You surprised me, too."

KEANE'S FATHER WAS FORTY minutes late. "That's okay," Keane told Dylan. "I don't mind."

They wore Janie down for another piece of Malinowski's cake and were surprised when she served it to them on paper plates instead of into their hands. They countered this disappointment by licking the plates clean and barking.

Janie was wiping the chocolate off their noses when the gleaming tan sports car skidded into the space behind Tug's truck. Keane's father was still bobbing his head slightly to the now-extinguished beat of some overly percussive song when he strode up the driveway.

"Whazup?" he said to the little group on the front steps.

"Where's my late fee?" asked Janie, smiling only with her mouth.

Keane's father chuckled and shook his finger at her. "You got me!" he said. "But maybe I could make it up to you some way . . ." He cocked his head to one side and gave her a moment to appreciate her good fortune.

"I got a buddy with a muffler shop over in Framingham," Tug said, a nail sticking out of the side of his mouth as he bent over a bracket. "If you were looking to get that pipe fixed."

"There's nothing wrong with my muffler. It's supposed to sound like that."

"Okay," said Tug. He lined up the nail and banged it hard with the hammer.

"Seriously, man. That's the way it sounds."

"Kinda loud," said Tug. "You might wanna check it."

Janie directed the boys toward the sports car. "Where's your booster seat?" she asked Keane.

"Dad says I'm big enough." He scurried into the back and buckled himself into the sea of champagne-colored leather. The chest strap lay across his face for a moment before he tucked it behind his back.

Janie closed the door and turned to Keane's father, now beside her. "They have a program down at the police station where they give you a booster seat," she said, "if you can't afford it."

"Bye, Keane!" yelled Dylan over the sound of the gunning motor.

9

SUNDAY, JULY 22

So Jake's practically moved in. Not really, but it seems like he drops by a lot. Or e-mails. I keep wondering if he talks to anyone but me about all this, but I never get around to asking. Not that we only talk about Father L. We usually start with that and then end up talking about other stuff. I don't even know what.

He did okay at Mass today. I think he was trying extra hard to look normal and stable after last Sunday. His homily had more little jokes than usual. They were pretty bad but they appealed to the older folks and that kind of mother that always wears a skirt to Mass, never pants.

When he came down to the church basement for coffee and donuts afterward, he came straight over to me, which I think may have ticked off his usual groupies. I smiled at him, and was about to say something nice about his homily, but then he smiled back, so relieved, and I didn't have to say anything at all. He reached out and gave my arm a quick pat, then he turned to the multitudes and did his duty.

Out of the blue, Aunt Jude invited him over for Sunday dinner, and us, too, of course. He accepted right away. I think he's just taking every opportunity not to spend too much time in the rectory.

The dinner was strange. I can't say why. More strange than just your average, eating-overcooked-pot-roast-with-your-nutty-aunt-and-a-guy-dressed-in-black-from-head-to-foot strange. Everyone seemed quieter than usual. Can you believe I'm saying this? Aunt Jude was quiet. For her. She still talked like her tongue was battery powered, but then at times she seemed to be watching him. I think she must know that this Father L. business is taking a toll.

And Jake, Mr. Smooth with the Church Ladies, of which my aunt is most definitely one, seemed like he didn't always know what to say, how to play it. I think maybe it's hard for him to do the Pastor Perfect routine in front of me. Because he knows I know.

Aunt Jude was watching me, too. She thinks she's sneaky but I can tell. Maybe she sees I'm not quite as wretched and pathetic. Probably patting herself on the back for sending him over to me back in the darkest dark days. Who knows what her agenda is.

Mum's got her itinerary set. She's flying in on Saturday the fourth, sliding in under the wire to make it for Dylan's birth-day. She better get here. Dylan will be so upset if she doesn't.

DYLAN WAS WEARING THE goggles again. Janie hadn't realized that he'd taken a break from this habit until she looked in the rearview mirror. "Hey, where'd you find those?" she asked as she drove him to Pond Pals camp.

"They were here," he answered.

"Do you need them for your swim lessons?"

"No, you can't see stuff, anyway," he said. "The water's too . . ." He wagged his hand around.

"Murky?" she asked. She had read online that they were try-ing to combat an invasive lake-weed problem with the use of a "weed harvester," a submersible machine that ripped the plants out by the roots. The article had said something about how the agitation had disturbed the generally clear waters of Lake Pequot. She was up on all the news these days. "So how come you have them on?"

"I just like to," he said. He took them off and stashed them behind his booster seat when they pulled into the Town Beach parking lot. Janie was tempted to put them away while he was at camp, but she thought it might upset him. She mentioned it to Jake later that morning, and after some consideration, they decided it was best to just let it be.

When she picked Dylan up that afternoon, he told her sullenly, "Keane already left. With his dad." He dug out the goggles and wore them for the short car ride home. He stayed out in the yard with Tug when Janie went into the house to change Carly's diaper.

The sound of breaking glass made Janie race down the stairs before she'd resnapped the baby's onesie. Shards of glass lay all over the kitchen table and an unfamiliar ball rolled into a corner of the linoleum. "What happened?" she called to Tug. "Where's Dylan?"

"He's okay." Tug's face emerged behind the sunburst of broken glass in the window. "He's fine. Dylan, you want to tell your Mom you're alright?" he called over his shoulder. There was no answer.

"Where'd that ball come from? Is that yours?" she demanded.

"No, never seen it," said Tug. "Dylan took it out of his backpack and threw it to me, but I had a board in my hands, and I couldn't catch it."

"Dylan, where are you?" she yelled coming out the front door with Carly on her hip, the flap of the onesie sailing out like the train of a strange little gown. Dylan was hiding under a rhododendron at the edge of the yard. "Come out of there right now." He scooted partway out and sat with his arms crossed against his narrow chest and his chin down.

"Whose ball is that?" she asked.

"Mine."

"Where'd you get it?"

"Keane gave it to me and he said it was mine and I could keep it so it's mine."

"Why did Keane give you the ball?"

"Because," he looked up for a moment to gauge her reaction. His eyes were red and his lips were tightly clamped. His chin began to tremble. "Because he said his dad could get him another one any time and I could have this one to practice because I throw . . . really . . ." the tears came now, " . . . bad."

"Oh . . ." Janie sank down on the grass next to him.

"I need Dad," he whispered.

"Oh," she breathed, and reached out to pull him toward her. "Oh, Dylan." *I forgot about throwing,* she wanted to say, *I forgot about all that stuff. I'm so sorry.* But her throat closed like a vise around her words and tears sprang to her eyes and she was too far from the bathroom to run and hide. Dylan buried his head in her lap and she hid her face in his black curls and they cried. Carly crawled a few feet away and found a stick to wave around like a baton, conducting the symphony of their sorrow.

WHEN JANIE'S SHOULDERS STOPPED heaving quite so much, she turned her head and wiped her face on the sleeve of her T-shirt. It left a dark, wet smudge like a makeshift badge. She knew Tug was watching even before she glanced up and caught his unblinking gaze. They both looked away. "I'll teach you to throw," she murmured to Dylan.

"Even if I broke a window?"

"Yeah, even then."

There was no avoiding Tug as they walked back toward the house. "Sorry, Tug," said Dylan. "I'm a bad thrower."

"Nah, you gotta be pretty strong to break a window," he replied. "Just need to work on that aim a little."

"Mom will help me."

He nodded and gave Janie the gentle edge of a smile, "Moms are good for that."

"What do you think about that window?" Janie said, stifling a sniffle.

"Actually, I'm kind of glad about this," he said.

"Really."

"No kidding. I've been meaning to mention it. This window, I think it should be replaced."

"Because?"

"It's old, it's not insulated, and it's too small. The kitchen won't get nearly as much light with the porch here now, and we could put in a nice wide one for not too much money. I know it's not in the plans, but it deserves a thought."

Janie sighed. She wasn't sure if she had a thought to spare. Tug helped her clean up the glass in the kitchen as they discussed the possibility. How wide. How expensive. In the end she said yes out of sheer exhaustion. And out of deference to Shelly, her soon-to-be-ex neighbor, who had said, "Of course you can trust him."

"ANOTHER BREAKFAST?" ASKED JANIE the next morning when Tug walked into the yard with his crate of tools at 9:15.

"Nah," he said. "Only so much of that a grown man can take. Ever eat with teenage girls? I mean, since you were one?"

"No, I don't think I have."

"They eat like they're at war. With the food. The food hates them, and they have to outsmart it. Deprive it of butter or salad dressing or the like. But no matter what they do, if they eat it, the food wins. So they put on more lip gloss and go after each other."

"Oh, sure," Janie laughed, "like it's so much worse than teen-aged boys, who slobber up everything that's not nailed down, and then ask why there's never anything good to eat."

"True," he grinned. He set down the tools and rotated one of his shoulders, unscrewing the lid of some ancient ache. "Actually

I was window shopping. Found you a beauty. Perfect size, discontinued model so I got it for a song, and they had it in stock. They'll deliver tomorrow. Which means today I'm going to rip a nice big hole in your front wall."

The noise was so bad, and the house was so small, there was no room far enough away from it. Janie ran as many errands as she could think of until Carly arched her back and screamed in the deli line at the supermarket, and she took her to Aunt Jude's house for a nap. Janie hoped that Aunt Jude would be "out and about," as she would say. But she was home, watching *The Ellen DeGeneres Show*, and ironing her wash-and-wear blouses.

"It was too loud at the house," Janie called over Carly's wails.

"You give that little lovie dove right over to me," Aunt Jude crooned as the baby lurched out of Janie's arms toward her. "That's my girl, yes you are, that's my baby. You come right upstairs with me to your nice, quiet nappy place . . ."

"You're watching this?" Janie asked when Aunt Jude came back downstairs.

"Oh, I never miss it. Unless I have somewhere to go, or Table of Plenty needs me to help out with lunch because somebody didn't come for their shift." Aunt Jude rattled on for a while about the irresponsibility of some people who'd rather get a manicure than help out, and the impermanent quality of nail polish, and her friend's husband's nail-color preference, though he rarely noticed if she bothered to wear any. Janie glazed over. She was quite certain that one day Aunt Jude's ramblings would contain a cure for cancer or a workable blueprint for world peace. But no one would ever know because no one could stand to listen to her for that long. " . . . But I do like this Ellen," Jude was saying. "She's very funny. She's a lesbian."

"You find homosexuality funny?" Janie could never pass up an opportunity to get under her aunt's skin.

"Jane Elizabeth Dwyer LaMarche! Of course I don't find it funny. A person's personal private life is not a laughing matter.

That's not what makes her funny at all, I never said that. She's very humorous and she happens to feel romantic toward other women for some reason. Those two are not connected in any way. At least I don't think so. Well, let's just think about that for a minute. Let me see, now. Those young men on *Queer Eye for the Straight Guy* are funny. Have you ever seen that one? It's very hilarious!"

Bored now with her aunt's verbal meanderings, Janie dropped herself like a bag of laundry onto the faded blue corduroy recliner. Time for a new subject. "What do you think of Barb?"

"Cormac's girl?" Aunt Jude picked up the iron and applied it in little dabs to a blouse collar. "I think she's nice. She's very . . . tall, isn't she? She must be six feet tall almost."

"She wears those high heels."

"It'll be a big change, won't it? Cormac's belonged to us for so long. Such a sweet, funny boy. Always trying to separate himself, but always staying so close. It'll be strange, but she's a nice girl and it's time."

"Time?" Janie sat up. "For what? What are you talking about?"

"Well, they haven't said anything, but I think this is it. Auntie's intuition. He's forty now. It's time."

Janie sank back, relieved. Auntie could intuit herself silly. Cormac wasn't getting married. They watched the end of *The Ellen DeGeneres Show* and then the midday news, which reported the ongoing investigation of Father Lambrosini, as well as the anticipated heat wave and two more burglaries. When it was time to pick up Dylan, Carly was still sleeping, so Janie left her with Aunt Jude and took Dylan to Pelham Ball Field to practice throwing. She had gotten him the smallest baseball mitt she could find, and still it flopped around on his hand as if *it* were wearing *him*. Nonetheless, Dylan was ecstatic to stand on the pitcher's mound and wing the ball in her general direction, then charge home plate and scream, "Home run!"

It should be Robby, Janie knew. Robby should be out here with his boy, his little window breaker. But he wasn't and he wouldn't ever be. This thought didn't startle and disable her quite as much as it once had, although it would never be okay.

See this? Janie sent up a prayer to her dead husband. *If you can't be here, at least keep watching. Don't stop watching over us.*

JANIE AND THE KIDS were eating apples and peanut butter in the kitchen when Tug hoisted a four-by-eight-foot piece of plywood that completely covered the hole for the new window. Janie came around to the front door. "Do we need that?" she asked.

"If you don't want raccoons raiding your Cheerios, you do."

"It blocks out all the light."

"Well, I think I have a sheet of heavy plastic in the truck. I could staple that up instead. Just don't leave any food out."

The kids were exhausted. Dylan had spent himself playing ball and was weepy with fatigue by the time he collapsed into his bed. He fell asleep midsentence, whining something about his mitt. Janie should have been tired too, but she lay in bed that night considering what other fatherly duties might await her. She threw the sheets off so the occasional asthmatic puffs of breeze could cool her and fell asleep to the distant crinkling of the plastic as it sighed in and out again.

IT WASN'T THE RANDOM snapping of the plastic that woke her. The sound was shorter, sharper, more purposeful. It stopped almost as soon as it began, and she wondered if she had only dreamed it. She rolled over, hoping to slide back into the muggy torpor from which she had been beckoned. But catching sight of the clock, she knew Jake would likely e-mail her soon, and she might as well get up.

When she reached the bottom of the stairs and rounded the corner into the living room, she was surprised to see a light on in the office. A figure emerged from the light, his face in shadow, and for a brief moment Janie thought it was Tug, back to make some further adjustment to the porch plans. She flipped the light switch, illuminating the living room and the man's face. It was not Tug.

This man was shorter and pasty-looking, not shades of caramel like Tug. He rubbed his latex-gloved hands in slow circles over his thighs and smiled as if he knew her, as if they were old friends who had chanced to meet in some unlikely spot, out of context from their prior relationship. Janie stared at him, momentarily wondering where she might have seen this strange, doughy face before.

"Hey there," he said. At the sound of his voice it became clear to her that she did not know this man. He was from nowhere. And he was standing in her living room in the middle of the night.

"What?" she asked, as the fact of the situation registered in its terrifying entirety.

"Hey there, pretty lady," he said and took a step toward her.

Robby, she thought, *get down here!* And then she remembered she was alone in the house, except for Carly and Dylan. And she became aware that if this strange man got past her to the staircase, there was absolutely nothing standing between him and them.

"Get out," she said, the tension in her chest making her sound small to herself.

"I don't think so," he said.

"Get the fuck out of my house," she wrenched out in a growl.

"Nah, I like it here."

The bile rose up in her throat and all she could think of was how fucking infuriating it was that this pasty little troll was talking to her like this, and her husband wasn't here to step in. *It's your job now*, she told herself, *even this*. The women from her self-defense class assembled in the back of her brain. *Yell!* they told her.

Janie yelled. "YOU'RE NOT GOING TO LIKE IT HERE IN A MINUTE YOU STINKING PILE OF SHIT. YOU HAVE NO FUCK-ING IDEA WHAT YOU'RE DEALING WITH. YOU WANNA

TAKE ME YOU GO AHEAD AND TRY IT BECAUSE I AM NOT GOING DOWN WITHOUT A FIGHT YOU'LL REMEMBER FOR THE REST OF YOUR MISERABLE GODFORSAKEN LIFE!"

This she screamed at the very top of her lungs, like she had no plans to ever use them again. Like her vocal chords had just been waiting for this moment to burn themselves out in one last blast. She gesticulated wildly, pounding on her own chest, pointing at him.

The strange man halted his forward direction. In fact, he took a step back, a look of startled panic on his face that seemed oddly incongruous, as if she were the attacker, not him. His nostrils flared, and he appeared to will himself forward, his hands snapping out and grabbing her wrists. It was exactly what Arturo had done in that silly-looking suit. And Instructor Debbie had taught her that when her wrists were grabbed it was the perfect opportunity to slam her knee into the guy's genitals. *Do it!* the women urged.

She reared back on her left leg to gain momentum, which served to fully focus his attention on maintaining control of her arms. Then she rammed her right knee so hard between his legs that her knee cap felt the impact of his pelvic bone behind the sensitive reproductive organs. He released his grip on her wrists and lurched forward to grasp his exploding testicles, practically an engraved invitation for her to slam her other knee into his downward facing nose.

And when he collapsed on her living room rug, he was still. Which was almost disappointing because she was just twitching to kick him some more. She had never experienced so much uncontrolled rage in all her life, and that was saying something.

Good effing work! called the Katya in her head.

OFFICER DOUGIE SHAW SLAMMED on the brakes of his squad car in Janie's driveway, leaped out, and ran for her front door, dodging lumber and piles of dirt by the light of his blue-and-red flashers.

The door was open and he lunged inside, drawing his gun and aiming it at the crumpled heap on Janie's carpet. He whipped his head left then right, finally locating Janie on the stairs wielding the phone and a large glass jar about half full of rocks and pine cones.

"You alright?" barked Officer Dougie. He squinted quizzically at the jar for a second, and then back to the perpetrator.

"Yeah," she said, knowing that her uncontrolled panting belied her.

The guy bleeding onto her rug began to moan and make futile little writhing movements.

"Shit, Janie," breathed Dougie, "what the hell happened?"

The entire Pelham police force and half the fire department arrived moments later, sirens screaming, lights flashing. The primal growl of the idling fire truck and ambulance announced their ominous wrath to the neighborhood. Janie darted up the stairs to check on the kids, certain that all the noise would have woken them. Carly was sitting upright in her crib, half-lidded eyes scanning blindly around the room. Then she slowly toppled back down onto her blanket. By the time Janie tiptoed across the room and peeked over the crib railing, the little girl had already fallen back asleep. Dylan, apparently still worn out from an afternoon of ball playing, snored lightly.

Janie went back downstairs and told what she knew, as the perpetrator was handcuffed and then hauled up onto his feet.

"Aw, Jesus," one of the officers muttered when the blood-bathed face came into view.

"My fuckin' nose," moaned the pasty little man, spitting red-streaked saliva. "Christ, my balls!" he whined, as two officers propelled him out the front door.

Janie's house soon cleared of the uniformed invasion until it was just Dougie again, asking what sounded like the same questions over and over. Finally he jammed the little pad of paper into his pocket and said, "I'm calling Cormac."

"I'll tell him tomorrow," she said. Her breathing had slowed and the panic subsided; weariness crawled over her, and her limbs went limp. It was all she could do to stay upright.

"Janie," he said. "You don't want to be alone after an attack." He scratched his crew cut with the capped end of his pen. "Course, you did beat the guy bloody. That puts a new twist on it . . ."

"My neighbor will be over here any second," said Janie, wondering why Shelly hadn't already arrived. With the fleet of rescue vehicles clogging the street, she could hardly be unaware of the spectacle. "Really, I just want to go back to sleep."

"Once the adrenaline stops pumping you get really tired," nodded Dougie. "You sure she's coming?"

It took ten more minutes of reassuring him that she was fine, just worn out, and that if Shelly didn't show up for some reason, Janie would call someone else. "You don't want to be alone right now," Dougie kept insisting, as if he were reporting from somewhere inside her head. As if he had any idea of what she wanted right now. What she wanted, in fact, was for him to stop talking at her and go check the lock on that bastard's jail cell. That's what she wanted.

FIFTEEN MINUTES LATER, JANIE was still slumped in a chair at the kitchen table, alone. Her exhaustion had migrated into nausea and a weird shaking feeling. She knew she could not sleep. She wondered if she would ever sleep again.

If Shelly were here, she would tell Janie to go to sleep and Janie would comply. That was the core of their relationship. Shelly showed up and told her what to do when everything was incomprehensible and terrifying. And though completely uncharacteristic of her, Janie obeyed. Where was Shelly now, when she needed instructions most?

Janie reached for the phone and found herself dialing not Shelly, but the rectory. Later she would rationalize this by saying Jake was the only person she knew who would be awake.

That he would understand her need to pull inside herself. That he had been assaulted and would know how to help her calm down. These things were all true, but much later she would admit to herself that, had they not been true, she would have called him, anyway.

"Jane?" he said. "Is everything alright?"

"Yeah, I just . . . this weird thing just happened, and I knew you would be awake . . ."

"What happened?"

"A guy . . . some guy broke in . . ."

"Someone broke into your house? Tonight?"

"Yeah, and he grabbed me . . ."

"Oh my God!"

"And I beat the shit out of him. Like they taught me in that class. I broke his nose and I kneed him in the crotch . . . I had to keep him from getting to the kids . . ."

"Jane, my God! Are you okay?"

"Yeah, I'm . . . uh . . ." She gulped in air before her throat closed up altogether. A sob escaped and she put her hand over her eyes. "I'm kind of . . ." She was weeping before she was even aware that she was upset, her shoulders shaking, her lungs heaving. *Oh,* she thought somewhere in her numbness, *I'm crying.*

He may have said something more, or he may have simply hung up. The next thing she knew there was banging at the front door. She stumbled blindly toward it, and when she opened the door she was suddenly enveloped in warmth, clutched against skin and well-worn cotton, rocked as her body spasmed and shook, as wails of anger and fear and sadness erupted from her. She heard whispering but couldn't make it out. Didn't care, anyway.

When the exhaustion overtook her again, and the sobbing slowed, she looked down. Still pressed against his body, all she could see was that his feet were bare.

10

JANIE ROSE TO CONSCIOUSNESS with the slamming of a car door.
Actually, the sound was too heavy for a car, the metallic *thunk*
too low in register. More likely a truck.

She mulled over the familiar smell of a man whose deodorant
was in need of reapplication. The vestiges of Sport Scent or Powder Fresh could still be detected, but this was overpowered by the
musky, reassuring odor of dried male sweat. She felt the pressure
of her cheekbone resting against his shoulder as they sat slumped
next to each other on the couch, his head tilted back toward the
top of the couch pillows, his mouth slightly open. She resisted the
temptation to slide her arm beneath his and entwine his fingers
with her own.

"Jake," she said, and he blinked. His hand slid up to scratch his
chest through the faded cotton T-shirt. Janie noticed the unrav-
eled edge of the sleeve. It matched the ragged hems of his jeans.

His yawn ended with the start of a smile when he saw her.
Then his eyes flicked down to their legs, thigh to thigh on the
couch, hers covered in thin pajamas, and he slid away. Turning to
face her, he made sure that none of their body parts touched. "I
didn't want to wake you," he said. "When you fell asleep, I meant
to just sit there for a minute and then go. I guess I dozed off." He
looked down at his bare feet, then up at her again, a vague panic
setting in around his eyes.

"You should go," she said, and noted the relief on his face. "I'm fine."

"You're sure?"

"Absolutely. The kids will be up soon."

He was on his feet and at the door in a moment, but halted his exit abruptly. Turning back toward her he asked, "Should I come back? It's Friday," he reminded her.

She thought for a moment, unable to come up with the right answer. "Um, yeah. If you want to."

"Alright," he said, and left.

A FEW MINUTES LATER Janie was scooping coffee grounds into a paper filter when there was a terrific ripping sound behind her. "Mother of Christ!" she gasped. The grounds flew from the filter and splayed out across the kitchen counter. Turning to defend herself, she saw Tug pulling the plastic off the window frame. "You scared the hell out of me!" she told him.

"Sorry," he said without any sign of remorse. He balled up the plastic and stomped away.

What's his problem? Janie wondered briefly, swiping at the grounds on the counter.

By the time she had started the coffee, he was back. "You might want to clear out today," he said inspecting a pair of pliers, for what, Janie couldn't determine. "Lotta banging."

"Okay." He seemed strangely irritable. Maybe he was just tired. "Coffee?" she offered.

"No."

Janie poured herself a cup and sat down. She would need to tell Cormac about the break-in, preferably before that blabby Dougie Shaw got to him. And then maybe she could convince him to pass it on to Aunt Jude. Janie dreaded telling her aunt. Which would be worse, she wondered: the sure-to-be-endless fretting for Janie's and the children's safety? Or the satisfaction that Aunt Jude would inevitably sling around at having been right about that stupid self-defense class? As if a home invasion itself weren't enough to put up with.

"I have to come in." Tug was looking somewhere past her shoulder. "I have to measure for reinforcements under the window."

"The front door's open."

He disappeared for a moment. "What the . . . what IS this!" he called from the doorway. Janie saw him staring at the hubcap-sized spot of dried blood on the living room rug.

"I forgot," she muttered, getting up. "Can you help me get this out of here before Dylan sees it?"

"Is everyone okay?" He stared at her incredulously.

"Everyone but the guy who broke in last night." She told him the details as they rolled the bloody rug and leaned it behind a tree by the driveway. She would have it cleaned while Dylan was at camp.

Back in the house, Malinowski poured himself a cup of coffee and sat down at the kitchen table. "So, what was . . . that guy . . . that priest . . . doing here this morning?"

"I just didn't want to call anyone who, you know, cares too much about me." Her own words sounded strange to her. She tried to make them make sense. "I didn't want anyone who would freak out. He's good in a crisis."

"He didn't have shoes on."

"Yeah," said Janie. "I can't explain that."

Dylan came down the stairs with Nubby the Hairless Bunny clamped under his arm. "I want juice," he said and curled into Janie's lap and closed his eyes again.

"I'll get it," said Tug.

"How'd you sleep, sweetie?" Janie ran her fingers through his unruly black curls.

"Good," he grunted.

"Did you have any dreams?"

"No." He twisted around to reach the juice Tug had placed on the table near him. "Just bad words."

"Bad words?"

"Bad guy words."

"Who was saying them?" Janie asked.

"A bad guy."

"Were you scared?"

He shrugged. "I want toast. Is it time for camp? Where's my ball?"

"Hey," she said. "We might go hang out in the park after camp. Tug says he's going to be doing a lot of loud banging."

"I like loud banging."

"It won't be that bad," said Tug.

"You just said it would," Janie said, questioning.

He shrugged and put his mug in the sink.

FRIDAY, JULY 27

There's been a police car down my street every half hour since the sun set. I never liked Dougie Shaw, but now that it's dark, I don't mind him so much. A guy broke into my house last night and, to use the Experiential Safety lingo, I disabled him. I don't really want to write about it because I've told the story too many times today and I'm boring myself. Shelly was at her boyfriend's house when it happened, and today she pumped me for every last detail.

Cormac is sleeping in the little twin bed in the back room, the poor guy. All bent up like a pretzel. I told him he didn't have to, but there was no stopping him. He's been on his cell phone since I came up to bed. He's talking low. Must be Barb.

I ended up telling Aunt Jude about it myself. She went so white I thought she might faint. Once she got over the shock she did natter on for a while about the state of the world and taking precautions and God's saving hand, but it wasn't as bad as I thought it would be. She rubbed my shoulders and I thanked her for making me take that class. I think I could hold up un-

der torture, but if I'm getting my shoulders rubbed I'll tell any secret you'd care to hear.

Tug talked me into letting him install an alarm system. A cheap one. At first he thought the guy got in through the plastic, but he didn't. The window in the office was pried open. Still, he feels bad. Not sure why.

Jake didn't end up coming over today. Something about meeting with a couple about a wedding. I think he might feel weird. I feel weird. I slept next to a priest! Jerry Springer will be calling any minute for his segment on "Ass-Kicking Widows Who Cozy Up to the Celibate." I e-mailed Jake and told him I'd be offline tonight because of Cormac sleeping over. He hadn't replied by the time I shut off the computer and came up here. Hope he doesn't feel too weird.

I'm glad Cormac's here. I'm so tired.

WHEN JANIE GOT UP the next morning, Cormac was long gone. The Confectionary opened at 5:30 a.m. even on Saturdays, and he liked to be the first one there. A rainstorm had come to break the heat, and the pungent smell of rehydrated lawns and rinsed asphalt filtered in through the windows. She checked her e-mail before making coffee. The one from Jake said:

"Jane, I'm glad your cousin is there. I was worried about you being alone and scared. You're going to be shaky for a while, and it helps to have someone you feel safe with. I find myself saying little prayers for you throughout the day. You've been given so much to shoulder, and somehow you seem to rise to the occasion. I admire that in you, Jane. As a man whose family life was something less than ideal, I can't help but think how lucky your children are to have you. Sleep well. Jake."

Carly was starting to talk to herself up in her crib, little singing, humming noises, playing with her voice like a toy. Then she called, "Ma? Ma!" and Janie went up to her. Dylan was just opening his eyes, so Janie took Carly with her into his bed, and the three of them snuggled and giggled. In the happiness of their little family heap, the coffee didn't seem so necessary.

WICK LALLY, A REPORTER for the *Pelham Town Crier* recognized the white truck as he pulled his Volvo up behind it. "Mal!" he called, crossing the lumber-strewn yard. "Mal, buddy!"

"Hey," said Tug, barely looking up from adjusting a piece of trim around the new window. "What's up. How's the back?"

"Ah, it's nothing. Little twinge."

Tug chuckled as he banged in a nail. "That's not how it looked last week. Looked like you were headed for a body cast."

"Well, you know, a walk-off home run has its price. You'll see when you get one. Someday."

"I just never got one that made me cry, is all," said Tug. "You here for Mrs. LaMarche?"

"Yeah, is she home?"

"Nope."

"Where is she, when's she coming back?"

Tug shrugged. "You should lay off her. She's been through enough."

Wick laughed and wagged his head. "Lay off her? I'm just hoping she won't break my balls! What is she, like six feet, two hundred pounds?"

"She's average. And she's been through enough."

Janie chose this unfortunate moment to pull into the driveway. Dylan and Keane scrambled out of the car and immediately began dueling with what had once been paper towel rolls, now brightly colored and festooned with crepe paper streamers.

"Those aren't for fighting," said Janie as she pulled at Carly's car seat.

"Get the pirate hats!" yelled Keane. The boys ran for the house, calling "Hi, Tug!" as they passed.

Janie looked at the two men in her yard. One was listing slightly to the left but smiling brightly all the same; the other was rubbing the butt of a hammer in the palm of his hand and looking annoyed.

"This is Wick Lally, a reporter for the *Town Crier*," said Tug. "He's a reporter."

"Well, now that my occupation is firmly established, Mrs. La-Marche, may I speak to you for a few moments?"

Janie looked back to Tug, whose hard gaze and barely perceptible head shake gave her the impetus to say, "I'm sorry I can't talk right now."

"I understand," said Wick, all sincerity. "I'll return in an hour when you've had time to settle in."

Janie glanced at Tug again and then back to Wick, "I'm not going to talk about it."

"I understand completely. However, many victims do say how much better they feel when they've discussed a harrowing event, and told their side of the story."

"First of all," said Janie, "I don't consider myself a victim. Second of all, there are no sides to this story. What happened is what happened. It's not up for interpretation."

"As a twenty-four-year veteran of the newspaper business, I can assure you there are sides to every story. Won't you feel more comfortable if yours is told in your own words?"

"Jesus, Lally," said Tug. "She said no."

"Thanks for your input, Mal," Wick said, "but if she's capable of beating the daylights out of an intruder, she's capable of making up her own mind without the assistance of her carpenter."

Janie's eyebrows went up. Tug's face locked into a blankness that Janie no longer mistook for passivity. "Wow," she said to Wick. "That was a poor choice of words. You can go now."

"Mrs. LaMarche, it's in your best interest—"

Janie took a quick step forward, and to the great amusement of her carpenter, Wick Lally flinched. "No comment," she murmured.

When the Volvo pulled away, Janie said to Tug, "I guess I've got a reputation now."

He grinned broadly and she could see tiny flecks of opalescent brown in the dark of his eyes. "Comes in handy sometimes," he said.

THE MONTH OF AUGUST announced itself with a thunderstorm, the heat crackling in the sky like kindling for a giant bonfire. The rain came too, however it sprinkled itself meekly, apologetically, succumbing to vapor almost as soon as it hit the ground. When the storm passed, Shelly Michelman happily pounded a For Sale sign into the damp soil of her meticulously landscaped yard. She positioned the sign so that purple and blue pansies surrounded the post, as if the flowers sprang from the sign itself and not the ground. It was calculated to beckon, to charm, to sell.

THAT CRACKLING IN THE air, that sense that a cloud could burst at any moment did not give Janie second thoughts about her Friday walk with Jake. She was relieved, in fact, that things were, in her assessment, getting back to normal. They had somehow managed to get past their initial discomfort over the events of the previous week. Whenever Janie thought about how she had called Jake rather than a member of her own family, cried to him, clung to him in his well-worn T-shirt and jeans, how the feel and smell of him had been the things that had calmed her, even more than the soothing words . . . well, she just put that right out of her mind. Mostly.

She heard Jake's car pull into the driveway and peeked through her new kitchen window. He got out wearing the standard black pants and collared shirt, but then he quickly unbuttoned the shirt, removed it and arranged it across the back of the driver's seat. Underneath he wore a black T-shirt. Janie hastened Carly into her baby backpack, adjusted her sun hat, and went out to meet him.

"I'll be back in a bit," she said to Tug, who was on a ladder, working on collar ties for the vaulted rafters of the porch ceiling.

He glanced at her, flicked his gaze at Father Jake, and did not respond.

Janie smiled at Jake. "Is there a Black Store somewhere where all you guys shop?"

He chuckled back, "Yeah, but it's also a Goth favorite, so we have to be careful to avoid the shirts with chains and the studded wrist bands."

"I don't know," she said, "those might be a big hit with the Prayers for Peace group."

They walked down the street on their usual route to Jansen Hill. Carly bounced along chewing on her fist and drooling on the back of Janie's neck. "She's teething," explained Janie, as Jake dabbed at the dampness with his handkerchief.

"What's happening with the intruder?" asked Jake when they resumed. "Will you have to testify?"

"Dougie Shaw says no, it doesn't look like it. They got a confession out of him at the police station before they took him to the hospital. He's locked up until the plea hearing."

"They didn't take him straight to the hospital?" said Jake. "You said he was bloody."

"Apparently they felt he was healthy enough to be questioned. Dougie says a broken nose speeds up an interrogation like you wouldn't believe."

They walked briskly, much faster than they had when they first started taking their Friday hikes several months before. Janie had begun taking strolls around the neighborhood without him a couple of times a week, and her muscles felt strong and steady. She was secretly proud that she could keep up with him even with a twenty-pound baby on her back.

Their speed was also a function of anticipation. When the road ended and the path through the unpopulated woods began, their conversations inevitably turned more relaxed and personal. Walking past houses, they looked straight ahead; in the trees they made eye contact.

"Your mother's coming tomorrow?" said Jake.

"Yeah, Uncle Charlie's picking her up at Logan Airport around noon."

"You don't seem excited."

Janie thought about this for a minute. "I guess I should be, but I think I might be kind of pissed."

"She hasn't spent much time here since Rob died."

"Exactly! And no one else seems to get that. Aunt Jude and Cormac and everyone—they don't seem surprised that she just went right back to Europe-as-Usual. Am I crazy, or is that weird?"

"It's hard to understand, I'll grant you. Sometimes people have their reasons for things, though."

Janie slowed and leaned over, hands on her knees, to rest for a moment. The baby felt heavy now. "You're siding with her."

Jake squatted down next to her and caught her eye. It was a look that said, *You know better than that.* He tucked a piece of Janie's hair back behind her ear, and ran a hand over Carly's silky head. She grinned at him around her drooly fist. "You've got a little monkey on your back," he murmured to Janie. "A sleepy little monkey."

The impulse to be too close to him overwhelmed Janie for a moment. She wanted to slide her arms around his waist and lock them across the back of his black T-shirt. She wanted to feel his hand in her hair again, to be embraced by him, baby and all. She stood up quickly and began to walk.

Jake fell in stride beside her. The path was wide, and appeared to have been originally blazed by a cart of some kind, perhaps a hundred years ago or more. Janie walked in one ancient wheel track and Jake in the other, divided only by wood grasses and the occasional sapling.

"I've often wondered if there might have been some sort of shelter up here at one time," said Jake.

"There was," said Janie. "Mike and I used to sit in the old foundation and play farmers."

"I didn't know you had an agricultural streak," he teased.

"Not much! If I recall, my main activities were churning imaginary butter and shooting imaginary bears. And Mike spent all his time planting pebbles and pine needles in elaborate designs."

Janie veered off and followed a lesser trail through some brush, careful to step over fallen branches. They soon came upon an indentation in the hill bolstered on two sides by decrepit rock walls. A half-rotted log lay at the base of one wall. "See that log?" said Janie. "We spent an entire afternoon rolling that thing in here. Mike didn't like to get his jeans messy sitting in the dirt."

"Fastidious," commented Jake.

"Like you wouldn't believe."

"Were there any farmer children?"

"Yeah," Janie laughed. "I was pretty strict, when I wasn't letting them eat their fill of butter." She lowered herself onto the fallen log and Jake sat down next to her. They didn't touch, but his hand rested near hers on the disintegrating wood. "Did you ever want to be a dad?" she asked quietly.

"I think I did in the abstract. I thought a lot about how I would protect them and teach them to stand up for themselves. But I don't have that longing to reproduce myself that some people have."

"You're very kind," said Janie, staring out into the pine boughs. "That's important in a father."

"I have a temper," he admitted.

"Join the club."

"Yes, but you seem to be able to use yours purposefully, in appropriate ways."

"Like beating the hell out of a burglar? Let me tell you, past the fear and the panic, I really wanted to kill him. I was almost disappointed when he dropped so fast. To me, that's a little scary."

Jake turned toward her and looked her full in the face. "You were protecting yourself and your children. You were in a terrifying situation and you handled it perfectly. How many people can say that? I can't. If I'm honest with myself I have to admit that I envy you."

"Jake, you were a child when you were assaulted. Repeatedly. By your own father. Do you think I could have done what I did under those circumstances? How could anyone?"

He was quiet and motionless except for the blinking of his eyes. Finally he said, "It's with me still." He shook his head and the motion dislodged a tear. "I can't get away from him."

Janie put her hands on his cheeks, brushing the tears back with her thumbs. "There are things that happen that can't be undone," she said. "But you, Jake Sweeney. You have figured out how to really piss him off. He may still be with you, but if he is, you kick his ass every time he sees the kindness in you. When he sees how you reach out to the most miserable of us and give comfort. That's not the man he raised. You're the man *you* raised."

The tears fell faster down his cheeks, and she pulled him toward her, wrapping her arms around his shoulders. She felt his hands reach for her waist, finally gripping the bars of the back pack in which Carly slept. His silent weeping went on for several moments and the shoulder of her T-shirt where his face was buried became damp.

When he stopped crying, he eased back away from her and pulled the hem of his T-shirt from his pants and wiped his face with it. Janie caught a glimpse of the soft, dark hair that swirled at his belly.

"Jane," he said finally. "Thank you." He patted her cheek and smoothed her hair. "I've never known anyone quite like you. I feel very lucky to count you as a friend."

She nodded. What else could she do?

When she got back to her house, and Jake drove away, she deposited a fragment of the old rotted log in her jar.

11

⚊

LATE AFTERNOON THUNDERSTORMS DELAYED Noreen Dwyer's de-
scent into Boston. This bit of intelligence was relayed by her
brother, Uncle Charlie, self-appointed official driver of returning
and exiting relatives. Janie often speculated that this designation
may have originated with her father's final ride to the bus station.
Or whatever vehicular transport Mac Dwyer's retreat entailed.

"Janie, honey, your mum's still up in the air," Uncle Charlie
told her. "Goddamned air traffic control won't let her down."

Janie imagined her mother floating among the clouds with
enormous bird wings strapped to her arms, just as happy to stay
aloft as land.

Because of the delay Noreen was driven straight to her sister Jude's for a big family dinner. They were all there to greet
her when Aunt Brigid, posted at the kitchen window, called out,
"She's here!"

"Thank goodness," muttered Aunt Jude. "These chickens are
drying out by the minute, and the mashed potatoes are hardening
into spackle. Barb, dear, hand me that baster."

Dylan was the first to reach Uncle Charlie's immaculate Ford
Tempo, and he threw himself at his grandmother before she'd
even gotten completely out of the car.

"Glory be to God, but you're enormous!" she teased him.
"What is your mother feeding you? Giraffe food?"

"Do giraffes eat peanut butter and banana sandwiches?" he giggled.

"I think they must!" Her knobby-knuckled hands ran over his head and squeezed his shoulders.

"Gram, guess what! There's only one day between today and my birthday. And I'm gonna have a party with my friend Keane, and you can come!"

"That's why I'm here, love," she said as she hoisted her purse and bag of quilting squares out of the car. "That's why I'm here."

AT BEDTIME NOREEN TOLD Dylan an Italian folk tale about a seam-stress who tamed a grumpy dragon by making him a beautiful vest, so when he flew off to live in the Alps he would feel proud and not so angry. Then she descended the stairs and sorted herself out in the tiny bedroom next to the office. In years past there had been struggles about where she would sleep when she returned to the house she had inhabited for thirty-five years. Robby had often tried to insist that she take her old bed in the master bed-room upstairs. While she appreciated his gallantry, Noreen stood her ground. The single bed was fine for her, she said, and as the downstairs bedroom was closest to the bathroom, she wouldn't wake anyone if she "took a little trip to the toidy" in the middle of the night.

Last Christmas, when Noreen had returned to Pelham for the holidays, Robby had pressed the point. His little French grand-mother would spin in her grave, he said, if she knew he'd rel-egated the grand-mère to such an inauspicious spot in her own house.

"It's not my house," Noreen had replied with surprising vehe-mence, "and it's not my room. I never liked that room when it was mine, so why should I be forced to take it now?"

Returning for Robby's funeral only two weeks later, Noreen qui-etly installed herself once again in the little bedroom. Janie slept on the living room couch. No one slept in the big bed upstairs.

"All set, Mum?" Janie now asked, peeking her head in the doorway.

"Fine and dandy," said Noreen. "Just working on these quilt squares a bit before my eyes shut."

"I didn't know you were doing quilts."

"The pieces are small. They travel better."

A code to live by, Janie thought. *If it doesn't travel well, leave it behind.* "Well, good night," she said.

"Janie, come in for a moment, won't you?" said her mother. Janie stepped reluctantly into the room and leaned against the waist-high dresser that sat opposite the bed. She sensed an issue.

"Um . . . have you heard from your brother since the funeral?"

"No." Janie could tell her mother was stalling. They both knew better than to expect Mike to call. He didn't use the phone if he could possibly avoid it. "He's probably up to his armpits with another massive sculpture or something. At least he gets paid for it."

"Yes, I suppose you're right, but . . ." Noreen trailed off, then started up again with, "I just wanted to know . . ." she seemed to be choosing her words carefully. "I just wanted to know how you are, sweetheart. I know Jude looks in on you all quite a bit . . ." A sly smile drifted across her face. "That's both a help and a burden, I imagine."

"No," said Janie pointedly. "It's no burden. Aunt Jude's great. She's there when I need her."

"Oh, well, yes, of course," Noreen sputtered. "Of course she is."

Janie took a step toward the door.

"But you're okay?" said her mother, dropping a quilt square as she gestured in Janie's direction.

Janie let a breath of air into her lungs and expelled it. "I'm a single mother now, Mum. You know how that is."

"Yes," she sighed. "Yes, I do."

"Good night," said Janie.

As she stepped into the hallway, she heard her mother mutter, "Blessed and cursed, all at once."

"THIS IS JUST THE way I like it, Gram," Dylan said. "Mom never makes it like this." He was down in the kitchen, and Janie could hear the gentle clacking of metal spoons against glass bowls.

"Well, everyone has their own way, dear-o. No two of us are alike."

"Couldn't you teach her *your* way? It has more sugar."

Everyone's way looks like it has more sugar than mine these days, Janie thought. She climbed out of bed and put on her jeans and the T-shirt her mother had brought her. It was bright pink, with "Italia" across the front in silvery script, and it smelled like the cargo hold of a jet. Janie reviewed it in the mirror. *Good God,* she thought, and rolled her eyes.

Dylan raised his bowl toward Janie as she came into the kitchen. "Want some oatmeal? Gram makes it with butter and lots of brown sugar. See? See how brown it is?"

"The shirt looks nice on you," said her mother, with a smile that Janie first took to be victorious, but then saw that it might be something else. More like grateful. "Let me pour you some coffee."

"You should wear that to church," said Dylan. "Father Jake won't mind if you don't wear a fancy shirt with buttons. He'll like to see you wearing stuff that's pretty."

THEY SAT IN THE usual pew. Carly entertained herself by sucking on Aunt Jude's necklaces, much to Janie's aggravation. But because the rest of the family sat between them, it was impossible to put a stop to it without raising her voice. Janie was half afraid that Aunt Brigid would shush her and tell her to stop being a distraction, as she had when Janie was young. Dylan sat snuggled up under his grandmother's proprietary arm, describing the donuts they would eat downstairs in artful detail.

"That's him!" he said in a loud whisper. "That's Father Jake! He's our friend! He comes to our house all the time." Janie found Dylan's claim on Jake amusing, since he seemed to have no particular interest in the priest outside of Mass.

Down in the church basement afterward, they stood and chatted, sipped their weak coffee, and chided Dylan about his third donut. The powder had sprinkled itself like soft snow across his chest, and Noreen took an intricately embroidered hankie from her purse to spot-clean him.

"Hello," said Father Jake as he approached their group, having satisfied the more strident of his admirers. "You must be Dylan's grandmother," he said smoothly to Noreen, extending his hand.

"Yes, Father, I have that honor," she replied courteously. "I understand you've become a great friend of the family."

"Yes," he said. "I have *that* honor." They all chuckled, pleased to have him claim such a distinction.

"Hi, Jake," said Janie, catching her mother's fleeting look of discomfort.

"Hello, Jane." He took in the T-shirt and glanced back up at her, a nanosecond of amused sympathy in his gaze.

Thank you for getting how silly I feel, she thought. *No one else here understands the sacrifice I'm making in the interest of goodwill.*

"It's my birthday tomorrow, Father Jake! Do you want to come to my party? You can come if you want to. It's right after I get home from camp."

"Well . . ." Jake hesitated. He looked to Jane.

"It's just family and one of his friends," said Jane. "You're welcome to come, though you may be required to play Twister and bob for an apple or two." The idea of him dressed in black down to his stocking feet, teetering in some contorted position on a Twister mat tickled her, and she laughed.

He narrowed his eyes at her. "It just so happens I'm very good at Twister."

"Well, then, by all means, come. Show us your stuff, Father!"

After he'd accepted the invitation and moved on to another group, they walked up through the church and out to the parking lot. No one talked until they were at their cars, wishing Dylan a happy day-before-your-birthday. Noreen said not a word the whole ride home.

THAT NIGHT, KEANE'S MOTHER called to say that she was taking the next day off from work for a long-overdue root canal. The desire to prove to her new boss that she was serious about her work, not some Twinkie who would put up with his low-level sexual harassment, combined with her secret phobia of dental work had fueled her procrastination. However, the time had come.

"I should be done by eleven at the latest," she told Janie. "That's plenty of time to feel normal again before I pick up the boys. It'll give you more time to get ready for the party."

Janie didn't like the idea. Heidi seemed far more responsible than her immature ex-husband, and yet . . . she couldn't put her finger on it. Heidi seemed strangely . . . desperate? It was hard to reconcile with her blond, bouncy cheerleader looks, but Heidi acted like one of those girls back in high school who could never quite get all the pieces together to be as popular as she hoped. Having never hoped for much popularity, Janie was slightly repulsed.

"Do you have enough booster seats?" she asked Heidi, thinking this would end the matter.

"I have one for Keane, and if you leave Dylan's at camp when you drop him off, that'll solve it," she said happily. "People do that all the time."

What you don't understand is I'm not "people." Some days I feel barely human. Janie was worried she might be particularly snarly with self-pity on Dylan's birthday. She was not looking forward to celebrating the anniversary of becoming a mother without the guy who had made her so. *And I'll rip your arm off and beat you with it if anything happens to my kid.*

But the options were either to concede or to make an unreason-
ably big deal out of it. Dylan would love riding in Keane's car, Janie
knew, and Heidi really did seem okay, if a little overeager. Janie
gave in. Heidi would drive the boys to the party at one o'clock.

VALENTINE'S DAY, EASTER, FOURTH of July. All had come and gone
without Robby, and they had been fairly miserable as a result.
But, nothing seemed as wrong as celebrating their child's birthday with his chair empty, the piano keys silent, the Robby-shaped
hole in their lives never more apparent.

He's really dead, she had told herself hundreds of times since
the afternoon of January fourteenth, a strangely warm day for
midwinter. That morning, Aunt Jude had spirited Dylan away
somewhere. Janie couldn't remember where, having been in a
semi-trance of sleep deprivation since Carly's birth three months
before. It was a Sunday, so maybe Aunt Jude had taken Dylan to
church. Janie had sat on the couch nursing the baby, and Robby
had said, "It's so warm out. Mind if I go for a ride?"

How had she replied? Hopefully it was something like "Of
course not, honey. Go right ahead." Or even just a generously
delivered, "Fine by me." She didn't remember feeling angry,
stranded with the ravenous baby while the laundry pile grew
and the crust hardened on the dishes in the sink. She only remembered feeling tired. Too tired to care about the state of the
house or who went where, as long as no one asked her to get up
and function.

Robby had caressed the baby's downy head, a promise of
Janie's black curls evident in kitten-fur form. And he had leaned
down to give Janie a quick kiss on the cheek. "Love you," he'd
said. But she couldn't remember if she'd said "Love you" back.
She hoped she had.

She really, really hoped she had said something loving to her
husband in the minutes before his death. But she couldn't be sure.
It still nagged at her.

He knew! she would tell that nagging thought when it tried to overwhelm her. *He knew I loved him! He knew that I was surprised to find myself in such a good marriage with such a good man.* But still she wished she would have said so just then, with his hand on their newborn's head and his lips at her cheek.

"Love you," she had silently said to him countless times since that day. When the kids were being adorable, or when she was cold at night, or when she sat on the back of the toilet tank with a hand towel pressed to her wet, aching eyes. "Love you."

And tomorrow, the fifth birthday of their first child, the one who had permanently altered their lives, their identities, their worldview . . . tomorrow would be a hard day to be without him. Possibly the hardest so far. It would probably be the second worst day of her entire life, a thought that did not induce sleep as she lay tense and lonely in her bed, awash in the permanence of his death.

Janie trod carefully down the stairs and closed herself into the office, taking every precaution not to wake her mother. "Are you really coming to the party?" she e-mailed Jake.

"Yes," he replied. "Are you worried about it?"

"I'm planning on spending most of it locked in the bathroom, so it should be a breeze."

"Sometimes the anticipation is much worse than the actual thing you dread."

"I just don't want to let Dylan down. And I really don't want to fall apart with all my relatives standing around like a Greek chorus, moaning about the demise of my sanity."

"Keep your mind open to the possibility that it won't be horrific. Anticipate sadness, yes. But don't plan a debacle. That's never a good idea."

"I'm glad you're coming."

"I'll be there."

PATHOLOGICALLY EARLY, UNCLE CHARLIE, Aunt Brigid, and Aunt Jude arrived for the party at 12:30, bearing macaroni salad and an orange Jell-O mold with blueberries suspended in it like juicy beetles in amber. Cormac arrived twenty minutes later with a black-frosted cake in the shape of a pirate ship. It sat low in the "water" of turquoise tinted confectioner's sugar and was topped by dismembered masts and sails from one of Dylan's toy ships that Janie had secretly handed off to Cormac. Tiny plastic pirates stood ready by their canons waving swords and stolen jewels. It was the perfect combination of scary and mouthwatering. Barb documented her boyfriend's genius by shooting an entire roll of film at it before the party had even started.

Up on the new porch roof Tug Malinowski was nailing down asphalt shingles. He watched this cast of characters parade by him into the backyard and waved when they called for him to come and eat when he had a minute. The midday heat had caused rivulets of sweat to darken the neck of his shirt, making him thankful he'd tossed a clean one into his truck that morning.

"Where's the birthday boy?" he asked Janie as she climbed the ladder to hand him a glass of chocolate milk. It was yet another of her ploys to avoid the party without retreating to the darkened bathroom to cry.

"His friend's mother is bringing him home," she said. "Do you really like this stuff, or would you rather have something more age-appropriate, like iced tea?" She felt bad for Tug, crouched up there in the squishy-wet heat. She had hoped for a cool, dry day for the party, but it was August, after all.

"No, I like this." He gulped it down and handed her back the empty glass. "You let someone else drive him home?"

"Why? You think I shouldn't have?"

"No," he said. "I think it's good. For both of you. It's good."

Janie looked into the calmness of his features for some indication of what the hell that was supposed to mean, but found no clues. *He watches me,* she realized, a thought that didn't alarm her as much as she supposed it should.

"Janie!" called Uncle Charlie. "The bucket's full of water, now where are the damned apples!"

"Don't forget to come down for some cake," she said to Tug.

"Wouldn't miss it," he said.

"He's here! The birthday boy is right here!" yelled Keane, as he and Dylan came galloping through the gate to the backyard. "This is the guy!" He pointed both fingers at Dylan, in case Dylan's relatives might not recognize him as a five-year-old.

"Look at you!" they called, and "You've grown since yesterday!" and, ruffling Keane's white-blond hair, "Who's this friend, here?" The boys' enthusiasm ramped up even further when they saw the cake.

"It's the wickedest cake ever in the whole universe!" exclaimed Keane, as Aunt Jude steered his fingers away from the icing. They ran to the game of Pin the Earring on the Pirate, which Uncle Charlie was affixing to the side of the house with duct tape. Being blindfolded and spun around was just the thing to keep the boy-energy at peak flow.

"Hi," said Heidi, catching Janie's eye. She stood by the gate surveying the party.

Janie walked over to thank her for picking up the boys. "How'd it go?"

"Horrible," she said. At close range, she looked pale and swollen, like some sort of albino bullfrog. "The anesthesia wore off too soon, and my jaw aches from keeping my mouth open for so long, and I feel like my face is vibrating. Is it? Can you see anything?"

"Oh, the root canal," said Janie. "No you look . . . fine," she lied.

"Don't lie."

"Okay, you're puffy."

Heidi's shoulders slumped in resignation. "I'm Alvin the Chipmunk."

Janie smiled at this—perfect Heidi was making fun of herself—and a sudden momentary sense of okay-ness came over her. *Miraculous, really*, she thought, considering the dread she had barely been keeping at bay. "Stay," she said to Heidi.

"I don't want to barge in."

"Barge," said Janie. "We've got Jell-O, and God knows *I'm* not eating it."

Heidi grinned an abnormally wide grin. "Under the circumstances, that sounds delicious."

The boys had finished sticking "earrings" of gold contact paper onto the unfortunate pirate, who had become perilously overaccessorized. They were especially pleased with the one that Dylan had unwittingly placed on the pirate's butt.

Barb held the baby, who was chewing on the camera strap as Barb snapped picture after picture, some seemingly aimed at random objects like the side of the house or someone's leg. Noreen and Aunt Brigid brought out the sandwiches, and Aunt Jude fussed with the paper plates and napkins, all festooned with a "Yo-ho-ho!" theme.

"What are we drinking?" Cormac murmured to Janie as they stood at the end of the table, handing out sandwiches. "Rum?"

"Not like I couldn't use it," she whispered, glancing at the three older women sitting together, united in their watchfulness. "The pity factor is extra huge today."

"True," sighed Cormac. "They're feeling pretty bad for me, chickie."

Janie hip-checked him. "Yeah, well, we all feel sorry for you, muffin man."

Cormac laughed and bumped her back. "You haven't heard about my newest hire. Big Bad Charlie McGrath."

"Uncle Charlie? What about the dump?"

"He's taking early retirement. He came to me and said: 'My ass hurts and my goddamned bursitis flares in the cold and I wanna work somewhere that doesn't smell putrid before I die.'" Cormac wagged his finger at her. "Now *that's* the attitude I'm looking for in an employee."

Janie burst out laughing, the sound rising above the murmur of the women and the snapping of the camera and the open-mouth chewing of the boys. They all looked at her, which made her laugh harder, eyes watering at the absurdity of Cormac and Charlie trapped together amid the cookies and pies. Through her blurred vision, she saw Dylan grinning at her. "It's a really fun party, Mom," he said, and she heard the relief in his voice, as if he'd been waiting for just that very sound.

FATHER JAKE ARRIVED AS they were singing "Happy Birthday" around the candlelit cake. He stood by the gate as Heidi had done, not wanting to intrude on the ritual, waiting to be invited in. The brightly colored paper on the gift he carried had creases at odd angles. He'd evidently bought a small, flat package of wrapping paper, not a whole roll.

Janie noticed her heart rate quicken when she saw him, something that had been happening for the last several weeks, but she had purposely ignored. *I'm just happy to have reinforcements,* she rationalized. *He understands what I'm dealing with here. He gets me.* And when he caught her eye and smiled, absorbing the sight of her like rain into dry soil, she inhaled quickly, an unbidden, barely perceptible gasp. That was harder to ignore.

"Hello, Father." Noreen was in front of him, flanked by Aunt Brigid and Aunt Jude. "It's wonderful that you could join our little celebration. Have you had lunch? There are plenty of sandwiches and Jude made a lovely Jell-O mold. Brigie, why don't you get him a plate?"

"Thank you, that's very kind," he said.

Vanishing cream, thought Janie. *He slides back behind that false front in the blink of an eye.*

"I don't think I've ever seen you without your collar, Father," said Aunt Jude. "You look so different! Of course, some priests do it all the time. Father Stone over at Saint Bart's almost never has his. I've heard he wears moccasins on the altar, too!" She laughed and then coughed. "Well, you're nothing like that. I'm always saying you're a good, traditional priest. Haven't I said that, Noreen?"

"Yes, you have," said Noreen, quietly.

Jake dug into the Jell-O mold as the women watched. "This is delicious. The fruit is a nice touch."

"You've never had it like this before?" asked Aunt Jude. "Didn't your mother ever make it?"

"No," Jake glanced quickly at Janie. "She never did."

Now you see him, she thought, *now you don't. Wish I could learn that trick. These days people see more of the real me than they ever wanted to.*

The presents came next, and with Keane's help, Dylan tore through them with ecstatic speed. A toy backhoe with levers to work the digger ("just like we use at the dump") from Uncle Charlie and Aunt Brigid; a blue polo shirt with matching blue and green plaid pants ("for church") from Aunt Jude; a set of muffin pans with holes shaped like dinosaurs ("I've got a great spinach muffin recipe we can try . . . just kidding") from Cormac and Barb; a pirate costume with a plastic sword ("Mom got me a sword, too, so we can fight") from Keane; and a quilt of Europe with appliqués for all the countries ("your first geography lesson") from his grandmother. From his mother and sister, Dylan got a new bike, green with black racing stripes. Most surprising of all, it had no training wheels. ("I don't know . . ." said Dylan, after the initial excitement. "I'll help you," said Janie.)

Janie was standing next to Jake as Dylan opened his present, a paperback book of children's stories from the Bible.

"Oh," said Dylan, his eyes wandering back to the pirate sword. "Thanks."

Janie felt her face go hot. "Dylan," she said. "Say a real thank-you to Father Jake. That's a very nice book."

Dylan flicked his glance to Jake and said, "Thanks. It's nice." Then he saw Keane and Heidi spreading out the Twister mat, and he ran over.

"Sorry," said Janie.

"Don't apologize," Jake replied, leaning his shoulder toward hers until they almost touched. "He just got some really exciting presents. I never expected a big reaction."

"Still, he needs to learn . . ."

"He's fine. The question is, how are *you*?"

Janie sighed and looked up into his face. "Okay. I was sad this morning, and I was sure I would be a wreck for the party. But I'm not. I think it's beginning to sink in that he's not here."

Jake studied her face for a moment. It felt as if he were taking inventory of every pore of her skin, every speckle in her pale eyes. "You've managed to handle such a difficult situation," he murmured. "You've held up under such grief."

A blush rose from her neck into her cheeks, and she had to glance away. "You've helped me," she said finally. "Nobody gets it but you."

Dylan called from across the yard. "Mom, look! We're Twist-ered!" The intrusion was both a relief and a disappointment. She glanced toward the boys, who had collapsed in a giggling heap on the Twister mat, then back at Jake.

He nodded. "I should be getting back."

"Thanks for coming," she said. "I mean it." He smiled at her, then turned to say his good-byes. Janie headed toward the Twister game, sorry to have the thin thread of connection severed. "I think you must be the silliest two boys I ever met," she called as she strode toward them.

After Twister, the boys were ready to bob for apples. "Couldn't I take a special picture first, before you get wet?" asked Barb. "Come over here for just a minute, Dylan, here next to your mom." Janie was sitting on the grass with Carly bouncing between her upturned knees. "Kneel right there behind her," instructed Barb. Then she started snapping. The others gathered to watch.

"Your hair smells like fruit," Dylan whispered into Janie's ear. "What does mine smell like?"

Janie turned her head and sniffed. "Well, I don't know what your hair smells like, but your neck smells like peanut butter. Did you try to eat your sandwich with your neck?"

Dylan giggled and squeezed her. "It was a neckwich!" *Snap, snap, snap* went the camera.

"Da!" yelled Carly. "Da-da!"

"Yeah," said Dylan. "Where's Dad? He should be in the picture, he . . ." He stopped.

Everyone stopped. No one moved, save to glance at each other for moral support.

"He's not . . ." Janie inhaled, prayed to keep her voice calm. "He's in heaven, Dylan. Remember?"

Dylan nodded. He remembered. And yet he still said, "But it's my birthday."

A sniffle escaped from one of the older women.

"Daddy knows it's your birthday," said Janie. "And he'd be here if he could. But you're not allowed to leave heaven, remember? Otherwise he'd be here. He would definitely . . ." her voice went breathy and tears stung the corners of her eyes. ". . . be here."

"Why are they crying?" Keane whispered loudly to his mother. "Why are *you* crying?"

"It's just sad, Keane."

"It's a birthday. It's not supposed to be sad."

"You're right, honey," said Heidi, hugging him against her hip. "It's not."

Barb's camera was silent. Noreen clutched Jude's hand in one of her own and covered her face with the other. Cormac and Uncle Charlie stood shoulder to shoulder like mute giants, staring into the grass at their feet.

"Hey, Dylan," came a new voice from behind them. "Happy Birthday, buddy."

Dylan crumpled. "I don't want it to be my birthday anymore," he choked at Tug.

"It's still your birthday, Dylan," Janie whispered, guiding him around to the front of her, both children now corralled between her legs. "We can still enjoy it."

"You're crying, too," Dylan accused.

"True. Okay, let's all cry for another minute and then have fun."

"What about Dad?"

"Dad loves you very much. That's all we know, Dylan. That's all we'll ever know." *And it's all I get from here on,* she thought. *The knowledge of love. Not the feel or the sound or the taste of it. Just knowing.* And the fit of self-pity she had tethered away from public view broke loose from its chain.

Her weeping was not quite the circus show of humiliation she'd anticipated, however, because she was not the only performer under the big top that day. Everyone cried. Carly cried because she wanted to touch Barb's shiny silver camera swinging unnoticed from Barb's neck, but couldn't get loose from her mother's grasp. Keane cried because a really fun party had just gone suddenly boring and a little scary. Everyone else was simply overcome with pity for the birthday boy missing his daddy on his big day, and for the baby who would have no daddy memory whatsoever. And for the mother, their Janie, who had been insufferably irritable and sarcastic for seven long months until now.

AFTER A FEW MINUTES, Carly squawked loud enough for Janie to let go, and she crawled over and pulled herself up on Barb's low-slung capris. Barb picked her up. Keane wiggled away from his mother and wandered toward the picnic table to help himself to more cake. Cormac and Uncle Charlie inhaled their sniffles and turned in unison to rake the sticky pirate plates off the table and into the trash. Aunt Jude pulled tissues from her big white purse and handed them out to Noreen and Aunt Brigid.

"Hi, Tug," said Dylan, wiping his nose on the shoulder of his T-shirt. "What's that?"

Tug was holding a box wrapped in the comics section of the newspaper, and sliding a handkerchief into the back pocket of his jeans. "A present I brought you," he said. "But maybe you'd rather open it another time."

"No," said Dylan getting up. "Now's good."

Janie went into the house to get the bag of apples for bobbing, and took the opportunity to hold a cold wet dishcloth against her cheeks and red-rimmed eyes. She heard someone come in the kitchen door, and then felt hands on her shoulders gently pressing and rubbing.

"There are so many things I could say, right now," murmured Aunt Jude.

Janie sighed and her arms went loose. "Thanks for not saying any of them."

"Oh, alright," said Aunt Jude giving Janie's shoulders a little shake. Then she went back out. In a moment Janie followed her.

"Whoa, that's sick!" she heard Keane say, and turned toward a low buzzing sound. Dylan was kneeling in the grass and wearing a set of plastic safety goggles that seemed to envelop his entire head. He was leaning over a small block of wood and holding some sort of tool.

"Hey, what's that?" she asked walking toward them. Tug watched her approach.

"A screwdrive!" yelled Dylan. "My own screwdrive! To keep! Now I can build stuff, too!"

"You gave him a power tool?" she asked Tug incredulously.

"Don't worry," he said. "It runs on two double-A batteries. It's got the torque of a pinwheel. And Dylan knows that he can only use it with a grown-up watching, right, Dylan?"

"Yep." He chewed his lip and guided the bolts in and out of the predrilled holes in the wood block.

"Tug, he's five, for godsake."

"Janie, it's safe. I ran it past a couple of my buddies' wives, and they gave it the thumbs-up. Fact, they had me make extras for their kids. You can put it away when you don't want him to use it."

"But—"

"Like some cake?" Heidi was suddenly with them, offering Tug a generous slab of ship's bow.

"Thanks," said Tug. He smiled politely, taking the cake in his left hand and offering her his right. It was then that Janie noticed he was wearing a clean shirt. "Tug Malinowski. Porch builder."

"Heidi Mathison. Mother of the friend of the birthday boy." She passed a self-conscious hand up to her almost normal-looking cheeks. "You're doing a wonderful job out front. It's going to add so much to the house. And how did you ever come up with this screwdriver idea? The boys can't get enough of it."

He smiled. "It's not that big of a deal."

"Sorry, but you're wrong there," she said, her smile looking more sparkly than Janie had ever seen. "I'm in marketing and we have several toy manufacturers on our client list. There's nothing with this kind of realism. If you ever wanted to take it to the next level I could put you in touch with some people who . . ."

Janie took one more wary glance at the mini cordless screwdriver, now in the hands of a begoggled Keane. *Her problem now*, she thought and went to the picnic table to help straighten up.

"Janie?" said Barb, the rims of her eyes still shiny and pink. "I'm so sorry," she exhaled. "I never thought . . . it never occurred to me the pictures would remind Dylan about . . ."

"It's okay," said Janie.

"I'm really sorry. I can just throw that roll right in the trash."

"What?" said Cormac, tuning in. "Don't throw them out, they were terrific."

"But they'll remind her of . . ."

"So? It's not like without the pictures we'll all just forget about Robby and never have another sad thought." He turned to Janie. "You've got to see them. It was so perfect. Promise me you'll just take a look at them." Cormac's arm slid around Barb's shoulder, a gesture of support, or perhaps protection from his ice-eyed cousin. He's belonged to us for so long, Aunt Jude had said. *Not for much longer,* thought Janie.

By 2:30 the heat had climbed another couple of degrees, and the boys were clamoring to get wet. By turns they plunged their heads into the tub of water, their small pink mouths rooting for the apples that slipped away as if self-propelled. Urged on by Cormac, Barb documented the activity from every angle. After three or four tries apiece, both frustrated boys were beginning to show signs of impending party-induced meltdown. Uncle Charlie surreptitiously slid his huge hand into the bucket and held an apple from below for each to bite.

"I did it!" screamed Keane. "I did it and I don't even LIKE apples!"

And then it was time to go. Janie was hugged mercilessly by all the grown-ups except Tug. Even Heidi, the last to leave, hazarded a quick squeeze, saying, "Thanks for letting me stay. The Jell-O was delicious." She shot a furtive glance toward Tug, and told Janie, "I'll call you later."

Tug followed Janie into the house, carrying the bag of trash. "You okay with that little screwdriver?"

Carly was slumped on her hip, and Dylan had already relegated himself to lying on the couch with Nubby Bunny, rubbing a soft worn rabbit ear over his nose. She nodded wearily. "Sorry I freaked out. You know how I get."

"Yeah." He smiled at her. His lips parted as if to add something, but then he closed them again.

"It really is a pretty cool gift." She shifted the heavy-lidded baby to the other hip. "And it came at just the right time."

He nodded. Then he went back outside and climbed the ladder to the roof. As Janie laid the sleeping baby in her crib, she heard the rhythmic tapping of his hammer against the new shingles. She went downstairs and curled herself around Dylan on the couch, and they dozed on dreams of black cake and spinning bolts.

12

NOREEN KNEW THAT HER daughter had been attacked ten days before. Jude and Charlie and Brigid had talked of nothing else when Janie was out of hearing distance: how Jude had procured the self-defense course for the fund-raiser, and then won the prize herself and given it to Janie. (This point had been detailed by Jude more than once.) How the intruder had broken into several homes in the area. How Jude's friend's son, the owner of Walking on Sunshine Carpet Cleaners, got the hideous bloodstain out of Janie's living room rug. How that Dougie Shaw ("Remember him, can you believe he's all grown up and carrying a firearm now?") responded to Janie's 911 call. How the attacker's guilty plea meant that Janie would not have to testify, and how that awful man ("goddamned evil bastard" Charlie invariably muttered) had gone straight to prison.

Noreen now knew everything her brother and sister knew, and yet some things still seemed unexplained. It was clear that Janie did not want to talk about it, and Noreen wouldn't press. But when the weekly *Pelham Town Crier* arrived on Tuesday morning, the questions it answered provoked even further uncertainty.

"There's an article in the paper about you," Noreen called from the kitchen when Janie returned from dropping Dylan off at camp. "About the attack."

"I don't want to see it," said Janie. She took Carly into the living room and set her up with a brightly colored toy piano, her current obsession. "Wait a minute," said Janie. "Who's it by?"

"The reporter's name is Wick Lally." Noreen came and handed the paper to Janie. While she waited for Janie to read it, she sat down next to Carly and straightened the straps of her sunsuit.

"Cripes," muttered Janie, straining to concentrate over Carly's piano playing. "What an ass."

"Is it true?"

"Well, yes, I suppose it's technically factual. But it sounds so melodramatic. And who cares about all these little details, anyway?" Janie was annoyed at how exposed she felt.

"Why did the priest . . ." Noreen fiddled with the slipcover on the couch, which seemed perfectly straight to Janie. ". . . why did Father come over? How did he know to come?"

The article stated that a neighbor saw a gray sedan in Janie's driveway shortly after the incident. It remained there until the following morning when Father Jake emerged from the house and drove away in it. The neighbor claimed he was casually dressed and "shoeless."

"I guess I called him," said Janie. She turned the little piano upside down and Carly thumped on the bottom like a drum. The sound was much less jarring.

Noreen picked a thread from the slipcover's hem. "Why not Charlie or Cormac? Or even Jude?"

"I don't know," Janie shrugged. "I didn't want to bother them. Jake's up half the night, anyway."

"Bother them?" said Noreen, turning suddenly to Janie. "They're family. You were attacked. They would never have considered it a bother. And how do you know Father's up at night?"

"Because we're friends. Neither of us sleeps very well, and sometimes we talk at night. It's no big deal, Mum." It sounded meaningless as she said it, but Janie knew it was not meaningless. It meant something. Carly flipped the piano right side up and began to bang on the tin-sounding keys again.

Noreen retreated to fiddling with the slipcover, smoothing the green-speckled print with her sun-spotted hand. "You're very friendly with him."

"So?" Janie flipped the piano again. Carly flipped it back.

"I'm not going to interfere in your life . . ."

"Good."

". . . but it seems to me that such a friendship might not be . . ."

"What?"

". . . the best idea."

"Mum, please. I don't know what you're worried about." Janie knew exactly what her mother was worried about, and if she were completely honest, she would have admitted to herself that she, too, had some concerns. She didn't like the quickening of her pulse when Jake came into view and she didn't like how much she thought about him when he wasn't with her. She certainly knew it was not a good idea to speculate whether he thought about her, too. And yet, like knowing where your mother hid the Easter chocolates when you were a child, it was hard not to think about it.

"Janie," said Noreen, above the baby's racket. "Sweetheart, please be careful."

Janie tossed the little piano into the toy bin and took the angry baby into the kitchen for a snack.

THE AFTERNOON HAD GONE better than the morning. Once Dylan was home, his dogged attempts to learn to ride his new two-wheeler had distracted Janie and Noreen from the disturbing thoughts that Wick Lally's insinuation-ridden report had aroused. Those concerns and their brief confrontation had not been laid to rest, however they had gone dormant for the time being. Noreen went over to Jude's after dinner. To Janie, the relief was palpable.

The phone rang shortly after Janie got the children into bed. It was Heidi, with a tone to her voice that made Janie wonder if she were going to ask for a loan. "So what's up?" Janie finally said.

"Well, nothing really. Just calling to say Hi . . . also, I was wondering if you know anything about your contractor's . . . personal life. He wasn't wearing a ring or anything . . ."

"You're interested in Tug?" asked Janie. She stopped unloading the dishwasher.

"Well, I don't know," said Heidi. "I might be. If he isn't married or involved or anything. I would never date a married man. Like ever."

"I don't think he's married." Janie held a mug in midair considering this point. "He's never mentioned a wife or kids. Just his nieces."

"He's . . . handsome. Don't you think he's handsome?"

"He's not bad looking." Was Tug married? Did he have a woman in his life at all? How had she missed this point, she wondered, tapping the bottom of the mug against her palm.

"He's very sweet with the boys," said Heidi. "And he seems smart. Is he a good businessman?"

"I guess so. He's not overcharging me or anything." Actually, he'd gone out of his way to keep her costs down, she remembered.

"Do you think he would be okay if I, you know . . . asked him out?" Heidi seemed almost in pain at this point. "He's not one of those macho guys who hates modern women, is he?" she asked, cringing.

"I honestly don't know." Janie put the mug on the counter and crossed her arms.

"Janie?"

"Yeah?"

"Could you find out?"

THE ROOF SHINGLES WERE done and Tug was working on a railing with balusters that would ring the porch. "The balusters aren't strictly necessary," he explained. "But with kids, you don't want them running into the screen and punching holes in it or banging their heads on the railing."

"Okay," said Janie. "Sounds good."

"I'm going to stain them cherry, so they're lighter than the mahogany on the floor, but the colors won't fight each other. You alright with that?"

"Fine."

"Really?"

"I said I was, didn't I?"

Tug chuckled. "You going soft on me? I expect more pushback than that."

"Let's see," she narrowed her eyes in mock anger, and stuck her fingers out dramatically as she counted: "The new back wall, the bigger window, the mahogany flooring, oh and let's not forget the security system that's not even part of the project. Now balusters. When—if ever—have you not gotten your way when you wanted to diverge from the plan? Huh? Never, that's when. So why should I waste my time questioning you about something you're just going to do, anyway?"

He laughed. "Guess you got me there." After a moment her smile faded. "What?" he asked.

"It's kind of embarrassing."

He frowned. "What?"

"Heidi. You know, Keane's mother? Blond, kind of perky?"

"I remember."

"She asked me if you were married. You've been at my house all day every day, for over two months, and I don't even know that about you."

"Well . . . ," he stammered. "It's not like we sit around shooting the breeze all the time. And you've been busy with your own . . . ," he searched for the word, ". . . life."

"So are you?"

"No."

"Seeing someone?"

"No."

"Would you ever be interested in a date? With Heidi? Because she might be interested."

Tug's tan skin became tinged with pink. "Oh."

"It's okay to say no. She's so . . . you know . . . cute. I'm sure there are lots of guys who would go out with her. It's not like you're the last chance she'll ever have for a date."

Tug let out a confused chuckle. "Okay."

"Okay, yes?"

"No . . . ," he said, and took a breath. "No. I'm not dating these days. I'm kind of on vacation from all that."

"Oh." Janie didn't know whether to ask for clarification, though she was vaguely curious. She was about to go back inside when he said, "Tell you the truth, she looks just like my ex-wife."

"Really?"

"Dead ringer."

"So . . . that's not good. In terms of dating."

"It'd be a little distracting."

Janie smiled. "I won't tell her that part."

"She's very nice," he said. "I'm just not . . ."

"In the market. Okay. And guess what? I changed my mind about those balusters." She flicked her thumb over her shoulder. "They're out."

He laughed and adjusted the baluster he'd been working on so it fit a little tighter. "Anything you say, Mrs. LaMarche. You're the boss."

THAT NIGHT, JANIE DREAMED she was trekking through a shadowy forest, muddy and scratched, as if she'd fallen down a ravine. Cold, wet clothing clung to her body, constricting her movement in every direction. The path she was following ended abruptly at the shore of a steam-shrouded lake. She pulled off her boots and tore at her clothes, aching to enter the warm water.

When she was finally free of every stitch of clammy, binding cloth, she dove in. The water was soft and warm and strangely buoyant. The scrapes on her aching limbs stopped hurting and she felt clean and safe. She was like a seal, skimming in and out of the water. Something swam up to her, another seal-person. He swam around and around her and she couldn't see his face. His hands glided up her body, touching her, healing her. And then his head rose above the water and his lips skimmed across her face. She felt herself grow warmer and warmer until he was kissing her, gently probing her with his hands, and she reached out to pull his smooth wet body toward her.

"Jake," she said, as their legs entwined and their heads slipped below the water.

When she became aware of the pillow under her cheek, Janie shut her eyes tighter and tried to dive back down into the dream. She wanted to be naked and warm and pressed against that seal-man's body, with every nerve ending throbbing in anticipation of feeling good for a change; without a thought except for what might happen in the next moment, subsequent moments being too far in the future to warrant consideration. Not caring, not hurting, not knowing anyone or anything.

No such fucking luck, she groaned to herself as the light behind her eyelids seemed to grow brighter. The illusion of happiness slipping away from her, melting back into the recesses of her limited imagination, made her breathless with frustration.

It was Jake, she had to admit to herself. He was in the dream, and he was in her head in a way that he shouldn't be. But what were her options? She knew she could not force herself to stop thinking about him any more than she could force herself not to dream about him. *What if he were married?* she asked herself. *How would I handle it?* She knew how—avoid him until the unwanted feelings subsided. It was the only way to deal with a stupid crush.

Unacceptable. She was barely getting through the days as it was. How would she vent her molten feelings, manage her hair-trigger temper, or feel the least bit understood without a daily dose of Jake? This . . . okay, yes, this crush—it would pass. It had only developed, like some minor localized infection, because her resistance was low. It had been eight months without intimacy of any kind, and her craving to connect—with anyone who could stand her long enough to understand her—had led her into this . . . infected crush.

Funny though. She'd never had an infection that felt this good.

"WHERE ARE YOU GOING?" Janie asked her mother as she came downstairs to gun the coffee maker to full throttle. "You're dressed up."

"To church."

On a Thursday? A vague tension settled into Janie's shoulders. "Morning Mass?" she asked. Noreen nodded. Janie turned to find the bag of grounds in the cabinet. "Well, pray for me."

"Every day," said Noreen. "The best I can."

WHEN JANIE DROPPED DYLAN off at Pond Pals camp, Heidi was there, taking longer than usual to get Keane settled, arranging his backpack with exacting precision in the pile of bags by the gate. "Oh, hi!" she said expectantly to Janie.

"Hi," said Janie, shifting the growing baby a little higher up her hip. She waved to Dylan as he scooted off to assume the seat on the story blanket that Keane routinely saved for him.

"What's new?" asked Heidi.

Janie shrugged. *I have a pus-filled, suppurating, infected crush on the parish priest*, she thought, *but other than that, nothing much.*

"Come on," urged Heidi. "Don't make me ask."

"What?"

"Did you talk to him?"

Jake? she thought. But she knew Heidi could have no idea about that. No one did. "Oh, Tug."

Heidi gave an embarrassed sigh. "It's okay. You've got a lot on your mind." She was doing that desperate, unpopular girl thing again, which was hard for Janie to make sense of in the context of the Gwyneth Paltrow looks and the Ann Taylor suit.

"No, I talked to him," said Janie. "He's divorced, but not looking. He's on vacation from dating."

"That's it?"

"That's pretty much all he said."

Heidi's face went slack with disappointment, then she nodded. "Must have been a bad divorce."

"I don't know, he didn't say."

"No, that's definitely it. People swear off dating when they've been hurt. His wife probably had an affair or something. There's nothing like that to kill your interest."

Janie was just getting used to the idea of considering Tug's love life at all. Had he been hurt somehow? He didn't show it. Come to think of it, he didn't show much of anything, other than a penchant for chocolate milk and an uncanny understanding of small boys.

"Well, I'd better get to work," said Heidi. "Thanks for trying."

Janie felt a flash of sympathy. "You know, you're a nice person. Smart and pretty. It'll happen."

"Thanks," said Heidi, fingering her car keys. She squinted in the direction of the parking lot. "I'd better get to work."

It was a quiet afternoon. Noreen took Dylan to Cormac's Confectionary for a snack after camp, leaving Janie with the napping baby and the hum of the washing machine. Janie loaded and unloaded, washed and dried, sorted and folded. It seemed as if she hadn't done laundry in weeks.

When, toward the end of the afternoon, the washer and dryer had stopped, the hum remained, and Janie recognized the crackling buzz of a coming thunderstorm. Tug went home early, pulling away in the white truck just as the rain started. Janie sat on the living room rug surrounded by piles of folded laundry, and listened to the *tack, tack, tack* of the first raindrops spattering on the roof. The familiar sound had changed slightly, was somehow more distant now that the new porch roof sheltered the front door from the weather. Tug had installed special gutters for the new section of roof and continued them on across the old. They were designed to resist the deposits of nature's detritus. They should never need cleaning, he'd told her, and offered to install them across the back of the house as well. She was still deciding.

The cozy sound of the rain made her wish for Robby's arms around her, as they had been for so many thunderstorms. She remembered one time early on, when they'd gone camping in the Berkshires. Instead of hiking in the rain, they'd spent the dreary day in the tent snuggled in their sleeping bag, alternately making love, sleeping, nibbling on trail mix and singing songs to each other. Janie didn't have much of a voice, so she chose camp songs she'd remembered from childhood: "Sipping Cider Through a Straw" and "Found a Peanut" and the like. Robby tried to harmonize, though he often didn't know the words, and the silly lyrics and off-key melody would make them laugh and roll around in the sleeping bag until they were kissing and clutching each other once again.

"Smell this," Janie had said when they'd gotten home and pulled the packs apart by the washing machine. She'd held out the open sleeping bag to him. "Take a whiff, if you dare."

"Whoa!" laughed Robby after he'd stuck his nose in. "And a good time was had by all!"

It had become a joke between them, something they'd say to each other after particularly exceptional sex. Now, sitting in the living room, wishing for the gazillionth time in the last eight months that she could feel him near her, she could remember that phrase. But, in her mind she could not hear him say it. The words were there, but not the sound of his voice.

No, she thought, slipping into the deep end of her sorrow. *Don't fade. Please, Robby, honey. Please don't fade away on me. What will I have when there's not even the memory of your voice? Nothing. I will have nothing.*

WHEN NOREEN AND DYLAN returned just before dinner with a pre-cooked rotisserie chicken from the market, Janie was dozing on the rug amid the clean clothes. She had cried so hard, and become so weak and exhausted, she'd fallen asleep right where she sat.

"Mommy's tired," Janie heard Dylan whisper as she was coming to. "She gets tired a lot."

"She works hard," said Noreen. "Try to help her when you can."

"How?" said Dylan.

"Just be the best boy you can be."

"I am," he said, as if it were obvious.

"Yes, of course you are."

"KIND OF A ROUGH day," Janie e-mailed Jake at 2:15 a.m. She read the *Boston Globe* online, stopping to check for his response every few minutes, until quarter to four. But none ever came.

13

JAKE WAS WEARING THE somber black sport shoes when he showed up at eleven o'clock on Friday morning, not the walking shoes. And he had his collar on.

"No walk?" asked Janie. She stopped fastening the chest strap on Carly's baby backpack.

"Not today," he said quietly.

"You have some sort of meeting after this?" she said indicating the collar. "You're all suited up."

"Oh." He fingered the collar, then clasped his hands firmly in front of him. "Let's go inside."

Janie took Carly out of the backpack and set her up with some toys in the living room. She felt a strange numbness come over her, as if she were watching herself take out the little toy piano and the blocks, but the hands weren't actually hers.

"Tea?" she asked when she went into the kitchen.

"No thanks."

Her heart began to pound, and she knew something was off. "Okay, what's going on?" she asked.

"Nothing. Everything's fine. As a matter of fact, I'm really happy with how well you're doing. You've really come through the worst of it."

She rolled her eyes. "You should have seen me yesterday, sobbing in the clean sock pile."

His face softened, and she realized that until that moment she'd been talking to the ghost twin, not the real Jake. How had she missed it?

"You had a bad day yesterday?" he asked.

"Yeah." She studied him. "Didn't you get my e-mail?"

"Oh. I guess I've been offline." He looked down at his hands, a finger tracing along the grain of the butcher-block table. "The party was wonderful," he began again. "Dylan seemed very happy."

Why is he painting this rosy picture? It suddenly seemed very important to prove that she was not doing well at all. "You left just before the meltdown. We had the whole place in tears. Even the contractor, who doesn't strike me as a weepy guy." She lobbed this at him like a rotten egg.

"Oh," he said. "Well, that's not really surprising, I suppose. But getting through this first year, that's the toughest. And you're almost there. Next year will be much easier."

"Yeah, okay," she said, a slow burn stoking up in her veins. "So we just have to get through Carly's birthday, Thanksgiving, Christmas, and New Year's. Piece of cake. Well, actually I guess you'd have to throw in Valentine's Day, Robby's birthday in March, and my birthday in April, since we didn't celebrate those at all. I guess technically we haven't gotten through those. But, yeah," she said, sarcasm pinching at every word. "You're right; we're in the homestretch."

He did not reply. He stared out the kitchen window into the quiet yard. Tug had gone to check on another job, so the comforting sound of his incessant banging felt particularly absent. Janie slammed her hand on the table. "What is WRONG with you today? What IS all this bullshit?"

He turned fully toward her and she could see that the switch had been flipped behind his eyes. Ghost Jake was gone, Real Jake was back again. "Jane."

"WHAT, for chrissake!"

"JANE!"

"Just SAY it! Whatever it is, just don't give me this Father Friendly crap!"

"I can't come here anymore. I can't . . . we can't do this."

"Do WHAT?" She knew exactly what, and yet in her mind, it had been a secret, even from him. She couldn't believe he knew the private struggle she was waging against the infectious crush.

"Have you even read the paper?" he demanded. "Do you have any idea of what those kinds of insinuations could do to me? *And* you. I was," he made little quote marks in the air, ' "casually dressed' and 'shoeless.' Mother of —" he bit back his words. "I shouldn't even be here now!"

"Oh, I get it. I see. You are turning your back on our friendship because it might LOOK bad. Father Jake with his big vow to serve humanity, but only until the gossip mill starts and a couple of old ladies tsk-tsk to each other over their morning Metamucil!"

He let out a sigh and stared darkly out the window. "One of those old ladies was your mother."

"Excuse me? What are you talking about?"

"Your mother came to the rectory to see me after Mass yesterday morning. She's concerned about how close we've become."

Janie was stunned that her mother had taken such a step, intruding so completely into something that wasn't her business. It wasn't like her. And yet, Janie had sensed her mother's reticence when it came to Jake. Now she knew why. "Goddamn her," muttered Janie. "What right does she have?"

"You're her daughter."

"All the more reason not to screw up my life in such a heinously embarrassing way."

A cheerless smile invaded his face. "You know I have no experience of parental protection. But I imagine it would be hard to watch a child who's already been through too much choosing something that can only cause more pain." And there it was. He knew. Silence throbbed around them.

"It's a crush," Janie said finally. "A stupid grade school crush. By definition it's temporary."

Jake began to twist in his seat. He crossed his arms tightly across his chest. "Well, I guess I should be the judge of that. But thanks for your insulting characterization."

Janie's head snapped in his direction. "Why are *you* insulted?"

He snorted derisively. "Because you just relegated my emotional state to a childish whim."

Janie's mind raced to reorganize the pieces of this puzzle into a completely different configuration. *His emotional state? HIS?* she wondered incredulously. "You have feelings for me?"

"Oh, for goodness' sake, Jane, don't act like you didn't know. It's embarrassing."

"I thought you were . . . you know . . . just being really kind."

He studied her, searching for someone who knew better. He glanced away. "I'm not that kind."

Her heart was pounding so hard and fast she felt it might seize and stop, like a motor revolving beyond its capacity. The last time her heart had beat like this she was facing an attacker, not the single person who seemed to understand her these days, the one person she wanted near her. She heard the faint voices from the self-defense class calling, *Do it! Do it now!*

"I have feelings for you, too." She was breathless, as if she'd just sprinted a long way toward him.

His gaze crept cautiously to hers, then sank to his hands. He shook his head. "This can't happen."

"Apparently it already has."

"Jane." He was looking at her now. "It's my fault. This is all . . . it's my responsibility."

"Oh, and what am I?" she asked. "Some little girl, some invalid who's been taken advantage of? I'm an adult, Jake. Don't treat me like a helpless child."

"No, you're not a child. But you are incredibly vulnerable right now. And I let things get out of hand because of my own crisis. I let it go too far."

"How can you say that? Nothing bad happened. No one can say we've done something wrong."

He looked away again, unable to meet her eyes, fingers gripping the edge of the table. "It's not what's happened so far that concerns me."

Janie felt vaguely light-headed. *There's an answer to this riddle,* she thought. *There's a solution that isn't an ending.* "Has this ever happened to you before?" she asked, hoping the answer was yes, as in Yes, it is fixable. And hoping the answer was no, as in No, I have never felt this way about anyone but you.

"Not really," he said. "Not like this."

The worst of both worlds, she thought. *Don't give up!* whispered the women from the class. *Save yourself!*

"Jake." She steadied herself. "There's another option."

He nodded. "I know. I've thought about it."

"You have? About me?"

"Yes, about you. I certainly haven't had these thoughts about anyone else. Which is why I am quite certain this is not a stupid fucking grade school crush, as you so eloquently described it."

His pass at humor, the break in the tension, the faint, clean breath of hope—these things conspired to make her reach out and brush the back of her knuckles against his, her palm facing upward, open. His fingers arched up and entwined with hers. They watched those fingers intently, as if an answer would stream out from the tips. Then he disentangled himself, laying his hand on top of hers, ending the motion. "I cannot have an affair," he said simply.

"And I'm not getting involved with a guy who wears black every day," she said. "I'm not talking about an affair. I'm talking about you being free."

He squeezed her hand. "I want so much to do this for you."

"Then do it. It's the only way we don't lose each other."

"I can't."

Janie whipped her hand away. "You can't? CAN'T?"

"No. I can't. I cannot. That's not who I am. You of all people know that."

"I know that? How the hell would I know that?" she demanded. And yet, somewhere down deep, she did know that. He had told her about his engagement, how it had tortured him, despite the love he felt for his fiancée. Janie batted this away, saying, "Okay, you like being a priest. But why? Is it because you're so in love with the Lord that you could never fall for someone else? No. Obviously not. No, the real reason is, you like the cover. You like being able to fade in and out without anyone noticing. You don't want the scrutiny of intimacy. What the hell kind of life is that!"

He was fuming now, eyes searching wildly around the room. "And you're such a paragon of intimacy! You snarl and snipe at people all day long. The people that love you the most, you treat the worst, as if they're disposable! And yet you need them and love them and fight with them and cry to them. That's not me! That's not my kind of life!"

"Bullshit! You need people just as much as I do!"

"Yes. I do." He looked exhausted all of a sudden. "In some ways maybe more. I'm not as strong as you are. But I also need quiet." He sighed. "I need to pray. I want and need to keep my eyes on God every moment of every day. That's what makes sense to me, Jane. It's the only thing that gives me peace. Loving you gives me no peace."

Tears began to slip down Janie's cheeks. "Since Robby died," she said, "it's the only thing that gives me peace."

They sat there in their last minutes together, motionless except for the rise and fall of their chests and the blinking of their flooded lids. A new life, a paler, sadder life would begin when one of them moved. It would be set in dull, grinding motion when he left her house for the last time.

"Jane." His voice hissed with the strain of emotion as he rose from the chair. "I'm so sorry."

She didn't care that he was sorry. It didn't matter now.

"Would you please . . ." he choked. "Could you go to Mass somewhere else for a while?"

Mass? she thought. *He's worried about Mass?*

"Good-bye, Jake," she whispered. "At least this time I get to say good-bye."

IT WAS DARK WHEN Noreen came to sit on her bed. "Sweetheart," she said, jiggling Janie's arm.

Janie was stuporous. Somewhere in her brain, the keys of Carly's piano were playing a cacophony of tin, random notes. She remembered that after the front door had closed on Jake and on the only good part of her life that was left, she had heard Carly crying. Janie had stumbled into the living room to find Carly wedged under the couch, reaching for the little piano that had found its way into the dark abyss beyond her insistent fingers. Janie had dislodged the baby, who continued to howl for her toy all the way up the stairs and into the confines of her crib. The noise. The ceaseless noise.

Janie had called Aunt Jude and said simply, "I'm going to bed." Aunt Jude had known to pick up Dylan at camp. Carly had cried herself to sleep.

Janie had been too spent to cry. She had lain on her bed, a twirling numbness overtaking her, until she succumbed to the black torpor that awaited. At some point, she'd become aware of Aunt Jude's grating enthusiasm as she babbled to Carly in the other room. And now it was dark out.

"Janie, dear."

Janie opened her eyes. Her mother was wearing a gray cardigan with an embroidered hummingbird that she'd likely made herself. *Hummingbird*, thought Janie. *That's what you are. You don't care how fast you have to beat your wings, as long as you can fly away.*

"Jude and I are taking the children out for a quick bite. Then we thought maybe they could have a sleepover with us at Jude's. That would get them out of your hair for a bit. You need some time to yourself."

Janie's tongue felt thick and pasty when she asked, "To do what?"

Noreen folded her hands in her lap. "Just collect yourself, dear."

Collect myself. Pick up all the broken little shards and plaster-of-paris them back together like a craft project.

"I hate you," said Janie. "You should have stayed in Italy."

Noreen rose and walked out, grasping the door frame with her knobby fingers as she passed.

THE NEXT MORNING THE sun blared in the window, coating Janie with a sticky dampness that made her unruly hair cling to her neck. The electric buzz of insects whined outside.

"Hey!" A woman's voice called, followed by the staccato rapping of footsteps coming up the stairs. "Hey, what are you, sick? What are you still doing in bed? Where are the kids?"

"Jesus, Shelly," Janie muttered, rolling away from the verbal barrage. "Can't you just shut the hell up for once."

"I heard that, bub. A girl who sleeps in her clothes does not get to tell me to shut the hell up. Where are those pajamas I got you? And when's the last time you washed your hair, it's all greasy."

Janie rolled back. "Shut UP!" she yelled, but her voice was scratchy and weak.

"What happened?" asked Shelly. She stood there in her pale blue suit with the opalescent buttons and her diamond stud earrings, hands on hips, the French manicure gleaming from the plastic nails. "I spend a few nights at Geoffrey's and all hell breaks loose."

Much to her shame and fury, Janie started to cry. Shelly lowered herself to the side of the bed. "Okay, baby," she crooned, patting Janie's knee. "Now what's all this about."

As Janie began to unwind the tale, wailing and leaking from her eyes and nose, Shelly pulled at her, gently excavating her from the bed and steering her down the stairs toward the bathroom. Occasionally, Shelly inserted one-word directives: "Walk," and "Blow," handing her a tissue, and "Strip," turning on the shower and stepping just outside the bathroom, door cracked so that she could continue to listen and give commands. "I'm going to the kitchen to make coffee now," Shelly called when Janie had finished her anguished tale. "Lots of shampoo."

When Janie got out and dried herself, she saw that Shelly had put a clean set of "construction pajamas" on the toilet lid. She dressed and aimed herself toward the sound of clacking heels on the second floor, where Shelly was remaking her bed with clean sheets. "Get in," said Shelly, lifting the covers, and Janie complied. "Okay, coffee's in a thermos on the bedside table. Here's what you're going to do. You're going to stay in bed all day. I mean it, do not get up except for the bathroom."

"The kids . . ."

"The kids are all squared away. Jude's set up for them, and your mother would probably babysit until they go to middle school, after what she did."

"I hate her."

"Of course you do. Now I have to go. The inspection's in a few minutes."

"On your house?" Janie's words came out in a pinched whine. "You have a buyer?"

"Yes, bub," she nodded. "I'm sorry."

"No you're not," muttered Janie. "You're fucking thrilled." She looked up, remembering, "You said you'd still come back, but you didn't even come to Dylan's birthday."

"Pfff," Shelly snorted, shaking her head. "I know. I could've kicked myself! Geoffrey and I took a long weekend on Block Island, and I didn't get the message till Tuesday."

Shelly stood and straightened her suit, licking her finger and stabbing at a tiny hair of lint on the lapel. "I mean it," she said pointing at Janie. "Do not get up. Stay in bed tomorrow, too, if you can. Monday will come soon enough."

AFTER CRYING AND HURLING curses at her pillow for most of Saturday afternoon, Janie went downstairs to the bathroom. She peeked into the tiny back bedroom. Her mother's things were gone. Janie went back to bed.

At 7:30 p.m., the phone rang, but Janie did not answer. At 7:32 it rang again, and again at 7:33. "Hello," Janie whispered into the receiver, now almost awake.

"Hi, Mom. You sound all scratchy. Are you better yet?"

"No, Dylan."

"Then can we stay at Auntie Jude's again? Carly fell asleep, and Gram and me are making snip . . . snit . . . ," his voice aimed away from the receiver, "what's it called? Oh, yeah, Snickerdoodles."

"Oh." *I hate her.*

"Mom? Don't get too sicker, okay?"

"I'll try. I love you, Dylan."

"Love you, Mom. Carly loves you, too. Everybody does."

JANIE DID NOT FEEL loved. In fact, at around 3:15 a.m. the arctic desolation she had been experiencing since Jake left thawed temporarily, exposing a reeling rage that made her want to break things. She stormed down the stairs, thankful for her children's absence, but simultaneously blistered with anger that they were with her mother. The fucking spoiler. Abandoner of despondent offspring. Dutiful just long enough to come back and ensure the permanence of their despondence.

Janie punched the Power button on the computer and composed a long, rambling e-mail to Jake that was alternately self-pitying, self-reproaching and accusatory. It was stalkerlike, a fact that Janie realized before she hit Send. *What's next*, she asked herself with disgust. *Getting drunk and trying to French kiss him in the Communion line? Try not to be any more of a cautionary tale than you already are.*

She stabbed at the Power button, with full knowledge that it would give her a stern rebuke about improper shutdown when she turned it on again, which made her want to preemptively toss it through the back window. But she was tired all of a sudden, and dragged herself back to her bedroom before any damage, either real or of the cyber variety, could be done.

When she woke again, it was 10:25 in the morning, and she knew with a leaden certainty that Aunt Jude and her mother had gone to Mass. The nerve, the shameless, red-panty-wearing gall of them to show up with her children in that church and take a wafer from that . . . that . . . what was he?

What was he, really? Peeling back a tattered corner of her shame and rage and hurt, Janie got a momentarily clearheaded glimpse of Jake. He was just a guy. And he was trying to live by his code, a code that neither she nor many others fully understood. And perhaps he was bound by a vow, and a love of solitude, and a level of self-protection that grew problems for him here and there. But didn't we all have coping strategies that worked most of the time, but in certain uncommon circumstances failed miserably? He was just a guy, after all, only human. Completely human, though she had fooled herself into thinking that he was somehow better than that.

This fleeting brush with objectivity did not last long. She was back to hating him and her mother, and to some extent, everyone else fairly quickly. And yet, having stumbled upon the truth of his humanness, she could not completely unknow it. Had he used her for a friendship that was not supportable? Had he led her on? Yes! Well, a bit, anyway.

Around noon, Aunt Jude stopped by. Janie was roused from dreams that were barren and vaguely violent by the sound of dishes clinking and jewelry jingling in the kitchen downstairs.

Her immediate reaction was to feign sleep. But she had somehow arrived at a point of boredom with herself and her pitifulness and reached for a hairbrush.

"There you are," exclaimed Aunt Jude when Janie entered the kitchen fully dressed, with nothing to belie her former state but bad breath. "How are you feeling?"

"Peachy," said Janie, her voice raspy from disuse. She sank weakly onto a kitchen chair and realized she hadn't eaten in two days. "Where are the kids?"

"With their gram at my house. I was just making you some pistachio pudding. It's the instant kind, so it should be set in another few minutes. There now," she clucked to herself as she put the bowl of gelatinous green goo into the refrigerator.

"You know what she did, right?" demanded Janie. "Behind my back?"

Aunt Jude was now rooting around in her big white purse. She pulled out a sleeve of saltines and began to lay them on a plate. "Yes," she said.

"Is she still leaving on Thursday?"

"As far as I know."

"What could have possessed her to go to him, someone she hardly even knows, instead of coming to me, her own daughter? That's all I want to know."

Aunt Jude finally stopped fussing with the crackers and faced Janie. "I don't think it's my place to get in the middle of this," she said. "But I suppose I already am, not because I want to be, but because I'm just trying to be helpful. That's all I've ever really wanted was to be helpful to people." She pushed the plate toward Janie, who ignored it.

"Help away," said Janie.

"She was just worried about you and Father. You seemed too close. And both being so lonely, it was just trouble waiting to happen, is all. Just trouble and heartache. You've had enough of that already. And she's your mother; she wanted to protect you."

"It was NONE of her freaking BUSINESS!"

"Yes, well," said Aunt Jude, helping herself to a cracker. "She did what she saw fit. Maybe others would have handled it differently, but she's got her own way. She can't help herself."

"Can't help herself from embarrassing me and ruining the one friendship that makes any sense to me these days? Can't help herself from prancing all over Europe instead of showing up for me? What exactly can't she help?"

Aunt Jude got up to check the pudding. "Not quite set," she reported, her ample posterior protruding from behind the refrigerator door.

Useless, thought Janie. *I'm going back to bed.*

Aunt Jude came from behind Janie and began to rub her shoulders. "Whatever you think, and whatever she does, just remember it's out of love. It's not always how we want it to look, but she does her best. She just wants a happier life for you than she's had herself."

"I hate her."

Jude's fingers stopped their gentle probing. "You don't."

"Oh yes I do."

"*Hate* is a very serious word, Jane Elizabeth." Her thumbs began to move slowly across Janie's shoulder blades, as if Aunt Jude herself were unaware. "It's too dark of a word to use against your mother. You have no reason, no reason on this earth to hate anyone, no matter what sorrow you're holding. I could tell you . . . I could show you . . ." Aunt Jude let out an exasperated sigh.

"You went to Mass this morning, didn't you?" Janie turned to face her, wrenching away from the trance-inducing hands.

"Of course. Why wouldn't I go to—"

"I knew it. God, I knew you'd just march in there with my kids like everything was sunshine and roses, except for me, the loser niece who's so humiliated she can't—"

"We went to Immaculate Conception in Natick—not Our Lady's! You're not the only one, you know," Aunt Jude sputtered.

"You're not the only one who's upset and angry. I know that's hard to see right now, but Janie, please, you've got to take a broader view."

A broader view of what? thought Janie. *I can't stand to look any more.*

Aunt Jude left her with the green pudding and saltines. Janie went back to bed. At seven o'clock that evening, her aunt returned with the sleepy children, who'd been bathed and fed and were already in their pajamas. Janie was glad she had clothes on, even if they were rumpled into spiderwebs of wrinkles. She was dressed, and her "illness" was over, no matter how she felt. She brought Dylan and Carly up to their beds and stayed with them for the few moments it took them to settle into sleep. She drew her fingertips across their silky heads and warm, smooth cheeks.

Blessed and cursed, her mother had called her. Wasn't it the truth.

14

G OOD NEWS!" HEIDI'S VOICE came over the phone like a gleeful
squirrel on Monday morning. "Lightning hit my office building over the weekend and the sprinklers went off. No work!"

"That's nice." The receiver was wedged between Janie's ear
and shoulder as she cut up pieces of pear for Carly and waited for
the toaster to pop. Up came the blackened bread. The toaster knob
had somehow gotten turned all the way to "dark." Dylan would
not eat this, she knew, yet she buttered it anyway.

"It's a paid vacation, is what it is," chimed Heidi. "There's a
sale at J. Jill—do you want to go?"

"I'm not much of a shopper," said Janie. *You can tell that just
by looking at me.* She wondered momentarily how old her underwear was, as she dumped tiny dunes of cinnamon onto the toast
to camouflage the charred sections. Pre-wedding, she realized.
That old.

"Well, at least let me have Dylan over for a playdate after camp.
Keane would love it. He keeps asking why he always goes to your
house."

"You work," said Janie, delivering the toast to Dylan, who took
one look at it and went back to driving his Matchbox car over the
bananas in the fruit bowl.

"I've offered to have him over on the weekends, but you're
always busy." Janie could hear the bristle in Heidi's tone, but she

couldn't make herself care. She motioned for Dylan to eat the toast and he picked it up. When Janie turned to Carly with the pear pieces, he put it back on the plate.

"Today might not be good, Heidi," said Janie, going back to the counter to pack Dylan's lunch. "My mother's around, so she'll probably want to see him."

"She saw me a lot!" Dylan was kneeling backward in his chair now, aiming himself at Janie, the Matchbox car left to idle in the bananas. "She saw me that whole time you were sick!"

"You were sick?" asked Heidi, concern smoothing her wrinkled pride.

"I want to play with Keane!"

"What did you have?"

"Keane's Mom!" yelled Dylan, pulling on Janie's elbow. "I can play! I'm available!"

"Nothing serious. Dylan, STOP!"

"Please! Please let me go to Keane's!"

"No!" she yelled. Then, "Fine! Go to Keane's."

The details were worked out before Janie could come up with any more excuses. Heidi would pick them up from camp and bring Dylan home to Janie at three. He would be off her radar screen for two hours. He had gone on playdates, supervised by mothers Janie knew even less well than Heidi. But that was before Janie had seen how quickly it all could change, how an innocuous activity like bike riding could be fatal. School and camp were exempt somehow—there was no real logic to it. Perhaps it was because they were routine. They were licensed by the state, run by professionals. They were necessary for Janie's tenuous hold on her temper and sanity. Playdates at other children's houses had slid off the grid of normal. And Heidi was no professional.

AT 12:45, AFTER A morning of food shopping and errands and trying to keep Carly from crawling up the stairs four or five hundred times, Janie felt herself itching to get in the car. She could just drive by the Pond Pals pickup line, make sure Heidi was there. And if she weren't there right on time, Janie could pick up the boys herself. In fact, she could even call Heidi and offer to take them from Pond Pals to Heidi's house, then maybe stick around for a cup of coffee.

You're gripless, Janie warned herself. But the scheme festered in her thoughts until she realized that she really was in no mood to spend any extended time with Heidi—with anyone, really—and that Carly, having missed her morning nap, was now nearly violent with fatigue. Janie took her upstairs and sat with her on Dylan's bed to read a story. *The Runaway Bunny* was lying on the floor by the bed. Janie picked it up and flipped to the first page.

Once there was a little bunny who wanted to run away. So he said to his mother, "I am running away."

"If you run away," said his mother, "I will run after you. For you are my little bunny."

Then the little bunny wanted to become a fish and swim away. His mother calmly replied that she would be a fisherman and fish for him. *Heartless little shit,* thought Janie. *She's just trying to keep you safe.* By the time the little bunny threatened to join the circus and the mother was turning into a tightrope walker to keep up with him, Carly had lost interest and Janie was ready to throw the book against the wall.

She put the baby in her crib and watched as the little hands flung away the stuffed dolly and grasped the rungs of the crib to pull herself along until her head was pressed up against the headboard. *No hesitation,* Janie realized. *No worries. No security item. Playdates at other peoples' houses are going to be small potatoes for this one. She'll probably be back-packing across Europe before she's ten.*

How had Janie missed it? This developing personality, this fury to get things out of the way so she could move? If Robby had been here . . . well, yes, if Robby had been here every single thing would be different. But specifically, Janie realized, they would have discussed their second child. They would have commented to each other on her independence and tenacity. They would have nudged each other so that neither missed the way this child put herself to sleep, or woke up talking, or played her little piano with such fervor that she was sure to be a pianist like her daddy.

Dear God. Janie had failed to notice even that. A wave of self-hatred washed over her so strong she felt she couldn't bear the weight of it. She slumped down onto Dylan's bed and watched the sleeping baby. *Sorry,* she prayed to Carly. *Mommy's so sorry.*

JANIE WOKE WITH A quick gasp of breath that startled her and set her heart to galloping. Her eyes searched the room, for what she couldn't quite name. Then it came to her. A clock. For godsake, what time was it? There was no clock in the kids' room because there had never been any need for one. But as she rose like a shot from Dylan's bed, it suddenly seemed like a gross oversight. Carly was still unconscious in the crib, both arms and one foot hanging languidly from between the slats as if she'd been trying to escape in her sleep.

Janie quick-stepped down the stairs into the kitchen. The clock said 3:20. Where were they? She dashed into the little office and scrambled through the file drawer until she hit the preschool family directory. Heidi and her ex-husband were still listed at the same address and phone. Janie dialed. No answer.

She felt her panic lurching against her insides like an intestinal bumper car. She redialed, hating Heidi for not answering and hating herself for losing control. No answer. Why didn't she have Heidi's cell phone number? Did Heidi have a cell phone? Of course she must. She was the type who had emerged from the womb texting the boy newborns as the doctor snipped her umbilical cord.

And what type was Janie? The type who lets her child go off with an amateur. The type who neglects to get the damned cell phone number. A neglectful failure of a mother. She dialed the home number again and left a disjointed, stuttering message, imploring Heidi to call her.

Now it was 3:30. Where, where, where was he? Her brain raced from one catastrophic scenario to the next. A car accident. Improperly buckled. Ejected from the vehicle. Bleeding and crying for her. Or worse.

She dialed 911. "Have there been any accidents?" she demanded of the dispatcher, in a voice that sounded screechy and addled even to her. No there hadn't, was there some sort of emergency? "My son, he's four, no he's five now, and he . . . he's on a playdate . . . and he . . . the other mother . . . she hasn't brought him home yet . . . she was supposed to be here thirty-five minutes ago . . ."

Half an hour late wasn't so long, suggested the dispatcher, a cretin who clearly had no children, no relationships at all, probably lived in a basement apartment with beer-stained indoor-outdoor carpeting and sports talk radio blaring. He offered to send over a squad car, while managing to make it clear that he thought this a gross misuse of taxpayer dollars.

"No," Janie said, and hung up.

She ran out the front door, past Malinowski who was on a damned ladder as usual, and into the street. Hands fisted at her hips, she searched up and down for Heidi's car. Nothing. Sweat trickled down her spine. She would have to find him. "Hey," she yelled up at Tug as she ran back into the house for her car keys. "Can you . . . the baby's asleep . . . can you . . . I have to go find Dylan . . ."

"Yeah, sure," he said, descending the ladder.

She leaped into her car, gunned the motor, wrenched into reverse, and narrowly avoided slamming into Heidi's car as she pulled into the driveway. As Janie jumped out of her car, she could feel the boiling blur of panic slow and congeal into something rancid, toxic. She stared at the three of them, straggling calmly out of Heidi's station wagon, giggling, sticky with some foreign, happy substance.

"We went to Dairy Queen!" called Dylan. His smile disintegrated when he saw the wild look on his mother's face. "It's okay. I'm still hungry. I'll still eat dinner."

"Go into the house, please, Dylan," said Janie. Dylan didn't move.

"I'm sorry," said Heidi, surprise rippling the surface of her perfect features. "It was just a little treat. I only got smalls."

"That's nice, Heidi. It's a nice treat, and frankly I wouldn't care if you got them a quart each. But now that you're," Janie flicked her gaze blindly toward a nonexistent watch, "forty-five minutes later than you said you'd be, do you think you might have thought to call? Would that be so much to ask?"

"Oh my gosh, are we that late? I had no idea . . ."

"You promised you'd have him home by three. Three o'clock. It's now almost four. I called your house. I didn't know what to think. I could only imagine the worst."

"Oh, Janie," breathed Heidi. "I am so, so sorry! I didn't realize you'd be so—"

"Out of my mind with worry? That's so surprising to you? That's such a shock? What mother wouldn't be?"

"I can't apologize enough." Heidi's shame rose in pink blotches all over her neck. She was starting to pant. "It'll never happen again, I promise. I'll never—"

"You're damned right, it'll never happen again," said Janie, straining now to maintain voice volume in the normal range. "I'd be completely negligent to ever allow it."

Keane burst into tears. He pressed his pale, thin fingers across his eyes and sobbed. Dylan stared at his mother in confused horror.

"Get in the house, Dylan," warned Janie, and he began to move woodenly toward the porch.

Her arms around her bereft son, Heidi, said, "I just can't . . . I'm so . . . I'll call you later?"

"Don't," said Janie, and turned toward the house.

Tug stood alone on the porch when she opened the screen door. He stared at her, his features calm, his hands resting in his pockets. But she knew. Janie could hear every word he wasn't saying.

"Don't. Say. Anything," she warned him.

"You can't do that," he said. Beneath the quiet tone, she heard the loud ring of disapproval. "You can't do it to Dylan."

"You," she hissed, pointing her finger at him. "You just shut up about Dylan. He's MY kid. Don't you act like you know better—you don't even have kids. You have NO IDEA how it feels to be so . . ." she sensed the eruption coming, but couldn't stop it, didn't even try. The words flew out of her like flaming birds from an inferno. "I've HAD it with you and your opinions about how I should do everything differently. You don't like how I parent, you don't like how I handle things, and you have NO RESPECT for my husband's wishes! My poor dead husband wanted to give me a porch, and you've changed every damned thing you could. I wanted HIS porch, not YOURS."

Janie's eyes darted around the structure as if she'd never seen it before. "I hate it," she said. "And you're fired. I'll send you the rest of the money, because I don't even care about that. I just want you out of here. Now."

ON TUESDAY MORNING IT was raining, not hard, but steadily enough so that Janie suggested that Dylan stay home from camp. She had no interest in bumping into Heidi. Actually, she had no interest in even leaving the house. Dylan didn't mind. He said he didn't really like that camp so much, anyway. He asked Janie to get his goggles from the car, and he wore them all day. At bedtime, Janie made him take them off. The red indented circles around his eyes seemed permanent.

On Wednesday, the weather cleared, and mist rose from the pine needles as Janie dropped Dylan off at camp. Keane was already there, saving a seat for Dylan. Dylan sat next to some other boy whom Janie didn't recognize. After dinner, he said he was tired and went to bed early.

Cormac and Barb came over and were disappointed to find that Dylan was already fast asleep. Barb had made a collage of pictures from his birthday party. In the center was a close-up of Cormac's ingenious pirate cake. The mat around it had openings cut off-kilter for the other pictures: Keane and Dylan laughing and pointing to the earring on the pirate's butt; the boys bobbing for apples with Uncle Charlie; a close-up of Gram and Aunt Jude singing "Happy Birthday"; Tug showing Dylan how to use the tiny screwdriver; Janie and Cormac passing out cake to Heidi and Father Jake; Carly pulling herself up on Dylan's new bike.

There was a separate picture, too. Beautifully matted and framed, it was of their little family sitting in the grass. Janie's head was turned toward Dylan whispering into his ear, and his mouth was wide with laughter. The only one looking directly into the camera lens was Carly. Steadying herself between her mother's upright knees, the baby graced the picture with a look of such confidence and purpose it was as if she were planning her first solo flight. At any moment she would soar above the backyard and head for parts unknown. Barb's photo had managed to capture the true Carly, not the lifelike doll who got toted from one errand to the next, whose mother barely even knew her.

It was a gut punch, as if every photo exposed Janie's shortcomings as a mother, a daughter, a friend, and an employer. For a brief moment she wondered if Barb had designed it for that express purpose. No, she determined, Barb wasn't that smart. Just monumentally insensitive.

Janie did try to hold her tongue. When Cormac offered to get a hammer and picture hook and put them up for her right away, she didn't immediately tell them that she had no plans to hang them, would likely store them in a distant corner of the web-ridden eaves. No, she had only said that she didn't want to wake the children with the hammering. But Cormac persisted, and Janie admitted that she might need some time to get used to them. Why? they asked.

She finally lost patience and told them. Because she didn't think that Dylan would want such a detailed reminder of the worst birthday of his life. Which, of course, was only part of the truth.

Barb left the house in tears. Cormac stayed long enough to express his disappointment in Janie's insensitivity. HER insensitivity! Janie replied that she would get right to work on a Pology scone for Barb, unless she didn't do carbs, in which case Janie could grow her some Pology lettuce.

EVERY DAY SEEMED TO end worse than the last, and Thursday was no exception. Noreen had an evening flight back to her Italian homeland, and Uncle Charlie had spent hours spritzing Armor All on the plastic interior of his Ford Tempo. Janie picked Dylan up at camp a few minutes early to avoid seeing Heidi, then drove to Aunt Jude's so the kids could say good-bye to their gram.

"I didn't see you that much," Dylan complained to Noreen. He'd worn his goggles for the brief car ride, and Janie could still see the faint pink rings around his eyes. She hoped no one else noticed.

"I was with you all weekend!" chided Noreen with a gentle smile.

"But then you moved in with Auntie Jude."

"Well, I wanted some time with my sister. Sisters are very special, Dylan. You'll see. When you and Carly are all grown up and don't live together anymore, you'll want to spend time with her, too."

"How come I won't live with Carly? Is Mom going to make her leave our house?"

Janie winced inwardly. *He thinks I make everyone leave.*

They sat shoe-horned into Jude's tiny kitchen and ate Stella d'Oro Anisette Toast cookies, while Noreen and Dylan reminded each other of every moment they had spent together during her stay. The bedtime stories and the trips to Cormac's Confectionary and swinging on the swing set in the backyard. Gram liked to swing. *Gets her closer to the jet stream*, Janie brooded.

Uncle Charlie went out to the driveway to warm up the Tempo, and good-byes were said.

"I love you very much, Janie dear," her mother whispered as they gave each other a quick hug.

Janie almost said, Love you, too. It was true, and yet she felt it was against her will, as if it were a condition of some sort, like eczema or a tendency to stutter. "Have a safe flight," she said instead.

After they watched the Tempo recede down the street and turn onto Route 27, Aunt Jude invited them to stay for dinner. Janie suspected that Aunt Jude wanted to talk about patching it up with her mother, so she made excuses about the kids being tired and left.

At a quarter to six, Janie found herself thinking, "Oh, good, Robby will be home soon." It had been over a month since she'd forgotten he was dead, and the slip stung her like a wasp.

Rice Krispies for dinner. It was all she could manage.

ON FRIDAY, AFTER DROPPING Dylan off at camp, Janie realized she had no errands to run. There was no one she wanted to visit, or, if she were honest with herself, even had the option to visit, without facing some tear in the relationship that required mending. She went home and tried to enjoy the absence of power tools buzzing at close range, but it just seemed quiet and boring.

Before Janie had a chance to choose some toys for Carly, Carly crawled over to the plastic toy bin and pitched every single item out. Janie slumped down with her back against the speckled green sofa and watched. Carly climbed into the bin and sat with her hands perched on the rim, as if it were about to take her on an amusement park ride. Carly looked at Janie. "Ma!" she yelled.

"Yes, I see you. You're in the toy bin."

"Mmmmm!" Carly growled, imitating Dylan's motor sounds.

"Are you going for a ride?" Carly giggled and growled even louder. Janie reached for the bin and pulled it across the carpet toward her, the baby's head swaying back for a moment as the ride took off. Her eyes went wide with excitement and she laughed, "Ma!"

Janie pushed the bin back and forth. Then, caught up in the child's delight, she got behind it on her hands and knees, steering it all around the room. When she made unexpected turns, Carly let out happy shrieks that made Janie smile despite her bleak mood. As the turns got more precarious, the baby's howls of approval grew louder, until the bin bumped too hard into the couch and spilled her out onto the carpet. Her face fell and her lips trembled.

I ruined it, was Janie's first thought. *Goddammit, I ruin everything.* She crawled to the baby and bent down to console her. "You okay, Carly? You alright? Mommy's sorry. I should be more careful. I wasn't careful enough with my baby."

The little girl wrenched back from the precipice of unhappiness and pulled herself up on her mother, pushing Janie down in the process. Carly climbed up on Janie and pressed her damp little lips against Janie's neck. "That tickles," Janie laughed in surprise, and Carly pressed harder, burrowing her face into her mother's soft, vulnerable throat. Janie tried to pull away, her whole body shaking with laughter, but Carly's chubby hands slid behind Janie's neck, capturing her, claiming her. Imprisoned by her drooling ten-month-old, it was the best Janie had felt in a week.

When the game finally ended, Carly lay upon her mother's chest for a moment, then climbed down onto her knees. Slowly she rose onto her feet, using Janie's body to stabilize herself. Then she turned and walked four steps across the carpet to the couch.

"Carly!" said Janie, sitting up. "Look at you!" She held out her hands and Carly lurched back across the short distance to her, falling into her arms. "You did it! You walked!" Carly staggered back to the couch, then returned to Janie. "You're not a baby anymore—you're officially a toddler!"

Who can I tell? thought Janie in a blur of excitement. *Who should I call first?*

The list, not long to begin with, grew shorter as she realized that her relationship with each person was currently . . . experiencing technical difficulties. Even the contractor was pissed at her. That left Uncle Charlie and Aunt Brigid—and no matter how Aunt Jude was feeling about Janie right now, if Charlie and Brigid got the news first, she'd be undeniably hurt. And Shelly. Who the hell even knew where Shelly was at the moment? Probably loving it up with her new handsome, rich, architecturally dramatic boyfriend.

Dylan. The goggled one. He should hear the news first. Hopefully he'd be excited about it. Janie realized that she wasn't sure if he would be—he'd been uncharacteristically unenthusiastic about everything since she'd blown up at his best friend's mother. In front of him. For taking him to Dairy Queen and consequently sending Janie into a hair-tearing panic.

But Janie didn't want to think about that. She finally decided to call Aunt Jude, who was so delighted, she said she was coming right over to see. An immediate visit was more than Janie had bargained for. "I could bring her to your house tomorrow," she offered.

"I can't wait that long!" said Aunt Jude, and hung up the phone.

By the time she arrived, Carly was droopy with fatigue, refused to show off her newfound skills for her auntie, and was soon put in her crib for a nap. When Janie came back down the stairs, Aunt Jude was helping herself to the pistachio pudding she'd made for Janie, which had remained untouched until now.

"It's so exciting," said Aunt Jude. "A toddler! She's growing up so fast."

"You didn't even see it," Janie reminded her.

"But you saw it. That's good enough for me."

"Why?" asked Janie. Why was that good enough for her? It wouldn't have been good enough for Janie, not by a long shot.

"Because you're her mother! I don't need to see—I've seen all I need to. I saw you and your brother walk—that was important to me. You two were my babies. Not my real babies, of course, but the realest ones I'll ever have. Your mother was good like that. She shared you."

"She was lucky to have your help," countered Janie.

Aunt Jude smiled appreciatively. "So we were both lucky."

Before she left, she worked on Janie about serving lunch with her at the soup kitchen.

"The kids," said Janie, hoping that would end it.

"Charlie and Brigie will take them. It's all set."

Janie rolled her eyes. "Aunt Jude."

"What?"

"I'm a grown-up. You can't just run my life like you did when I was little."

"I'm not running your life. I'm giving you opportunities. I can't make you go."

"But you always do."

"No, Janie, I don't. I'm just watching you walk, like I always have. If you don't want to walk, that's your choice, just like it always has been."

Friday, August 17

Carly walked today! Only ten months old. Dylan was thirteen months, I think. He's more cautious—probably had to think it through first. Carly doesn't seem to feel fear (yet). Lucky girl. I called Aunt Jude. What were the options? (My fault, I know.) She came over and I didn't fight with her. At least that's something.

A Jake-less Friday. The first in five months. Get used to it.

———————

"IT SMELLS FUNNY," WHISPERED Dylan, as Janie buckled him and his booster seat into Uncle Charlie's car. Carly and her baby seat were already installed. She had refused to walk since the previous morning, a fact that made Janie wonder if it had really happened at all.

"It's Armor All," Janie whispered back. "It's supposed to make everything shiny."

"Oh," said Dylan. "Well, that's good, I guess."

"Ready for our magic carpet ride?" boomed Uncle Charlie as he maneuvered his massive frame into the driver's seat of the Tempo.

"Like Aladdin!" giggled Dylan.

"I guess that makes me Princess Jasmine," said Aunt Brigid, securing an errant strand of wiry gray hair with a bobby pin behind her ear. To Janie she said, "I hope you don't mind us taking them on a royal trip to the dump. Charlie hasn't shown them off to his buddies in a while."

"I thought he was working at Cormac's now."

A wry smile came over Aunt Brigid. "Oh, he is . . . but it's a bit of an adjustment."

Janie waved as the car backed cautiously down the driveway.

Jude insisted on driving them to Table of Plenty. "I know the way," she said.

"So does everyone who's ever been down Route 27," said Janie. "You just want control of the keys in case I try to leave early."

"But you're not leaving early, so why would I be worried about that?"

The soup kitchen was on the south side of Pelham, just before the Natick town line. It was housed in a former shoe factory that had been purchased through a federal War on Poverty grant by the Mass Bay Food Bank. Though recently painted a cheery salmon color, it hadn't been properly scraped beforehand, giving the building a smeary, bubbled look, like a war refugee with lipstick on.

In the parking lot behind the building sat a handful of vehicles, not one of which was less than a decade old. (Volunteers with nice cars learned very quickly to park at Brooks Pharmacy across the street.) A line of patrons sat on wooden benches waiting, mostly patiently, for the doors to open. A few younger men congregated by a decrepit Lincoln Town Car, leaning on it and smoking cigarettes. One elderly woman walked determined laps around the perimeter of the parking lot, humming and occasionally exclaiming to herself about the state of her hair, which was pulled back in a tidy bun. Though it was August, she wore a heavy sweatshirt and what looked to be several pairs of pants. Janie saw the outer layer slide down the woman's narrow hips until she hitched them back up.

Aunt Jude knocked on a small side door of the building, and was let in by a round, sweaty older woman in a hairnet and apron. "Judy, Judy, Jude!" exclaimed the woman, wiping the perspiration from her cheeks. "You get right in here! And who's this curly-headed child?"

"This is my niece, Jane LaMarche. Janie, this is Vonetta Driscoll. She's the volunteer coordinator, and she makes the best egg noodle soup in the world. I could live on it!"

"You sweet talker," cooed Vonetta. A moment later, she looked past Janie. "Beryl, now you know I can't let you in this way. You keep on walking, honey. I'll let you know when it's ready."

"Did I hear someone say eggs?" asked Beryl politely. "Because I'm just a bit concerned about my cholesterol today, and I might decline to partake of eggs."

"No eggs, just tuna casserole. You alright with mercury?"

"Well," smiled Beryl, shyly. "I have been characterized as mercurial, so I suppose it's fitting."

"Wonderful," said Vonetta. "Glad we're on the same page. I'll give a shout when it's ready."

Vonetta ushered Janie and Aunt Jude back to the volunteer office, where Jude stashed her laptop computer and Janie was admonished to put her long black curls up into a ponytail.

"Look at those eyes," Vonetta commented to Jude. "They're so light, it doesn't hardly look like she could see out of them." Waving her hand in front of Janie, she teased, "You can see, right?"

Janie chuckled, unsure of how to respond. It had been so long since she'd been with someone who wasn't inspecting her for signs of anguish, she almost didn't recognize the feeling. After a moment it came to her. Relief.

Aunt Jude showed Janie where to restock the napkins and plastic utensils while Aunt Jude helped load the trays of food onto the folding tables that formed the buffet. At noon, they took their places behind the tables, ready to serve the patrons who surged through the scuffed double doors.

Aunt Jude seemed to know most of them, if not by name, by some detail they had shared with her about their lives. "Hello, Mary . . . Hi there, Antonio . . . Hi, would you like a little extra? I know you've got a healthy appetite . . . Now, Mr. Jones," she addressed one elderly gentleman in a tattered Red Sox cap, "where is your friend, Mr. DiFilippo?"

"Ahh, he's taking a nap. Little siesta. He'll be 'round later."

Janie smiled and scooped, garnering grins from some of the younger men. Others seemed strangely suspicious, and one even made quite a show of inspecting his casserole after she served him. Most, however, nodded and avoided eye contact, staring blankly into their paper plates.

"Just a half portion, please," murmured Beryl, the walker. "I don't metabolize cream-based cooking as I did in my younger days." She moved quickly down the line to the salad and breathed a barely perceptible sigh of disappointment. A wide metal bowl of limp iceberg lettuce was speckled with shaved carrots and the occasional pale tomato wedge.

After the meal was served, Janie helped Aunt Jude and a handful of other volunteers ferry the serving trays back to the kitchen. The leftovers were shoveled into plastic containers while the volunteers stopped to serve themselves. Several took their plates out to the large room to eat with the guests. Others, like Aunt Jude and Janie, had just a quick bite in the kitchen.

"Mmm," said Aunt Jude. "I love your tuna casserole, Vonetta! Don't you, Janie? Don't you just love it?" Janie smiled and nodded toward Vonetta, wondering how quickly she could ditch the rest of the ample serving Aunt Jude had given her.

After they set the kitchen in order, Aunt Jude went back to the volunteer office and retrieved her laptop computer. "This is my favorite part," she told Janie as they walked out into the dining room. Most of the tables still held the debris of the meal, but one table in the corner had been meticulously cleared and wiped. Two middle-aged men sat at the table waiting patiently for Jude.

"Well, I see my foreign correspondents have gathered faithfully!" Aunt Jude said to the men as she booted up the computer. "Any news, Malcolm?"

"She's holding her own, God bless her," said the man called Malcolm. His face was lined and pitted with blackheads. Janie thought he must be in his sixties, but she couldn't be sure.

"Has hospice been called in?" Aunt Jude asked.

"Oh, I, uh . . . hospice? Can't remember. Maybe they don't have that out in Oregon."

"Where's the letter?"

Malcolm's eyes dropped penitentially to his lap. "I had it," he said. "But when I woke up it wasn't there. Think it must have blown away."

"Oh, I know what you mean," said Aunt Jude, patting the arm of his stained shirt. "I lose things all the time. They're right there, and then they aren't. Have you met my niece? This is my Janie. This is Malcolm, and this is . . . oh, remind me one more time?" she pleaded with the other man.

His lips, held tightly closed over bucked teeth, parted to answer, "Jimmy. 'S alright. I only been here once before."

"Jimmy, that's right. Sorry. Well, now Malcolm, you just fire when ready. I'm all set to go."

"Dear Mary Alice," he began, and Aunt Jude's fingers flew across the keyboard. He was writing to his sister, who was sick with cancer, and past the point of treatment. Malcolm was at least happy to hear that she could still drink her favorite A&W root beer, but wished he were there to make her one of his famous Ovaltine and graham cracker milk shakes, like he did when they were kids.

"That sounds delicious," commented Aunt Jude.

"It's god-awful," chuckled Malcolm, "but she'll get the joke."

He went on to say that he hoped his nephew was taking good care of her, since Malcolm couldn't be there in person, and it was lucky that good-for-nothing ex-husband of hers hit the road way back when he did, because he would have been useless. Worse than useless.

"Are you sure you want to say that?" said Aunt Jude. "It might be a little harsh for someone in Mary Alice's condition."

"Nah," said Malcolm. "She's a tough old chicken. 'Sides, no one knows better than her what a rotten bastard the guy was." He gritted his teeth and shook his head. "No good rotten bastard."

He finished his letter by telling Mary Alice that in his dreams he was holding her hand, just like he always used to, like when they'd hide in the basement closet on their mother's "bad nights." He was holding her hand and telling her that everything would be okay, and that soon they'd be away from there. But it looked to Malcolm like Mary Alice would be making her escape early, and it was hard for him to think of being left behind in a world without her.

"I know I haven't seen you but once or three times in all these long years, but in my dreams I'm always holding your hand. And you're holding mine. And that's the way it'll be until I come to join you in our new home above the stars. Love, your big brother, Malcolm."

Aunt Jude finished typing and glanced over at Janie. A look passed between the two women that, Janie realized, had never been transmitted before. It wasn't about either of them or their struggles with each other. It wasn't anger or disappointment or dismissal. It was a simple recognition of the real world in which they lived, both of them, together.

"Malcolm," said Aunt Jude, turning her attention back to him. "This is just lovely. Mary Alice will be so happy to hear from you. When I'm done with everyone's letters, I'll just go in the office and print them all out at once, and then you can address it yourself."

"Thanks," said Malcolm. "I know her address by heart."

"I've no doubt."

"Uh, Jude? You got that nice paper you always bring? My sister said she never got letters on such nice paper before. Made me feel kinda . . ."

"Proud?" said Aunt Jude. "Yessir, I brought it. Matching envelopes, too. And stamps."

"Thought of everything," smiled Malcolm. "Like always."

NEXT IN LINE, JIMMY wanted to write to the White House, indicating his advice on domestic matters as well as foreign policy. "I don't know what we're doing in the Middle East, Mr. President, sir, when it's those crazy motherfuckers in North Korea we should be worried about." It was Aunt Jude's policy never to scribe curses, of which she had to remind Jimmy on several occasions.

"Oh yeah," said Jimmy. "How 'bout 'crazy motherfornicators' instead?"

Several more guests stopped by at the table in the corner and dictated their letters. Aunt Jude said her fingers were getting tired (which Janie knew to be patently false, since Aunt Jude spent practically every free moment on the Internet) and asked Janie to take over. Janie was reminded of the first time Aunt Jude let her get behind the wheel of her car, back in high school. Janie had soon learned to tune out the constant barrage of driving tips and notifications of any other car within a quarter mile. But for now, it was good to have Aunt Jude as her guide to the world of scribing letters for the hapless, the sad, the angry, and the mildly psychotic.

When everyone else had gone, Beryl was still lingering near the table.

"This is my niece, Jane LaMarche," said Aunt Jude. "She'll be doing the typing."

Beryl studied Janie. "You have a tremendously auspicious name, Miss LaMarche."

"Jane?" said Janie. It was about the most inauspicious name she'd ever heard in her life.

"No, LaMarche. It means 'the walk' in French. You must be a traveler like myself."

Janie was unsure of how to respond, and Aunt Jude stepped in for the save. "That's her married name, Beryl. The last name she was born with was Dwyer."

"Oh!" Beryl's eyebrows shot up. "Even more impressive. You *chose* to be a LaMarche."

Janie offered to scribe a letter for Beryl, who politely declined. "I'm very old-fashioned," explained Beryl. "A typed letter is so cold and impersonal. It can be sent to so many people at once! Only a handwritten letter can convey the sense that the writer is actually with you, saying the words to you alone. When you write a letter with your own hand, you give a tiny piece of yourself."

"I see your point," said Janie. "How about this? What if I make you some stationery? Then you could handwrite your letters on nice paper with your name printed on it."

Beryl lightly touched her own cheek, then her hair. "I am overcome," she murmured. "It is a most apropos solution to my conundrum. You are, indeed, a true LaMarche."

Janie smiled. "How would you like your name printed?"

"Miss Beryl Ann Bishop."

"And your address?" The words were out of Janie's mouth too fast, and she nearly kicked herself for it. However eloquent her words, it was clear that Miss Beryl Ann Bishop was homeless.

Beryl pursed her lips in thought for a moment, "I think it best to say . . . En route, will advise."

15

⚊

THEY WENT TO MASS at Immaculate Conception in Natick, a gothic-looking minor cathedral with a serious pigeon problem. So many nooks and crevices in which the nuisance birds could nest, and no way to stop them, short of casting wire mesh over the entire ornate building. An awning had been erected across the entrance to the church to shelter parishioners from pigeon-generated mishaps.

The pastor was eighty-three, Aunt Jude informed Janie. Well past retirement age, but he didn't want to leave, and the Archdiocese of Boston wouldn't make him go because of the shortage of priests. His throat required clearing approximately every minute and a half, Janie calculated, and he did so with a grumbling *ehhhhhh, heh* sound that made it seem as if he were heckling himself.

There were no donuts after Mass. Everyone just went home.

In the car there was some discussion of going to Cormac's Confectionary to rectify the lack of post-Eucharistic pastries, but Janie didn't feel like ordering cupcakes from Barb and acting like everything was copacetic. She was able to convince Dylan that it would be more fun to make their own cookies and have beaters to lick.

"Could you please not wear the goggles?" she asked Dylan on the way home. "Just for this short little ride?" She hated that she was begging. He caught her gaze in the rearview mirror, then hesitantly lowered the goggles so that they hung from his neck. He chewed on the end of the plastic head strap until they pulled into the driveway, when he tucked the goggles neatly behind his car seat.

It took Janie some minutes to find the cookbook with the recipe that Dylan had requested: Peanut Butter Blossoms. They were essentially peanut butter cookies with chocolate kisses perched in the middle. Janie didn't have any chocolate kisses, however.

"No flowers," said Dylan. "I guess that's okay."

Things picked up when the beaters started whirling the butter and brown sugar into a creamy sandstorm. Janie let Dylan hold the small hand mixer and he giggled as the vibrating appliance made his arms feel tickly. "Let Carly try!" he yelled over the sound of the mixer. So Janie held the little girl next to Dylan and all three sets of hands engulfed the whirring motor.

The addition of each ingredient required a taste, and Janie wondered if they'd have even half the batter left to bake. But Dylan was happy and engaged, two things she'd seen precious little of in the last week, so she allowed his fingers to slip into the bowl over and over again. As they dipped their forks in sugar and pressed them across the balls of dough on the cookie sheet, Dylan said, "Hey, I got an idea! Let's bring some to Keane. He loves peanut butter, and he never had these before!"

"How's it going with you two?" asked Janie. "I haven't seen you sitting together for story time at camp."

"Yeah, we weren't friends this week."

"No?"

"No." Dylan pressed a cookie too hard and it splayed out over the edge of the baking sheet. "I felt bad to him."

"What did you feel bad about?" Janie picked up the smashed batter and rolled it into a ball again.

"His mom scared you, and you yelled and he cried, and I was very not happy."

Janie studied the wad of dough. "That happens sometimes. People don't always get along."

"So I guess we should just eat the cookies all ourselves."

She sighed. *Pology Cookies,* she thought, *a first.* She remembered Malcolm and his Ovaltine-graham cracker shakes. "Well, let's see if they're home."

THE LOOK OF ECSTATIC surprise on Keane's face when he saw Dylan made Janie wince. He leaped at Dylan who laughed and tried to hug Keane back until he remembered what he was there for. "Don't crush the cookies!" he yelped. Janie rescued the plate from his outstretched hands before the two boys tumbled against the doorjamb and into the foyer of the house.

"Okay, boys," Janie had to say several times while attempting to extricate them from the oversized basket of shoes they had fallen into. "Keane, where's your mom?"

"Exercising! Downstairs! Did you bring those cookies for me? To eat?"

"Keane, go get your mom."

"What flavor are they?"

"Keane, get your mom and then we can have some cookies."

Keane bolted toward a doorway in the foyer. "DYLAN'S HERE! HE HAS COOKIES!"

Janie, Dylan, and Carly moved toward the doorway and peeked into the kitchen. It was larger than Janie's living room and had a giant island in the middle. The satiny maple cabinets were perfectly complemented by the blond speckled marble of the countertops.

"How many people live here?" asked Dylan.

"I think just Keane and Heidi," said Janie.

"Fancy."

Heidi emerged from the basement in exercise shorts and a gray T-shirt that was splotched with dampness around her neck and waist. Her pale hair was pulled back in a lopsided ponytail, tendrils of which were pasted to her pink, sweaty face. "Hi," she said. It was half greeting, half question.

"We brought you some cookies," said Janie matter-of-factly.

"Thanks." Heidi reached for a paper towel and dabbed at her face and neck. "How are you?"

"Good," said Janie. "Better."

Janie hadn't realized that Heidi was holding her breath until she exhaled. They set up the boys with cookies and milk and let them eat way too many as they chatted carefully about which camp counselors the boys liked best and whether those swimming lessons were just glorified splash time. Carly cruised around the kitchen holding onto cabinet knobs, until she suddenly turned and walked across the ceramic tiled floor to Janie, supplying the mothers with more safe subject matter. Eventually Carly got fussy, and milk got spilled, and Janie was ready to go.

"I'm really sorry about Dairy Queen," ventured Heidi, as the boys ran outside.

"Sorry I flipped out. It was a really bad week, and I'm just . . . you know . . . extra . . . I just need to know where he is." Janie took a deep breath, surreptitiously pinched the back of her hand and said, "I hope you'll have him over again."

"Yes! Great! Any time." Heidi looked so enthusiastic that Janie almost laughed out loud. With her hair a mess and no makeup on, Heidi was the grown-up-girl version of her son.

JANIE PULLED INTO THE driveway after dropping Dylan off at camp Monday morning, and strange men were hanging around her yard. Maybe not quite hanging around, but not working terribly hard, either. One, his long, thin arms covered with rust-colored freckles, was cutting a piece of wooden molding with a handsaw. The other, dark and shorter than the molding cutter, was snapping the measuring tape in and out of its casing and smoking a cigarette.

"Oh, hi," he said, flicking the cigarette butt under the nearest rhododendron. "Mrs. . . ." He looked to the other guy for help, but only got a shrug. " . . . Laverne?"

"LaMarche," said Janie. "Who are you?"

"Uh, well, Tug sent us over to finish up here. Won't take long. Day, maybe two. Being as there's two of us." A sly grin came over his face and he looked at the other guy. "And we got no reason to, you know, extend things." A harsh little snort of laughter erupted from his friend. Janie noticed a green tattoo on his freckled fore-arm that read "Greg the Grate."

"Terrific," said Janie, and went into the house. Tug was show-ing her up. Clearly. He wasn't going to just take her money and leave her alone. He'd sent over his most annoying workers to make sure the job was finished—his way. She thought of phon-ing him and telling him to call off his minions, but Carly needed a diaper change and the breakfast dishes were putrefying in the sink, and somehow the phone was never quite handy when she thought of it.

The reassuring sounds of hammering and small motors whir-ring were coming from her porch again, and Janie felt her shoulders slide lower into their sockets. It was disturbing how comforting it was. Damn him. She put Carly down for her midmorning nap and went to empty the dishwasher. The power tools had stopped and by the sound of the hammering overhead, she knew the men were on ladders working on the porch ceiling.

"Jesus, would you look at this?" she heard one of them say. She guessed it was the short dark-skinned one. "Two-by-eights instead of two-by-fours. Thing's built like a brick shit house."

"Fuckin' gold-plated," grunted the other one, Greg-the-self-proclaimed-Grate.

"Took his time, too. He's been here all summer. Coulda thrown it up in about four, five weeks. Less if he'd brought in the crew." A few more slams of the hammer. "You know why, though. You get it, right? He likes the LO-CA-TION. He likes the VIEW."

"What view? Fuckin' street, is all."

"It's those eyes, man, I'm telling you," he crooned. "They're like ice. They're so cold their HOT!"

"What, the lady? She's freaky, Ignacio. She practically back-handed you before she went in."

"That's the best kind!" This was followed by some hoots and some *heh-heh-heh*s and a Jesus! when one of them must have lost his footing for a moment. Finally they started hammering again.

Needing a little space from the two stooges, Janie took a cup of coffee out to the picnic table in the backyard. She brought some children's clothing catalogues with her, knowing that in a month or so the weather would turn cooler, and Dylan had not one pair of pants that fit him anymore. But she flipped through the catalogues without paying much attention.

It had been a while since she'd been assessed for her sex appeal. Or maybe not so long, but being married, with a ring on her finger and a live husband, the attention of other men had always seemed like just so much verbal dust, flying around but having no actual meaning. She still had the ring, but it didn't seem to hold its former powers of filtration. Men ogling women, making assumptions about attractions that had no basis in reality . . . *Standard stuff*, she told herself.

And a gold-plated brick shit house? What was that about?

DYLAN NEGOTIATED AN AFTER-DINNER trip to Dairy Queen in return for putting his own clothes in his own dresser drawers. He was able to accomplish this task with almost no whining and very few stops to play with his toys or lie on his floor with Nubby the Bald Bunny and stare at the ceiling. As Janie had required virtually nothing in the way of helping out from Dylan over the past seven months, she considered it a step in the right direction for both of them.

A disagreement ensued over whether they would do the drive-through or park and wait in line with the hordes of other ice-cream-needy patrons, then dally over their dripping cones at one of the sticky picnic tables nearby. In the interest of a reasonable bedtime, Janie put her foot down, promising to go home the long way as a concession.

The long way took them by Pelham Ball Field where the Men's Over-40 League had pitted the Pelham Stealing Geezers against the Natick Trophy Husbands. Janie's car seemed to slow of its own accord.

And there he was, in a stop-sign-red shirt and gray baseball knickers, hands hanging on the fence near the Geezers' bench, shoulder to shoulder with one of his teammates. The two men conferred momentarily and then burst into laughter. Janie pulled over.

"Why are you stopping? What's this game?" asked Dylan.

"It's softball. Take off your goggles."

By the time she had ushered them out of the car, wiped their sticky hands, and disposed of the cone wrappers, the Stealing Geezers had taken the field. Carrying Carly and holding Dylan's hand, she climbed the stands to an empty spot on the end of the third row. Dylan wanted to sit on the very end of the bench, but since there was no railing, Janie insisted she take the end.

"But it's not high!" whined Dylan. "If I fall off I'll only get a bump or something!"

"Hey, look over there," said Janie to distract him. Dylan followed her finger out to third base. "Who's that guy?"

"It's Tug. That's Tug! He's got a red shirt, like the other guys! HEY TUG!"

He was only about fifty feet away, so his head turned at the sound of his name, soon focusing on the small boy waving and bouncing on the balls of his feet. Tug gave a thumbs-up to Dylan, who threw his two little thumbs into the air in return. Tug's gaze turned to Janie—hard to be sure at that distance, but she knew, all the same—and she gave a little wave. She didn't plan it. It just happened.

Tug smiled back, narrowly missing a pop fly that was generously covered by the left fielder, who'd had to run his hardest toward the infield to make the catch. He gave Tug a friendly whack
in the back of the head with his mitt and trotted back out to left
field.

The Trophy Husbands were not to be trifled with, and gave
the Geezers a solid workout. Toward the end of the inning, Tug
lunged to field a speeding grounder and fired it to first base before
tumbling sideways into the grass. It was a courageous play and
fans in both sets of bleachers jumped to their feet in appreciation.
Janie noticed that he waited for the attention to wane before he
allowed himself to give his shoulder a rub. He glanced up to see
if she was watching, and a barely perceptible grin graced his face
before it was replaced with the standard issue glare toward home
plate.

At the third out, the Geezers jogged toward their bench. Tug
walked past the bench to the stands and greeted Dylan with a
high five. Then he took off his mitt and let Dylan try it on. "Hi,"
he said to Janie. "Passing by?"

"On our way home from Dairy Queen. Thought I'd take the opportunity to talk to you about the crew you sent over."

"Rosencrantz and Guildenstern? They seem like clowns, but
they do good work. You'll see."

"Okay, Shakespearean references aside, you didn't have to
send them."

"I know. But I have your money and I want the job finished
properly. That's only right."

"Malinowski!" called a member of the team. "You're on
deck!"

"We're not finished," she warned him.

"Hold onto that glove," he told Dylan, who cradled it tightly to
his narrow chest.

Tug approached home plate swinging the bat every other
step. The catcher said something to him and he grinned, but

then turned his attention to the pitcher. His body was facing Janie across the plate, which seemed strange until she realized he was batting lefty. *He's left-handed*, she thought, and stored the information as if she might have some occasion to retrieve it. She frowned at herself.

He let a high pitch go by, then swung at the next, fouling it up toward the Geezer stands. Dylan jumped up with Tug's mitt flopping on his hand, but the ball landed in the dirt well in front of them. "Darn it," muttered Dylan. Janie had never heard him use that phrase before. *Must be Keane,* she thought offhandedly, and once again aimed her attention at the batter.

The next pitch was low and outside, and Tug let it pass. Janie glanced at Dylan, the mitt still on his hand, his mouth slightly ajar, his eyes focused intently on the arc of the ball being thrown back to the pitcher. The next pitch was straight down the middle, and Tug's whole body twisted to meet it. The ball sailed high and far, and the crowds stood to see if it would make it past the fence.

"Home run," whispered Dylan desperately.

But the center fielder got his glove under it just before it passed from view, and Tug dropped the bat and walked toward the bench. "You got robbed, man," Janie heard one of his teammates say. Tug picked up a water bottle and tipped back his head as he gulped. Then he walked back to Janie and the kids.

"Why did that guy catch your ball?" asked Dylan.

"Because he could," said Tug.

"Are you sad?"

"I'm a little disappointed, to tell the truth. But I'll just try harder next time. You still got my glove?" Dylan held it up like a trophy. Tug turned to Janie, but said nothing.

"Last week," she started, not entirely sure of where she was headed. "I was . . ." She glanced at Dylan. "I wasn't very well behaved."

"I butted in. It was none of my business."

Janie nodded, then shrugged. "Still." Tug waited for more, his eyes so dark she couldn't see the pupils. What more should she say? "I'm sorry."

Tug smiled, looked away for a moment, then inhaled and turned back. "Me, too," he said. "And I'd really prefer to finish the job myself. If it's alright with you."

The relief she felt at his offer to return, despite the horrible things she'd said—and she knew they had been horrible and mostly unjustified—flooded her brain, making it hard to compose any response other than, "Fine," and a moment later, "Thanks."

The Stealing Geezers were going back to the field, and Dylan reluctantly handed over the glove.

"We'll probably go soon, so I can get you guys to bed," she warned Dylan.

"No!" he whined.

"Don't worry, buddy," said Tug. "I'll see you tomorrow and I'll tell you all about it."

THERE WAS A TINKLING sound, almost like wind chimes, when Janie woke. It levitated her up from a satiny black sleep into the feel of her construction pajamas and the covers pulled over her shoulders. It was cooler, a welcome relief from the tepid puffs of spongy air that she'd come to expect.

The tinkling sound grew louder as she descended the stairs, and it organized itself into voices murmuring to each other outside. *Rosencrantz and Guildenstern-the-Grate*, she thought. But one of the voices was too high, and when she peeked out the kitchen window she saw Tug and Dylan sitting on the mahogany floor of the front porch. Each was eating half a bagel plastered with globs of cream cheese that Tug must have brought with him. There were two sippy cups beside them, and Janie knew without a second thought that they were filled with chocolate milk.

" . . . so the next guy gets up and swings at the first pitch, which isn't always the best idea . . ."

"Why not?"

"Well, because you kind of want to see what the pitcher's going to give you, you know? You want to let him show himself first."

"Why?"

"Uh . . . let's see . . . okay, maybe you were thinking 'This pitcher is really tough. He's only going to throw me curve balls. That's what he does. He's a curve ball pitcher.' But then, you stand there in the batter's box and you look at him. I don't care what anyone tells you, you never know what a pitcher is made of until you're standing in the box, looking down the line at him, eye to eye. And then you watch a pitch. You see just exactly how he stretches back and snaps his arm. You see the look on his face, the way he recovers afterward. That way you know the real guy, not the guy you made up in your mind when you watched him from the bench."

"Ohhhh," said Dylan.

Dylan did not really understand, Janie could tell. But maybe there was some piece of it that he could take away, like don't make snap judgments about people until you know them, or give yourself a moment to think things through before you take a swing. She could use a little remediation in those areas herself, she knew. Or maybe it was just good for Dylan to have the chance to sit with a nice guy and talk sports.

Turn around and make the coffee now, she told herself, *or in about fifteen seconds you'll be in the bathroom with a hand towel over your face.*

JANIE WAS PUSHING CARLY in the baby swing in the backyard when Tug came looking for her. "Hey," he said, "can I get up under your eaves?"

"Sure, why?"

"I just want to check the seam where the new roof meets the old one, make sure there's still no bowing. I might put in a little extra reinforcement just so you don't have trouble down the line."

"How far down the line?"

He chuckled and colored a little. "I don't know, like a hundred years?" He followed her up the stairs into her bedroom, glancing quickly at the muddle of sheets and pillows.

"Okay, so I don't make my bed," Janie said in defense.

"Me either," he said. "Why bother?" Janie leaned down to undo the latch on the three-foot-square door into the eaves, Carly clinging to her like a baby koala bear. "Hey, I can get that," said Tug and squatted down next to her. He yanked open the door as Janie turned to let the squirming girl out of her arms and onto the floor. "What's this?" he asked. When Janie looked back, Tug was holding the collage of pictures that Barb had made of Dylan's birthday pictures. "Why's it in here?"

"Oh, I . . . ," she stammered. "I don't know, I guess I just didn't . . . like it."

"Why not? They're great pictures. This one with the two boys and the pirate's butt is priceless."

"Oh, come on," she said. "You were there. It wasn't exactly the world's happiest party."

"Because your husband wasn't there."

"Yes, my dead husband failed to make an appearance, which I think was pretty obvious by the way we were all sobbing." She couldn't seem to keep herself from saying, "Even you."

"So I shed a tear," he said, narrowing his eyes at her, "it was a sad moment."

"One I don't need to remember every day in dazzling color," she said. Carly was going for the door and Janie scrambled after her, barricading the doorway with her body.

"But what about Dylan?" He was still squatting at the entrance to the eaves. Why wouldn't he just go into the spidery darkness with his little flashlight and leave her alone?

"Jesus, Tug, what are you, his agent? He was sad, too, if you'll take a second to remember. No one was crying harder than him."

"Yeah, but then he was bobbing for apples, and eating too much cake, and having fun. He's okay, Janie."

It blistered her, the way he seemed to think he knew Dylan better than she did. But the look on his face wasn't superior or preachy. He was smiling in that subtle way he had, where you weren't even sure if it was a smile, except that you could feel it. Why was he smiling, for godsake? There was nothing to smile about. "Tug, I swear . . ." she warned. It was the only thing she could come up with to say that wouldn't end with Ignacio and Greg, the dynamic dimwits, on her property again.

"Show it to him," said Tug, the soft little grin still lingering around his eyes. "Let *him* decide." He turned and started into the eaves, but stopped again, then turned and came back out with the other picture in his hands, the one of Janie, Carly, and Dylan sitting in the grass together. Tug knelt on the floor of her bedroom and studied it for several seconds. "Wow." He held it out to her. "Hang it."

DYLAN FOUND THE PICTURES propped against the wall in Janie's room. She hadn't purposely shown them to him, but she hadn't banished them back to spider world either. It was a roll of the dice, she realized, home decor roulette.

He loved the collage. In fact, he spent about twenty minutes trying to decide which picture he liked the best. In the end he couldn't choose, and Janie had to reassure him several times that it was okay to have two favorites, just so he would move along to putting his pajamas on.

"The cake picture is the best because it's like it's back together again, not all broken up in our stomachs." He fingered the glass over the picture enough that Janie knew she'd be taking glass cleaner to it on a regular basis until he outgrew that sense that if he just touched it enough it would become real again. "But the apple one is good, too. Keane is laughing with his lips big like a clown, and I have water dripping all over!"

The pictures really weren't so bad; it had been a mostly good party, after all. She was relieved that Dylan wanted to hang it in his bedroom, however. She wouldn't have to pass by the one with Jake in it quite so often. Dylan took a long look at the other picture of just the three of them. "Was this after we cried?" he asked.

"Before."

He looked back at the collage, to the picture of Tug helping him with the screwdriver. "But this one is after," he said.

"Right."

He turned to the family photo again. "What were you whispering to me?"

"I think I was saying you smelled like peanut butter."

"Because I ate my sandwich with my neck!" he remembered. "That was so silly! Look at me laughing."

"You thought that was pretty funny," she nodded.

"Where should we put it?" he asked looking around her room. "I know! In the kitchen, where that one is of the two people . . ." Dylan wrapped his arms around himself and puckered his lips, as if he were being forced to eat raw squid.

The Gustav Klimt print, Janie realized. *The Kiss*. Robby had given it to her when they were dating. It was a message as big as skywriting to Janie: this is serious. I want you like this guy wants this girl—completely. Opening it on her thirtieth birthday it was the first time she had really allowed herself to think This Is The One. If she hung the photo in its place, where would *The Kiss* go?

"That's not such a good spot," she said to Dylan. "We already have something there. How about if we put this picture of us in the bathroom."

"The bathroom!" Dylan exclaimed with horror. "I don't want everyone looking at me when I poop, Mom!"

She almost said "It's just a picture, Dylan, no one's actually looking at you." But bedtime was long gone by now, and she knew he wasn't going to budge on this no matter how clearly and patiently she explained it. "We'll talk about it tomorrow," she said.

He put on his pajamas and brushed his teeth (the front of them, anyway) while Janie changed Carly's diaper and wrestled her into a clean onesie. Dylan finally climbed into bed. "Thanks for those pictures, Mom," he said.

"Well, actually they're from Cormac and Barb."

"Thanks, Cormac and Barb," he giggled.

IT HAD BEEN A week since Janie's mother had left Pelham and flown home happily (so Janie assumed) to her Tuscan villa. Okay, it was really a small apartment in Turin, but having never seen it, Janie often imagined her mother living in a Shangri-la of ancient splendor and crusty bread. *Easy for her,* was the phrase that came to mind. What exactly was so easy, Janie had never fully identified.

A letter came addressed to Janie alone. Usually Noreen's letters and cards were addressed to Carly and Dylan, with Janie's name added as an apparent afterthought. The text of those letters was directed toward the children, not Janie. When she saw the blue aero-mail envelope in the stack of catalogues, sale notices, and house-painting flyers, a funny feeling came over her. It was part excitement; finally her name had been culled from the others to receive a beam of motherly attention. And it was part dread.

What could you possibly be worried about? she chided herself as she walked the mail into the house. After all, Janie wasn't the one who'd left her daughter high and dry after the briefest possible mourning period. And she wasn't the one who decided to spend the summer in fucking Naples, Italy, instead of boring, sad old Pelham, Massachusetts. And she CERTAINLY wasn't the one who sent her daughter's only true friend packing.

Though the temperature had climbed into the high seventies, Janie braced herself with a hot steaming cup of Sumatran Java and sat down at the kitchen table with the letter. *My Dearest Janie,* it began. Dearest Janie rolled her eyes.

I'm on the plane back to Europe now. We should be landing
at Heathrow in about three hours. Then I'll make my connect-
ing flight to Rome and take a taxi to the bus station. The bus is
much cheaper than a flight to Turin.

Janie knew what she was doing. It was her mother's private
rosary, reciting her itinerary as a kind of prayer to Saint Christopher, the patron saint of travelers. He supposedly earned his
saintly stripes by carrying people across a raging river. Noreen
was just looking for a safe place to cross.

I know you're not happy with me for speaking to Father Jake. I
want to apologize for any embarrassment or sadness that I may
have caused in doing so. And I will admit that I am not entirely
sure if I've done the right thing. I thought about it for a long
time, and I came to the conclusion that, while neither one of you
would intentionally "go the wrong way," neither did you seem
to understand how easily that could have happened.

A mother does everything in her power to shelter her children from harm. I have always tried to live by that. And perhaps
I spent so much time looking out for Mike, I didn't worry much
about you until now. But a mother's worries don't end at adulthood. You'll see. You're very protective. If I've done the wrong
thing, as I've said, I apologize. Maybe it seems like the wrong
thing now, but will have been the right thing once time passes.

We're over the open ocean now. There are no clouds, so even
though we're up very high, I can still look down past the wing
of the plane and see the dark blue water beneath. There doesn't
seem to be anything else on this earth but water! But I know
there must be, because you're out there. You're in my old house
in Pelham, and now you're living a life that is very much like
mine was, alone with two small children.

The pain I feel about your having to live my life is overwhelming. I've always prayed so fervently that you would have

more opportunities, more excitement, more love. And since
January it's seemed like all those prayers were just funny jokes
to God. He didn't take me seriously. Or maybe He never even
heard them in the first place.

I worked so hard. For what? So you could be the me I left
behind? So you could take my place at the table, eating franks
and beans with Jude on Saturday nights? Venturing no farther
than Jansen Woods or Town Beach?

I am deeply ashamed of myself for staying away. A child
needs her mother when tragedy strikes. And yet, my dearest
girl, I simply couldn't watch you turn into me. The old pain
overtook me and made me run. I told myself that my misery
would compound yours, not lighten it. I'm too sensitive, I know.
(Hasn't Jude told me so a thousand times!) I hope someday
you'll forgive me.

There is something I've been meaning to ask you since January, but never saw the right moment. Here, over the ocean, I feel
I can say it. Would you ever consider coming to live in Italy? I
could get you a part-time job at the American School. The children would be so happy, and we could travel every summer. It's
such a happy life, sweetheart, and I want to share it with you.

Please consider this opportunity. I know it may seem a little
outlandish, but think it through. It would be an answer to all
those prayers I've been saying to a God who didn't seem to
listen.

All my love,
Mum

16

⚊

Weird letter from Mum. Said the reason she basically abandoned me this year is because she couldn't bear to watch me turn into her. Am I her? Is that what happened?

It made me think of that homeless guy Malcolm. The only person he ever cared about and felt safe with in this world is dying, and he can't even be with her. All he has is the memory of his hand in hers and the promise of being reunited when they're dead. I may be a self-pitying, miserable nerve-jangled freak, but at least I recognize that he has it way worse than me. Mum would never make it in the soup kitchen biz.

She wants me and the kids to come live with her in Italy. I guess it's an option if I ever permanently dismantle my life here, which was actually starting to happen last week. Always good to have a backup plan when Pology Cookies lose their magical powers.

Speaking of which, Dylan has a playdate with Keane today. At Keane's house. Or possibly they'll hop a flight to Disneyworld if Heidi gets it into her head they need a little something extra. (Keep those cookie sheets ready for action, chickie, as Cormac would say.) Speaking of Cormac . . . blah. I know. I need to do something. No brainstorms yet.

*Tug's out there staining the porch. He gave me way too
many details about what colors he was going to put where and
how and when and why, and the names were all like "honey
oak" and "chocolate mahogany" and "fish sticks and a bag of
chips birch." Someone in the stain company marketing department was hungry, is all I can think. I kind of stopped listening.
But it was nice sit there and have someone to drink my coffee
with.*

HEIDI RETURNED DYLAN HOME from the playdate ten minutes early,
which was just about when Janie realized she was checking the
clock about every thirty seconds, and she was grateful for the
reprieve from this compulsion. His face was painted with a wispy
goatee and a black patch over one eye.

"I did it with eyeliner," explained Heidi. "In the kitchen, at
home," she added purposefully. "It'll come off with a little makeup
remover."

Like I have makeup remover, thought Janie. But she nodded and
admired her surly-looking swabby, and responded "Avast ye!" to
his "Argh!" Dylan wasn't allowed on the porch with all the cans
of stain sitting around waiting to be spilled, so he contented himself with fighting bad guys in the front yard and doing the play-
by-play on his activities through the screen to Tug.

"There's another one . . . there's two bad scary pirates now, but
I am fighting them very hard . . . *fyoo, fyoo, fyooooo!* My sword is
all fire . . . You bad pirates . . . don't come in my house and scare
my mom . . . she is very brave and she will punch you in the nose
so all your blood comes out . . ."

Tug leaned close to the kitchen window and said, "Janie, come
listen to this."

She had been staring into the refrigerator, hoping to be inspired. Actually she'd been hoping that an entire meal had magically appeared in there, complete with drinks and after-dinner

mints. She closed the fridge and turned toward the window, but never heard Dylan. What she focused on was the Ford Explorer in her driveway with "Cormac's Confectionary" written on the door panel.

Janie glanced from the truck to *The Kiss* on the kitchen wall. She slid it off its hook. Another quick look told her Cormac was now swashbuckling with Dylan, and he would have to come all the way around to the back door to avoid being spattered with stain. This gave her just enough time to rush up the stairs and back down again before she would have to greet him.

"Hey, chickie," he said as he came in, and she rose from the chair into which she had just planted herself seconds before. He seemed tired, and there was something about the particular way a smudge of flour clung to his temple that made her notice how his hairline was receding.

"Hey," she said. "What's going on?"

"Brought you some day-old muffins. Mixed variety, except no banana almond. For some reason everyone was in a banana kind of mood today." He reached up to the top of her cabinet and brought down the blue-flowered plate. "Needs a wipe," he said. It was covered with a fine layer of sawdust.

"I haven't used it much lately," she said, and ran the plate under warm water. She wiped it and put it on the table. Cormac laid out the muffins. "OJ?" she asked.

"You know it," he said. She nearly spilled the juice watching to see when he would notice. He pulled the top off a muffin and opened his mouth. And stopped. "You hung it!" he said.

"Yeah, it's nice." She turned to put the juice away, smiling to herself at having surprised him.

"You hate it."

"No, I never said I hated it. I said I had to get used to it."

"You said it was the worst birthday of Dylan's life."

"Well, it was. So far. He'll probably have worse ones. Like that birthday of yours when you hitchhiked all the way up to Colgate to see that girl that you thought you had something going with, and she only pecked you on the cheek when she saw you, and you turned around and tried to hitch back but you couldn't get a ride. Didn't you spend like eighteen hours on the road that day? That was definitely worse than Dylan's."

They ate muffins, and Carly showed off her new vertical skills, and Dylan came in complaining of a yucky taste in his mouth, having smeared eyeliner onto his lips. A pineapple coconut muffin turned out to be the perfect antidote (after Janie scrubbed his face with a washcloth. "What, no makeup remover?" teased Cormac.)

Tug's face appeared behind the screen of the kitchen window. "I'm taking off," he said.

"You'll be back tomorrow?" asked Janie.

"Yeah, the floor's not done yet."

"Want a muffin?" asked Cormac. "There's plenty."

Tug didn't respond immediately. He looked to Janie, and the eye contact went on a little too long.

"Come in," she said, turning away to give a piece of corn muffin to Carly, now seated on Cormac's lap. What was Tug waiting for, anyway?

When he appeared in the kitchen a moment later, she could see a tiny splatter of stain on his left cheek like a constellation of freckles. He offered a handshake to Cormac. "Tug Malinowski."

"Cormac McGrath, Janie's cousin. You were at Dylan's party, right?" Cormac steadied the baby on his lap with one hand and shook with the other. "Nice job out there, by the way. Not too many contractors will paint."

"I don't mind," said Tug, giving Janie a quick glance and seating himself in the chair next to her.

Cormac pushed the plate of muffins toward Tug. "Try the pistachio," he smiled. "Janie's favorite."

Barb's collage of party pictures had been hung in Dylan's bedroom in a place of honor over his collection of camp art projects.

Cormac was urged upstairs to admire it, Carly dangling from one floury hip and Dylan from the other.

Janie and Tug had sat alone together at the kitchen table any number of times over the previous months, going over the porch plans, discussing changes, and sometimes just sitting there drinking coffee. But now Janie felt a certain unrest, perhaps because Cormac was in the house, and she had the strange sensation of being watched.

"What happened to the other picture?" Tug asked. His voice was quiet, as usual, and yet it seemed to bounce off the creamy yellow walls of the kitchen. "The one with the couple kissing."

"Oh, I just put it in my closet. I guess I'll hang it when I figure out where it should go."

"I can hang it for you."

A quick smile. "I know I'm not exactly Bob the Builder, but I can manage something that minor. I should probably find a book on home maintenance, though. Remember when you helped me with the gutters? I was making such a mess of it." She shook her head and nibbled at her muffin.

He nodded, remembering. "You weren't too bad for a rookie. Most of this stuff isn't astrophysics, you'll pick it up. And you can always call me if you get in a tough spot."

Call him? Like on the phone, not out the window? "Tomorrow's your last day, isn't it?"

"Pretty much. Once the floor's stained, the job's done." He pulled off a piece of his muffin and dabbed at the crumbs sprinkled around his napkin, but he didn't complete the action by putting it into his mouth. He put the piece down, then picked it up again and dabbed some more.

TUG LEFT, ALREADY A few minutes late, he explained, for softball pregame warm-ups, a practice that was once incidental but was now necessary for muscles that didn't leap from rest to action like they used to. He made a mildly self-deprecating joke of it, but Janie could sense both regret at his being forced to coddle a now-less-cooperative body and also pride at getting out there nonetheless. She noticed his ropy forearm tighten as he grasped the napkin and muffin remnants and released them to the trash basket. The scar on his arm had ripened from an irritable pink to a resigned tan color over the time she had known him.

Cormac, Carly, and Dylan straggled back down the stairs together, Cormac now holding not only the baby but a Popsicle stick structure that Dylan had given him. They plunked back down at the table and went for another round of muffins, Cormac eating only the top, as usual.

"Why do you just eat the tops?" asked Dylan.

"It's my favorite part. I like to save my stomach room for the stuff I like the best," said Cormac. He glanced at Janie. "And speaking of what I like best . . . I have some big news." Janie felt her own stomach clench, as if it were awaiting a death-defying drop into unknown territory.

"What?" said Dylan, bouncing in his chair. "What is it?"

"Barb and I are getting married."

A sound escaped Janie's open mouth, part gasp, part synthesized happiness.

"At a wedding?" asked Dylan. "With a cake?"

"Cake will definitely be involved," said Cormac, his eyes on Janie as he transferred Carly, now reaching for the muffin plate, to the other knee. His head tipped one notch to the side. "Chickie," he said. "You up for it?"

Don't be a jerk, she told herself. *Right now. Stop being a jerk.* She reached her hand up to the back of his head and into his hair, grasping it and giving it an affectionate tug. "Yup," she nodded, "Definitely." She leaned over and kissed him on the cheek. "Cormac's getting married!" she said to Dylan.

"I know, Mom," said Dylan, wagging his head at her. "He already told me."

THE SALE PENDING SHINGLE seemed to have grown out of the top of Shelly's For Sale sign overnight, like a whitewashed weed. Janie noticed it as she backed out of the driveway to take Dylan to his last day of camp. She was still getting used to the news that Cormac, the perennial Happy Bachelor, had suddenly folded his tent and moved to another campground, or so it felt. Also, it was her second Jake-less Friday, and though she had so far resisted the urges she felt to contact him, or even just to drive by Our Lady, Comforter of the Afflicted Church hoping for a glimpse of him, Fridays were particularly hard. Everything seemed to be ending.

The bathtub, streaked with many days of boy grime, needed scrubbing, and the vacuum had nestled quietly in its closet for too long, but Janie felt limp and lonely and sat in the open doorway to the porch, watching Tug stain the remaining few boards of her mahogany—not pine—floor.

"You know why my cousin came over yesterday?" she said. "To tell me he's getting married."

"When?" asked Tug, carefully guiding the stain-soaked rag along the grain. It was Australian Timber Oil, he had told her, a special formulation. She couldn't have cared less.

"New Year's Eve. Can you beat that?"

"A buddy of mine got married the day my wife had me served with divorce papers. I was one of the groomsmen. Had to smile for the pictures and everything."

"Did you?"

"Sure. What choice did I have? Can't ruin another guy's wedding just because your own marriage crashed and burned."

"She served you?" asked Janie, tentatively. So far she had no data that Tug was anything other than . . . well, than not-a-bad-guy. Shelly trusted him. And Janie couldn't ever remember him doing anything wrong or mean. Annoying, intrusive, and over-bearing, yes, but not actually bad. However, she didn't really trust her own powers of observation these days. Her instincts had been haywire, scrambled like some sort of foreign military intelligence signal, since Robby's death.

"Yep," he said. "She served me."

Janie got the feeling that if she asked him for further information, he would give it. But, scrambled though she felt she was, she understood that divorce details were a whole new level of interaction—at least for her. Maybe he was used to recounting the grisly scenes of his marriage to whoever hired him to build so much as a doghouse. Perhaps it was how divorced people washed the bad taste out of their mouths, by talking to strangers who wouldn't know any better if the story were spun, here and there, to the teller's advantage. Did Janie really want to up the ante with this guy, who was likely just passing the last few moments of his employment with her by smoothing out the lumps of his prior bad behavior? She got up to refresh her coffee.

The dishwasher had finished its cycle, and she unloaded the steaming-hot glasses and plates to their assigned places in the cabinets. She scrubbed a solidified spot of ketchup off the side of the refrigerator. She straightened the napkins in the blue ceramic napkin holder. Tug's wife served *him* divorce papers? Returning to lean in the doorway, Janie asked, "She beat you to it?"

It had been some number of minutes since the conversation had abruptly ended with her departure to dawdle in the kitchen, but Tug picked it up as if it had been a matter of seconds. "No, I was hoping we could hold it together. But Sue was done. She made it pretty clear."

Janie remained standing in the doorway, paralyzed by indecision as to whether she would sit back down, ask any further questions, change the subject, or resume her meandering patrol of the kitchen, searching for semi-pointless tidying activities.

Tug glanced up at her from his crouch on the mahogany planks. "I don't have any real need to go into it," he said, "but I'll tell you if you're interested. As long as you're not just being polite."

She felt silly, but in a sort of comfortable way. "You know me," she said. "Polite isn't really the first adjective that leaps to mind." A burst of laughter came from deep in his chest, and his head went back, his eyes nearly closed. It was a surprised, tickled kind of laugh and it satisfied something in Janie that she didn't even know was hungry. It made her laugh, too. "Well, it's true!" she said.

"I'd have to agree with you there," he nodded, still grinning at her. It should have been insulting but it just wasn't. "Listen," he said. "I forgot my cooler, and I was going to do takeout at Carey's Diner. You and Carly should meet me there and we'll have a nice lunch to celebrate your porch."

CAREY'S DINER WAS NOT really a diner, and the Carey family hadn't owned it since the 1980s. A local named Mel Gunther had bought it and upgraded it to a café motif, with sponged yellow walls and European-looking pottery displayed in folksy clusters on the walls. In back, overlooking the parking lot, he had installed a brick patio with glass and wrought-iron tables shaded by large green canvas umbrellas. Mr. Gunther had toyed with changing the name of the diner to something slightly more urbane; however he noted quite shrewdly that the steady stream of his customer-neighbors had taken nearly six months to stop commenting on how much the diner had changed. For the better, he hoped they meant, but they never used explicitly positive phrasing. It was better—he knew it was. All they seemed to notice, though, was that it was different from what they were used to.

"So is Dylan going to kindergarten?" asked Tug, glancing up from his menu. They were seated on the patio where the shade made the heat feel merely summery, rather than oppressive.

"No," said Janie.

"He could go, though. He's five."

"Yeah, he could go," said Janie. "But since his birthday's in August, he'd be the youngest kid in the class, and I just didn't think another year of preschool would be the worst thing."

"It's a big step, kindergarten," Tug nodded, studying the menu again. "Whole new world."

"You're talking about me now, aren't you?"

He gave a quick shrug, "Partly. I'm agreeing with you, you know. Neither of you needs something else to get used to right now."

The waitress, a middle-aged woman in a white polo shirt, which was stuffed into the elasticized waistband of her khaki pants, hurried over to the table. "Hi, Rena," said Tug. "How's it going?"

"Oh, Tug, hi!" she panted. Her pitted skin and noisy inhalations made Janie think she must be a heavy smoker. "Didn't recognize you with your new friends, here! Such a little sweetie girl!" she said, giving the baby a chuck under the chin. "What's your name, honey?"

"That's Carly," said Tug patiently, "and this is her mother, Janie."

"Oh!" said Rena, grinning a little too broadly.

"I just finished some construction at their house, so we thought we'd celebrate."

"Well, that's wonderful! What a generous employer!" Rena nodded at Janie, who looked startled.

"I'll have the turkey club," Tug said quickly, "fruit instead of fries, and a chocolate milk. Janie?" She ordered a spinach salad, and Rena scurried away.

"Hey," Janie said, taking a jar of baby food out of her purse. "You actually like chocolate milk?"

"Absolutely," said Tug. "Who doesn't?"

"I don't know, I just never heard anyone over the age of twelve order it at a restaurant before."

"Their loss."

They chatted about the diner and how things in general had changed over the years. Tug had grown up in Natick, the next town over, but had inherited the cottage his grandfather had built on the shore of Lake Pequot here in Pelham. He had gutted and rebuilt it himself when he'd moved back from Worcester almost a year ago. He liked that only two pairs of hands had ever worked on the house—his grandfather's and his. Janie told him about buying the house she'd grown up in, and her mother's now apparent disaffection for the place. She even told him about the letter, and her mother's offer to have Janie move to Italy with her.

"You're not going, though," said Tug. "I mean, does that even appeal to you?"

"A little, it does. You know, it's Italy, so that's pretty interesting. And the kids are young enough to make the transition. And we wouldn't be surrounded by so many reminders of what we've lost." She fed Carly strained carrots, sliding the rubberized spoon around the messy little chin to wipe up the overflow. "But when I actually think about going, I can't imagine it. Everything we know is here. And . . . I don't know . . . I just like that house. My mother thinks I've turned into her, but I don't feel like her. I don't feel trapped. I feel a lot of other miserable things, but not that. And I'm pretty sure misery is portable, so in the end, moving doesn't really solve anything."

He looked at her for a moment.

"What?" She swiped a hand across her mouth in case some vestige of her salad had detoured.

"Nothing. It's just you're pretty clearheaded for someone who thinks she's such a wreck."

"I have moments of clarity," she said. "But, trust me, they're brief." It was a nice compliment, though. And even though she didn't really believe it, she retained it, tucking it away to remember later, in private. She changed the subject. "Why the fruit?" she asked as he popped a grape in his mouth. "You drink chocolate milk, but fries are a little too adolescent?"

"Nah," he said. "Fried food slows you down. In my line of work I have to stay nimble. Doesn't help much on the ball field, either." He sliced a grape into quarters. "Can she have them?" he asked, nodding at Carly.

"Oh . . . uh, I haven't given her grapes, yet . . . and I can't re-member when that's supposed to be okay," she stammered. "With Dylan I was so on top of stuff like that."

"She'll be fine as long as they're cut up."

"How do you know?"

"We babysat my nieces all the time when they were little. The younger one would eat as many grapes as you'd give her. Man, those were some nasty diapers. I didn't make that mistake too often!"

They watched as Carly studied the grape sections, pinching one tightly between her thumb and forefinger and taking it to her lips. She rolled it around in her mouth, gnashing at it with her mostly toothless gums, then swallowed. Immediately she went back for another.

Tug smiled. "Better get to the market and pick up some grapes. Bigger diapers might be a good idea, too."

They finished up the last bites of lunch. Rena brought over the bill and handed it to Janie.

"That's for me," Tug said, taking it from Janie's hands.

"Oh, sorry!" trilled Rena. "My mistake!"

"I'll pay my part," said Janie.

"I invited you." He quickly tucked a credit card into the plas-tic folder and handed it back to Rena. "Besides, I'll write it off as a business expense. 'Lunch with client.' "

"Am I still a client?" she asked. "All the work is done."

"You are until I pay this bill."

In the parking lot the heat engulfed them, rising off the asphalt like vaporized tar. Janie started her car to get the air conditioner running, and put the baby in her seat. Tug was giving her final in-structions about letting the stain dry for twenty-four hours before stepping on it or placing any furniture. *Furniture?* she thought. It hadn't even occurred to her that she'd need to put something out there once it was built. And who would help her decide what to buy? Tug would be long gone. She stared at his face, which had grown so familiar to her, as if he were now part of her house, like a door or a post that was always there. Except that he would not be there, perhaps ever again. His lips were moving, but she wasn't making any sense of what came out of them.

"So . . . ," he said, with dismaying finality. "Thanks for hiring me."

"I didn't," she responded dumbly. "Robby did."

"True," he said, squinting away for a moment. "Well, thanks for rehiring me, then."

It was a joke, but Janie couldn't find the humor. "Thanks for everything, Tug," she said quickly, before her chin began to tremble. "Really, it's great." She got in the car and drove home.

17

FRIDAY, AUGUST 31

It's been a long week. No camp, and school doesn't start till next Tuesday, so Dylan hasn't had much to occupy him. He was wearing his goggles all day every day, until I finally couldn't take it anymore. I told him he could wear them an hour in the morning and an hour before dinner. He whines for them at odd times during the day, which is even more annoying than having to look at him with the stupid goggles on, but I had to draw a line somewhere.

I took him and Keane to Town Beach yesterday. They must have raced in and out of the water six zillion times, throwing their little bodies around like they were made of Silly Putty. And Dylan didn't ask for the goggles even once! At the beach, for godsake!

It's been so quiet around here. No banging. No requests to change the roofline from basic triangle to geodesic dome or anything. I found Dylan sitting on the new porch one afternoon (goggles on, of course) right where he and Tug had been talking baseball that time. Just sitting there. When he saw me he took the goggles off, but he didn't get up. He's only a little boy, but sometimes there seems to be an ache inside him that's grown-up sized. Or maybe it's more of a reflection of my own ache. Which seems to be getting worse, not better. So much for the healing effects of time.

Aunt Jude hijacked me yesterday and took me back to the soup kitchen. Beryl wasn't there—en route to parts unknown, I guess. Malcolm was, though, and this time he wrote to his sister's son, mostly to give instructions. Make sure she has enough root beer and don't let her be alone too much, stuff like that.

Then he talked about how Mary Alice loved beach roses, always picked them whenever there was a rare trip to the ocean when they were young. Malcolm guessed that his nephew didn't know this. He said kids only know what they need to know about their mothers, like how much trouble they'll get in if they get caught pinching cigarettes from the drugstore. But they don't pay too much attention to the things that give "some small comfort against the daily heartache of motherhood." He had no idea of what might have consoled his own poor mother, and wished he had. The bitter tenderness of this comment has stayed with me all day.

Malcolm asked whether Oregon even had beach roses, and if so, did Oregon have the same seasons as we do here in Massachusetts, where it is now summer. (Clearly didn't pay too much attention in geography class, but as I get to know him, I can see that he may have been dealing with much tougher issues than whether Oregon, though part of North America, might nonetheless be in the Southern Hemisphere.) In any case, if it happened to be summer there on the West Coast, Malcolm asked his nephew to go to the beach and pick some roses for Mary Alice.

There were backup suggestions, like, if not, grab some regular old roses from a neighbor's yard, but do it just before sunrise when people sleep the deepest, so he'd be less likely to get caught. I wondered if I should be typing instructions for petty larceny, but I looked to Aunt Jude and her eyes weren't blinking fast, like they do when she gets worked up, but were soft and sad, so I figured it was a go.

Beach roses. Comfort against the heartache of motherhood.

AFTER CHURCH AT IMMACULATE Conception in Natick, Dylan begged to go to Cormac's for a cupcake, and Aunt Jude was no help. "Get the boy a cupcake," she whispered to Janie, but loud enough for Dylan to hear her and take heart. "You want him to like church, don't you?"

"How is going to Cormac's for cupcakes going to make him like church, for godsake?"

"He associates it with something nice, for *goodness'* sake," said Aunt Jude, raising those over-penciled eyebrows in such a way that almost made Janie laugh.

Janie was not ready to bump into Barb yet, but she realized that bumping was inevitable, given their constant proximity, and given that soon they would actually be . . . related. But Barb wasn't there when they came through the heavy glass door of the confectionary. Janie was annoyed at how relieved she felt. *What are you—twelve?* she scolded herself.

They were greeted by Cormac, and the sight of a cookie flying through the door of the kitchen behind him, and Uncle Charlie's unmistakable "GodDAMN this goddamned thing!"

"*Eeeeasy* Charlie," came a woman's voice. "It's a spatula, not a snow shovel."

Cormac rolled his eyes. "He's a gross motor guy in a fine motor world."

ON LABOR DAY, UNCLE Charlie threw his annual cookout. He invited his old buddies from the dump, and, with encouragement tinged with blackmail from Aunt Brigid, the employees of Cormac's Confectionary, his "new place of business." The blackmail to which Aunt Brigid vaguely referred had something to do with a picture of Charlie from their younger days, possibly doing something not-so-masculine. Janie and Cormac peppered her with questions, but she locked her lips and threw the imaginary key over her shoulder.

Of course Barb came, too. Janie was fairly certain that Cormac had relayed the fact that her pictures were now prominently displayed. Half the apology had been delivered. It was the other half, the face-to-face, let's-all-be-friends-now part that made Janie itch.

It had been tempting to arrive late and, with the proximity of other guests for cover, whip off a quick, "Sorry about the last time I saw you, I was having a bad day." But Janie knew it was spineless and relied shamelessly on Barb's pitying the poor widow.

When Janie entered the McGrath kitchen with a platter of veggies and Carly on her opposite hip, Aunt Brigid and Barb had just finished shaping spiced ground beef into burgers. She greeted them both with quick kisses on their cheeks and asked how the preparations were going.

Barb turned to scrub her hands in the sink, looking self-consciously out the window at Uncle Charlie and Cormac who were carrying a picnic table, each attempting to walk to a different spot. When she had dried her hands, she turned to Janie. Her look was unmistakable. It said, *I may streak my hair to an alarming degree, and I may pay too much attention to my accessories, and I may seem like a lightweight in every category you can come up with. But I am here. And I am in it for the long haul. And I am not putting up with any crap from you, no matter what you've been through.* Or so it seemed to Janie. An act of consequence was required.

Janie told Barb, "Carly has something to show you." She stood Carly on the floor, and said, "Go get Barb! Go get your new auntie!" Seeming to sense the importance of this particular performance, Carly stormed toward Barb, arms outstretched, a slender thread of drool escaping from her openmouthed smile. The women erupted into applause as Barb caught her up and covered her soft cheeks with congratulatory kisses. Barb's nod to Janie indicated the peace offering had been accepted.

Later in the afternoon, while Cormac was spinning Dylan around by his arms, and Carly was asleep on Barb's shoulder, Janie told her, "The pictures are beautiful. Sorry I was such an ass."

Barb's gratified smile belied her casual, "You just needed to get used to them."

"I appreciate your giving me some slack," said Janie. "But don't give me too much."

"Don't you worry about that," said Barb, rubbing her cheek against the baby's black hair.

Cormac had been conscripted, as was tradition, to bake a cake for the Labor Day bash. In years past there had been cakes made in the shapes of dump equipment (like the giant trash compactor), cakes made with the likenesses of retiring employees, and one memorable cake decorated with favorite quotes. These included: "Stevie, get that pile over there. Oh, wait. That's Bob"; "Where's the Take It or Leave It for naughty children?"; "Smells like my wife's Baked Bean and Cauliflower Supreme"; and the perennial favorite, "Do I need a dump sticker if I'm only taking things home?"

This year, when the cake was brought out of hiding, it had been fashioned in the shape of a huge, muscular arm, flexing its bicep. Grasped in the fisted hand was an oversized chocolate chip cookie. Uncle Charlie groaned. His dump buddies made merciless fun of him. One of Cormac's baker ladies gave him a little pat on the shoulder and said, "Welcome to hell, big guy."

BY EARLY EVENING, CARLY had been awake long enough to be sleepy again, and Dylan's icing-sticky cheeks were drooping with fatigue. Janie gathered up the kids and the diaper bag and the empty veggie platter and loaded the car. The drive home led them past Pelham Ball Field, where the Pelham Stealing Geezers were playing some new opponent.

Dylan perked up at the sight of the red shirts. "Is that Tug's team? Is Tug playing?"

"He might be," said Janie. "I'm not sure." She, too, had scanned the Geezers bench for Tug, but was too far away to make out one player from another.

"Can we stop? I want to watch the game!" insisted Dylan, removing his goggles for a better view.

"No, honey, we need to get to bed. Tomorrow's the first day of school, remember?"

"But I want to see Tug."

"I know, and we'll see him sometime," said Janie. Feeling compelled to adjust his expectations so he wouldn't be let down, she added, "Dylan, Tug doesn't come to our house anymore. He was only there to build the porch, and it's all done now."

"Is he still our friend?"

"Well, I guess," she said. "But it's not like it used to be."

Dylan put his goggles back on and rode silently home.

THE COFFEE WAS BREWING by 5:45 the next morning. The entire family had been awake since 5:30, fluttering and scurrying as if they had three and a half minutes, not hours, to get ready for school. Dylan decided that he didn't like his *Clifford the Big Red Dog* backpack anymore, and Janie had to dig through the eaves for an old backpack from her camping days. By the time she found it, Carly was hopping around in her crib, screeching to be fed.

Janie felt the need to give the kids something hearty for breakfast, so instead of Rice Krispies and apple slices, it was scrambled eggs and turkey bacon, which seemed to take ages to get crisp. Dylan loaded his lunch box and emergency clothing bag into the old backpack, said it smelled funny, and wanted his Clifford backpack back. Somehow three and a half hours flew by, as they managed their excitement and trepidation by doing everything the hard way.

Dylan was not with Miss Marla this year; he was in the pre-kindergarten class with Miss Sharon, who was known for being very good at getting kids ready for kindergarten. Miss Sharon

was big on self-help skills. Her students zipped their own jackets
and were responsible for making sure their artwork made it to
their own cubbies. The word in the parking lot, where minivans
vied for the choicest spots, and where mothers and nannies lingered before speeding off to the supermarket, workplace, or gym,
was that Miss Sharon was a hard-ass.

"What's my teacher's name again?" asked Dylan. "Keane's in
my class, right?" as he skip-walked toward the front door. Janie
had answered these and 150 other questions all the way to school,
so she knew he was just talking for talking's sake. *Maybe questions are a child's rosary,* she mused.

"Dylan, you had a nice breakfast, and you have all your stuff,
and your teacher, Miss Sharon, will take good care of you. Keane
will be there, and I'll pick you up after lunch just like I always do.
Okay, sweetie? It's all going to be great, so let's just get in there
and check it out."

And it was great. Miss Sharon had put out all the best art supplies and blocks and dress-ups. The room was organized down to
the last Magic Marker cap. She greeted each child and parent as
if they were visiting dignitaries. She had warmth and enthusiasm
and competence down pat. First day of school was a Fourth of July
clambake for Miss Sharon.

"Parents," she called to the milling adults, "don't forget to send
in a picture for our Here's My Family bulletin board. It helps to
see those familiar faces when we're learning to transition!"

Learning to transition, thought Janie. *Now there's a class I
should audit.*

Dylan clung to Janie like a barnacle for the first five minutes,
then his grasp slowly released until he was only holding her finger. Even before Keane blew in with Heidi, Dylan was waving to
kids he knew from last year, and leaning toward the sensory table
filled with shaving cream and Matchbox cars. "Okay," said Janie,
when his little fingers let go completely. "Have a ton of fun and I'll
see you at pickup. Love you, Dylan."

"Love you, Mom," and he was off.

Janie dawdled at the sign-in desk, waiting for Heidi to say good-bye to Keane. It took a minute or two, because Heidi had to catch him before she could kiss him. When they walked out together, Janie asked, "So what are you going to do about the picture?"

"I have no idea," groaned Heidi. "I suppose I could manage to stand next to that philandering doofus long enough for someone to snap a photo. But what does that say to Keane? I don't want him to feel like we're covering something up—or worse—that we might actually get back together." She nudged Janie with her elbow. "You'll use a copy of that one Barb took of the three of you at Dylan's birthday party, right?"

"I guess," said Janie.

"Why wouldn't you? It's gorgeous."

"I don't know . . ." Carly wriggled to get down and Janie let her walk, holding her hand to keep her from inevitable trips and spills. "It's just kind of out there, I guess. Hey, look at us, no daddy."

Heidi gave a sympathetic shrug. "We are what we are," she said. It was no practical help, but it gave Janie a sense of not being alone in the matter. She was about to ask Heidi if she had time to grab a cup of coffee when Heidi glanced at her watch, gave a wilted little shriek, and broke into a jog toward her station wagon, calling good-bye to Janie over her shoulder. Janie went home.

Carly was in the process of dropping her morning nap, a fact that tapped its watch at Janie, reminding her once again that milestones don't wait for mothers to be ready. The changing naptime flustered Janie, making it hard to plan when to be home and when she and Carly could be out somewhere. Not that she had anywhere important to go. This morning, however, since Carly had already been up for almost half a day, she conked out on the car ride home.

Janie transferred her to the crib, poured the last dregs of coffee into a mug, and carried a kitchen chair out to the new porch. She had intended to simply enjoy the view, but found herself scanning the porch itself, noticing details she had overlooked amidst the clouds of sawdust and smell of stain.

The walls that extended out from the house were each composed of two five-foot-wide panels of mesh screens, separated by cedar posts. The front wall was made of three such panels. The leaves of the red maple in the front yard were still, yet Janie could feel a subtle current of air around her. This porch would be cool even on the hottest days.

The back wall, which extended from the far end of the kitchen by the driveway to the other side of the front door, had been paneled in beaded fir and stained (Janie was surprised she had retained this detail) in "butterscotch maple." The rotted house shingles that Robby had intended to keep were long gone, now probably buried under several months of garbage in the town dump. The great majority of any civilization ended up in its own dump, Uncle Charlie liked to say.

The vaulted ceiling of the porch had also been finished in beaded fir, but was stained a slightly darker color. ("Caramel chestnut"? Or was she making that up?) It loomed fifteen feet high, crossed by three cedar beams that matched the uprights. The ceiling was studded with an antiquey wood-slatted ceiling fan, the light like a broad sepia-toned bowl in the center. Had she picked that out? Sort of. Tug had pointed to it in a catalogue and she'd agreed. Acquiesced? Did it matter?

Possibly the best feature was the screened door that led to the yard. It was wooden with some delicate scroll accents in the corners, and sat diagonally across the corner where the lawn met the driveway. It added a touch of the uncommon and kept the room from feeling boxy. Two broad mahogany steps led down to the yard.

The porch was beautiful, she had to admit. Simple, artistic, somehow cozy despite its openness. It needed furniture, maybe a rocking chair or two. Things that would defer to the porch as the main attraction. A lamp so she could sit out here in the evening and read. Or just sit.

Thanks, Robby, she thought. *Thanks for my birthday or Mother's Day present, or whatever you meant this to be. Thanks for starting something beautiful before you left. Thanks for all the times you thought of me, considered what I would want, put my needs before your own. So many times. Such a good man. Thank you.*

CARLY SLEPT AND SLEPT. Janie had lost all sense of time when she saw the white truck pull into the driveway. Tug's arm rested on the open window, then raised to greet her. He climbed the steps onto the porch with a long flat box, grinning at her on the lone chair with the empty coffee mug on the floor beside her. "Thinking about furniture?" he asked.

"I am now," she said. "Any suggestions?"

"What am I—your interior decorator?"

"No," she said, squinting up at him in mock irritation, "you're the Idea Guy. Like every five minutes, 'Hey, Janie, I have an idea . . . let's . . . paint the whole thing gold and call it a ballroom!'"

He laughed and looked around. "Gilded? Nah, too nineteenth century. But it's not bad for dancing, if that's what you had in mind."

Her face softened. It was so good to see him. "What's in the box?" she asked.

He looked down at his hands. "Oh," he said giving it to her. "I saw this at a little shop on the Cape last week. I didn't pay much for it, so if you don't like it, don't feel like you have to—"

Janie lifted the cover off the box. It was a set of wind chimes. The chimes were long and thin and were suspended from a delicately carved piece of wood. A pear-shaped piece of the same wood, about the size of her thumb, hung in the middle. She glanced back up at him, her eyes wide.

"I tried it out," he said quickly. "It's not very loud. The chimes are spaced far enough so they don't bang into each other, they only sound when the wooden clapper touches them, so it's soft. And the notes are low. It shouldn't keep the kids up at night or anything. . . ."

She tugged it from its box by the looped hanger and listened to the gentle tinkling sound for a moment. "It's so nice," was all she could think to say.

"Really, it's okay if you don't like it."

She looked around. "Where should I hang it? From the beam over there, that's perfect. I wonder if I have a hook somewhere." Tug produced one from his pocket and held it out on his palm. She had to smile. "You knew I'd like it," she chided him.

While he stood on the chair and screwed the hook into the beam, she went into the house and brought out another chair and a glass of chocolate milk. They sat, and she asked him about his trip to Cape Cod. He had a house there in Orleans; he'd put the down payment on it from his first serious construction job almost twenty years ago. It wasn't very big, only two bedrooms, and didn't have a water view, but it was near enough to the ocean to hear the surf crashing on Nauset Beach at night, which was his favorite thing about it. He'd gone down there the day after he'd finished her porch and stayed for a week, his only summer vacation.

"Must be pretty relaxing," said Janie.

He nodded. "My brother and his family came for Labor Day weekend. My nieces, you know, they're like most kids—only relaxing when they're sleeping. But they're teenagers now, so that's the better part of their day." He drank up the last of his chocolate milk. "It's good to have them nearby again, since I moved back." He spoke matter-of-factly, even affectionately, but Janie sensed a faint eddy of resignation, too. A breeze kicked up and the chimes rang softly.

"Listen to that," said Janie. "And they go so well with this room, it's like you built it just to hang them here. I feel like I should pay you for them, though."

"Absolutely not," he said. "They're a gift."

But why? she almost asked. *Contractors hand out gifts now? Did Shelly get a gift?*

"I should go." Tug rose quickly, strode into the house and placed his glass in the sink. A moment later he was standing on the porch again, hands in his pockets, face blank. "Listen," he said, "the Geezers are playing tomorrow night—that's my team."

"I know," said Janie.

"Well, the games are earlier now since it gets dark sooner, so I thought maybe you might want to bring the kids. Dylan really seemed to like it."

"He practically reported me to the Mommy Police when I made him leave the last time."

Tug chuckled for a second. "Well, maybe this time we could, you know, maybe grab an ice cream or something afterward."

Janie felt a strange clenching sensation in her chest. A fragment of conversation flickered in her inner ear; it was Tug's workers saying he enjoyed "the view." They were wrong, though. A man might enjoy the view, but that didn't mean he wanted anything more. Tug was off the market. He had told her so himself. Her mind stuttered in response to his suggestion, and she said only, "Okay."

His hands seemed to tense in his pockets momentarily. "Great. I'll see you tomorrow."

"So, you know that monstrosity Shelly sold over in Pelham Heights?" Tug was leaning an elbow on the edge of the stands where Janie and the kids had set up camp for the game. There were snacks and drinks and baby toys strewn about. Carly was sitting in Janie's lap gumming a teething biscuit; Dylan was wearing Tug's glove and tossing a tennis ball into it, whispering "Out!" to himself.

"Yeah, the one that basically funded her retirement?" said Janie.

"That's the one. Guess what—they're gutting it."

"Come on!" snorted Janie.

"No kidding. It's a palace, but not the right kind of palace, apparently. Too modern. They want more charm. And not just molding and a couple of beams. Hard-core charm."

"How do you know?"

"I got the job."

"No way! That's huge!"

Tug bristled. "I do big jobs, you know. That porch is the smallest thing I've done in years."

"No—I meant it's great!" She nudged his elbow. "And don't go fishing for my undying gratitude because you lowered yourself to do my itsy-bitsy porch. Even Michelangelo painted houses on the side."

Tug considered this for a moment. "Is that true?"

She shrugged. "How should I know?"

He laughed hard, tipping his head back in that way that he had, and Janie had to laugh with him. He gave her hand a quick pat before heading back onto the field. They didn't end up going for ice cream after the game because it was getting dark, and Dylan was fairly spackled with ballpark dirt, requiring a bath before bed. But before they left, Janie agreed to come to Friday night's game and let the kids go to bed late, a concession she made with a minimum of encouragement.

JANIE WAS STILL ON the phone when Heidi arrived to pick up Keane.

"No!" the two boys whined at her in unison. They had built a fort in the living room with couch cushions and sheets, and numerous small toys had been squirreled away under its drooping roof.

"Go talk to Dylan's mom," begged Keane. "Go talk to her a lot."

"She's on the phone, Keane, and we have to get home and figure out something for dinner."

"Wait!" said Dylan. "Hear her? She's saying 'Uh-huh.'" The three of them stopped to listen.

"Uh-huh," said Janie, writing something on the calendar in the kitchen. "Uh-huh . . . uh-huh . . ."

"That means she's almost done! Go!" he said, wagging his finger toward the kitchen. "Go quick!"

Heidi gave them a serious-business look, and said, "Five minutes." The two boys scrambled back into their fort, pillows listing with the strain.

"Sorry about that," said Janie hanging up the phone. "Dylan's been begging me for swim lessons again. Robby always took him, and I couldn't even remember where they were held."

"Swim lessons?" said Heidi.

"Yeah. I'm still checking it out. Are you interested?"

Heidi would have to clear it with her ex-husband, but she wanted to make it work. She was worried about Keane knowing how to swim, since his father had just bought a boat, and was, as Janie knew, not terribly safety-conscious. "I wish he would get transferred to Japan, or something," said Heidi. "I hate how little control I have. He's irresponsible and immature, but because he's the father, he can take Keane out on the open seas if he feels like it."

Janie tossed out a sympathetic look, but privately she had to wonder if a self-absorbed adolescent for a father wasn't better than no father at all. She was also struck by the fact that it wasn't so long ago that she would have felt compelled to voice that opinion. "Scrambled eggs and toast for dinner again," she said quickly, in an effort to maintain her slowly rehabilitating sense of discretion.

Heidi groaned in agreement. "I just can't make a real dinner when I know I'm the only one eating it. We live on chicken nuggets and pancakes."

Janie studied her for a moment; her makeup was still fresh, her silk blouse was uncreased, her hair hung in that precisely haphazard style that Janie had seen in magazines. *Beach roses,* thought

Janie, *some small comfort against the heartache of motherhood.*
"Let's order out for pizza," she said.

Heidi slumped into a kitchen chair, a blissful smile gracing her unblemished face. "Brilliant."

FRIDAY, SEPTEMBER 7

The kids have finally settled down. I don't know if ice cream before bed is such a good idea, but they had fun. Dylan was practically wagging like a happy dog in the line at Dairy Queen. It was a good game—they played the Weston Midlife Menace, the team that idiot reporter, Wick Lally, is on. Tug got him out when he tried to steal third. The guy jumps up, all friendly, and gives Tug a big pat on the back—No hard feelings, or something good-sport-ish like that. Tug ignored him. I saw him roll his shoulder after, like he was wiping off the guy's cooties.

Afterward, when they won, the team went to The Pal for beers, but Tug kept his word about ice cream. I felt bad for him, I'm sure he probably would have rather gone with the guys. I told him it was fine, we could do ice cream another time, he should go celebrate. But he said No, he's been there a hundred times and it's just the same old thing.

I have this funny feeling about him. He seems pretty happy. Well, maybe not happy, exactly, but content, anyway. He likes his life—he's good at what he does, loves his house, his family. Talks about his nieces a lot, mostly complains, but you can tell how much they mean to him. And he loves softball, told me he hasn't missed a game or a practice since he moved back. He says he likes the aches and pains he gets from a good game, and when he can feel them the next day he knows he played his hardest. Now that's just weird.

But he's also unhappy. When he's ticked off he gets quiet (which I know from experience because he's been ticked at me plenty). And he's lonely, which must be why he seems to want to spend time with us. He's attached to us in a funny way, maybe because he's seen so much of our drama. Maybe it's like getting hooked on a soap opera—you want to know if the young stud (who's always named something like Dirk or Drake or Dakota) is going to realize that the girl he loves but also hates because she's on trial for murdering his mother isn't really the killer, but merely a pawn in the game of intrigue being played by a soulless, unaccountably rich guy named Franco.

Tug laughs a lot when he's with us. I think we take his mind off things. I'm glad I know he's not looking to date. That would make it uncomfortable.

I went for a walk up Jansen Hill today. My first in over a month. It was a beautiful day and I had nothing better to do (except take the car in for an oil and filter change, which I don't think has been done since last fall, so I guess it'll keep for another couple of days). I'm out of shape. Plus Carly's bigger.

I went to the old house foundation where Jake and I sat on the log and he cried. I wonder how he's doing. I didn't sit there long. It was too hard to miss him. I have enough missing to do without looking for more.

Walking back down I saw a maple leaf on the ground. It was thick and green in the middle, but the edges were that translucent red that you see in the fall. I put it in the jar, which, yes, I still have. I'd get rid of it, but I can't think of where.

IN CHURCH ON SUNDAY, they sat behind a couple with two teenagers, a boy and a girl, who had perfected their lack of enthusiasm with a slouching kneel. The parents, in their early fifties, Janie guessed, sat close together. During the Offertory, the man leaned over and whispered something into his wife's ear. She turned and beamed him a sparkling grin. His eyebrows shot up, and they both laughed silently.

I used to have that, thought Janie. *That used to be me in fifteen years.*

WHEN TUG PULLED INTO the driveway at a quarter to twelve on Tuesday, Janie was only mildly surprised. It was just Tug, showing up again. It seemed almost normal.

"Hey," he called, walking toward her with his cooler as she met him on the porch, wiping her hands on a dish towel. "Have you had lunch yet?"

"No, I just barely cleared away the breakfast stuff. Is it that time already?"

"Well, I'm up around five, so I eat when old people do, an hour or so ahead of everyone else."

"Is that the early bird special?" she asked pointing at the cooler.

"You might say," he smiled. "Got extra if you want to join me."

They brought kitchen chairs and an end table from the living room out onto the porch, and Tug unpacked his cooler: a turkey sandwich on rye bread with Havarti and roasted red peppers, a vegetarian wrap with alfalfa sprouts sticking out from the end, apple slices, a pint of chocolate milk, a thermos of coffee and a baggie of quartered grapes.

Janie looked down at the spread, then up at Tug. He had brought two entire lunches, one for him, and one clearly designated for her. Coffee, which he never drank. Grapes for Carly. This was premeditated, no matter how much he tried to act as if he had just happened by spontaneously. That clenching feeling grew in her chest and she wondered what would make him do this.

"Eating with a bunch of guys every day gets old," he said, as if he were reading her mind.

Lonely, she thought with relief. *Bored and lonely just like me.* "Which sandwich is yours?" she asked.

"Either one," he said. "Take your pick."

"So if I take the turkey, you'll eat the veggie with sprouts."

"Yep."

"Liar."

"Well," he admitted, "I'd have to pull those little hairy guys out, but I'd eat it. I'm not picky."

Not picky, noted Janie, and reached for the veggie wrap. *Or so he claims, anyway.* "So were you good and achy after that game on Friday?" she asked.

"Yes, I was, thanks for asking," he smiled. "My right shoulder was throbbing for most of the next day. Very satisfying."

"Have you always been such a big fan of pain?"

He thought for a moment and licked a sliver of roasted red pepper from his lip. "No. It's grown more appealing lately."

"Since your divorce."

He nodded and took several gulps of chocolate milk. "Would it be weird if I asked you how you met your husband?"

"Would it be weird if I told you and maybe got a little choked up?"

"Not that much," he said, and settled back in his seat.

Janie took a breath, exhaled. "It was on this cross-country trip I took . . ."

At twenty-nine, Janie had quit her job at Beth Israel Hospital in Boston, feeling a certain restlessness, a certain compulsion to do something—almost anything—that was not work-eat-sleep-hang-with-friends-work-again. And she'd developed an allergy to latex gloves that seemed like an omen. Aunt Jude checked the latex allergy website and gave her a list of alternative glove products. Janie decided to drive cross-country instead.

She was living in Somerville, just outside of Boston, with a houseful of roommates, all of whom signed on for the adventure, and all of whom eventually came up with excuses, such as car payments, dates on the verge of becoming relationships, and the necessity of wisdom tooth removal, not to go. Janie was disappointed but undeterred. She sublet her room for the summer, packed up her Toyota Tercel, and headed west on the Massachusetts Turnpike.

"My twin, Mike, lives in Flagstaff," she told Tug, "so I decided to end up there, half thinking I might even stay and look for work. I felt this need for a drastic change. You ever get like that?"

"Definitely," said Tug. He glanced away from her, nodding slowly, and she could tell that he was thinking of something specific. Then there was a faint buzzing sound and he jumped up, wrenching a cell phone from his pants pocket. He studied the display, and let out a snort of frustration. "Sorry," he said to her. "It'll be quick."

It wasn't though, and he stood at the other end of the porch, staring through the screen, running his hand back across his head in that way he had when he was agitated, and saying things like, "No, I told you about this last week," and "The inspector cleared it." While she waited, Janie found herself drifting back to her first glimmer of the drastic change she had been headed for almost a decade ago.

Driving through Albany, New York, she had noticed a motorcycle traveling at about the same speed she was. It wasn't one of those bullet bikes, with the rider practically prostrate in order to reach the handlebars; nor was it a souped-up "hog" with the front wheel out so far that he reclined as if sunning himself. This bike was the big clunky kind, the rider sitting upright, feet squarely below him. The gas tank was no distinct color. The rider's helmet had no noticeable enhancements. He wore sunglasses and the stubble of a man who had recently decided to stop shaving.

If she slowed, he passed her, but she always seemed to catch up again, sometimes passing him if she didn't watch her speed. They leap-frogged like this across upstate New York, and Janie remembered enjoying the sense that she had some company on the road, even a stranger with whom she would never share a word. At one point, near Utica, he gave her a quick grin when he passed.

Approaching Syracuse, her quart thermos of coffee was empty, the contents now weighing heavily on her bladder, and she decided to pull off at the next rest stop. She felt a moment of regret that she would lose her road buddy, until she saw him pull off ahead of her into the Chittenango Travel Plaza. She almost didn't stop. It was one thing to enjoy the disconnected company of another driver while secure in your own vehicle. It was another thing altogether to breach the void by actually meeting. At a rest stop no less. It was the opening scene of your standard slasher movie.

Then again, she was about to wet her pants, Janie remembered, approaching that point where it's scary to stand up because it seems possible that the dam might not hold. At the last minute, she yanked the steering wheel to the right and careened into the Chittenango lot, parked in the fire lane, and made her way gingerly to the ladies' toilets. The ensuing relief was worth the risk.

As she pulled away from the yellow-striped curb, she noticed a picnic area in a grove of pines at the far edge of the rest stop. Time to stretch her legs and tuck into one of the pita pocket sandwiches she had made for herself back in Massachusetts. The only people there were a family with several small boys, whose noise level and proclivity for punching each other made it obvious why their parents had decided to feed them outside rather than in the cramped food court. They were polishing off a sleeve of Chips Ahoy! cookies, when Janie sat down at another table. The family left soon thereafter, a squalling fight breaking out in the backseat that blasted through their open car windows. Even now, Janie could almost hear how the sound of the brawl faded as their car made its way to the highway on-ramp.

Moments later motorcycle guy pulled up. It took him four tries to get the bike securely situated on its kickstand, by which time Janie's fear was tinged with embarrassment on his behalf. He pulled his helmet off and rolled his eyes in self-disgust. "It's not my bike," he said defensively. Janie shrugged and averted her eyes. Although by then she had noticed that he was kind of cute, despite the fact that his regular-boy haircut blew the whistle on the attempt at cool-guy stubble.

He approached her hesitantly with his bag of takeout from the food court and told her he'd been on that godforsaken motorcycle all day without even a radio to listen to. "It would be great to sit at your table and spend the next twenty minutes lying about our identities," he said, but he didn't want to creep her out, so if she preferred that he leave her alone, there were no hard feelings.

"I have a loaded gun in my bag," she told him.

"Of course you do," he said with an amused grin. "This is America. Who doesn't?" And he sat down.

For years afterward, she interrogated him about why he had taken it as an invitation and not a threat. To her, at the time, it had been a threat, a bluff to keep him at a safe distance, if not exactly locked on the other side of her car door. "It was a lie," he would say. "It was just your opening lie."

It ended up being her only lie. There were things that she declined to tell him, like where she was going, her last name, and the like. But the rest didn't seem to hold much quarry for misuse. Wasn't that why she had undertaken this adventure in the first place?

He began by telling her that he was the studio keyboard player for U2, but had gotten sick of the brogues and all the foreign policy talk. That was his only lie. Then he admitted he had been a branch manager for BayBank during its merger with Bank of Boston, and when they offered him a transfer or a layoff, he had picked layoff. His brother, who had owned the motorcycle since high school, had recently moved to Phoenix with his wife and baby. The motorcycle was supposed to be sold, but was priced too high ("on purpose" he confided to Janie) so that his brother could eventually reclaim it. He, Robert Pierre LaMarche, was taking the opportunity of his layoff, his brother's baffling adoration of the bike, and the disintegration of a recent relationship to make this trip.

The lunch at the Chittenango Travel Center picnic area lasted almost two hours. By the end, he had convinced her to meet him at Niagara Falls, which hadn't really interested her, but he was so enthusiastic, she decided it might be a waste to go right by the thing and not stop.

After convoying to Buffalo, they ate dinner together at a road-side burgers and ice-cream stand, and later got separate rooms at a tattered motel with a flashing neon sign of a barrel going over a waterfall. Several of the light tubes had blown, however, making it seem as if the barrel was rolling down a blue road. Now, as she picked at the remnants of her veggie wrap, Janie wondered if those lights had ever been fixed or, if she were to go there now, would it look exactly the same.

The two of them went on like this, agreeing to meet at the next attraction on Robby's list, eating together and sleeping in separate motel rooms. Each night they stayed out later, each morning they lingered longer over breakfast, each attraction seemed more interesting or ridiculous, either case requiring a more thorough perusal. The trip took seven days, not the four that she had planned on.

It was on the sixth day that he first kissed her—nervously, and without much in the way of follow-through. While she felt fairly certain that he would not have minded if she had joined him in his hotel room, he hadn't pressed the point. "The trip was so much better with you along," he explained later. "I didn't want to mess it up."

Robby followed her all the way to Mike's tiny apartment in Flagstaff, Arizona. He met Mike, stayed for dinner, slept on the couch, and stayed up half the night talking with Janie. When Mike left for the art studio the next day, they made love all morning, and Robby didn't end up heading south to Phoenix until after lunch. He told her on the phone that night that when he arrived, his brother had hugged the motorcycle first, and then him.

Janie was thinking of that phone call, her hand gripping the receiver only a few short hours after they had kissed good-bye over the sputtering growl of the motorcycle engine. It had felt drastic. Good and drastic.

"Sorry about that," Tug said, snapping his phone shut. "It's one of the things I like and hate about construction—lots of problem solving." He sat down again, ignoring the apples and chocolate milk. "So you were on the Pike, jobless, homeless, looking for something completely new . . ."

Janie recounted the story of the cross-country trip, leaving out the more personal details. She almost felt she could tell him, had a sense that he was wondering at what point the relationship had become romantic. But it would have been inappropriate and also somehow insensitive.

"How did you end up back here?" he asked.

"Well, Robby already had a new job lined up that he was going back to in a month, and I spent way too much time hanging out with him all over the Southwest to actually job hunt myself. So I came back, too, and picked up a position at Newton-Wellesley Hospital. We got married two years later and ended up buying this house when my mother moved to Italy."

As she finished the story, Janie was pleased at her ability—finally, it seemed—to talk about Robby without getting weepy. There had been a moment or two when she'd felt emotional, but she never shed any tears. Maybe she would cry later, after Tug had packed up his cooler and left. "Why did you want to know about that?" she asked him.

"I don't know, just wondered. We got together a couple of times down at The Pal to go over the plans for the porch, and he seemed like a good guy. Steady, good sense of humor."

Robby went to The Pal? More than once? With Tug? These were small things, things her husband would have told her eventually, had he lived. And yet it was the revelation of small things, not the seemingly more important story she had recounted, that made her eyes sting and her breath short.

As she blinked back tears, she caught sight of Tug's watch. The crystal was so scratched she couldn't see the face, but it reminded her about picking up Dylan at school. "What time is it?" she murmured, trying to keep her voice even.

"Five of one."

"Shit!" she leaped up, almost knocking over the little table. "I'm late for pickup!" She turned to run into the house.

"Where are you going?" he asked, standing.

"To get Carly!"

"Janie, don't wake her up. Just go. I'll stay here."

"What? No! You can't . . . she'll freak out if she . . ."

"No, she won't. Just go."

Janie grabbed her keys off the hook inside the front door and sprinted for the car. When she careened into the school parking lot, she almost forgot to turn off the motor before she got out. *School's only been open for a week,* she chastised herself, *and already I'm late . . . Bad mommy, bad mommy . . .*

When she got to the door of his classroom, all the kids were gone except for Dylan, who was holding Miss Sharon's hand and chewing on the strap of his backpack.

"Sorry, sorry, sorry!" gushed Janie. "I am so sorry!"

"Did you go to the doctor?" asked Dylan.

"No, I just . . . lost track . . ." Her heart was pounding and she had to reach for the doorway to steady herself.

Miss Sharon gave her a look of forced patience. "I know the start of school can be a bit of a transition, but we really need parents to be on time. It's best for everyone."

"Yes, I know. I'm really sorry," said Janie, taking Dylan's hand and leading him out of the classroom. Miss Sharon's condescending tone rankled her, but she was more concerned about Dylan. "Sorry, sweetie," she whispered.

"It's okay." He gave Miss Sharon a quick backward glance. "Wait till Keane's father does pickup," he said, and put a cupped hand over his mouth to cover his smile.

Carly was sitting in her highchair when they got home, her face still crinkled with sleep lines, eating the grapes that Tug had brought her. He was leaning against the kitchen counter and saying things into his cell phone like, "They have to have it . . . they always have it . . . so call Sudbury Lumber . . ." He snapped the phone shut. "Gotta go," he told them.

"Thanks so much," she said. "For lunch, too. Next time it's on me, and you're doing all the talking."

Without actually smiling, his face seemed to take on a faint glow of accomplishment. "Deal," he said.

18

~

FOR SOME REASON IT was the swim lessons, not the mortgage payments or preschool tuition, that made Janie take a hard look at her finances. They were just so much more expensive than she expected. She wondered if she should postpone them until she went back to work and there was some inbound cash flow.

It had been Shelly, with her compulsive attention to detail and divorce-honed sense of self-preservation, who'd set the course for Janie's financial security. A week after Robby died, she had come over with Chinese takeout (which was never eaten because Janie could ingest nothing more than an occasional pistachio muffin, and it was midweek so Shelly ate only kale or some other odd green vegetable). Shelly had stayed long after the General Gao Chicken had gone cold, sprinkling Janie with gentle but persistent questions about her "safety net." Robby, the banker, had always handled the finances, so Janie's answers were, as she now remembered, clearly subpar. She didn't know how much they had in savings, CDs, stocks, mutual funds, college accounts, IRAs, or 401(k)s. She wasn't entirely sure where those accounts were, and in some cases, if they even existed.

Shelly grabbed the loose and flapping monetary reins. She discovered that, yes, there were savings, a few CDs, and two 401(k) accounts. She contacted Robby's employer and negotiated an additional three months of health insurance coverage. She automated almost all the bills—mortgage, utilities, telephone, etc.—so that Janie would only have to move money into her checking account and pay off her credit card every month. This Shelly had handled herself until around April, when Janie began to seem somewhat less stuporous during their semiweekly online banking sessions.

Shelly had also done all the paperwork to collect on Robby's life insurance policy and had increased Janie's own policy significantly, in case it were ever needed, "God forbid." The payoff from Robby's policy had seemed enormous—too much, in some ways: Janie had never aspired to wealth and did not have expensive taste in clothes or home furnishings, her main luxury being premium coffee beans. But no amount of money was any compensation for the loss of Robby, and in that sense it seemed a snickeringly small sum.

The swim lessons cost more than she'd paid for anything that hadn't been on Shelly's budget spreadsheet, except for the porch, which had somehow never seemed optional. The lessons fell into that "discretionary purchases" column that had remained benignly blank since its creation eight months ago. Janie was now struggling with her discretionary spending skills, blunted from disuse.

"Mom?" said Dylan, standing in the doorway, goggles swinging from an outstretched finger. "Can I wear them now?"

It was time for Dylan to have an actual reason to don his favorite eyewear, Janie decided in that moment. Maybe if he wore them in a swimming pool, he wouldn't need to wear them around the house quite so much. It would be worth the money just to find out.

THE NEXT MONDAY, JANIE picked up Keane and Dylan and brought them for their first lesson. Dylan had been oddly concerned about which of his two bathing suits to wear. He liked the blue one with the sharks the best. That had been apparent all summer on the rare occasions when both bathing suits were clean (rather than

one or the other of them found balled at the bottom of his backpack like some small, wet sandy animal).

"Come on, Dylan, just grab one. We're going to be late for
school," Janie had said.

"It's important!" he'd replied with a tremor of panic in his
voice. Finally he chose the red one with the orange waist band.

After pickup, the boys were buzzing with silliness in the back
of the car, their booster seats shoehorned in next to Carly's toddler
seat. They poked at each other and howled with laughter when
one of them passed gas. "Toot, toot, tootie!" called Keane.

"You're a fart head!" Dylan sang out.

"No potty talk, please," warned Janie, knowing that it was all
but useless, like sending compulsive poker players to Las Vegas
and saying, "No gambling, please." The boys giggled in the back
and whispered their bathroom words to each other.

"Who's excited about swim lessons?" asked Janie, trying to
derail the toilet talk.

"Me!" they both yelled.

"Well, kinda," added Keane. "I maybe might sink."

"Yeah, I'm kinda nervous," said Dylan.

"Why are you nervous?" asked Janie.

"I just am."

Keane did sink on numerous occasions, his pale white arms
slashing at the water as if he were engaged in battle. The swim
instructor, a young man with a thick nest of curly hair that he
seemed intent on keeping dry, plucked Keane from the chop of his
own waves over and over again. Watching from poolside, Carly
asleep in her arms, Janie saw that Dylan took these moments to
lift his goggles and scan the deck. When his eyes alit on her, he
would give a little wave, then keep on looking.

The lesson was over and Janie escorted the boys to the wom-
en's locker room.

"Let's have these two showers," said Keane. "They're right
next to each other. I'll knock on the wall and you knock back."

Dylan complied, but Janie couldn't help but notice how quiet he was. Not sullen exactly, but working out some puzzle, perhaps, that distracted him from Keane's announcements that he was knocking with his elbow, his knee, his butt. When they finished rinsing off, Janie knelt down, Carly still draped limply over her shoulder, and wrapped them each in their towels. Keane sprinted toward the changing room, racing to see who could get dressed the fastest.

"Hey," said Janie, hanging on to Dylan's towel for an extra moment. "What's on your mind?"

His eyes blinked rapidly as he tried to conjure up the right words. "Dad . . . ," he said.

Janie tucked and retucked the towel. "Yeah?" she said.

"I thought . . . he always was here before. I know he's in heaven and he can't come back, like you said. But we always put our goggles on together, and went swimming together. And it seemed like he might be here . . . even though he can't. I wore the red bathing suit so he could see me better . . . if he came . . . in case he didn't recognize me from his trip to heaven."

Janie nodded, smoothed the towel, readjusted Carly over her shoulder. Tears welled in her eyes.

"Sorry to make you cry, Mom."

"You didn't make me cry, honey. It's just sad. It's always going to be . . . disappointing when he's not here. Even though we know he can't be here, we're still sad and disappointed when he's not."

"Are you always going to cry?"

"I don't know. I might sometimes. Does it make you worry?"

"A little."

She nodded again, pushing at the twisting tension in her throat. This is what the book had said, this is what she knew. You had to keep reminding them. You had to keep talking. "You know how sometimes there's a right answer and a wrong answer to things? Like your name is Dylan. That's the right answer. If someone calls you Bob or Bill, that's wrong."

·"Yeah." He fingered his goggles, sending them around and around through his hands like worry beads.

"Sometimes crying is the right answer. For me, right now, it is. And then I'll stop, okay?"

"Okay." His pale eyes watched her face, studied her tears, a towel-skirted weatherman checking the precipitation. His hands were still now, clutching the goggles, waiting.

"Hey," she said, her face relaxing, turning to wipe her drippy chin on her shoulder. "Maybe goggles are the right answer sometimes."

A smile, half embarrassed, half relieved, bloomed on his face.

"I win!" yelled Keane, appearing at the doorway to the dressing area, white-blond hair an electrified frenzy around his face.

"No fair!" called Dylan. He ran to get his clothes on, the tight-wrapped towel causing him to scuttle penguin-like, the goggles flapping through the damp human smell of the locker room.

EACH WEEK, TUG CAME for lunch. Sometimes he brought his cooler; other times he might arrive with wicker furniture catalogues or a little toy for Carly or a bag of particularly burly-tasting coffee beans. Janie found herself stocking sliced turkey; a jar of roasted red peppers now sat in the door of her fridge. Tug's appearances weren't exactly planned, but nonetheless seemed to be settling into a Tuesdays and sometimes Thursdays tempo. He always made casual mention of his softball schedule. Janie and the kids usually made it to the home games, though they rarely stayed until the end.

"How'd you get the name Tug?" Janie asked him one day, as Carly fingered pieces of Muenster cheese on her highchair tray. He would beat the sawdust out of his jeans as he walked toward the house, and Janie could see faint lines across the thighs, a fingerprint here, a darker palm-shaped spot there.

"From Sue," he said, leaning back in his chair. "My parents always called me A.J.—Augustus Junior."

"Well?"

"You really want to hear it?" he asked. He ran a hand back across his head. It lingered there a moment then flopped back into his lap. Janie knew this meant he was hesitating for some reason, perhaps because it was painful to talk about, or merely because he didn't know where to start. Her curiosity about him had grown over the last several weeks. She remembered when he told her that Sue had been the one to initiate the divorce, and at the time it seemed like far more information than she wanted or had a right to. But now he wasn't just that guy with the power tools out in her front yard, creating maddening clouds of sawdust with the hum of his saws-all. Now he wiped other people's sawdust from his jeans before he came in. "Up to you," she answered.

He shrugged as if it didn't matter one way or the other to him, but she could see two things: it was painful, and he did want to tell her. It reassured her, this quandary he was in. It was her own quandary—being attached to the past, constrained by a rupture that might never fuse; and yet the mail still arrived, children continued to outgrow their clothes, the house demanded maintenance and repair. Connections with other people continued to occur, despite all her intentions to shut them out. Unlikely connections at that. The countless stories that made up her life—and his—hadn't evaporated, as almost everything else had seemed to. Might as well tell them.

"You probably wish you'd stuck with A.J.," she said to get him started.

"Nah," he said. "It's not like that."

He and Sue had grown up together in Natick. "Always had a bit of a thing for her, even before I really, you know, thought about girls." As he described her, Janie saw that she was like Heidi, in that every-hair-in-place, always-wearing-just-the-right-thing kind of way. She was friendly and smart and, unlike Heidi, so rock-solid sure of herself that she was the one most often chosen to lead the class in reciting the Pledge of Allegiance or to take a sick friend to the nurse's office.

"Teacher's pet?" asked Janie.

"Not really," said Tug. "Teachers loved her, don't get me wrong. I don't think she ever handed in even one assignment late, including the time her family went to Florida for February vacation and got stuck there for three extra days because the airline went on strike. But she wasn't a goody-goody either. She was just driven to do things right, be the best. People admired her for it."

Tug had gathered sufficient courage to ask her out in the seventh grade, after a summer of bamboo-like growth, with a voice that was now an octave lower. She had taken a week to think about it. During that week, Tug could feel himself being pulled into the vortex of her correctness. He studied more, got his hair trimmed, and spent far less time playing desk football with folded-up wads of lined paper during study hall. Suddenly he was aware of how ridiculous he looked with his fingers formed into a mini goalpost when it was the other guy's turn to try for the extra point.

After thorough consideration, she accepted him, and they dated all through junior high, unlike most of their friends, who changed partners like school was one big square dance. Sue didn't approve of that. Waste of time, jockeying in and out of "relationships" based on little more than whether your friends thought you looked cute together.

The summer between junior high and high school was a different story, however. Sue calmly explained to him that she thought it was for their own good to date other people and try the many new activities that high school had to offer. She was considering joining the debate team and wanted to be able to concentrate her full attention on being Natick's first female debate champion.

Tug had assumed there was another guy, and accordingly dated up a vengeful storm that summer and throughout the fall. He was surprised to find that he never got turned down, and attributed this at least in part to Sue. Any guy deemed good enough for her must be something. And he was something. He could see how she'd molded him into someone with higher standards and aspirations beyond what had been expected of him by others. His grades were good and he had become an excellent third baseman, fairly confident that he could make the high school team in the spring. Sue would have expected nothing less.

But spring was a long way off, and he was having a hard time distracting himself from the rumors of Sue dating the captain of the debate team. The first night of Christmas break, one of his friends had a party, and Sue showed up with the debate captain. Tug was mortified, having come without a date, and proceeded to try and correct the situation with whoever was handy. From across the room, with his fingers safely entwined in those of some girl he barely knew, Tug was stunned to see Sue take a swig from a bottle of beer. Sue didn't drink.

"She used to say, 'Alcohol is for people without ambition.' I found out later she hadn't done well at a debate. She hadn't done that badly, you understand, but she hadn't come in top three, either."

A few days later there was a huge snowstorm. Almost two feet of snow fell overnight, and the only thing that made it slightly less exciting was that, being vacation, it hadn't resulted in a school cancellation. Most of Tug's buddies spent the morning sitting on lunch trays, testing the durability of their spines as they sped down Walnut Hill. Well-trained by Sue to seize opportunity, Tug was making fistfuls of cash shoveling his neighbors' driveways.

He always shoveled out the elderly Mr. and Mrs. Bellows for free. "Fixed income," Tug explained to Janie, "hadn't made a home improvement in about twenty years." Besides, Mr. Bellows always came out with his bent, rusted old shovel and tried to help. Tug was working on the driveway while Mr. Bellows chipped away at the front path, clearing it in spoon-sized chunks. All of a sudden the old gentleman was lying on his back in the snow, face half covered with tiny avalanches of sparkling flakes. Tug screamed in to Mrs. Bellows to call an ambulance, and ended up giving Mr. Bellows CPR until it arrived. Sue had previously convinced him, in that calm, smiling, relentless way she had, to take a CPR course with her. It was every citizen's duty.

A week later, the day before New Year's Eve, Tug found himself on the front page of the *Natick Bulletin:* A HERO IN THE SNOW. Sue, as well as the mothers of most of his friends, called to congratulate him. She seemed strangely stuttery and nervous when she asked him if they could meet on a bench at the Natick Green. "She brought a thermos of hot chocolate and two mugs."

"She knew how to butter you up," teased Janie.

"Yeah," he chuckled. "I guess I'm a sucker for a woman bearing chocolate."

A flutter of anxiety went through Janie. *What's that supposed to mean? Does he think I purposely . . . he knows I'm not trying to . . . he likes chocolate for godsake, everyone knows that . . .* But Tug was talking again, so Janie had to leave off worrying about the implications of her beverage offerings.

Sue had read the article about him, how he had likely saved old Mr. Bellows's life. ("For the time being, anyway," Tug added. A couple of months later, Mr. Bellows had died in his sleep of a more thorough shuttering of his ancient aorta.) Sue went on to say that she was reminded of what a good influence Tug had on her and was hoping that he might consider getting back together.

Good influence? On Sue? It was the first time Tug had considered that he might have any effect on her whatsoever. Sue was Sue. No one influenced her. Except, he was now learning, maybe him.

It was very flattering, and yet there was something missing from her proposal. In retrospect, it still surprised Tug that, at fifteen, he'd had the wherewithal not to jump at the offer he'd lain awake imagining for the previous six months. She had done the cost-benefit analysis and determined him to be the appropriate choice for her. He waited to see if he meant anything more to her than that.

In the silence, her chin began to tremble. "She wasn't a crier. Ever. Times when she should have, she didn't," Tug explained to Janie. And Sue didn't cry, there on the bench that day. But he could see her strain against emotion, a sight that was almost frightening to him.

"You tug at me," she whispered, finally. "Even when I should be focusing on other things, the thought of you tugs at me."

That was it. "I was a goner," he told Janie with an embarrassed little smile. And what sealed the deal was that Sue began to call him Tug, effectively announcing to him and to everyone else, that she, the most beautiful, ambitious girl in the sophomore class, had fallen in love like any other fool. The name caught on among his friends, first as a taunt—one he didn't mind all that much. Eventually, as with most nicknames, the meaning behind it faded and it was just what he was called.

"That's really sweet," said Janie. He shrugged and began to tidy up the table, tightening the lid on the kosher dills and brushing potato chip crumbs into the palm of his calloused hand. "Does it ever feel strange," Janie asked, "that she named you, and you're not together anymore?"

"Only once," he said. "The day she told me it was over, and she was still calling me Tug. Seemed like a joke."

"But it didn't bother you enough to do anything about it."

"Nah, it bothered me alright. But a guy doesn't go changing his name in his forties. Plus . . . I don't know. It's my name. It doesn't belong to her."

"Good point." Janie nodded, thinking that what belongs to who in a relationship is always up for interpretation. It was that muddling of gifts—impalpable as a name or immovable as a porch—that caused the most confusion.

He crumpled up his napkin and dropped it on his plate. "Think you'll make it to the game tomorrow night?"

"Not like I have a choice, now that Dylan's practically the team mascot," she said warmly, feeling somehow grateful for his gift of the story of his name.

He smiled and patted her hand.

THURSDAY, OCTOBER 4

Shelly is moving this weekend. I hate even writing that, and then I can't believe how much I hate it because we've lived next to each other for years and I didn't like her for most of that time. Sometimes I don't even like her now. She's so bossy and weird, with her plastic nails and her one-vegetable-only meals. But she saved me so many times, financially and otherwise. And I just love her.

How is it that the Shellys of the world—the people who you avoid because they're strange and have nothing in common with you—are the ones that show up when you need them, and my own mother can't even pull herself together to visit for more than a week and a half?

Shelly came over this morning to ask me if I wanted her "moonstone blue" leather couch with the matching chair and ottoman and coordinating striped suede pillows. Apparently she conceded them in the Great Furniture Treaty of Rhode Island, in return for getting to bring her wrought-iron patio set. She told me that combining two households is almost as hard as splitting one up. The big difference, according to her, is that the sex is better. Better? She was having not-so-great sex with her ex-husband while they were divvying up the dish towels? Yikes.

Taking her couch makes no sense. It will barely even fit in my living room. But here I am, saying yes to the couch and the chair and ottoman. I can't help it. They're Shelly's. I want them.

She asked me how my finances looked, now that the porch is paid for and preschool tuition is starting up again. I showed her the numbers. We agreed that I should start looking for a part-time slot at a local hospital after the first of the year. Just enough hours to get on the health plan. I'm going to talk to Aunt Jude about watching the kids. Another person who drives me crazy that I can't live without.

It feels too soon to start working again, Carly especially seems too young. But her birthday's next week. For Dylan's first birthday, we went camping in Acadia National Park. It was a beautiful clear day, and you could practically see the entire Maine coastline. We felt like we were giving him the world. No relatives, no balloons, no hoopla. Just the three of us, needing no one else, happier than I ever thought I could be.

I better call Cormac and order a cake.

WHEN JANIE CALLED ABOUT the cake, she also asked Cormac if he would come over on Saturday and help her move the enormous leather living room set from Shelly's. She mentioned this in passing to Tug between innings, and he said simply, "What time?"

Early Saturday morning, with Dylan and Carly circling their legs like cats, Tug and Janie took her small sofa and her mother's old wingback chair out to his truck. He would bring it to the take-it-or-leave-it at the dump when he brought his own trash. While they waited for Cormac to arrive after the morning rush at the bakery, Tug disappeared for several minutes. She spied him hauling her garbage bags and recycling to the truck from the little unattached garage in the side yard.

"You don't have to do that," she said when he came back in.

"Might as well. I'm going anyway."

"Well, thanks. It's very thoughtful."

A look came over his face then—barely a look, only the slightest modification of his features. A slight crinkling of the spray of crow's-feet around his eyes, a brief play of muscles around his lips, a minor shift of his head to one side. He looked at her, the beams of his pupils dilating, taking in every inch of her, and then after a beat, he looked away.

It sent a spasm of panic through her almost as intense as the night she faced the intruder in her living room. She turned and walked quickly away from him, finding herself in the darkened bathroom. *Shit*, she thought. *Shit, shit, shit.*

It had been the shadow at the back of their friendship, this look. A silent, barely perceptible edge to the questions he asked and the stories he didn't want to think about but nonetheless wanted her to hear. In certain light, even a shadow can be caught unawares.

The whole picture came into focus as she sat on the edge of the tub pinching the back of her hand. The lunches and the little offerings—not quite gifts, but also not necessary in the course of a purely platonic relationship. The easy contentment as he leaned against the stands chatting with her while the rest of his team sat on the bench. The pats on her hand. More than anything, the way in which his presence had come to be expected. He hadn't asked whether his help was needed today. There was furniture to be moved. Of course he would come.

"Janie!" she heard Cormac boom through the house. "We're here!"

Get a grip, she told herself. *Get one huge hell of a serious grip.*

"Tug and I are going over for the chair," said Cormac clapping his hand on Tug's shoulder when she emerged. "You sure all of this is going to fit? How wide's this door?"

"Two foot ten," said Tug. His face was as blank as sheet rock. "The one on the porch is a three-footer." Measuring tape in hand, the two men left for Shelly's with Dylan in tow.

Barb came around the corner from the kitchen. Carly was standing on her feet, her little hands stretched upward to meet Barb's, giggling as they clomped into view. "Are you excited?" Barb asked Janie.

"What?" said Janie sharply, feeling as if her jangling nerves might somehow show.

"About the new furniture—don't you just love redecorating?"

"Oh." Janie inhaled deeply and exhaled, finally managing a friendly smile. "Yeah, it's just . . ."

"I know," said Barb, walking Carly all around the nearly empty living room. "I always get a little wigged out when I make a major change, too."

Janie nodded and leaned against an empty wall, willing herself to calm down. *It's just Tug*, she told herself. *He's just lonely. It'll pass. He knows I'm not . . . It'll pass.*

"Hey," said Barb, swinging the little girl up into her arms. "I'm glad we have a moment alone. I wanted to ask you something." Janie forced herself to focus on Barb with her best I'm Listening face. "Would you . . ." Barb stammered, took a breath and started again. "I'd really like it if you'd be one of my bridesmaids."

You've got to be kidding me, thought Janie. "Sure," she said. "Love to."

"I promise not to make you wear anything silly—no hats or bows or anything!"

Janie sighed. "I'm sure anything you pick will be fine."

"Ooo, this is so great!" Barb said, giving Carly a squeeze.

"Bah!" squealed Carly and clapped her hands.

WITH BARB CORRALLING THE kids, Janie, Tug, and Cormac got the couch into the house. The living room was more crowded with all the new furniture, but the coolness of the color and the rounded smoothness of the leather softened the room. It begged to be sat on.

Tug remained standing while the others sank to their seats. "I should run," he said. His dark eyes transmitted nothing as they flicked to Janie. "I'll catch up with you next week."

"Thanks for all your help," she said.

"Thanks, man," said Cormac, standing to shake his hand. "Couldn't have managed it without you, no kidding."

After Tug left, they sprawled out on the couch and chair, the kids climbing over the arms of the furniture like fleshy lizards. Cormac and Barb squabbled happily about what kind of cake they would design for Carly. "Is Tug coming?" Cormac asked Janie.

"No," she said. "Just family."

TUESDAY MORNING, JANIE SWEPT up any errant cake crumbs missed the night before, and moved the remains of Carly's piano cake into the oven. She brought the balloons up to the kids' room and took out the trash, though the bag was only half filled with festive paper plates and napkins.

Even still, Tug had not so much as unpacked his cooler before he was asking, "Carly's birthday is this month, right?" He smiled down at the little girl as she grasped the knee of his jeans.

"Uh, yeah." Why was Janie feeling so guilty? It was a family party. She hadn't invited Heidi. And she had only invited Shelly because Shelly had instructed her in no uncertain terms that she was to be apprised of all Janie's festivities. But it was clear that Shelly would be too busy arranging and rearranging her new home in Rhode Island to come, so it didn't really count. And just because someone keeps showing up, that doesn't entitle him to a season's pass to your life. She didn't have to make excuses. "It was yesterday."

Tug glanced back up at Janie as if to determine if this could possibly be true. "How'd you celebrate?" His tone was overly neutral.

"Little party here last night. Just pizza and cake. And relatives."

"Huh," Tug grunted, the least possible indication that he'd heard her. He ran a hand over Carly's soft black curls. "Happy Birthday, birthday girl," he murmured. Carly grinned up into his blankness, then turned and wobbled away, in search of someone or something more engaging.

Janie ground her molars together. It was unreasonable that a grown man would be disappointed at not being invited to a child's birthday party. It was insane, actually. He couldn't just puppy dog around like some adoption candidate, for godsake. And if he had a . . . a thing for her . . . he would just have to get over it.

Tug glanced back at Janie, nodded once, and began to unpack the cooler. Sandwiches, potato chips, grapes . . .

"Uhh!" Janie groaned.

"What." There was a warning in his voice but she ignored it.

"You can't do this!"

"Do what, exactly."

"You can't want so bad to be here! It's too hard!"

Tug slammed down the thermos with the chocolate milk in it. He shook his head, struggling for words. "Do you think I like this? This was not what I had in mind when I took this job, believe me! I didn't even want the damned job once I knew . . . what . . . that he . . ." He jammed his hands in his pockets, took a breath.

"What do you mean you didn't want the job. You showed up here with a signed contract and told me you were starting the following week! Which you didn't, by the way. You blew me off for a month!"

"That's right, I gave you a whole month to back out. Why do you think I did that?"

"Because my little porch is so inconsequential and you had bigger fish on the line!" Janie said pointing her finger at him.

"No, because your husband was dead. And my wife of twenty-some-odd years was divorcing me, and I couldn't stand to be around someone else in pain. I had enough of my own."

Janie's mouth dropped open. "Well . . . then why did you take the job?"

"Because he wanted you to have it!"

"And how was that your responsibility?"

"Jesus, Janie!" He shook his head in frustration. Fury clamped around his eyes and jaws. "Jesus," he muttered again, then took a deep breath and exhaled. "I was somebody's husband once. And if I had died with a gift for my wife in my pocket, I sure as hell would have wanted someone to take the damned thing out and give it to her before the lid closed on my coffin."

Janie felt weak all of a sudden, and her eyes began to sting with a warning of tears. She sank down onto a kitchen chair. Carly was in the living room, the discordant notes of her little piano floating through the house.

"I'm sorry," Tug muttered. "I don't mean to be the guy who wouldn't go home."

"No," Janie shook her head, stared at the coarse-grained oak table. "You're not mostly."

"Mostly."

Her face softened and she glanced over at him. "You just have to be clear that I'm not . . . looking for more than friendship."

"I know," he said. "Neither am I, really. I should stop coming by so often."

"No!" She said this with a vehemence that surprised them both. She did want him around. And while she knew that misunderstandings and hurt feelings were possible—probable even—it seemed to be the going price for having him to talk to on Tuesdays and sometimes Thursdays. And for a standing invitation to all his home games. And for those pats on the hand, which she really didn't mind so much.

"Listen," she said. "If I tell you something, can you take it the way I mean it?"

He nodded, watching her and waiting, she knew, for a bomb to drop. She didn't like it, this power she now seemed to have to hurt him. But if she wanted the balance of power restored between them, she had to hand over a little piece of herself, an embarrassing fact that would offer him some small protection from the damage she could do. "I missed you at the party last night," she admitted, barely able to look at him. "I wished you were here."

His relief was palpable, and a slow smile started around his eyes.

"Don't smile!" she cringed.

"Then next time," he said, leveling a gaze at her like a dare, "invite me."

19

FOR HALLOWEEN, DYLAN WANTED to be a knight.

"Not a pirate?" asked Janie.

"No, I'm bored of them now."

So she cut cardboard into the shape of a shield and stapled a cardboard strap to the back. She fashioned an empty wrapping paper tube into a sword. And she covered these and his bike helmet with aluminum foil. Dylan was so excited that he convinced her of his need to "try it out a little bit." Within twenty-four hours, the foil was off the helmet, the strap was off the shield, and the sword was bent in so many places it looked like a large, shiny elbow macaroni.

"Can't we just buy one?" he asked, after a brief and unconvincing expression of regret for ruining all her work.

"There's a ton of costumes at Target," offered Tug. His noon lunch with Janie had been delayed until two o'clock by a surly plumber, whom Tug had eventually fired. Tug had to admit to himself that the guy's making him late for lunch had played a small but pivotal role in the termination.

"What were you doing at Target?" asked Janie. She could imagine him at any hardware store in town, but Target, with its comforter sets and Crock-Pots and entire aisle of hair accessories, seemed completely un-Tug-like.

"When a man needs new boxers, he needs new boxers."

"Too much information!" she said, putting her hands over her ears.

Tug laughed. "Oh, get over it."

"Did you get a costume?" Dylan asked Tug.

"Uh, no. I don't usually go out for Halloween, buddy."

"Why not?"

"Uh . . ." He looked to Janie for help.

"Yeah, why not?" she teased.

"You could come with us!" said Dylan.

Again, Tug looked to Janie. Did he want an out or an invitation? she wondered. And what did she want? "Come," she said. "You can help me carry all the costume pieces when Dylan gets tired of holding them."

MONDAY, NOVEMBER 5

It can't possibly be November. But it's getting cold and rainy, and the supermarket has turkey basters and cans of pumpkin in the center aisle, so maybe it is.

Halloween was fun. Dylan was a "nice knight, not the bad kind" and very happy with his plastic sword and shield. Aunt Jude came across a toddler-sized ladybug costume in the clothing donations at Table of Plenty. Not exactly what the well-dressed homeless person is wearing this season, so she nabbed it for Carly. Barb came over with her camera. Among the close-ups of antennae and sword handles, I'm sure there are some very cute pictures. Tug came, too. He was dressed as a guy who's not covered in sawdust with a tape measure clipped to his jeans. He looked nice.

And now we have more Milk Duds and Tootsie Rolls than we could ever eat in a lifetime. Tug stuck around and took care of a couple of chocolate bars after I put the kids to bed. He still hasn't told me why Sue divorced him. The obvious reason is infidelity, but I just don't see it. He doesn't seem like a cheater. Maybe she wanted to have kids and he didn't? But he loves kids, couldn't be more thoughtful with mine. There's always money, I guess, but he seems to be making a pretty good living. The longer he doesn't tell me, the more I want to know.

I went to the soup kitchen with Aunt Jude on Saturday. I brought a bunch of the candy Dylan collected but doesn't like (and even some he does). I've learned that alcoholics like sweets, and eating sugar helps stave off the craving for booze. So I was very popular for a few minutes there.

Beryl was back. She told me about her recent travels up north. She stepped across the border into Maine and stepped back into New Hampshire again, then crossed and recrossed. She likes the feeling of getting to choose over and over where she will be. She likes to change course suddenly, just because she can and no one can stop her.

But then apparently someone did change her course. "A distinctly indecorous gentleman" who caught her sleeping beneath the awning of an office building tried to "press his advantage." It sounded pretty scary, but she preferred not to say too much. She did leave Portland "posthaste" and returned to the relative safety of Pelham.

I have this strange notion that I could take her home, give her a shower and a haircut, put her in one set of clothes (not three), and take her to tea at the Ritz. No one would know that she wasn't some genteel older woman with season's tickets to the ballet. My question is who was Beryl before she was homeless and a little crazy and incapable of staying in any one place for more than an hour? Was she like this as a little girl? Did something happen that traumatized her so much that her brain chemicals got flowing in the wrong direction? Who was Beryl before she was Beryl?

Malcolm's younger sister in Oregon is getting worse. He had me write a sad, desperate letter to his nephew begging him to stay by her side and be good to her. He hinted that he knew his sister hadn't always been easy to live with, that perhaps she *wasn't the best mother she might have been under other, better circumstances. Malcolm implored his nephew to set all that aside, to imagine her in her earliest days, "unstained by hardship." Malcolm remembered her as a very beautiful, sweettempered child and wished that he could give these memories to his nephew so he would know that his mother had been good. A baby is the purest thing there is, he said, and everyone was a baby once. "She was my baby, the only one I'll ever get, so please, please take care of her."*

I cried. I couldn't help it. The impulse to avoid pain, even other people's pain, is so great. And yet there we are, Aunt Jude and I, almost every Saturday. Otherwise who would type the letters?

LATER THAT WEEK, CORMAC and Barb stopped by with the pictures from Halloween. "Just a few," said Barb. "The ones you'd like."

"What about the ones I wouldn't like?"

"Oh . . . No, I . . . ," stuttered Barb. "There aren't any you wouldn't like, so much as they wouldn't . . . interest you."

"Artsy shots," interjected Cormac, giving Janie a Watch Yourself look. "You know, antennae and stuff."

"They might interest me," Janie said. "Who doesn't like antennae?"

Barb looked to Cormac for interpretation, and found him rolling his eyes and smirking at Janie. "You wouldn't know antennae if they bit you on the ass!"

"At least I know that antennae don't *bite*, biscuit boy!"

Cormac turned to Barb, "That's it, she's out of the wedding."

"What?" said Barb. "It's only seven weeks away—"

"Oh please, Cousin Cormac, please," Janie mock whined. "PLEASE can I be in your wedding?"

"I hate it when she begs," he said to Barb. He swung an arm around Janie's neck and pulled her in tight, grabbing her chin in his other hand. "Okay, but you better be good, understand? No bad girls in the wedding, chickie." It was all in fun, but the message was clear.

"I swear on a stack of cookbooks," she puckered at him, "I'll be good."

They looked through the pictures, and it wasn't hard for Janie to be enthusiastic and appreciative. Barb seemed to have an uncanny knack for making her subjects show themselves: Dylan, sword held high, practically channeling King Arthur; Carly hurling herself across the room, looking for all the world as if the ladybug costume were meant for actual flight.

There were sweet pictures and funny pictures of various groupings, and one last picture of Tug coming in the door. He was looking at Dylan, who was prepared to engage him in battle, the two of them facing each other with an unlikely combination of aggression and warmth.

That's right, thought Janie, *his shirt was plaid.* It was a button down, with pale tracings of green and tan intersecting each other in pleasing combinations. And it smelled good, she remembered from standing next to him on countless doorsteps, as she held Carly, and Dylan practiced his trick-or-treat manners. *He must use laundry detergent with a nice scent.*

It took a moment for Janie to realize that she was in the picture, too, standing to the side and a little behind Tug, her gaze directed toward him. She was smiling, but there was more than that. There was a look of . . . what? She remembered feeling happy, almost relieved, when he arrived. His enthusiasm for the kids' costumes had been very sweet. And he wasn't intrusive with them, the way so many adults were with other people's children. He didn't force interaction. Dylan talked to Tug if he felt like it, and if he didn't, Tug let him be.

It was easy, Janie realized, looking at that picture. Tug's cautious but steady march toward further involvement in their lives had mostly been easy, save for the occasional minor skirmish between the two of them. Not so minor, really, but over now, and each one had served to clarify their relationship, to make further contact easier.

Gratitude, she realized, studying the picture. *That's me being grateful.*

IT STARTED OUT WITH a headache, the kind that made Janie momentarily wonder if she was experiencing some sort of rapid-onset blindness. Her eyelashes hurt. It was painful to turn her head. As heavily caffeine-dependent as she was, however, the feeling was not completely unknown to her. It was the kind of headache she'd had a couple of times before when, for various reasons, she'd neglected to drink her usual three or four cups of coffee.

One time, she and Robby had been camping, and the coffee grounds had been "forgotten." Robby thought it was a good opportunity for her to "detox." Janie responded by climbing back into the tent, dosing herself with the emergency Benadryl from the first-aid kit, and sleeping for six hours. That was after she broke up with him and hit him in the back of the head with her hiking boot.

This time, Janie had had her coffee. But she drank another two cups just to be sure, and took some Tylenol. The headache got worse and spread to her back and arms. By the time she got the kids off to bed, she was shivering and pale. Her dreams that night came in snapshots: the kids and her on a rotting raft at night in the middle of a river; pellets of rain beating down on their unprotected heads; Dylan's horrified face, beads of sweat exploding from his pores; Carly biting her own arm.

As the sun began to blare through her bedroom window, Janie roused, wrapped her comforter around her and reached for the phone. "Aunt Jude." Her voice sounded as if she had recently been dug from a glacier and defrosted.

"Janie? Janie? Is everything alright? Are the children—?"

Janie winced and held the phone away from her ear. "I'm sick."

Aunt Jude began a relentless litany of her sick friends, the illnesses she'd heard about, and the illnesses her sick friends had heard about. "Do you want me to come over? I could get the children dressed, feed them some breakfast, do you have any milk, I could bring some—"

"Just come."

Some time later, she had no idea how much later, Janie heard the snap of the screen door on the porch. Some time after that she heard voices on the landing outside her bedroom. "Mommy's sick, honey, she needs her rest."

"Can I see her?"

"We don't want to wake her."

"But can I just SEE her? With my EYES?" Her bedroom door opened slowly, and Janie squinted across the room at them: Aunt Jude holding Carly in her little pink Easter dress; Dylan with his black curls wet-combed across his head from a newly made side part.

"Hi, Mom," Dylan whispered loudly. "You're sick, right?"

"Yes, sweetie," she croaked.

"I'll take him to school, and Carly can come home with me," said Aunt Jude. "I've got the car seats and the diaper bag. Are you okay?"

"Probably just a twenty-four-hour thing," Janie murmured, though neither of them really believed that.

After they'd gone, Janie wished she'd asked for a glass of water. Then she was rafting again with the kids, who were tied to a mast without a sail. The rotting wood was slippery and Janie kept losing her balance and sliding to the edge of the logs, the swirling water black as tar by her feet.

Later, a man's voice came from the bottom of the stairs, and Janie thought, *Thank God*.

"Tug," she said, trying to raise her voice, knowing she hadn't.

His work boots made hushed thuds on the stairs. "You alright?" he said from the doorway.

"I feel like hell," she said.

He came forward into the room, moving across it tentatively, as if crossing the border of an unknown country. Stopping by the bed, hands in his pockets, he asked, "Fever?"

"Can't find the thermometer."

She saw him hesitate for a moment, then decide to sit on the edge of her bed. He reached out a hand and placed it gently on her forehead. It was cool and leathery, and she could feel her own heat seeping into it. Then he had both hands on her cheeks. Again the coolness, the momentary relief. He reached under the blankets, searching for something, and took her hand. His fingers pressed on her wrist while he studied his battered watch. "Janie, girl," he said shaking his head at her, "you are in tough shape. Your pulse is racing and you're putting out enough BTUs to melt your hair."

"Just put your hands on my face again," she murmured. He smiled as he reached for her cheeks.

He asked her about her symptoms, if she'd taken any medication, was she drinking water, did she have any ibuprofen, where exactly would it be? He left and returned. Ice water, a cool wet washcloth, little reddish-brown coated pills. As she struggled to sit up, he arranged her pillows behind her so she could lean back and still be sufficiently upright to drink.

"These blankets have to go," he said. "You're cooking yourself." One by one he pulled them off, folded them neatly and laid them on the chair, which was still covered with all the clothing and undergarments she'd peeled off the night before. He left her only the top sheet.

"Freezing," she said from under the cold damp of the washcloth.

"Sorry. It'll be okay once the ibuprofen kicks in."

"How do you know so much?"

"Sue was a nurse."

A few of her languid brain cells began to spark. "Was?" It was easier to ask from beneath this wet cloak of pseudo-anonymity.

"Her license was revoked. Drink some more." He handed her the cup. "Can you sleep?"

"No," she lied. "Bring your lunch up here and keep me company."

"I didn't bring anything this time," he said. "I'll eat later."

"There's turkey and cheese and peppers in the fridge. That rye bread you like is in the freezer." Janie could feel her body starting to cool, and the piercing pain in her back and arms becoming blunted and dull. Tug didn't respond, so she lifted a corner of the washcloth to peek at him. "What?" she asked. "Oh, you don't want to get sick."

"No, I don't worry about germs. It's just nice," he gave a little shrug, "you keeping that stuff on hand for me."

"You're my best lunch customer," she said, and put the washcloth over her eyes again.

He went downstairs and Janie pressed the washcloth across her face and around her neck. She rummaged in the drawer of her bedside table for a hairbrush and organized her curls into a topknot. It felt good to spruce up a little.

She fell into an easy doze, comforted by the far-off sounds of the refrigerator door thumping closed, the ding of the toaster oven, the clack of a knife on a plate. He brought her toast and encouraged her to try and eat a little so the ibuprofen wouldn't bother her stomach. He asked about the kids. It was tiring to talk, she wanted only to listen. She wanted him to talk a lot so he would stay longer. And she wanted to know about Sue.

"How'd her license get revoked?" Janie asked. It seemed like a non sequitur, yet the question had been hanging there between them since he'd mentioned it.

He didn't answer at first, then he said, "That's kind of a long one."

"Oh," she said, nibbling at the toast. "You probably have to get back to work. How's the Pelham Heights house coming?"

"No, it's not that," he said. "I'm just not sure how much you want to know."

That was a fair statement, she had to admit to herself. She'd been nothing if not tentative with him. But he knew so much about her. He had the details on the beginning, ending, and a good deal of the middle of the most meaningful relationship she'd ever had. And he'd been witness to half the major events of her life over the last six months.

And . . . well, it was clear that he'd wanted to tell her for some time now, dropping little hints like hookless bait. Somehow his wanting her to know had become important to her, too. "All of it," she said. "Tell me."

BECOMING A NURSE HAD been Sue's plan since she was old enough to pin her mother's nursing cap into her baby-fine blond hair. Her older sister had gone to nursing school at Fitchburg State. The goal, it became apparent to Tug, had been to go to a better nursing school than either of them. When she got accepted at Boston College, he and Sue celebrated with a trip to Canobie Lake Park to ride the big roller coaster. "Not the new twisty one they have now that turns you upside down. Back then the biggie was that one on the huge rickety lattice of white two-by-fours."

"The Yankee Cannonball," said Janie.

"That's the one. She liked to sit up front, first car. Had to get there faster than everyone else."

Janie knew the type. "Did you go to college, too, when she did?"

"That's a whole 'nother story."

"So?"

Sue had encouraged him to go to business school. He was ambivalent, having worked on his friend's father's construction crew for several summers. He liked being outside, and he liked building things, making something grow from a hole in the ground into a building that sheltered people as they went about their lives, working, sleeping, eating lunch. His only problem was that he was too slow, and the foreman would hassle him to do things faster. "I liked the process too much."

He applied to only one school, University of Massachusetts–Boston, and got in. For two and a half years he commuted to classes, spending a good deal of his time at Boston College with Sue. But then his mother died right after Christmas of his junior year. "Dad kind of fell apart. Things weren't getting done." He looked at Janie. "You know how that goes, right?"

"You know how well I know."

So he took the semester off, much to Sue's everlasting disappointment. He picked up hours with the construction crew again. And he became the one to buy the groceries and pay the bills and empty the mousetraps. When he didn't register for classes in the fall, Sue was furious. "It was the first time I said a big, honking 'No' to her, and she wasn't used to that."

"You didn't want to go back?"

"I didn't really see the point. I had learned some things about business, which has definitely helped me along the way, don't get me wrong. But I knew I was never going to go corporate, like all those other guys were. I had what I needed, so why waste the money?"

"Sue wanted you to have the degree."

"In a big, bad way." He stopped for a moment, ran his hand over the scar on his arm, a private little smile edging in around his jaw.

Janie laughed. "You did it to piss her off!"

"A little, I guess," he grinned. "It was about time, you know. I was twenty-one years old. I had to stop living for her approval."

As expected, she dumped him. And while it wasn't the happiest time of his life, it was important for him to see that he could live without her. He dated other girls, got serious with one or two, but then backed out. He bumped into Sue at a Christmas party in Natick, and they talked. There was no mention of getting back together, but it felt important to be on good terms again. She asked him to come see her graduate from Boston College in the spring. She thought she had a shot at valedictorian.

With the best grades in the whole School of Nursing, Sue won the coveted roll of class speaker. But she got edged out for vale-dictorian by a communications major. Tug learned all of this from her at a party she took him to afterward, where she got as drunk as he'd ever seen her. He half carried her back to her apartment, and held her hair while she threw up. He put her in the shower, helped her brush her teeth, and guided her to her bed. "I know it's crazy, and I probably need years of therapy to figure this one out, but I always liked her better when she was low."

"Sounds like she was more human. You slept with her?"

"Nah, she wanted me to, but it seemed too . . ."

"Opportunistic?"

"Yeah, and kind of disgusting. Hard to get excited when you've just watched a girl puke."

"Good point. But you wanted to be with her again."

"Like a moth loves a flame."

Within a year they were married. Sue got a job at UMass Medi-cal Center in Worcester and Tug built them a house in Northboro. With all the construction going on in the late '80s, he decided to set up his own company. It was a good time for them, their happi-est. Sue moved up the ladder, eventually becoming known as the best nurse in the cardiac care unit.

"Any thought of kids?" asked Janie.

"Bingo," he said.

Sue always wanted kids "someday"—but not until after she got out of internal medicine and into cardiology. Then she wanted to wait until after she got off the outpatient floor and into sur-gery. Then it was after she graduated from bypasses to electro-physiology. Or after Dr. Esteberg, the most respected, demanding cardiologist in the department started regularly requesting her for his surgeries. "She liked kids. We always had a great time when we babysat for my nieces. But she was never quite ready for her own."

"You were ready."

"We were in our late thirties. I was to the point of begging." He felt himself slipping away from her, thinking about other women. He started going to bars with the guys from his crew when Sue was working the evening shift, which seemed to be pretty often. He would dance with a woman if he was asked. He would slow dance. It felt good to have someone in his arms, someone pliable, who let him lead. He kissed one once when he walked her to her car. His eyes flicked to Janie. "I shouldn't have told you all that."

She shrugged, hoping to seem unfazed. "It's not cheating, exactly."

"Yeah, it kind of was. Sex isn't the only way to cheat."

"Were you thinking about leaving her?"

"I don't know what I was thinking. Things just seemed to happen. Time passes and then you're forty." Sue's goal—she promised him, the last—was to become nurse manager of the cardiac care unit. The current nurse manager was due to retire in less than a year, and Sue was certain she was most qualified to take the position, even though others were more senior. Then she hurt her back lifting a patient. She could barely move, but she insisted on finishing her shift. An MRI showed a herniated disc in her spine, requiring weeks of rest to heal.

Tug anticipated a battle to make her stay still that long, but once she was on the pain medication, she almost seemed to enjoy the time off. It was a relief, she told him. A relief from working so hard and caring so much what others thought of her performance. A relief from being her, he realized.

He stopped going out—had to be home to take care of her. He went by the house when he could during the day to check in, see if she needed anything. When he wasn't with her, he found himself thinking about what he could get for her or do for her that would make the waiting more bearable. They passed the evenings stretched out on the bed together, talking. It was the last good time.

Once she was better, she went back to work with a vengeance. Had to make up for lost time. Had to show everyone she was the most knowledgeable, most dedicated, most reliable. The nurse manager gave notice, as expected, and Sue applied for the job.

"I knew she didn't get it when I got home one night and she was already there, having a glass of wine." When Sue told the hiring administrator she planned to challenge the decision, the woman gave it to her straight. She was highly competent, yes, and completely dedicated. But none of the other nurses liked her. She was too intent on showing them up. How could Sue manage the nurses when she was so unconcerned with their feelings? She was a good nurse, but she was no leader.

"Looking back," Tug said, "I think she got depressed. It wasn't real obvious, and I think I was just so happy about finally trying to start a family, that I wasn't looking too hard. But the signs were there." After a while she seemed better, more relaxed, even kind of silly sometimes. But it wasn't like when she was confined to her bed, with her goals still intact. She could be scatterbrained and annoying. This new Sue was not a better Sue, just different.

On their way to his brother Dave's house for Christmas one year, they had to turn back twice for things that Sue had forgotten to put in the car. When they finally arrived, Sue helped the girls open their presents and sat on the floor with them, intently dressing and redressing their Barbie dolls with the new outfits she and Tug had brought them.

Dave's wife, Christa, a social worker, took Tug into the spare bedroom and asked him what the hell Sue was on. Tug was shocked, told Christa she was crazy. Christa wasn't buying it. "Go out there and look at her—she's lying on the floor with her hair all askew, playing with dolls! That is not Sue!"

It took Tug a while to be sure, but the time came when it was undeniable. Nonetheless, when he confronted Sue, she denied it. She straightened up after that, and he hoped (more than believed) that she had stopped. But one day, it all caught up with her. Postsurgical patients in her care seemed to be experiencing a surprising amount of residual pain. The new nurse manager, a longtime co-worker of Sue's, set up a sting, and other nurses were happy to assist. They caught her in the act of pocketing a patient's pain medication. A careful chart review determined she'd likely been doing it for over a year. "My wife, who prided herself on competence and correctness above all things, had left hundreds of patients with chest wounds in horrible pain so she could get a buzz on."

She was fired, her nursing license was revoked, and she was indicted for narcotics theft with intent to distribute. Hospital administration didn't believe she was taking them herself. Even high, she still did her job as well as anyone. She pled guilty to the lesser charge of theft and got five to ten years in MCI Framingham.

"But wait a minute," Janie said, as Tug finished the last bites of his sandwich. "You said she served you divorce papers. Why did she want a divorce from *you*?"

"Yeah," said Tug, setting the plate on the floor. He leaned back in the chair, ran a hand back across his head. "I was all set to leave her. She'd lied to me, hurt people. She was in jail, for chrissake. And she didn't ask me to wait. Nope. She knew I had every right."

But then one day, a month or so after she was gone, he was watching the news. In fact he'd been watching it for days. Hurricane Katrina was busy battering the Gulf of Mexico, and selfishly, Tug admitted, it was a welcome distraction from his own trouble. "Gave me a hell of a perspective, too. Here I was, safe and sound, drowning in nothing more than my own self-pity, and down South people were literally drowning in their own homes."

The thing that impressed him the most were the emergency workers. "Guys were lowering themselves from helicopters, dropping into that toxic water, trying to find and rescue people they'd never even met. And here I wouldn't drive in the comfort of my air-conditioned truck over to Framingham to visit a woman I'd loved all my life."

He started going to see her on Saturdays. If he couldn't visit, he wrote. He sent her things. She accepted all of this with gratitude, even humility, which he'd never seen in her before. She was changing, he could tell, and he had hopes that it wasn't too late for them. After several years of exemplary behavior she was released early. When they got the word last December, he went for his Saturday visit with a head full of plans for their future. She put an end to that right away. She thought they should separate. He couldn't understand it, couldn't believe he'd spent years waiting for her, only to be cut loose. He'd jumped into the toxic water, and she was waving him off.

But she hadn't led him on, he had to admit. She'd never talked of a future with him. Purposely, almost superstitiously, they had talked only of the present, her computer skills classes, his work on his grandfather's house. Now he fought with her, railed about the effort he'd made to mend their marriage. She hadn't known that was his intention, she said. She thought he was just lonely.

Still, he couldn't believe that she preferred a life without him. Finally she said, "You know what, Tug? You remind me. And I just don't want to be reminded."

"HOLY COW," murmured JANIE. She shifted onto her side, stiff and aching, she realized, from having sat in the same position listening for so long.

"Yeah," he nodded. "I think she must have headed for a divorce lawyer straight from prison because she had me served about a week after her release." He didn't contest it—what would be the use? They divvied things up pretty quickly. He gave her the house in Northboro and moved into his grandfather's place here in Pelham. "Want to hear something funny? The divorce became final on my birthday in July. You brought me that cake, remember?"

"God, I had no clue."

"I wasn't exactly advertising."

"It was Dylan's idea."

"I know," he said. "Still, it felt pretty good to have a beautiful woman bring me chocolate on such a hell of a day."

Janie lowered her chin, gave him the warning look.

"So I think you're attractive. So what," he countered, rising. "It's not like it's late-breaking news." He leaned over toward her, felt her forehead. "Still a little warm. You should take more ibuprofen in—" he looked at his watch. "Dammit."

"What?"

"It's three thirty. I gotta get over to the job before the crew takes off and leaves power tools all over the yard."

"Sorry I kept you so long."

"My fault."

"I asked," she said. "I'm glad you told me. Have a good week if I don't see you."

"Maybe I'll make a quick stop tomorrow just to check up on you."

"On a Wednesday?" Janie raised her eyebrows in mock surprise.

"Okay, maybe not!"

"No," she said. "Come."

THE NEXT DAY, JANIE was no better. She knew it was a bug of some kind, the flu maybe, but she couldn't help but worry that it was something worse. Perhaps it was the opening salvo of some sinister disease, nibbling at her now in anticipation of the larger bites to come. *How do single mothers manage not to panic every time they sneeze?* she wondered. She thought of Christopher Reeve, the actor who was paralyzed by a fall from a horse and died young from complications. His wife died of cancer not long after, leaving their thirteen-year-old son an orphan. *It happens to people with every possible resource,* she thought. *It could definitely happen to me.*

Aunt Jude was busy with the Book and Knickknack Swap she had organized at the Senior Center, so Cormac picked Dylan up for school. He said he didn't worry so much about leaving the bakery, now that Barb was there for backup. "She can find the register tapes faster than I can these days. And she's better with snotty customers, God knows."

Janie crawled into the shower for a quick rinse while Cormac fed Dylan and Carly a breakfast of day-old crullers. In clean pajamas, she dragged her quilt downstairs and set herself up on the huge leather couch. It enveloped and soothed her, in part because it was so cool and soft, and in part because it was Shelly's. Janie missed Shelly and vowed to dislike the new boyfriend no matter how handsome, rich, and well-housed he might be.

Cormac left with Dylan, and Carly was happy to have free reign of the living room, playing with her toys, switching the TV off and on, crawling up into Janie's lap and then right back down again. She liked to sit and look at her board books, turning the pages with her thumbs, her little back so straight and noble looking. *At what age do kids learn to slouch?* Janie wondered. Her listless brain offered no answer.

Tug came by just before noon. He sat on the edge of the couch and checked her temperature with his hands. "Poor girl," he said. "You showered?"

"Yeah, I was grossing myself out."

"Your shampoo smells good." He brought Carly's highchair into the living room and fed her.

"There's avocado in the vegetable drawer," said Janie. Tug made a face. "What? It's healthy!" she said.

"Then you climb out of your little nest there and give it to her," he said. "It's too slimy for me."

"You're telling me you handle rotten boards and insulation and that nasty smelly window caulk and you won't touch avocado?"

He shrugged. "Complex, I know, but you'll get it all straight."

She smiled and closed her eyes for a moment. *Such a comfort to have him here.*

"Hey," she said suddenly, "I know it's silly, but you don't think this is anything . . . like . . . serious, right? It's just a bug?"

He gave Carly a couple of crackers and came to sit beside Janie on the couch again. "There's no way this is anything serious. In a couple of days you'll be hopping around like a jackhammer."

"Okay."

"There's a million what-ifs in life. You just have to keep yourself from thinking about the bad ones."

He couldn't stay long. After he left, Janie carried Carly up to her crib for a nap. She was completely exhausted ten minutes later when she made it back down to the couch. She fell into a dream-ridden sleep, rafting once again through black waters. This time she really did fall in, leaving the kids alone and adrift. The water wasn't wet, though. It turned into soil around her, enveloping her, suffocating her like dirt thrown into a grave.

HEIDI HAD PICKED UP Dylan from school and brought him to her house to play. At three o'clock Janie heard the boys clomping and giggling on the porch, and Heidi shushing them. The front door opened slowly and Heidi peeked in.

"It's okay, I'm awake," said Janie from the couch. "Carly's still asleep, though."

Heidi sent the boys around to the backyard to play. "I would have kept him longer," she said, bringing a grocery bag into the kitchen, "but I had told you three, and I didn't want to call and disturb you to extend it."

"It's fine," said Janie. "Carly will be up any minute, anyway. And it's good to see you."

Heidi sank into the leather chair and put her feet up on the ottoman. "I brought some dinner—homemade mac and cheese—and some salad." She studied Janie's pallid complexion. "But you don't seem like you'll be eating much of it."

"Maybe tomorrow," Janie said. She reached for the washcloth and wiped her face.

"Should I go?" Heidi sat up. "Do you need to rest?"

"No, I just woke up. And I don't really want to sleep, anyway. I've been having these bizarre nightmares about death. I keep worrying that this isn't just the flu, it's some fatal illness and the kids will be orphaned."

"Oh yeah. I used to do that. Right around when the doofus and I were separating. I couldn't stand the thought of Keane being raised by him alone."

"When did it stop?"

"I went to my doctor and had her do every test the insurance would pay for. I thought about getting one of those body scans, you know, the ones that are supposed to pick up every little thing you might have? But it was really expensive, and I realized that just because I don't have anything now, doesn't mean I wouldn't five years from now."

"So once you had a clean bill of health from your doctor, you stopped worrying?"

"Well, that and I called our marriage counselor and had a couple of sessions. He couldn't save the marriage, but he helped me get control of my intrusive thoughts." Heidi laughed. "You're not going to believe this, but you know what it came down to? He basically just told me to cut it out!"

Janie chuckled. "That's pretty much Tug's take on it, too."

"Tug?" said Heidi, her laughter pulling inward, like a humor vacuum. "The contractor?"

"Yeah," said Janie, feeling self-conscious. "We've become friends. He stops by for lunch sometimes."

"Oh."

"What do you mean, 'Oh'? We're not dating or anything. He just comes by. The kids and I used to go to his softball games sometimes until the season ended."

"I'm not implying that you are. I'm just . . ."

"What?"

"Jealous, I guess."

"Heidi, trust me. There's nothing to be jealous of. We just hang out."

"That's plenty to be jealous of! What do you think I'm looking for, a hot date every night of the week?"

"No, I only meant—"

"God!" Heidi shuddered in frustration. "I would kill to have a guy just to talk to!"

Janie exhaled. "You're right. It's nice."

"And he's okay with that? Just hanging out? Nothing more?"

"Well, I think maybe he'd like something more, but he knows I'm not up for it."

"Not even a little?"

"No! Robby hasn't even been gone a year."

"So maybe after January?"

"Heidi, stop! I can't think about this!"

"Oh, alright. Don't freak out."

Listen to her, Janie thought, amused. *Miss Insecure is telling me to be cool.* Carly began to stir upstairs, and without asking or being asked, Heidi went up to get her. It was funny, really, how someone so unlike Janie had become so familiar.

"I changed her diaper," Heidi said when she returned with Carly in her arms. "P-U! What are you feeding this child?"

Not avocados, thought Janie.

20

I T WAS 9:15 P.M. and Janie was in bed. The plan was to sleep, but she had napped too late in the day. Her flu seemed to be dissipating; she had been only intermittently feverish that day. She'd had enough energy to get up and feed the kids leftover macaroni and cheese for dinner.

A thought came to her as she lay there unable to sleep. She would get up and e-mail Jake, see what he was up to. A moment later she was embarrassed. She had forgotten that she and Jake no longer spoke, had no relationship at all, not even priest and parishioner. Why should it embarrass her, this momentary forgetting of the status of things? It was just a tiny lapse, never spoken aloud, with no one to see the stinging blush that crept up her neck.

How had she come to feel so strongly for a man—a celibate man, no less—that even after three months of radio silence, she could still idly consider contacting? Had her instincts become so tangled and short-circuited that she would subject herself to such a gaffe? Was the damage permanent? She had to be more careful, she told herself—of what, she hadn't quite worked out.

The phone rang and Janie reached for it quickly, grateful for a reason to change the channel in her brain. "Hello?"

"Hey, how're you feeling?"

The muscles at the back of her neck, pulled taught by self-doubt, released. "Better. I think I turned a corner."

"Sorry I didn't get over there today. The architect on this job is making me nuts. He changes the plans about every fifteen minutes."

"No kidding," she laughed. "What's *that* like?"

"Ah, don't start," he chuckled. "You love that porch."

"True."

They talked about any number of things. There were five units of 40B affordable housing going in on Old Connecticut Path. The developer had just fired the builder and was calling for new bids. Tug was thinking about going for it. Did Janie have any further thoughts about picking up her old job at Newton-Wellesley Hospital? How would the kids take it? Tug reminded her that his nieces babysat all the time, and might be willing to commit to a weekly stint if she needed it. The call went on for a while as they rambled through the funny moments, minor concerns, and action items of each one's day. Janie thought briefly of Heidi. *A guy just to talk to*, she had said.

"So, where are you going for Thanksgiving?" Tug asked, the cadence of his words changing slightly. "Your aunt's?"

"Yeah. Cormac and Uncle Charlie will go over the day before and clear all the furniture out of her living room. She has one of those puzzle tables."

"The kind that fold up small but have a bunch of leaves?"

"You've heard of them?"

"I have one. It was my grandparents'. One of the things I kept."

"So where are you going?" she asked.

"My brother's probably."

"Keeping your options open? It's only a week away."

"You might say." He was quiet for a moment. She could hear the gentle *swoosh* of his breath on the mouthpiece. "I was kind of thinking about us spending Thanksgiving together," he said finally.

Of course, Janie thought instinctively. *Makes total sense.* But then she started second-guessing herself. What would he think? What would it mean? What would he think it means? The blush rose up again, and she said merely, "Oh."

"Okay, it was just a thought." A thin line of disappointment underscored the apparent dispassion of his words.

"Well . . ." Now she was second-guessing her second-guessing. And wanting to be with him. "I mean . . . where?"

"Anywhere. Your aunt's, my brother's, your house, my house."

"You know how to cook a turkey?" she stalled.

"No, but it can't be that hard."

"Why?"

"Because it's just a turkey and an oven. I have one, I can get the other."

"No, I mean why do you want to do Thanksgiving together?"

He didn't answer for a moment, and she was certain that he was working out how to say it, more than why he wanted it.

"I'm thankful for you," he said quietly. "I want to be thankful *with* you."

Of course, she thought. *Me, too.*

THE ELDERLY FATHER GILROY, Pastor of Immaculate Conception Church in Natick, stood hunched and gently quaking at the lectern. Over the past three months, Janie had grown used to his throat clearing and his lackluster homilies. She usually spent a good deal of Mass keeping the kids from annoying the other, mostly older, parishioners, so it wasn't like she listened all that much. She often read to Dylan in a barely audible whisper from the children's Bible Father Jake had given him, full of simplified, white-washed stories and cartoon pictures. Dylan was transfixed. Carly liked to balance like a gymnast along the kneeler, her tiny hands gripping the pew in front of them. Back and forth she would dance. Aunt Jude would retrieve her if she got farther than an arm's length away.

"Don't read," Dylan whispered to Janie on this particular Sunday. "I already know it. I just want to look at the pictures." He was studying the too-brightly-colored depiction of David slaying Goliath with his little slingshot. Janie knew that Dylan was making the story much more dramatic and dangerous in his head than the words on the page did. It gave her a moment to tune in to whatever Father Gilroy was prattling on about. Turns out it was the Gospel of Luke:

> And he said to them, "Suppose one of you has a friend to whom he goes at midnight and says, 'Friend, lend me three loaves of bread, for a friend of mine has arrived at my house from a journey and I have nothing to offer him.' And he says in reply from within, 'Do not bother me; the door has already been locked and my children and I are already in bed. I cannot get up to give you anything.' I tell you, if he does not get up to give the visitor the loaves because of their friendship, he will get up to give him whatever he needs because of his persistence.

> "And I tell you, ask and you will receive; seek and you will find; knock and the door will be opened to you . . ."

"Now our Gospel today is a story from times of old," quivered Father Gilroy when he'd finished with the reading.

They're all stories from times of old, thought Janie.

"How-ever," persisted Father Gilroy. He said it as if it were two words, in his distinctly Boston accent: *How evah*. "We can exTRAPolate from this story given to us by our Lord." *Owah Lawd*.

"It's about PERSEVERANCE, perseverance in the face of AD-VERSITY. Well, let's see now . . ." Father Gilroy seemed to lose his train of thought for a moment. "Yes, well, uh, it's about friend-ship, too. Sometimes a friend wants more from us than we want to give. That friend wants something that seems UNREASONABLE. Come over in the middle of the night for a loaf of BREAD? When we're sleeping? That's UNREASONABLE!

"How-ever, that friend keeps knocking. That friend keeps ASK-ING us for something he NEEDS . . ." Father paused and brushed a hand over his mouth, wiping something away. "You ever notice how darn near half these stories have to do with HOSPITALITY? It's all about feeding and sheltering people, for Pete's sake! It's all about fish and bread and who's cleaning up after!

"Well, I'll tell you why. It's because back in the times of old, when they didn't have garage door openers and microwaves and all those fancy gadgets you women want these days, if people didn't feed and shelter each other, THEY DIED! So here's that friend, banging on your door in the middle of the night, trying to keep his visitor from starving to death right there in his living room. GET UP, for the love of Mike! Give the guy some bread!"

Father Gilroy turned away from the lectern then and took a step down as if the homily was over. But before the other foot hit the floor, he turned back, remembering something. "We don't always know what our friends need. And they usually don't bang on the door and yell it. It's all so much more COMPlicated these days. We have all these newfangled gadgets, like those cellular telephones that don't even plug into the WALL, and still we aren't too good at listening. And when WE'RE the guy that needs the bread, we have to persevere. Because sometimes people don't know how to listen, and we gotta keep asking.

"We gotta keep knocking on each other's doors, because oth-erwise," Father Gilroy glared at the congregation, "WHAT'S the POINT."

BARB FUSSED OVER THE kids as Janie and Aunt Jude waited for them to pick out a cookie from the Confectionary display case after Mass. They leaned against the high counter that spanned the bakery's front window. Customers sat on stools and sipped their Chai and French roast, stoking up to meet the icy blast of air that awaited them outside. An older man approached them, tentatively at first. He tightened his trench coat and fingered the end of the belt nervously. "You're Mrs. LaMarche," he said.

"Yes . . . ," said Janie.

"I'm Ed Martin. From the bank. I worked with your husband. I remember seeing you and your son come by a couple of times."

"Oh," said Janie, straining to be gracious. "Hi."

"Yes, well, I don't want to bother you . . . I just wanted to say that . . ." His words came out faster now, as if he were propelling them from his mouth, "Well, your husband was a good boss, a good man, and we all remember him fondly."

It was obvious that he had had to gather up all his courage to approach her, and this, in addition to his kind words, softened her. "Thanks, Ed," she said. "Thanks for telling me."

"I hope you and your family are . . . are doing okay?" he stammered.

"We're hanging in there." And they were, she realized. So slowly she had barely noticed, their status had been upgraded from "still shitty."

"Oh, that's great," he exhaled. "I'll tell everyone I saw you. They'll definitely want to hear." He nodded and excused himself and was out in the street in moments, nearly at a jog.

They watched him recede down the street, and Aunt Jude reached her bejeweled hand around Janie's shoulder and gave her a squeeze. "Good," she whispered. It was the shortest sentence Janie had ever heard her utter.

"So," Janie said after a moment. "Thanksgiving."

"Oh yes!" said Aunt Jude. "I've ordered the turkey from Stop & Shop. They have those free-range turkeys now. I know you like that kind of thing. It's a happy bird right up until it's . . . well, it'll be delicious, I'm sure."

"Think you'd have enough for one more?"

Aunt Jude's face went wide, on full alert. "Well, YES! Of course! Did you want to invite someone? Is it that nice blond woman, Dylan's little friend's mother? It's so hard when couples part. Her husband has the boy and she's all alone."

"Uh, actually the three of them are going to her in-laws' in Ohio. Her ex-husband's mother called crying and begged her to come."

"Isn't that so kind!"

"Of Heidi or her ex-mother-in-law?"

"Both!"

"I suppose," said Janie. It all seemed a little nuts to her, and yet she had to admit it was kind, too. Weird and kind. "No, I was thinking of asking Tug Malinowski, the guy who built my porch."

"Oh, Tug! Of course!" Aunt Jude was a little too excited about this. Janie ground her molars.

"It's just that he's all alone and I kind of feel sorry for him." The lie caught in her teeth but she spit it out, anyway. If Aunt Jude got all revved up about this, Janie would chuck the whole idea.

"Well," said Aunt Jude, looking away, suddenly focused on untangling her necklaces. "He seems like such a lovely person. I'm sure he has many friends with open doors. It would be our pleasure to have him." She glanced pointedly back up at Janie. "*Our* pleasure."

JANIE DECIDED TO PICK Tug up at his house on her way to Aunt Jude's. If he came on his own, the whole family would watch her greet him, like scientists studying the introduction of a new specimen into the habitat. There was nothing to see, really, she told herself. Just two friends happy to see one another. Nothing so out of the ordinary. Still, why subject herself to more scrutiny than necessary?

When she pulled into the gravel driveway, she saw that his house was a little smaller than hers, probably two bedrooms, she figured. It had an upscale log cabin feel to it, without the actual logs. The clapboards were cedar, and had apparently been applied with some protectant to retain their warm reddish-brown hue. In the center of the wall facing the street, there was a large cedar door with three bull's-eye glass windows along the top.

She could see part of the back of the house from the driveway. A deep porch ran across it with a spectacular view of Lake Pequot. The lot was modest, and there were houses within thirty feet on either side, as was common for lakeside cottages. But the windows on the sides of his house were small, some with rippled glass that would let light in but not the prying eyes of neighbors. All the sight lines led out to the lake. Tug's renovation of his grandfather's cottage had preserved privacy amidst the press of so many other houses. *He got it right,* she thought.

Dylan wanted to be the one to ring the doorbell, so she let him jump out while she stayed in the car with Carly. His unzippered jacket flapped in the wind off the lake. When Tug opened the door, Dylan hugged him. Tug squeezed the boy and rubbed his hand over Dylan's head. "Someone got a haircut," she heard him tease.

"Me! I did," said Dylan. "It's for Thanksgiving."

Tug went back in the house for a moment and returned with a bottle of wine and a covered dish. When he got into the passenger seat, he leaned over and gave Janie a quick kiss on the cheek. "Happy Thanksgiving," he murmured, and turned immediately to set his items on the floor. She could smell the wool of his navy blue V-necked sweater.

He fingered the tiny button on the collar of his shirt. "Should I be wearing a tie?"

"No, you're fine." She twisted around toward the rear window as she backed out. "We're business-casual for holidays."

"You look very nice."

"Thanks." She smiled self-consciously. It had taken her a good twenty minutes to choose the outfit: a pale blue silk blouse and a pewter-colored skirt scattered with tiny blue and black spirals, the diaphanous printed layer clinging to the satiny monotone slip. It was a distinct departure from the jeans and T-shirts she'd worn exclusively in the previous months. Not overly alluring—she'd been careful about that—but flattering to her figure, which had begun to remember the shape it had held before two pregnancies. It was at first infuriating, and then, finally, funny to her that she'd spent so much time on what to wear. Once the decision had been made, she'd hastily hung up the rejected outfit pieces, covering the tracks of her ridiculous indecision.

"What's in the dish?" she asked.

He squinted and shook his head, "Ah, it's probably terrible."

"What is it?"

"Well, I tried to . . . you know . . . come up with something a little more interesting than a bottle of wine. I brought that, too, of course. But I figured your aunt probably had all the bases covered, so I tried to think of something that she wouldn't maybe have."

"Tug," she laughed, swinging onto the main road. "What's in the dish!"

"Indian Pudding. It's a mess. I almost left it home."

"I've had that before, I think. With the cornmeal and the molasses, right?"

"Yeah, I found the recipe online." He shook his head. "I might leave it in the car."

Janie had to laugh. The thought of him, normally so competent and self-assured, leaning over a stove with a wooden spoon, squinting at a recipe, maybe with an apron on, trying so hard to please people he barely knew . . . and ending up with, as he put it, "a mess" . . . it just tickled her.

He began to chuckle. "You should see my kitchen. Looks like somebody threw a grenade."

"Bring it in," she cajoled. "Please? I want to see one thing you don't do well."

He smiled at the compliment. "Maybe."

AUNT JUDE FLUTTERED AROUND them too much when they arrived. She welcomed Tug like he was a returning war veteran, and it got under Janie's skin. She glanced at Cormac, who clasped his hands in front of his chest and made a simpering "My Hero" face behind Aunt Jude's back. It had the desired effect of lowering the voltage of Janie's irritation.

"Hey, it's my old furniture-moving pal," Cormac said to Tug, shaking his hand. Cormac glanced over at his father and then turned back to Tug. "Speaking of which, can you hang around and help me put this room back together when dinner's over?"

"Sure."

"Good, because the old man isn't really up to it anymore." Cormac raised his voice just a little. "He's gone a little soft, you know, now that he never lifts anything heavier than a pound cake."

"Shut your trap," Uncle Charlie growled from across the table. "I'm in the best shape of my life."

"Okay, Toughie," placated Cormac. "Remember your blood pressure."

"My blood pressure's lower than yours, ya little snot."

"Come on," Cormac said to Tug, "let's get a beer. Budweiser, Pop?"

"Get it from the back of the fridge. They're colder."

WHEN THE TURKEY LAY carved in generous slabs on the worn patterns of Aunt Jude's serving dishes, she began to hand bowls and platters to the adults to bring out to the table. "Careful, now," she chattered at them, and "Don't forget the serving spoon!"

"Now let's see, this would be, um . . . Tug?" she trilled. "Does your dish go with dinner or dessert?"

"After dessert," he said. "I'll use it to seal up any cracks you might have in your driveway."

"Cracks?"

"He's kidding, Auntie," said Janie. "It's dessert."

Choosing seats became a barely polite fire drill, with Dylan insisting on sitting between Cormac and Tug, Barb offering with particular vehemence to have Carly by her, and Aunt Jude being none too discreet about seating Tug next to Janie. "I'll sit in the damned kitchen!" Uncle Charlie muttered, impatient to land somewhere, anywhere, and get to his food.

With an exhortation from Aunt Brigid that everything was getting cold, they took their seats. Aunt Jude said grace. "Bless us, O Lord, as we enjoy this feast of your gifts, and help us, dear Savior, to know your grace in all things, in sorrow and in joy." Hands started to unclasp around the table, but Aunt Jude went on. "It's been a difficult year, Lord. A member of our family has gone to his reward in heaven. He was a loving father, husband, and friend and we miss him so much."

"She's talking about Dad," Dylan whispered to Tug, who nodded.

"But, as always, you have given us so many things to be thankful for. Our bodies are healthy and we have work and activities that we enjoy. Most importantly we have each other and we know how fortunate that makes us in a world where everyone seems so cut loose from each other. We have our dear Barb joining the family," she gave a smile to Cormac's betrothed, "and we have new friends that lighten our load and remind us of all that life has to offer."

Janie cringed at this obvious reference to Tug. He seemed so still next to her, not the barest twitch of a muscle in his hand as it held hers. In all of this getting-together-for-Thanksgiving business, she'd only been aware of her own hesitation. His utter stillness, a seemingly immutable intent not to be thrown by the insinuations of others, gave her an inkling of what it must be like for him, appearing new on such a scene as this.

"We praise you, Lord, and offer our sincere thanks for all your blessings. Amen."

IT WAS ONLY WHEN she'd pulled away from the house with no one but Tug in the car that Janie realized she'd chosen her fury purposely. There was nothing to be angry about, really. Everyone had behaved themselves, if you ignored the TV-ad-worthy looks of rapture the aunts gave as they sank their spoons into Tug's Indian Pudding. And Cormac had merely mentioned that if Tug stirred constantly over a low flame next time he wouldn't get so many lumps. Tug nodded and said maybe he shouldn't have been watching the Patriots game. He gave a hilarious impression of himself holding an imaginary spoon stock-still as he stared in disbelief at Tom Brady's fourth-quarter game-loosing intercepted pass.

"I saw that!" said Cormac. "Pop, did you see it? It was like something out of a Greek tragedy!"

"Oh, I saw it alright," said Uncle Charlie, shoveling up another wad of lumpy pudding. "The guy's had too many damned actress girlfriends, is what I say. He's distracted!"

Everyone was laughing, but Janie was still stuck on how Tug should have worked harder to make the pudding smooth. Why did Cormac have to criticize? Did he think Tug was the kind of guy who hangs around cooking treats all day? No, he came up with this idea to try and please them. . . . She looked around the table. Everyone was laughing and eating Tug's dessert like they'd had nothing but dry toast and thin soup all day. Maybe it wasn't such an insult, after all.

It was when the dishes were being washed, and last bits of meat were being extricated from the turkey, and the men were reassembling Aunt Jude's living room that Janie slid into a slow boil. Dylan sat at the kitchen table licking the drips from the ice-cream scoop while they all worked. "I don't want to go home," he said. "I want to stay here. Please, Mom? Can't me and Carly have a sleepover with Auntie Jude?"

"Aren't you tired, Dylan?" Janie stalled. Was there a reason for him not to stay? She couldn't think of any, but there was some sort of weird alarm going off in the back of her brain nonetheless.

"A little, but not that much. Please, Auntie Jude?"

Aunt Jude was very happy to have them. A little too happy, Janie thought. But she had already agreed before she realized the repercussions. Her response was fury, as if the whole family had manipulated a five-year-old to send her off with Tug alone. She could barely contain herself as she kissed everyone good-bye and watched them shake Tug's hand and pat his shoulder and express their falling-down ecstasy at his having joined them.

Out on Route 27, Tug inhaled and heaved a great sigh. The sound of his relief pulled her out of herself and away from stewing about the humiliation she'd suffered. Or might have suffered. Maybe. *Anger is so easy,* she realized. *It's being scared that's hard.* And if she were to heave her own great big sigh of relief, she knew it would be fear she exhaled, not rage.

"That was great," Tug said, glancing out at the houses they passed, some dark, some with their own holiday scenes appearing in the windows. "Your family's really nice."

"I'm glad you had a good time. The pudding was a huge hit."

"Ah, they were just being polite."

"Uncle Charlie's not polite, and he ate about a quart of it."

When they turned onto his street, Tug said, "Why don't you come in and see the house? I'll give you the nickel tour."

Janie didn't answer right away. Her heart began to throb in her chest. *My God, it's just Tug!* she told herself. *You've been alone with him a hundred times!* She pulled into the driveway and stared out at the lake. The moon lay behind a cluster of thin clouds, and threw a muted reflection onto the darkened waters. Tug didn't get out of the car. He waited for her reply. "I don't know," she said finally.

"Nothing's going to happen," he said.

"I don't know what to do."

"Janie," he said gently. "Just come in the house."

She glanced over at him, expecting to see a no-big-deal smile on his face, but found none. His eyes were as black as Lake Pequot; he was pulling inward, cloaking his emotions. And he wasn't setting out other, more digestible, ones in their place. He wasn't trying to fool her—at least there was that. She got out of the car.

Inside the front entryway to the left was a pane-glass pocket door, partially open. In the room beyond, Janie saw a tidy desk and a dark cork wall covered in photographs. Pictures of people were haphazardly interspersed with photos of roof lines, copper trimmed windows and intricately designed paving stones. The room had only two small windows. "Couldn't expect to get any work done if I had a view of the lake," he murmured as he stood beside her.

To their right ran a long black slab of marble countertop that separated the kitchen from the entryway. Beyond the kitchen was a sizable wooden table—teak, she thought—and eight matching ladder-back chairs. Past that was the living room, with a couch facing a wall of glass, beyond which was the porch.

As he showed her through the house, he gave her little details: the marble countertop came from a now-abandoned quarry in Vermont. His piece had been the last to be excavated. The dining room set had been ordered by his grandmother in the sixties, when teak was all the rage. It was a little dated, but it reminded him of his visits here as a child. The small maple table in the corner with the leafy red-striped coleus on top was the puzzle table he'd mentioned.

The tour progressed up the open wooden stairway that ran along the left wall of the living room. Here was the guest bedroom right at the top. Down a short hall toward the back of the house was his bedroom. She stood in the doorway and peeked in, as if she were at a museum and the room were cordoned off with a velvet rope. He had a blue-and-white-patterned quilt on his double bed, which faced a row of tall windows looking out onto the lake.

"I thought you said you never made your bed," she said.

"I don't usually." He looked at the bed, as if it might know why he'd made it. "I guess maybe I just figured it's Thanksgiving."

"You're a holiday bed-maker."

"Seems so." They glanced at each other for the first time since they'd come upstairs. It was a relief to see that they were still themselves. "Come on," he said. "I saved the best for last."

Back downstairs, Tug unbolted the door to the porch, stepped back, and let Janie out first. Then he switched off the lights in the living room. With no light source behind them, the lake suddenly came into detailed view. Janie let out a little, "Oh!"

"I know," he nodded, stepping up beside her, his arm brushing her shoulder.

"Tug," she said. "You must just . . ."

"Yeah, I'm out here all the time."

After a few minutes he leaned away from her and switched on a standing lamp. The lake faded and she could see the porch itself. It had wicker furniture—again, his grandmother's. But he'd painted the pieces a soft gray and bought new cushions. The fabric looked like striped blue-and-white bed ticking. There were several low lamps on end tables, and to the left a sturdy table with thick carved legs, painted white. This is where he ate his breakfast every morning, he told her, unless it dropped below 32 degrees. He didn't like when the milk froze in his cereal, otherwise even that wouldn't stop him.

He sat down on the wicker sofa and she followed. It was chilly, but there was no breeze. She tucked her legs up under the bell of her skirt and wrapped her thin sweater a little tighter.

"Something to drink?" he offered. "Cup of coffee? Glass of wine?"

What would he want? she found herself thinking. "Got any hot chocolate?"

He smiled as he rose. "You know I do."

Well here you are, she told herself, alone now on the porch. *In Tug's house.* She thought back to their first few meetings, that time when she was cleaning the gutters, steamed because he hadn't come when he was supposed to. He had climbed up onto the roof to talk to her, and ended up cleaning half of them himself. He had a way of diffusing her, even back then. Well sometimes, anyway. The bomb squad couldn't have diffused her the day Heidi brought Dylan home late. That time she had gone off with a mighty blast that had sent bits of mortar into every relationship she had.

But she'd gone to the ball field and apologized. And he'd accepted, even though she had said some really mean things, like *I wanted* his *porch not* yours. It made her cringe in shame even now.

And yet there had been some truth to it. She had wanted this last gift of Robby's to be fully his, undiluted by anyone else's influence. And now when she sat out there, she couldn't think only of Robby. Tug was all over it. The wind chimes he'd hung even made it sound like him. Shouldn't this bother her? It hadn't in a very long time. *It's too soon,* she thought. *This is all too soon, right?*

When Tug came back, he gripped two mugs by their handles in one hand and carried a canvas jacket in the other. He held it out to her. "You looked cold," he said as he sat down. The inside of the jacket was lined in flannel. The corduroy collar rubbed up against her cheek when she put it on. And there was that look from Tug, that scanning-every-pixel-of-her look. "I never was crazy about that jacket," he said. "It's a lot more appealing with you in it."

Janie's heart started the painful throbbing again, and her first reaction was to run, as if she were being attacked rather than praised. Then there was a surge of anger. He knew it made her uncomfortable—it was rude, really. But that wasn't right. She wrapped her icy fingers around the hot cup, gripping it like an anchor. "Tug," she started to warn him, but her thoughts wouldn't coagulate into words.

He nodded and took a sip from his mug. "I kind of liked it when you were sick." His eyes had locked onto something far away, on the other side of the lake, perhaps. "You didn't worry so much about me caring for you. You were just glad to see me."

The heart thumping stopped. In fact, she couldn't feel it beating at all for a few seconds. "I'm always glad to see you," she said. It felt so true it hurt. He disengaged from the far shore and turned toward her. She forced herself not to flinch. "I'm sorry if it doesn't show," she said. "I don't always . . . handle myself well."

"We're all just making it up as we go, I guess."

"It feels so dangerous," she told him. "Like there are land mines in every direction."

"I'm not a land mine."

She pulled air into her lungs, let it out again. "Maybe not. Maybe I'm the land mine."

"Oh, I get it," he smiled. "When you take time off from being scared for yourself, you spend it worrying about me."

Maybe this was true. He deserved good things, and she knew he had struggled through some very . . . not-so-good things. The question was, to which category did she belong? "Can I ask you something? When did you stop being in love with Sue?"

"I don't know," he said. "It's not like I just stopped one day. I was thinking once that I'm like one of those trees that gets planted too close to a chain-link fence. Over time the trunk starts to grow around the wires. You can take down the fence, but a little part of it will still be inside the tree. You'd have to cut down the tree to get rid of that last bit."

THE TEMPERATURE DROPPED SLOWLY as they sat together talking, and the wind began to pick up, blowing in off the lake in short bursts, teasing them into thinking it had died down, when it was only recharging for the next gust. Janie pulled the corduroy collar of the jacket up around her neck, and crossed her arms tightly around her to keep from shivering. Tug showed no awareness of the cold. He toed off his loafers and propped his sock-clad feet up on the coffee table in front of them. His arms lay loose in his lap, moving only to pat her hand from time to time.

When her teeth began to chatter, he took her inside, apparently hoping the conversation would transplant itself onto the living room couch. There was a wooden figure of a lighthouse on the wall, painted in broad black-and-white horizontal stripes. Three brass-rimmed disks mounted in its body told the time, the tides, and the barometric pressure. Janie saw only the time: 2:13 a.m.

"I should get home," she told him. "I have to get some sleep before I pick up the kids."

"Okay," he said, not hiding his disappointment all that well. "What's on for tomorrow?"

"Not much really." She saw him run a hand back over his head. "What?" she said.

"Well, it's supposed to be a nice weekend. Warm, sunny." He reached out to button her into his coat. "I had this thought maybe you and the kids might come down the Cape with me."

"Oh . . . um . . ."

"We could just go down for the day. Or we could stay over if you felt like it. The second bedroom has twin beds for you and Dylan and plenty of room for a port-a-crib for Carly."

Janie had not one thing planned for the next three days, other than weeding out some of the unloved toys and sending them to Goodwill. Of course, that was better accomplished when Dylan was at school and couldn't defend his need for every plaything he'd ever owned. There was church with Aunt Jude on Sunday.

No one in their right mind would turn down a weekend on Cape Cod for that. "Okay," she said, feeling slightly light-headed with fatigue. It had been a long, full day.

"Really?"

"Yeah, it sounds nice." They made plans to head out at noon the next day and stay for one night. Or maybe two. Janie wasn't sure. She'd think it through in the morning and call.

He walked her out to her car. Before she could open the door he hugged her, pulling her in close and holding her for a few extra seconds. He smelled of wool and shirt starch and very vaguely of chocolate. He was warm and strong and she felt comfortable supported there in the circle of his arms. "Happy Thanksgiving," he whispered into her hair.

And it was.

As she rode home through the darkened streets of Pelham, the car seemed to steer itself, like a horse trotting instinctively back to its own paddock. Janie rubbed her cheek against the upturned collar of Tug's coat. It was the middle of the night and the town seemed abandoned, with no other vehicles, no pedestrians strolling down sidewalks, no lights but the solemn glow of a single fluorescent tube from a storefront.

But there was movement in the distance, indistinct at first, like a shadow moving across the walls of buildings. As she came to an intersection, she stopped for the red light and saw a figure waiting to cross, stationary though somehow also in motion. As her headlights hit the reflector tape on his running suit, she saw that the person was jogging in place.

Her light turned green, and she proceeded slowly through the intersection, her eyes drawn to the familiar shape by the crosswalk. His head turned toward her as she neared, and she looked straight into the gaze of Father Jake Sweeney. Her foot released itself from the accelerator, and the car slowed. It was him, the real him, her onetime friend, and it had been three full months since their paths had intersected.

How are you? she wanted to ask. The very question she'd spent the past ten months dodging. *Really, how are you?*

She stopped the car right there in the middle of Route 27. But he turned away and ran past her, plunging himself into the darkness beyond the traffic lights. She understood completely.

WHEN JANIE ROLLED OVER and squinted at the clock the next morning she couldn't believe it: 10:05. When was the last time she'd slept later than six or seven? Years, it seemed. She picked up the phone to call Aunt Jude, and the dial tone stuttered, indicating a voice mail message. Janie ignored it and placed her call. The kids were fine, slept late, and were now eating toaster waffles with honey. "I had no idea I was all out of syrup!" said Aunt Jude. Janie asked for some extra time, and Aunt Jude was happy to have the children a while longer. She had her Gentle Joints exercise class at noon.

"I'll be there by 11:30," Janie promised, as she loaded up the coffee maker.

In the shower, her thoughts ran to nothing more complicated than, *The Cape . . . I love the Cape . . . which eave is the port-a-crib in?* A comfortable sluggishness remained with her while she packed, as if she were still just a little bit asleep. She eventually remembered to call Tug. "Should I bring any food?"

"Nah, the house is stocked. Plus I went out this morning and picked up a few things."

She loaded the car, locked the house, and went to pick up the kids, humming along to the radio as she drove.

"I might not be around for Mass on Sunday." Janie mentioned her plans to Aunt Jude as the kids scrambled around the car.

Aunt Jude was startled. "The whole weekend," she said.

A twinge ran up Janie's neck. "It's just two days," she said. "It's the Cape."

Tug was tossing a small duffel bag into the back of the truck when they pulled up. Dylan barreled out of the car and threw himself at Tug. "What's a cod?" he asked breathlessly.

"It's a kind of fish," said Tug, thumping him gently on the back. "Want to try and catch one?" Dylan did a little happy dance around the driveway.

"We're taking the truck?" asked Janie. Another twinge. Not driving her own vehicle. No getaway car.

"It's a four-wheel drive," he said. "We need it for the outer beach." Apparently there were two seats tucked behind the main bench. Tug had the kids' car seats set up before she could think of any reason to stop him. When she returned from taking Dylan to the bathroom one last time, her bags had been stowed and the motor was running.

Carly was soon fast asleep, the all-business hum of the truck's powerful engine and the snug quarters into which her car seat was wedged conspiring to lull her into an openmouthed, head-hanging torpor. Dylan spent a good deal of the trip studying and murmuring to the pack of baseball cards Tug had picked up at the grocery store that morning. "Swing, batter, swing, batter . . . no don't swing, that's a bad one . . . ," he muttered as he flipped from one card to the next.

"It's warmer down here," commented Tug. "Midfifties."

"Too cold to swim," said Janie.

"Maybe for some."

"You're not going in the water."

"Might," he said. "Did you bring your suit?"

"Are you kidding?"

"Do I sound like I'm kidding?"

"Mom," chimed Dylan, "are we almost close?"

"No, honey, we've got a while to go."

"Hey, Dylan," said Tug. "Pretty soon we're going to see a huge bridge, the Sagamore. When we cross over, we'll be on Cape Cod.

Can you watch for that bridge? That'd be a big help, because I
don't want to miss it and end up in Rhode Island or something."

Janie could feel Dylan's breath by her ear as he peered around
her headrest. "Is that it?" he asked as the totem pole at the Plym-
outh Information Center came into view. Though it looked nothing like a bridge, it was foreign to Dylan, Janie realized. Maybe
in this strange new world of trips to the Cape, that tall, pointy
carved thing could be used to traverse a divide.

"Nope," said Tug. "The bridge we're looking for is a lot bigger
than that."

When the Sagamore Bridge rose up in front of them like a
metal giant looming out of the scrub pines, Dylan screamed in
Janie's ear, "I SEE IT!" It set off a ringing in her head that didn't
clear for a few minutes. She could still feel it clanging like an
alarm as they drove over the huge bridge high above the Cape
Cod Canal.

Tug was telling Dylan something about the canal, how the
Cape was really an island now because of it, but Janie only caught
snatches of the conversation. The ringing in her ear and the panic
she was now feeling as she looked through the seemingly endless
row of gray bars that encased the bridge made her dig her fingers
into the seat cushion.

What is wrong with you? she scolded. *Cut it out!* But all she
could think was that she'd brought her children to a distant place,
in someone else's car, with no exit strategy. *What if I hate it?
What if the kids can't sleep? What if Tug and I get into a fight about
something? I'm trapped. Trapped on Cape Cod.*

"You alright?" murmured Tug.

"Yeah," she breathed. "I just all of a sudden felt kind of . . .
weird."

"Have you gone anywhere since January?"

Janie sucked in a huge lungful of air and let it rush back out of
her mouth. "Does Natick count?"

"Janie, girl," he chuckled. "You need to see the ocean."

They didn't even go to the house first. Tug drove straight out Beach Road to Nauset, the lavish blue of the ocean expanding before them as they came over the Heights. The parking lot was speckled with vehicles, most with Massachusetts plates, but one from as far away as Canada. All irresistibly drawn here by the last good Cape weekend of the year.

Carly woke when the truck stopped, and Janie freed her from her seat. Dylan climbed out and Tug went around to the truck bed to gather up some things. They followed the main boardwalk out to the shoreline, where the waves crashed relentlessly and the seagulls circled overhead. They hiked down the beach a little ways, and Tug spread out an old frayed quilt. Carly practiced walking in the sand, falling over, and pushing herself back up. She studied the sand grains stuck to her fingers. Dylan pulled off his sneakers and socks and ran to the water's edge, chasing the sea foam that surged out from each spent wave and then retreated into the ocean again.

Janie sat on the blanket and watched them while Tug cut slices from a hunk of cheese with his jackknife. He handed her a piece on a cracker, watched her take a bite. His eyes lingered idly on her, and she looked back at him, feeling drawn in, as if at any moment she might lean over and kiss him.

"I meant to bring back your jacket," she said.

He shrugged. As if a jacket mattered.

THE HOUSE WAS SMALL and squat and covered in weathered gray shingles that curled up at the edges like split ends. Inside the walls were white and the floors were bare.

"Used to be all kinds of god-awful wallpaper, but I took it down to the studs about ten years ago and pulled out the carpet." One of his nieces was allergic to mold, and the place was damp. If you could make money off mold, he told her, Cape homeowners would be millionaires. "Course, some of them already are." He had gutted it and installed insulation, new wallboard, and a dehu-

midifier in the basement. It was winterized now, and it smelled a
lot better.

The large kitchen had old wooden cabinets with wrought-iron
pulls and a shallow white enameled sink. In the middle of everything sat a 1950s-style table with metal legs and a yellow Formica
top. The metal chairs had matching plastic-covered yellow seats.
He'd never bothered to update the kitchen, he said, because he
liked it "Cape-y."

His bedroom had a large bed with a cranberry-colored down
comforter on it. The only other piece of furniture in the room was
a dark wood dresser with a huge oval mirror attached above, the
glass speckled with age. The other bedroom, just past the tiny
bathroom, had two twin beds, both with trundles underneath.
There was a long, low chest of drawers covered in yellow antiqu-
ing paint.

"You don't see this kind of thing anymore," Janie commented.

"Not unless you have some really elderly friends."

The living room was home to the only carpet, a hunter green
Oriental. "Fake," he said, when she admired it. There was a cane-
seated rocking chair and a tan upholstered couch, both of which
faced a huge stone fireplace that Tug had built himself. "I love a
fire, even in the summer," he told her.

By the time Tug had finished showing them the house, and
Dylan had inspected every inch of the yard, and Carly had been
given a bath, it was dinnertime. Tug grilled chicken that he had
marinated that morning back in Pelham, while Janie set the table
and assembled a salad from the fixings he gave her. She was chop-
ping red pepper at the kitchen counter when he came in to get a
serving plate for the chicken. He rested one hand on the small of
her back as he reached up into a cabinet with the other. The feel of
his hand vibrated on her back for several moments after he'd gone
back out onto the deck. The arousal she felt stunned her.

I'm not ready for this, she thought. But her back declined to
heed this warning and continued to tingle shamelessly.

THE KIDS HAD A hard time falling sleep. "I only sleep at home and Auntie Jude's," Dylan informed her. He had already been moved from the twin bed across the room to the trundle attached to Janie's bed. Carly squawked and gave plaintive calls of "Mama!" when Janie left the room. In the end, there was nothing to do but lie there until they fell asleep, by which time she began to drift off.

"Hey," she heard Tug whisper from the hall. The child-sized snores told her she was free to go.

Go and do what? She lay there for an extra moment. Then she became so nervous she started to giggle. Fear of waking them propelled her carefully out of the bed. She went directly into the bathroom, bypassing Tug with barely a glance. She brushed her teeth. Flossed. Washed and moisturized her face. It was almost nine o'clock, no reason not to get ready for bed. She wasn't tired, though, and she guessed Tug wasn't, either.

What does he want, for godsake? She knew what he wanted. He'd been subtle, but clear. And she had responded, she had to admit to herself. She'd stayed up half the night with him, accepted his invitation to a weekend away. *With the kids,* she thought, in her own defense. But the kids, now sleeping soundly, had been quickly reduced to a factor of zero.

It's just Tug, she told herself. *He's on your side.* And she marched herself out to the living room, where a fire licked up around a pile of dry, cleanly chopped logs. Tug was sitting on the couch with a glass of white wine in his hand. Janie's wine, which she'd only sipped down by half at dinner, had been freshened. She looked at the glass, looked at Tug, raised her eyebrows.

"Not like I need to get a woman drunk . . . ," he said, laughing at himself.

She laughed, too. It was funny. In a terrifying kind of way. "I am not sleeping with you," she said.

He nodded, thinking about this for a moment. "Thanks for the heads-up."

"Come on, you didn't really expect me to." She sank down onto the opposite end of the couch.

"No. You're still wearing your wedding ring."

Janie looked down at her hands. She hadn't even thought of that. In fact, she had never once considered when she might take it off. It was a part of her hand; removing it seemed akin to severing a finger. She looked back up at him. "Look, something's happening here, and it's not all you. I know that." He was so still, she thought she could almost see dust settling on him. "Tug."

"Hey, if it's not . . ." He shrugged, took another sip of wine.

"Don't!"

"Don't what."

"Pull all into yourself. Don't go dormant on me."

"Alright, then. What do you want me to do?"

"Just be patient."

"Are you kidding me? Like I haven't been patient? I am more patient with you than I have ever been in my life. You hire me, you fire me, you yell at me and tell me to mind my own business. You apologize, you fight with me some more, you might want to be with me, you might not. Jesus, Janie. I think I've proved my patience!"

"Uhhh!" she groaned. "Okay, so you're Saint Tug! I'll alert the fucking Vatican!"

"Look, just don't tell me to be something I already am, times ten."

"You were the one who said we're all making it up as we go along. That's what I'm doing. All I know right now is, if you brought me down here for some big lovefest, I'm not ready."

"You know why I brought you down here? Because I like to be with you. I like you near. And I knew if I came alone, I'd be thinking about you about fifty times a day. What's the point of being on the damned Cape if you're always thinking about something else?" He put his wineglass down on the end table, sloshing a few drops over the rim. "And if that makes me as pathetic as it sounds, then so be it."

He stared into the fire trying to pull inward, go dormant, as she'd put it. But his lungs still seemed to require too much air to quiet them, and his face couldn't quite lock down into blankness. She watched him struggle for composure. *Pathetic? No,* she thought, *not him.* Just unfortunate enough to have feelings for someone who was as much of a pain in the ass as she was, at a time in her life when it showed the most.

She slid her hand under his, grasping it slowly. She remembered how cool and comforting those hands were on her cheeks when she was sick. Now his hand was hot and tense. He wouldn't look at her. Well, he'd earned the right to ignore her, for a few minutes, anyway.

He was wearing a long-sleeved T-shirt, heathered blue with "Cape Cod Baseball League" in gray lettering across the chest. The sleeves had been pushed up to his elbows, exposing that long scar he had on his right arm. The curly auburn hair had grown in around it, but the pale line was still visible, as it always would be.

She did something then that surprised even her. She curled herself around until her back was pressed up against his side, and pulled that arm around her neck, down between her breasts until his hand rested on her hip. She snuggled back against him, and felt him shift to accommodate her. His head turned toward her, breath tickling the back of her neck. His chest expanded against her. He was breathing her in.

But he wouldn't comment.

She traced her finger up and down the scar on his forearm, exploring it. It was more jagged on one side and slightly wider at the top. "Who did this to you?" she asked.

"Did it to myself."

"How?"

He shifted again, put his other arm around her. "After she served me the papers," he said, "I was a terror. Hard on the crew, pissy with my family. An angry guy with power tools is a bad combination. I got irritated when I was cutting a board one day and the saw bit back."

"Sounds like me, the day Dylan ran out to see your backhoe. You had told him to get in the truck so he'd be out of the way. Remember how I went ballistic?"

"Yeah," he chuckled. "That's the thing about you. Right from the start you were so familiar to me."

"You think we're alike?"

"In some ways. Though, you tend to lash out when you're threatened, and I tend to go quiet. But . . . I don't know. I guess I always felt I could understand you. Even when you were throwing a fit about something, I could see why."

"Sue wasn't much of a fit thrower, was she?"

"Nope. Looking back, I wish she had been. Might have helped."

They sat there in silence, their bodies at rest, except for the cellular-level notes each was making of the other: the precise temperature of her back against his chest, the exact pressure of his arm across her shoulder, the soft tickle of her hair against his cheek, the taste of the air around him.

The wood in the fire burned and fell, the pile of red coals growing larger, the flames licking lower. "Want to throw another log on?" she asked.

"Are you going to be here when I get back?" he answered. She leaned forward and he got up. He put three more pieces in, adjusted them, and came back to the couch. They resumed their position. He kissed the back of her head.

"Here's the problem," she murmured. "I'm trying to figure out how to live life on a whole new planet from the one I used to live on."

"I know," he whispered.

"I'm not that good at it."

"You're doing fine."

"No, I make a lot of mistakes, and I get frustrated and angry, and it's a really good thing I don't own any power tools or I'd probably be limbless."

"This is some sort of a warning, right?"

"Yeah, I guess," she sighed. "If I was one of your buddies, I'd tell you to stay away from me."

"Too late," he said. "But thanks for your concern. Buddy."

JANIE WOKE BRIEFLY IN the early morning. A breeze blew through the window screen, bringing with it the smell of salt marsh grasses. It took a moment for her to realize that the distant rhythmic thumping she felt, more than heard, was the vibration of waves crashing along the shoreline.

Dylan's face was close to hers, breathing his mysteriously sweet child's breath toward her. His arms were wrapped protectively, possessively around Nubby the Fur-Challenged Bunny. She pulled the faded comforter up over his shoulders. Then she rolled over and went back to sleep.

When she woke again, Dylan and Nubby were gone, and Carly was calling "Mama!" as she stood and rattled the railing of her port-a-crib. Janie rose, scooped up the impatient toddler, and walked barefoot and bleary-eyed toward the sound of voices in the kitchen.

"Does the hook hurt the fish?" Dylan was asking.

"I'm not really sure," came Tug's reply. "I think it might be kind of like getting a splinter, because when you take it out, they just swim off like nothing happened."

Janie put Carly down on the floor. "Din!" she said and ran to her brother, pressing her face against his thigh.

"Ew! You're all slobbery!" he scolded her. "Here, eat this," and he handed her his toast crust.

Tug was frying bacon on the stove. Janie went over and leaned against him. He kissed her cheek. Glancing at Dylan, Janie saw a vague look of interest on his face, like he was trying to gauge the size of something that wasn't in full view. Janie shifted away from Tug. "You don't like bacon?" he asked.

"Not a big fan," she said. "But I kind of like the smell. Weird, huh?" Tug shot her a little grin, with no particular message other than he was glad to have her near him, and he didn't much care about her food-related eccentricities. They ate eggs and toast and sat around the breakfast table in their pajamas until the kids got squirrelly and a plan was determined. They would drive to the outer beach and fish, maybe even swim. It was warmer today than the day before, the temperature threatening to reach up and grab onto the 60 degree mark.

When they'd packed and loaded up the truck, they headed for Nauset Beach again, crossing the parking lot to a hardly noticeable dirt road at the far corner. Tug stopped to let some air out of his tires, and then they were off, bouncing along the rutted sand path, Dylan peppering Tug with questions: about the blue boxes (greenhead flytraps); about the fences along the dunes (to stop people from climbing up and eroding the sand); and about the roped-off sections of the beach (piping plover nests—federally protected).

Janie had never driven a car straight onto a beach before, and she had the strange sensation of doing something illicit. "Are you sure this is legal?" she asked him.

"It is if you've got a sticker." He took his fishing pole and tackle box out of the back of the truck while Janie spread out a blanket and set up beach chairs. He showed Dylan how to thread the bait onto the hook and cast the line. They stood together for a long time, Tug on his knees behind Dylan, guiding the pole back and out, releasing the catch, watching the hook plunk into the waves. Eventually Dylan got more interested in chasing the ebb and flow of the minor swells, and Tug stuck the pole in the sand. He poured charcoal briquettes into a little hibachi grill and lit it, the smell of lighter fluid transfusing the briny air.

The afternoon passed at just the right languid pace. They ate hot dogs from the grill and washed their ketchupy hands in the surf. Carly napped on a towel in the shade of the truck. Dylan dug holes until he reached water, just to watch them fill up and slowly obliterate themselves. Then he and Janie tossed a tennis ball around, until a wild pitch from Janie landed out beyond the crashing surf. "Mom!" whined Dylan.

"The waves will bring it in," she told him. But the little bobbing ball never seemed to make it past the crests, and Dylan eyed it with growing anxiety. Tug pulled his T-shirt off and waded out knee deep. Janie watched his shoulders tense and the muscles clenching in his back.

He turned back toward them. "You sure you need this ball?"

"Is the water cold?" Dylan asked.

"Just a tad."

"Not too cold for you, though," Janie teased. She told Dylan, "Tug *likes* cold water. He *always* swims in November."

"Really?" asked Dylan.

Tug dove in, coming up on the other side of a wave with a pained whoop. He grabbed the ball and made for shore. Janie watched him approach, the water trailing through the hair on his chest and over his hard, flat stomach. He was clearly enjoying this. "Are you going to get me a towel, or just watch me shiver?"

She tapped her chin, pretended to consider the question, and then he was running at her. She turned but didn't get very far before his arms caught her from behind and his cold wet body pressed against her back. She let out a laughing screech.

In a moment, Dylan was standing beside them, trying to make sense of it. "Mom's all wet now," he told Tug. "You got her wet." Tug released her.

"It's okay, honey," Janie said. "I don't mind."

"You don't?"

"No. We were just being silly."

Dylan took the ball from Tug and went to play in the sand by himself.

THEY DID CATCH A couple of fish, a bluefish and a striped bass. Dylan studied every movement as Tug pulled the hook from the blue's glossy dark lips, Dylan's own mouth unwittingly opening wider and wider as the fish's did. He sprang up and down on his toes, and let out a "Yes!" when it swam away. Tug had intended to keep the striper, but the idea of its demise did not sit well with Dylan. "We're going to keep it? And *eat* it?" Tug let it go. They stopped at Captain Eldon's Seafood and picked up scallops for dinner.

After dinner, Tug lit a fire. "Let's go find some roasting sticks," he told Dylan, and they went out into the yard.

When they came back, Dylan told Janie, "We're going to cook our own dessert! In the fire!" Tug brought out a bag of marshmallows, a box of graham crackers, and several bars of milk chocolate.

"S'mores?" said Janie.

Dylan's mouth fell. He looked at Tug.

"She must have had them before, buddy," Tug said.

"Not in a really, really long time," Janie said quickly. "How does it go again? You put the graham cracker on the stick?"

"Mom," Dylan rolled his eyes. "That wouldn't work!"

Dylan watched Tug skewer a marshmallow, and pierced his own as if he were performing surgery. At first he held it too far away from the flames. When Tug corrected him, he held it too close. The marshmallow burst into a tiny orange puff of fire. Dylan let out a horrified screech. "I killed it!"

"Nah, it's just what they call well done," said Tug. He pulled the black and bloated wad off gingerly with his fingers and held it out. "Taste it." Dylan wouldn't. Tug popped the whole thing in his mouth. He handed Dylan a new marshmallow and said, "Burn me another."

Eventually, Dylan was able to toast something to his satisfaction, and he assembled a little sandwich of marshmallow and chocolate pieces between two graham crackers. When he bit into it, the warm marshmallow oozed from the sides and left a big white smile across his lips and cheeks. "I never did this before," he told them, chewing happily. "I never had something like this."

JANIE GOT THE KIDS into bed and sat beside Dylan on the trundle, arranging Nubby's ears away from his face. "You had a lot of fun today," she told him.

"Yeah," he sighed. "I really like fishing. Except for the hook."

"And S'mores—you tried that, too."

"Sometimes they get burned, but that's okay. Tug will just eat them."

The children settled down easily into sleep, and Janie tiptoed out to the living room. Tug was drinking ice water. "No wine?" said Janie, sinking down onto the couch next to him.

He put a hand on his stomach. "Jesus, I'm so full of marshmallows I could heave."

She laughed, and all she could think was how profoundly happy and grateful she was at that moment. It had been such a good day, so uncomplicated by worry or aggravation or loss; the best day in ten long months—all courtesy of Tug Malinowski, a truly good man with the most beautiful dark brown eyes.

Then she was reaching out a hand to his chest and another to his face, brushing her fingers over his lips, leaning closer, moving toward him. For a few moments he let her explore him, and then his hands went to her shoulders and up the back of her neck and into her hair.

She felt her lips parting and the need to taste him. One of her fingers slid inside his mouth, and the feel of the tip of his tongue sent a shock of such intensity through her body she could barely breathe. She took her fingers from his mouth and pressed her lips there, gently at first, taking in his lower lip, then his upper lip, then lower again. He groaned and slid one hand down to the small of her back, pulling her in until her stomach pressed against his. This sound, this primal growl of need for her—she could feel it in her chest and her belly and between her legs. She opened her mouth and his tongue flicked in and she thought she might faint or go blind or melt completely into him.

Her hand roamed across his chest and down to his waist and up under the soft cotton of his shirt. She felt the swirl of hair at his stomach and he groaned again, louder, more insistently. Her hand continued to explore the landscape of his body and reached up farther until her fingers found the hard little knot of his nipple. "God, Janie," he breathed. And he was rising up, pushing himself against her, laying her onto her back. He took his shirt off in that way men have of reaching up and over to grab the back of the shoulders and pulling it off over their heads. Janie watched the muscles working in his upper arms, and could only think, *I need to touch those.*

He lowered himself back down to her, pushing her shirt up so that his stomach lay warm against hers. And they were kissing and pulling each other closer, and she could feel the press of his erection against her thigh. *This is happening,* she thought.

He kissed her chin and throat and breathed in her ear, "Take off your wedding ring."

"What?" she said, though she'd heard him.

"Janie. Please. You have to take it off." His hands were moving slower now, and he was no longer kissing her.

"No," she said.

He rose up on his elbows above her. His eyes traced over her like the beam of a search light. "Janie. I can't . . ."

"I'm not ready. Can't we just . . ."

"No," he said, and rolled off her. He sat on the edge of the couch, pulled his T-shirt back on. He brushed his mouth with the back of his hand.

"Tug."

He shook his head. "It's alright," he said. "I'm going for a walk." And he left the house.

JANIE WAITED THERE IN the living room for a long time. The next thing she knew, the house was dark and there was a blanket over her. She felt her way toward the bedrooms, stopping by Tug's closed door. No sound came from behind it, no snoring or even deep breathing, but she knew he was there. She almost went in.

But how fair would that be? *I'll seduce you in the living room, but I won't take off another man's ring. Then I'll try to talk to you about it in your bedroom in the dark?* No, she'd wait until morning. Maybe she could get up early before the kids. It would be better to consider it all in the light of day.

But Carly woke with the birds and demanded loudly to be attended to. This roused Dylan who found to his great embarrassment that he'd wet the bed. Janie was instructed to sneak the sheets and wet pajamas down to the washer in the basement before Tug found out. "He won't care, Dylan. A lot of five-year-olds still have accidents."

"Mom, PLEASE."

Janie was coming down the hall with the pee-soaked laundry in her arms when Tug's door opened. Unshaven, pale, and weary around the eyes, he seemed suddenly old to her. The bristle on his chin was gray, not auburn. Her memory flashed to the father of a childhood friend who grew a beard when he was having what Aunt Jude had referred to as "The Crisis." The beard had come in gray, and the father soon shaved it off again.

"Morning," Tug said, and walked past her to the bathroom.

The lazy placidity of the previous day had been replaced, Janie quickly found, with a strange frenetic energy, as if a joint decision had been made to which everyone had agreed. Dylan was obnoxious, overcompensating for his shame at wetting himself. He poked at Carly, who fell against the dresser and screamed furiously for several minutes. A pink lump arose on her forehead. Janie realized she was short on underwear and had to turn yesterday's inside out, which made her feel icky and irritable. Tug busied himself with recaulking some chipped grout in the bathroom.

"I think I'll take them out," she said to Tug as he squatted by the shower. He looked at her for the first time that morning. It made Janie feel weak and sad.

"Mom," whined Dylan from the other room. "Make her stop!"

Tug's face softened. "I'll be done here in a minute." He took them to the Hole in One donut shop, which despite the sugar and caffeine involved, had a much-needed calming effect on them all. They sat at a booth by the window. Perched in an industrial plastic highchair, Carly decimated a cruller, half of Janie's blueberry muffin, and all of Dylan's scrambled eggs, while Dylan was busy charming the elderly couple in the booth behind him with tales of his fishing prowess.

Tug leaned back in the booth, calmly eating his bacon and cheese omelet. The color was back in his cheeks, Janie noticed, and he'd shaved. He saw her studying him, took another bite of his eggs, waited.

"We need to sort this out," she said.

"Janie, you need to sort this out." He put down his fork. "I'm sorted."

"Hey," she said, "if there's one thing I know from seven years of marriage, it's that it's never just one person's job to sort."

"And from twenty-one years of marriage, I know that sometimes people have no idea how much sorting there is to do. You start. I'll catch up."

"Jesus, Tug! That's a hell of a—"

He gave her a fierce look and tipped his chin toward Dylan, who had stopped talking all of a sudden. After a moment, he started again.

Tug's voice was low, almost subsonic. "Janie, I can't do this one. I can be patient, like you asked, but I can't be the one to help you figure out if you're still completely in love with your husband."

IT WAS OVERCAST AND windy, and the house felt too small. They packed up around noon and drove home. When they got back to his house, he helped her transfer the bags and port-a-crib to her car. He hugged the kids and strapped them into their car seats. It was a bigger good-bye than Janie had bargained for. "I don't like this," she said as she stood by the car.

"Me either."

"Are you coming for lunch on Tuesday?"

He squinted out across the lake. "I want to. But I don't know. I think I have to play it by ear."

"So you're leaving me hanging."

"We're leaving each other hanging."

She slid her arms around his waist and laid her cheek on his collarbone. He wrapped his arms around her, pulled her tight. When they let go of each other, Janie felt she might float out over the lake. She got into the car and buckled her seat belt.

21

W HEN JANIE CHECKED HER voice mail that night, there was only
one message, and it was from Thanksgiving Day. She remembered having ignored the indicator before she left for Cape
Cod. "It's Mike. Uh . . . Happy Thanksgiving . . . Just thinking
about . . . you, I guess . . . Happy Thanksgiving."

It was shocking. Her brother hated the phone. For several years
he didn't actually have a phone. Then he burned himself badly
with a blowtorch one day and had to stumble down the road to
the neighbors to call an ambulance. So, now he had a phone, but
he never used it, didn't even know his own number. If it rang,
he didn't answer. His studio assistant checked messages occasionally.

Janie had once happened to read a magazine article about
Asperger's syndrome. It was described as a mild form of autism
often characterized by weak social skills, tendency to hyperfocus
on a particular area of interest, sensory issues like hypersensitiv-
ity to touch or sound, and excellent spatial skills. *Hello, Mike*, she
had thought. The article went on to say there were likely many
adults with Asperger's who had never been diagnosed. "Think
of that kid in high school who would rather study geometry than
go to a party, who wouldn't eat in the cafeteria because it was too
noisy, who never looked anyone in the eye," it had said. Janie
didn't have to look too far.

Mike had excelled at two things in high school: art and track. He did passing well in math and science—brilliantly if it were something that grabbed his attention, like physics or graphing, terribly with algebra and earth science. He all but flunked English and history. His two passions were sculpture and long-distance running. He once confided to Janie that while he ran he liked to think about the patterns his footsteps were creating all over town.

"What else do you think about when you run?" she'd asked.

"That's pretty much it."

Robby had had the brilliant idea to get the family to pitch in for a watch-band-sized GPS system for Mike's birthday one year. Mike could talk of nothing else the next time he visited. Robby had had an affinity for mathematical constructs, especially number patterns, and he and Mike could sit together for hours and discuss them. Robby was patient with Mike's eccentricities in a way that most people, including Janie herself at times, often weren't.

Mike had come home for the funeral (after his assistant had been tracked down to give him the message about Robby's death). He had said almost nothing for the four days he was in Pelham. Janie had not heard from him since then. Not that she expected to.

"Hi . . . uh . . . is Mike there?" she now asked when a woman answered his phone. It never occurred to her that someone might pick up.

"Mr. Dwyer is working. If you'd like to leave your name and number I'll give him the message."

"It's his sister," she said, then added, "Janie." There was the underwater sound of a palm being place over the mouthpiece, and distant undulating noises.

The palm was released. "Janie. It's me."

"Mike! I got your message. How are you? Everything okay?"

"Yeah, I just . . . you know . . . wanted to wish you a Happy Thanksgiving. How was it? Sad?"

"Uh, not too bad. It was at Aunt Jude's."

"In the living room?"

"Yeah. How was yours?"

"Good."

"What did you do?"

"Went to a friend's house."

"Sounds nice. What's his name?"

Mike didn't respond. This, too, was typical. He talked about what he thought about, and he wasn't thinking about his friend's name. "I just couldn't stop imagining you having Thanksgiving without Robby," he said, finally. "It was all over my brain. How could he not be there, you know?"

"Yeah." But it hadn't been all over *her* brain. In fact, she realized, Thanksgiving was the first family gathering of any kind where she hadn't completely freaked out about Robby's absence. How did that happen?

"He was such a great guy, Janie. He was so . . . you know. Just . . . so . . ."

"He was. He was amazing. He really loved you, Mike."

"I could always talk to him. He was such a good . . ." Janie could hear the crackle in Mike's voice, the closest he usually ever came to crying. It occurred to her that maybe Robby hadn't really died for Mike until then. He'd been emotionless at the funeral, responded appropriately when asked, but never made any spontaneous acknowledgment of Robby's passing. "Janie," he whispered desperately. "How can you do it? How can you not have him?"

"I don't know," she said, the familiar ache starting behind her eyes. She pinched the back of her hand. "What choice do I have?"

"I'm so sorry," Mike said. He was crying now. "Janie, I am so sorry for all of us."

Tears rolled down Janie's cheeks. She pulled her sleeve down over her fist and wiped her chin. There was a murmuring in the background on Mike's end, to which he responded, "Thanks." He gave his nose a quick blow. "How are Dylan and the baby?" he asked.

"They're . . ." Janie had to think a moment. *They're fatherless,* she almost said. But it would have been too cruel. "They're okay. It's hard sometimes. We really missed him on Dylan's birthday. In August," she reminded him. She had to switch to the other sleeve. Mike blew his nose again, too.

"I got Cormac's invitation," he said miserably. "How can he get married when everything's so awful?"

"Well, people have to keep living."

"Do I have to go?"

"I think you should. You'll be home for Christmas, anyway, right? Just stay for New Year's."

"I hate weddings."

"You hate anything with more than three people in a room."

He laughed a little. "That's the truth."

"You'll come, right? Don't bail on me, Mike. I mean it."

"Yeah, alright."

Janie cried for a long time after she hung up the phone. She took *The Kiss* out of her closet and cried some more. She lay in their bed missing Robby so hard she thought she'd never be right again. *We need you,* she kept thinking. *We all need you.*

MONDAY WAS A TRUDGING, colorless, desiccated day. Janie drove Dylan to school, picked up milk at the grocery store, forgot to get cheese and bread, took Carly to the tot lot, sat on the bench, and stared into the pine boughs. *Christmas and a wedding and New Year's Eve,* she thought. *A perfect storm of reminders, all in one week.* Carly crawled through the big red plastic tube and over to the sandbox. She picked up handfuls of sand and studied the grains as they trickled through her fingers.

Rice Krispies for dinner, and early to bed. She was exhausted, and the kids were correspondingly cranky. She didn't sleep well.

Kept waking up gripping handfuls of sheets. Kept dreaming of seeing Robby at a distance, but when she ran to him, he'd disappeared.

IN THE MORNING, THERE was a kind of relief. Not actual relief, but the anticipation of it. It was Tuesday. Tug would be there. It took Janie a few moments to remember he'd said he wasn't sure if he would come, but she guessed that he would. He always seemed to know when she needed him. Not that she could actually talk with him about how badly she'd been missing Robby since Mike's call. He had made it clear that he couldn't help her with that, and she knew it was fair. *It'll be enough just to see him,* she told herself.

Normally Tug rapped lightly, in case Carly was asleep, and let himself in. Today he waited for her to open the door. His hands were empty. No cooler, no little toy or designer coffee drink. "Hi," he said.

"You're here." The anticipation ended; the relief was real.

"Yeah."

"You said you weren't sure."

"I decided about ten minutes ago."

"Are you hungry?" She wished she'd remembered the cheese and the bread at the market.

"No." They went into the kitchen and she made him chocolate milk, anyway. The coffee had gone cold in the pot, so she just filled a glass with water for herself. She asked him about the Pelham Heights house. He gave very brief answers. For a while, they just sat in silence.

Finally she said, "I can't take off the ring."

He inhaled, exhaled. "Ever?"

"Not right now. Not for a while."

"Okay," he said. He pushed back from the table and stood up.

"Tug."

"Yeah?"

"That's it?"

"That's it for now, I guess." He tried to keep his voice even, but the clenching of his jaw and the shoving of his fists deep into his pockets gave him up.

Guilt spread over her like a rash. "I led you on," she told him. "I let myself get way too carried away. It's all on me."

"Am I too old for you?" he asked quickly. "Too much of a working stiff? He was a banker, right?"

"God, Tug! It's not you!"

"I'm just trying to figure this out, because, for the life of me, I can't make any sense of it."

"It's too soon—it hasn't even been a year!" she was feeling defensive now. She'd taken the blame; why did he have to make her feel worse?

"Okay, so let me get this. He died on January fourteenth, right? So on the fifteenth, you're good to go? Is that how it works?"

"Jesus, I don't know!" She crossed her arms, chewed at the inside of her cheek. "I don't know!"

"You do know."

"What the hell is that supposed to mean?"

"You know how you feel, and you act on how you feel, and then you feel bad, so you consult some imaginary manual that tells you the rule is One Fucking Year!"

Janie stood up. "You know what? I don't have to listen to this. If this is how you think you can treat me, go find someone else to abuse!"

His mouth dropped open and his eyes went wild. "Okay," he said. "I'll go right out and do that. You know how many times a week people are trying to fix me up with their sister or their hair dresser or their kid's teacher? Hell, one guy's been trying to get me to go out with his ex-wife because he says I'll treat her better than he did!"

He let out a breath that it seemed he'd been holding for a long time. He shook his head, looked out the big bay window that he himself had installed. Then the fists unclenched in his pockets. "I love you," he said. "I'm so in love with you I can't even think straight. I have to keep myself from thinking about you at work because if I do I make mistakes. One of these days I'm going to put in a home theater where the master bath is supposed to go."

The urge to go over and put her arms around him was so strong she almost took a step. He loved her—no great surprise, although there was something startling and thrilling and also frightening about hearing him say the words. But it was causing him pain. She was hurting this good man, who, no doubt, would treat any ex-wife better than she'd ever been treated. Janie had to protect him from her confusion, and all she could think of at the moment was to stay put.

"The thing is," he went on, "I know I couldn't possibly be this far gone if there wasn't anything coming from you. I'm not the kind of guy who falls for someone from afar. And when I'm with you, Janie . . . I just feel so . . . loved."

The pressure in her chest twisted up into her throat, and it seemed impossible to say anything. After a few moments she was able to push out some words, but they sounded strangled to her. "I could take off this ring right now. And I would if . . . if it would magically make all my feelings fit into the right box. But it won't . . . They'd spill all over like they have all year . . . I'm trying to find my way . . . and I really . . ." she sucked in a ragged breath, "really want to stop hurting you."

His eyes filled. He tried to swallow several times. "Okay," he said, and left.

JANIE KNEW SHE SHOULD start Christmas shopping, but she couldn't seem to bring herself to do it. She did try once. She went to the Natick Mall. But it was too noisy and the lights seemed so bright, she couldn't make any decisions. She left without buying a thing. *I'm turning into Mike,* she thought.

SHE TRIED TO BEG out of going to the Table of Plenty on Saturday, but Aunt Jude wouldn't budge. "It's December!" she admonished Janie. "Everyone's so busy shopping, they've forgotten to feed the hungry and shelter the homeless! Thank goodness Mary and Joseph weren't trying to find food and lodging during the Christmas rush . . . Though I suppose a case could be made that they actually created the Christmas season, so . . . Oh, never mind. We're short on volunteers, you can't back out!"

When Vonetta the volunteer coordinator let them in the back door, she took one look at Janie and said, "You alright?" She turned to Aunt Jude. "She look alright to you? Her skin's so pale, it's starting to match those crazy eyes of hers!"

Aunt Jude put her ringed fingers on Janie's shoulder and said, "It's a difficult time of year, Vonetta. We're doing the best we can."

"Well, you're at the right place then. Every last soul here is just trying to get through."

"I'm fine," said Janie.

"Mmmhmm," said Vonetta.

"Of course you are," said Aunt Jude.

After lunch, Janie and Aunt Jude set up their letter-writing station. Business was slow. This seemed strange to Janie—it was the holiday season, after all. Why was nobody talking? Aunt Jude could handle the few guests who straggled over. Janie went for a walk.

Out in the parking lot, Malcolm was sitting up against the tire of an old, paint-chipped Lincoln Town Car. All the tires were flat. Malcolm smoked an unfiltered cigarette, his half-lidded eyes almost closing with each drag. He inhaled so fully that he nearly fell over with the effort. She sat down on the cracked asphalt next to him. "Hey, Malcolm."

"Hey," he said. "Got any smokes?"

"No."

"Poor thing. Here, have a drag." He reached out his blackened fingers to her.

She hadn't smoked a cigarette since high school, but it seemed the neighborly thing to do. *Besides, what the hell,* she thought. She took a tiny puff, and felt the searing blackness fill her lungs. It hurt, but somehow that seemed just about right. "How's Mary Alice?" she asked, handing back the cigarette.

Malcolm was in the middle of guiding his two fingers out into midair to catch the sacred butt, when he turned abruptly toward her. "How'd you know about that?" he demanded.

"It's me, Janie," she said. "I type your letters."

"Oh, it's you!" he said with a grin that blew out as fast as it lit. "Oh . . ." He reached inside his scarred jacket and pulled out a piece of paper. The letterhead said, *Jacobson, Herlihy & Ostrow, LLP.* Down the left side was a list of principals in the partnership. The address included a suite number.

Re: Your sister
Dear Malcolm:

Thanks for your letters. Mom died last Thursday. She said to tell you, "I'll leave a candle in the window of our new home above the stars." I'm not sure quite what that means, but I assume you do.

Regards,
Dean Ostrow

"Oh, Malcolm," said Janie. "I am so sorry."

He handed her the cigarette and she took another puff. "Yeah," he said. "All's I keep thinking is, 'Now what?' Isn't that the stupidest thing? I can't figure out what to do next. Like there *is* something, but I just don't know what."

Janie nodded. She stared out across the parking lot. He smelled like booze and pee and smoke and the most incredibly rancid body odor. But she didn't even care. *Now what?* she thought. *What other question is there?*

———

IT SNOWED ON WEDNESDAY, the weak flakes huddling together on the frozen ground. Not enough to make snowballs, much less a snowman. Keane came over for a playdate and the boys rolled around in their jackets and snow pants and hats with earflaps, claiming all the white they could. They came in wet and tired and unsatisfied.

"The fitting's tonight," Janie groaned to Heidi when she came to retrieve Keane.

"The bridesmaid dress? God, is there anything worse?"

"Oh, like you'd know," said Janie. "You'd look good in a painter's tarp."

"First of all, that is completely untrue. Second of all, the next time I see you, I will bring you PROOF."

"Oh, what? A ball gown that was a shade off?"

"No, smart-ass. You'll have to wait and see."

"And what's with the trash talk?" said Janie.

"Hanging around you too much, I guess," Heidi smiled.

Aunt Jude came over to babysit, nearly pushing Janie out the door to make the appointment. As she drove down Route 9 looking for the dress shop, she considered buying a pack of cigarettes. *Now what?* she thought, remembering Malcolm. *How can House of Happiness Bridal Salon possibly be the answer to that question?*

When she walked in the door, the satiny pinkness of it, and the remnants of a hundred women's perfumes hit her like a rogue wave. *Please, God, help me,* she found herself praying. *Keep me from the temptation to scream out bad words. Or purposely rip my dress. Or hurt Barb's feelings. Please God, help me be good.*

"Janie!" Barb called giddily from a doorway across the room. The sound went up Janie's spine. *Smile,* she ordered herself. *Approach.*

Once inside an even pinker room, Janie was introduced to the seven other bridesmaids. *The pews will be empty,* she thought. *We'll all be up on the altar.* She immediately forgot all of their names, but she did not fail to notice that they were all approximately a decade younger than her. Most were taller with perkier figures and better haircuts. Two were light-pole-thin and had clearly had some work done. Those breasts were just too round and high.

"And this is my godchild, Stephanie. She's a junior bridesmaid, right honey?" said Barb, drawing out a girl of about twelve from behind a high-backed shiny upholstered pink chair. The girl's brown hair hung like broom-bristle around her face. She looked miserable.

Janie delivered her only genuine smile of the evening. The girl smiled back, flicked her gaze around the room, and rolled her eyes to Janie. *You and me, both,* thought Janie.

The dresses were unveiled with more pomp than an inauguration. They were brought out by a phalanx of bridal salon workers and hung on tall mirrors around the room. Janie had to admit they were beautiful. And surprisingly simple. Sheath-style with delicate lace straps, and made from several different pastel-colored silks, they hung there just begging to be tried on. The other women began to disrobe immediately. Stephanie gave Janie an imploring look, and Janie replied by cocking her head in a surreptitious "come over here" gesture. Stephanie scurried over behind her.

Before either of them could catch up, the other women were completely naked. *What the hell?* thought Janie. The bridal workers were handing out "body stockings," panty hose that rose up to the armpit, creating what Barb referred to as "a sleek line."

An older woman, apparently the manager, approached Janie, still standing there in her bra and underpants. "Wait, just a moment," she said politely in a foreign, possibly Portuguese, accent. "I will get you something with more . . . support."

Janie glanced down at her stretch marks and slightly drooping breasts. Many curse words formed in her head. She looked at Stephanie, who hadn't even taken off her shirt. "Let's just get through this," Janie said.

"Okay," breathed the girl.

When the manager returned, she held out the "supportive" body stocking to Janie.

"You know—" began Janie.

"Follow me," said the manager, sweeping up two pale blue dresses as she walked.

Janie and Stephanie were ushered into a smaller dressing room. When the curtain swished closed behind them, they both began to laugh. "I'm going to kill my mother!" said Stephanie. "I didn't even want to be in the stupid wedding. And SHE doesn't have to be in it because she's PREGNANT!" Stephanie puffed out her cheeks and hooped her hands in front of her.

They struggled into their body stockings, Janie's with extra tension around the stomach and breasts, and helped each other into the dresses. She studied Stephanie, her tender body budding through the smoothness of the silk. Janie felt emotional all of a sudden. The sweetness of the moment, the imperfect, authentic beauty of the young girl. "Your mother must be so proud of you," she murmured. And she thought, *This is why I'm here. This is Now What*.

Stephanie smiled shyly and nodded. "You look really hot," she added.

"For an old lady," Janie teased.

"No, really. For anyone."

She dreaded Tuesday. It had been two weeks since she'd seen Tug, and she'd spent the previous Tuesday struggling mightily not to be home. She knew he wouldn't come. Why should he? And it was just too hard to be there, in the absence of him. It was harder than six o'clock was anymore. She went to a paint store and spent an hour and a half choosing new paint for her living room. Not that she had any plans to paint her living room.

This Tuesday, Carly had fallen asleep uncharacteristically early. Janie was trapped in the house. She was actually starting to consider painting when she saw the mail truck pull up. There was never anything good, just bills and flyers and credit card offers, but she went out, anyway. It would kill a minute and a half.

A letter was addressed to her in what she thought of as nun's handwriting; perfectly formed letters, curling daintily at the ends, knit together in perfect lines of art. The return address on the back flap of the stationery was raised, and gave the sender's name as "Mrs. Frances J. Seagrave." She lived on Pelham Heights Lane. "Dear Mrs. LaMarche," Janie read as she walked back toward the house.

I hardly know how to begin. I suppose it is my duty to inform you as to my identity so that you may determine whether you have any further interest in this letter. My brother is Emmett Daly, the man who caused the death of your husband.

If you continue to read, please first let me express my family's deepest, most heartfelt sympathy about the loss of your dear husband, and our profound regret on behalf of my brother at having been the cause of such an unimaginable tragedy. It is well within the bounds of reason if you were never to have anything to do with us.

However, I write to inform you that I fear for my brother. Since the accident, he has become unable to care for himself, not because he can't but because he seems to have no desire to do so. I have insisted that he come to live with me so that I may do my best to insure that no serious harm comes to him. This is becoming progressively more difficult. He eats and sleeps very little. He refuses to engage in almost any activity whatsoever. His wife passed away several years ago and his children are far flung across the country. I believe, Mrs. LaMarche, that my brother has lost the will to live.

Not withstanding the event of January past, he is a kind and decent man. When his good old dog, Nancy, was at the end of her natural days and unable to rise, he could not bear to have her put down. I had to take the animal to the vet myself. All this to say, please do not, under any circumstances, think that your husband's death conformed to a pattern of recklessness or lack of concern on my brother's part. To the contrary, I know of no other man who would be less likely to be involved in such an act. Needless to say, he no longer drives. He will barely ride in a car at all. Not that any of this is the least concern of yours, of course. I understand you have two very young children. It fills me with pain even to think of it.

Mrs. LaMarche, I do not know you, or anything about you. But I find myself wondering—hoping desperately, in fact—if you might be the kind of person who would be able to forgive my brother. I know that this favor may be unimaginable. I tremble as I ask it. And yet, I love my brother. I would do anything to ease the excruciating mental anguish he experiences every day, even if it involves a request of such magnitude to a stranger. If I have overstepped the limits of decency in your eyes, I hope you will find it in your heart to understand.

> Most sincerely yours,
> Fran Seagrave

Janie had sunk down onto the floor of the porch. Her fingers ached with cold, and yet she could not move farther into the house until she'd finished reading. Emmett Daly. That name came back to her. He was an older man, the police had told her, but not too old to drive. He'd called the paramedics himself from his cell phone, and he was sitting on the ground, holding Robby's lifeless hand and weeping when they arrived.

It was unknown as to whether he'd gone through the stop sign or if it had been Robby who'd blown through his own stop sign on the cross street. Mr. Daly couldn't remember, and wouldn't defend himself. He'd been charged with manslaughter. It was unlikely that he would serve any time, they had warned her, given that there was no evidence of recklessness.

Not reckless. That's what his sister had said. It was just an accident, like Robby forgetting the helmet.

We need that day back, was all Janie could think. *More of us than I ever realized.*

SHE PUT THE LETTER on her dresser. She had every intention of responding, and yet when she thought of what "responding" might mean, she got a little queasy. Should she write him a letter? That would be the easiest way, if she could think of anything at all to say other than, "You're forgiven." Who would even believe a note like that? She could call, but that seemed even weirder, like some disembodied voice coming at her over the phone: "I killed him." Then she would say, "It's okay. I forgive you." It wasn't okay. Nothing was okay. Maybe she didn't really forgive him after all.

THURSDAY, DECEMBER 13

I got this letter. The sister of the guy who hit Robby thinks he needs forgiveness. Well, actually, it seems that he might need a lot more than me forgiving him at this point in the game. He's in pretty tough shape.

The more I think about it—and I seem to be obsessed with it since I got the letter—the more I'm not even sure I really know what forgiveness is. Is it some big cosmic do-over? Like no harm, no foul? But there was harm—big, hairy, serious harm. Robby doesn't get a do-over, and neither do I or the kids. Things are broken now that can't be fixed. How come the other guy gets a Get Out of Jail Free card?

Alright, but it's not like he hasn't paid. His life is decimated, I get that. He will never not be a guy who killed someone. And when I think about it that way, it's worse than jail, and there's no free pass, no matter who says nice words to you.

So what does forgiveness really do for you? Is it even a real thing? Or is it something humans just made up to make our-

selves feel better? Or is it like the concept of time, something that actually exists, but our little brains can't really comprehend it, so we just measure it and give the pieces names until we've dumbed it down for ourselves?

SUNDAY, SHE WENT TO Immaculate Conception in Natick with Aunt Jude, as usual. Father Octogenarian gave a mercifully brief homily about it being the third Sunday of Advent. The pink candle in the Advent wreath could now be lit. "And for those of you who've already gone ahead and lit the pink candle," snarled the priest, "well, you've ruined it."

The pink candle was for Joy.

Fuck joy, thought Janie.

BY TUESDAY MORNING, EXACTLY one week after the letter had arrived, and three weeks since she'd last seen Tug, Janie had had about enough. *I AM turning into Mike,* she told herself. *I'm obsessive and hypersensitive, except without the world-class artistic talent. It sucks.*

Lunchtime was fast approaching and she had no errands to get her out of the house—except Christmas shopping, which any normal person would do, but Janie couldn't even force herself to consider. She had the admittedly certifiable idea that if she bought presents, Christmas might actually come.

She needed to be done with this whole forgiveness thing. She wanted an end to it, and there was only one way she could see to accomplish that, short of a home lobotomy. She checked the address on the envelope, strapped Carly into her car seat, and drove over to Pelham Heights Lane.

The Seagrave home was on the far end of the road, so Janie was forced to pass the impossibly large house that Tug was, at that moment, gutting. She saw his truck in the long winding driveway. Her foot pressed harder on the accelerator. One mind-warping dilemma at a time, if you please.

When she rang the doorbell, an older woman answered in a corduroy shirtdress that tied above her rounded belly. She wore pearl studs and sheepskin slippers. "Yes?" she said.

Janie's heart began to pound. *What in God's name am I doing here?* she wondered. "I'm Janie LaMarche." The old woman gasped. Her fingers flew to her mouth. Janie was afraid she might have a heart attack right there on the spot. *Oh, great,* she thought. *That's all we need.*

Janie took a deep breath and tried to smile, hoping the effort would diffuse the ticking bomb of Mrs. Seagrave's distress. She shifted Carly to her left hip and held out her right hand to shake. "I got your letter." Mrs. Seagrave was still looking at her like the fifth horseman of the apocalypse, so she tried a different tack. "This is my daughter, Carly."

Tears began to well in the corners of Mrs. Seagrave's wrinkled eyelids. "Oh, dear, yes," she said finally. "Isn't she lovely. Please come in." She closed the door behind Janie and leaned against it for a brief moment.

Janie glanced around. The house was large and elegant. A little overdecorated with dark antiques, but Janie could see that it was comfortable, lived in. A chess set lay on a small table by a window. The pieces were set up as if a game had been going on and then paused indefinitely.

"You have a lovely home," said Janie.

"Thank you, dear."

"Mrs. Seagrave —"

"Fran. Please."

"Fran, I'm sorry I scared you. I should have called first. But I've been thinking about this way too much. I had to just act. Can you understand that?"

"Certainly."

"And now that I'm here, I don't really know what to do next."

Fran took a breath and nodded. "Do you want to talk to him right away, or should we sit and have some biscuits first?"

Janie smiled apologetically. "Maybe biscuits."

They sat at an oversized oak table, bitten along the edges by the thousands of meals that had occurred there. Fran served strong coffee and large, grainy cookies that she referred to as digestives. Carly ate four.

Fran asked carefully, tentatively, about Janie's life. How did she feel the children were doing, did she have activities that she enjoyed? Janie found herself telling Fran about the porch. They shed some quiet tears together over the notion of Robby's gift coming long after his death. "A thoughtful, generous man," Fran said with a delicate sniffle.

"Yes," said Janie. "He was." She told Fran about Shelly and Aunt Jude and Heidi, and even briefly mentioned Tug and Father Jake. "You know the strangest thing about the last year? All these people that I started out not liking—I think I was just too angry to like anyone—and now they mean so much to me. It was the people I least expected could help me that have been there the most."

"You must have been willing, on some level, to let them."

"I think I was, even despite myself." She thought about this for a moment. "Maybe I could see your brother now."

Fran led them out to a sunny room at the back of the house. An elderly man, much older-looking than Fran, sat slumped in a cushioned chair in the far corner. His gray skin hung in drapes from his face. He'd shaved, but there were patches of whiskers here and there that he hadn't seen or perhaps hadn't bothered with. There was a book in his hand with soldiers on the cover, a history of some kind. But he wasn't reading it. He was staring at the floor tiles.

"Emmett?" said Fran. "There's someone here to see you." He looked up, struggled to make his eyes focus. Fran squatted down beside him and patted his arm. "Now I don't want you to be up-set with me . . . but this is Mrs. LaMarche." The old man put a hand quickly over his face, and his shoulders began to shake. Fran looked back up at Janie, as if to apologize.

Janie shifted Carly around off her hip and sat down on the unused ottoman by the man's feet. The little girl slumped in her arms, and Janie cradled her close. "Mr. Daly? Emmett? Your sister is so worried about you . . . and to be honest, I can see why. You seem like you're kind of . . . wasting." He gripped his sister's hand and shook even harder. Janie thought, *Well this isn't working.* But here she was, what could she do? Walk out?

"It's been a tough year, I know. For both of us. The worst year. We have every right to feel like hell. You should have seen me last spring. I was a holy wreck. I was not fun to be around, I promise you." His shaking quieted as he began to listen to her, but he still held his hand over his face. "We've had some really bad luck. The worst luck. Well, not so bad as some. You read the newspaper these days and people in these war-torn countries, they have it worse. They're losing people right and left. And living in hell. We have it better than them, don't we?"

Where exactly was she going with this?

"Emmett, please. Please look at me. I want you to see my face." Slowly he took his hand down. Janie could see the dampness on his cheeks and the tiny streams in the folds of his skin. He glanced up at her, then back down again. "Well, I don't know how much you saw in that quick look, but I hope you saw me. And I hope you saw that I'm okay. And my daughter here is so content, she's passing out in my arms with a belly full of cookies."

Emmett's face squeezed up into a ball of wrinkles. "No father," he gasped.

"No," said Janie, and she felt the tears come to her own eyes. But she wasn't sure if she was crying for Carly or for the old man who felt so responsible. Maybe both. "Sometimes life is just . . ."

"Suffering," he muttered.

"True." She rocked Carly back and forth, and soon the breaths came in smooth even passes.

Emmett reached out and touched her elbow very quickly, then pulled back as if he had risked too much. "There was no soft place to land," he whispered.

"No," said Janie. "Sometimes there just isn't." Carly's face, smooth and slack, seemed to glow up at her. *Blessed and cursed,* she thought. *Every one of us.*

"Emmett," she said gently. "I want you to stop beating yourself up. It was an accident. And you're making it worse by letting it ruin your life. You're making the accident happen every day. Let it be over, now, Emmett. Please. For all of us."

She stayed a little while longer with Fran and Emmett. When Fran walked her out to the front door, the older woman suddenly burst into seismic sobs, barely able to catch her breath before another overtook her. Janie held her arm, afraid she might fall.

"Oh, dear," Fran gasped, as her crying finally slowed. "Oh, my dear. Thank you."

Janie nodded. "You know," she said. "I need to thank you, too. I think this was a good idea."

"I'm so glad," Fran beamed through her tears. She patted Janie's cheek. "Your mother must be so proud of you."

When Janie drove back down Pelham Heights Lane, she looked for Tug's truck, but it was gone.

22

THURSDAY, DECEMBER 20

My mind is full of Emmett. Poor old guy. Poor, misera-
ble, guilt-ridden, practically suicidal guy. I keep thinking that
while I've spent the last eleven months climbing out of a hole,
he's spent it digging his hole deeper and deeper. I had no idea.
I never even thought of him.

I'm not sure if I actually forgave him. But I told him it was
over. I hope it helped. I really hope I helped someone for once
in the last year. So many people helped me. I didn't realize that
either, until I was talking to his sister, Fran.

I picked up Dylan from school that afternoon, and Miss
Sharon sent home her little class newsletter, which mentioned
how they were practicing their manners. (It's like finishing
school for five-year-olds, I swear.) One of the things she's been
trying to teach them is to think of others. The kids are supposed
to ask their parents and siblings, "How was your day?"

So, of course, Dylan asked me about my day and what I did.
It was pretty cute, actually. Except how do I tell him, "Well,
I went to see the guy that killed your father." Kind of hard to
explain. I started out saying I went to visit an elderly man who
was very sad. Dylan wanted to know why he was sad. I said
the man did something by accident that hurt someone and he

was feeling very, very bad about it. Did he say he was sorry? Yes, he's so sorry.

It went on like this for a while, and little by little, the truth leaked out. Dylan already knew that Robby had been hit by a car while he was riding his bike, so that part wasn't a surprise. What surprised him was that I hadn't gone to see Emmett sooner! "Didn't Dad die a long time ago?" he asked me. "How come you let the guy be sad for so long?"

So add that to the list of things I've screwed up this year.

Then, Dylan asked—demanded, really—to see Emmett himself! I called Fran to see if poor Emmett was up for another excruciating visit, she said fine, and we went over today. We didn't stay long because the kids got fidgety. But Emmett and Dylan did talk for a few minutes, and Dylan asked him, "Did my dad say anything?"

Poor Emmett almost lost it. But he pulled himself together, and he told Dylan that Robby died very quickly, so he didn't get a chance. But Emmett said he thought that if Robby had had the chance, he would have said how much he loved his family.

Dylan smiled. And he said, "Yeah."

Then we all cried (not the kids, just the grown-ups). I think partly I was crying because I was happy that Dylan heard it from a guy who seemed to have some inside information. Dylan knows Robby loved him, but today he got a sweet little reminder. He wore his goggles on the way home, but he took them off without a word when we pulled in.

So I guess that's my miracle for today, as Jake used to call it.

JANIE'S MOTHER WAS DUE to arrive on Sunday the twenty-third, but Janie still hadn't heard from Mike about his plans, so she called. The same woman answered the phone. "Hello?"

"Hi, this is Janie, Mike's sister."

"Hi."

"Are you Mike's assistant?"

"Well, no, but I do help out in the studio."

"Oh," said Janie. *And that makes you what, exactly?* she wanted to ask. The woman put Mike on the phone.

"Hi!" Mike always sounded surprised to hear from her, as if a call from his sister was a bolt from the blue.

"Hey, when does your flight come in?" Janie asked. "Uncle Charlie needs to know when to start spritzing Armor All on his dashboard."

Silence on the end of the phone. Her sense of humor rarely made sense to him. He murmured something away from the receiver, then said to Janie, "Alicia says Saturday the twenty-ninth. We're going to her parents' house in New York the day after Christmas, then we'll rent a car and drive up."

Alicia says?

"So is Alicia your girlfriend?" Janie asked.

"Yeah," said Mike, and Janie could practically smell the pride wafting through the phone line. "I can't wait for you to meet her."

JANIE HAD A STRANGE reaction to Mike's news. She felt duped somehow, as if it were a trick he had played on her. Mike didn't play tricks; he didn't even get fairly simple jokes. Why was she so bent out of shape?

She lay in bed that night trying to talk herself out of her agitation over The Girlfriend. Mike had had girlfriends before, but they usually didn't last very long. They were often artists themselves and dazzled by his talent. The relationships lasted as long as it took for them to realize that Mike's lack of social grace did, in fact, matter, and was not that appealing on a day-to-day basis. Janie usually found out about them by accident. Mike almost never even mentioned them.

This was different. Mike was bringing Alicia to meet her, for one thing, a feat never before attempted in their thirty-eight years of twin-hood. He seemed excited about it. Janie assumed he would bring her to Cormac's wedding. They would dance together while Janie sat alone at the table looking wistful . . .

Ah, now she was getting somewhere. *You're jealous,* she realized. *For once in your life, Mike has a date and you don't, not the other way around.* But there was more to it than that. When she'd talked to Mike at Thanksgiving, he was so upset about Robby. It had fanned the flames of her own anguish and had been a factor in her pulling away from Tug.

Why couldn't she take off the ring? Partly she had worried that it would be a shock to Mike. It would be a shock to everyone when she showed up without it someday. It would seem as if she were over Robby. And while she herself knew she would never be over him completely—as Tug had said, like the bit of fence that remained in the tree trunk—it was a very different thing to make such a public statement that she was moving on. Her improved mental state seemed shameful to her.

She had the strangest urge to call Jake and ask his advice. He was always so good at helping her clarify things.

Hi, Jake? she imagined herself saying. *It's me, Janie. Yeah, the woman who had that infectious crush on you and practically asked you to leave the priesthood for her? Well, forget about that, I'm into this new guy now, and I really want to get together with him, but I can't seem to take my wedding ring off because I'm ashamed that I might be feeling too good. Your thoughts?*

Janie rolled over and buried her face in her pillow.

THE DAY THAT NOREEN was due to arrive, Uncle Charlie had a back spasm and was unable to sit up straight, much less drive to the airport. Janie ended up making the trip with the kids. It wasn't so bad, not as much of a burden as she expected. The kids loved watching the planes taking off and landing, and there was no baggage claim to deal with. Noreen, ever the efficient traveler, only brought carry-on luggage.

On the ride back to the house, Noreen chatted with the children about Italian Christmas traditions. "Have you heard of La Befana?" she asked. "The story goes that when the three wise men were looking for Jesus, they stopped at the cottage of an old woman to ask directions to Bethlehem, and invited her to come along. 'No,' she said. 'I have too much housework to do.'

"Can you imagine that?" Noreen asked them. "She turned down a trip to see the Baby Jesus so she could sweep!"

Janie chuckled to herself, knowing her own mother would never make such a mistake. Miss an opportunity to travel? Noreen was the anti-Befana.

"That night," Noreen went on, "she saw the star in the sky that told her it was all true. The King of Kings had been born, and she'd missed it because she was too busy with her own little worries! Quickly she gathered up some toys to bring to the Baby Jesus, but without the wise men she couldn't find him. Now she leaves presents for all the good boys and girls in Italy, because she's sorry she didn't see what was really important."

"I want to live in Italy and get presents from that lady!" said Dylan.

Noreen looked to Janie. Janie kept her eyes on the road. "Maybe next summer we can go and visit," she said. "It will be warm then and we can wear shorts."

"Italy shorts?" asked Dylan.

"Any kind of shorts you like." She glanced at her mother. "Maybe this week we can go online and price a trip together."

Noreen sighed victoriously and settled back in her seat.

That night, after Noreen had tucked the kids in with promises to make them an Italian Christmas treat called struffoli, Janie paid a visit to the little back bedroom where Noreen was unpacking her clothes and quilting supplies. "Mum, I need your help with something."

"Of course, dear-o, anything."

Janie admitted that she had done not one shred of shopping for Christmas presents. She couldn't face it, she explained. Christmas hadn't really seemed real to her.

Noreen's face went dark. "I remember that first Christmas after your father left. Jude bought all my presents for me."

"I'm alright, Mum. I just need a little help."

The next day they shopped together while Aunt Jude watched the children. It wasn't so bad after all. Noreen had some good suggestions, and they ended up laughing over some of the more ridiculous items for sale: a home body-piercing kit; a T-shirt that said "Fishermen Do It with Baited Breath"; a slightly maniacal-looking Mrs. Claus doll that sang "I Saw Mommy Kissing Santa Claus" in a high-pitched whine. It was Christmas Eve—most shoppers wore signs of half-desperate, half-delirious panic.

"Okay," said Janie, when they'd finished. "I just don't have anything for you, yet."

"Well, you've let me help you, for once—that's a very generous gift, to my mind."

"Come on, Mum. That's not much to open tomorrow morning."

"Then research the trip with me tonight, and let me tell the kids about it when they wake up," said Noreen. "That's all I ever wish for."

THERE WAS NO CHRISTMAS Eve Mass offered at Immaculate Conception Church in Natick. By way of the church bulletin, the elderly Father Gilroy announced that he had detected a distinct "lack of interest," and simply canceled it. Janie didn't want to go to Mass on Christmas morning. It broke up the day. It wasn't how they did it. And besides, she wanted her old church back.

"Let's just go to the five o'clock at Our Lady's," she told her mother and Aunt Jude, who agreed as they shot quick glances at each other. Janie pressed her lips together to keep from saying anything snotty.

And there they were, in their usual pew at Our Lady, Comforter of the Afflicted Church. Thankfully they had gotten there early—people were standing three deep at the back. CAPE Catholics, Uncle Charlie liked to call them. Only came to church on Christmas, Ash Wednesday, Palm Sunday, and Easter.

Father Jake processed up the aisle with several more candle bearers and book holders than usual, with all the solemn joy of a Christmas Eve service. Janie wondered what he was thinking, how he was doing. He rose and sat, blessed them and led them in the "Gloria." He adjusted his round wireless glasses and checked the tiny microphone attached to the collar of his vestments. She missed him. Not this priest, but the man she knew under all the robes and rituals. Jake, her friend.

Songs were sung, the Host was consecrated. Janie shuffled obediently toward him in the Communion line. "Body of Christ," he said as his fingers dipped into the dish for a wafer. When he glanced up to deliver it, he registered her face. Memory softened his features, and the real Jake surfaced momentarily from behind his sacramental duty.

"Thanks," she said, rather than the requisite "Amen." She gazed at him for an extra second, just long enough to cause a stutter in the shuffling feet behind her. Then she stepped away from him and toward the chalice.

AFTER MASS, THEY WENT home and made struffoli with the kids, rolling out the ropes of dough, cutting them into little balls and frying them in oil. Dylan's favorite part was dipping them in warm honey and rolling them in the tiny colorful candy sprinkles. He didn't mind sampling about a dozen of them either. When the kids were asleep, Janie and Noreen stayed up late wrapping presents, making preparations for Christmas brunch, and trolling the Internet for deals on airfare to Italy. Janie was so tired when she went to bed that night, she was certain she would fall asleep before she could think one more thought.

But as soon as she burrowed into her bed and closed her eyes, the secret despondence she'd held tethered at the far fringes of her awareness throughout the day pulled up its stake and lunged. Missing, missing, missing. The dull ache of Robby's absence throbbed in her chest.

Where are you now? she wondered. Heaven, so comforting to a five-year-old, seemed like a made-for-TV concept in the dark press of her sorrow. *Where are you right this very minute?*

Somewhere, everywhere, nowhere. No answer satisfactory, and no way to know. She was slipping toward the hem of sleep now, where surreal images and half-sensible sentences dangle at the edge of consciousness. Sad, old Emmett was there, asking her to dance, singing to her in his grieving, gravelly voice, "Let it be over, now."

WHEN SHE WOKE SHE knew she'd been dreaming of Tug, the smell of chocolate almost real to her still. She felt for her wedding band and was both relieved and disappointed to find it. She wondered if she could possibly be good enough for him. Then the kids rushed in.

It was a mostly happy Christmas. However, there was a distinct absence of men: Robby, of course, and Mike, who'd been with them for every Christmas morning until this one. Janie tried to remind herself that it never would have occurred to him that it might be good to show up for this one in particular. Not just them, though. Uncle Charlie's back had gotten worse, so he came for a short while, but then went home. Cormac, too, made an appearance, but left for Barb's family's holiday celebration after brunch.

And Tug was missing. Very much missing, Janie realized.

Noreen and Aunt Jude stayed, but when Shelly showed up unexpectedly in the early evening, they took themselves to Brigid and Charlie's. Shelly brought overly expensive gifts—toys from FAO Schwarz in New York, and dangling crystal earrings for Janie.

"I didn't get you a gift," Janie apologized. "I didn't expect to see you."

"Pfff," Shelly waved her hand. "Not necessary."

"Still, I feel bad."

"Tell me some news. Tell me all about your life. That's what I want." Janie smirked, shook her head. "Ooo, what's this?" said Shelly. "What have I missed?"

"Let me put the kids to bed first."

"That good?" prodded Shelly. "That BAD?"

"You'll have to judge that for yourself."

Once Janie got the kids tucked in, she came back down, thinking on the way about how she might tell Shelly about Tug without getting too specific or personal. It turned out to be a waste of fifteen seconds. As the story began to unfold, Shelly fired well-timed questions at her, surgical strikes that reduced her strategy of nonspecificity to rubble.

"Wait, so he took you out to lunch when he finished the porch? Did he pay? Did you try to pay and he insisted?" she asked.

Then later, "Where did he stand when you came to the softball games and his team was on the bench, with you or with the team? Did he *ever* stand with the team? How close did he stand? Was he touching you?"

Shelly became so engrossed, she began to pick absentmindedly at the plate of crackers and cheese that was still sitting on the end table from brunch. "What's he like when he gets angry? Does he swear? Does he get a wild look?"

They had moved into the kitchen and were cutting themselves pieces of leftover quiche when Shelly said, "WAIT a minute! Just HOLD ON! You're telling me he asked you to have Thanksgiving together? He came to your FAMILY'S THANKSGIVING?"

By the time Janie told her about the weekend on Cape Cod, Shelly was eating mint Oreo ice cream straight out of the container. She was completely silent except for the licking of the spoon.

"So that's how we left it," Janie concluded. "It's four weeks today since we've talked. I miss him so much, Shelly, I can barely stand it. But he's made it clear that he won't see me until I have all my feelings tucked neatly into place. I just don't know if I can do that . . ."

Shelly tossed the spoon and empty container into the sink without a word. She left the room and came back with her cell phone. "What's his number?" she asked.

"What? Why?"

"Because there's this really cute girl in my office who just got divorced. I'm going to see if he wants me to fix him up. What's the number? I can call directory assistance if you don't have it."

"Shelly!"

"What?"

"That's not funny!"

"You think I'm being funny? You think I'm joking?" Shelly put the phone down and spread her hands flat on the table, the shiny pink nails splayed out like a Barbie doll's cutlery. "Oh no," she continued. "This is no joke. This man, whom you love—and yes, he's right, you absolutely love him—who loves you to the point of insanity—because he'd have to be NUTS to put up with all of this! You think you can just leave him hanging on some hook in your closet, waiting for you to take that damn piece of metal off your hand? You're wearing that thing like some sort of armor, like it will protect you from something, like it will keep bad things from you. It's keeping GOOD things from you! Tug Malinowski, is what!"

She stood up, stalked up and down the room, hands flying. "I've never heard of anything so insane in my life," she muttered. "It should be illegal, this kind of crazy." She turned on Janie, pointing a finely honed finger. "YOU have happiness by the BALLS, and you don't even know what to do with it! If you can't take that thing off right this minute, and go over there on CHRISTMAS—so important to you, your peace and goodwill and jingle bells all over the place—if you can't go over there right now and tell him you love him, and you're sorry, and to please give you a second chance, then I don't even KNOW what."

Janie started to cry. Shelly sat down and cried a little, too. "Janie, baby, please," she sniffed. "I taught you better than this." She put out her hand, palm up.

"Shelly, it's my wedding ring, for chrissake! You can't just command me to hand it over!"

"It might be your wedding ring," Shelly said gently. "But you're not married anymore, bub."

"I miss my husband," Janie whispered as tears dripped from her chin.

"Of course you do. We all miss people. I miss my parents, may they rest in peace. I miss my marriage when it was good. You don't have to stop missing. You just have to accept that missing doesn't mean you turn away happiness. Missing doesn't mean you have to miss Tug, too. You can have him!" She held her open palm a little closer to Janie. "So . . . how is he with the hands? Because I've always thought his hands were very sexy."

"Jesus, Shelly!" But she started to laugh.

JANIE DROVE DOWN ROUTE 27, a bowl of struffoli on the seat next to her, wondering what her mother would think when she arrived home and found Shelly there by herself. What would Shelly tell her? Good Lord, it could be anything. She was glad she would miss that particular conversation, which would likely include some none-too-delicate comment about not expecting Janie home any time soon.

Four weeks. Time enough for Tug to have moved on himself. Or to be so angry he'd want nothing to do with her. As she climbed his front steps she tried to consider the worst.

Nevertheless, she was not prepared for the door to be answered by a very attractive, very young woman. She was wearing a skin-tight, low-cut burgundy-colored blouse, and her dark eyes seemed impossibly large and liquid. It took Janie half a moment to realize that the effect was enhanced by expertly applied eyeliner.

"Uh, hi," said the woman, who was clearly taking in every

thread of Janie's decade-old gray peacoat and the hole in the fin-
gertip of her black leather gloves. With the bowl of struffoli in her
hands, Janie felt like Oliver Twist, begging for gruel.

"I'm sorry," stammered Janie. "I didn't mean to barge in . . . I
just wanted to tell Tug . . ."

The woman turned and yelled into the house, "Uncle Tug!"

Janie exhaled so hard it made her cough.

When Tug came up behind the young woman, she pointed to
Janie and said, "Uh, she wants to, like, tell you something."

"Merry Christmas," choked Janie. She handed him the struffoli.

"Merry Christmas," said Tug. He looked down into the bowl at
the sticky balls covered in tiny candy pellets. He looked back up
at her. "Come in," he said.

He put the bowl on the dining room table and introduced her
to his brother, Dave, sister-in-law, Christa, and nieces Tracey and
Sophie. Janie took off her coat and shoved the gloves in the pocket.
Tug reached for the coat and watched her hands come toward him
as she held it out to him. He went still for a second, then took the
coat and hung it in the closet behind him.

They had been finishing up dessert when she arrived, so they
invited her to sit with them at the table. "Here, I'll cut you some
birthday cake," said Christa, slicing into a lopsided mountain of
fudgy black chocolate.

Janie's brain seemed to be crisscrossing the room like a roving
camera, flicking from face to face, searching for hints of anger or
dislike. Did they know about her, and if so, were they wishing she
would leave? "Whose birthday is it?" she asked, trying to sound
normal.

"That would be our Lord and Savior," said Dave with a stiff-
ness that paralyzed her for a moment. Then he broke into a grin.

"Dad!" groaned Tracey, the one who had answered the door. She
was eighteen—"going on twenty-eight," her father teased her—and
a freshman at Rhode Island School of Design, studying textiles.

"Fashion," said Sophie executing a perfect teenaged eye roll. Sophie was fifteen, a sophomore at Natick High School, on the junior varsity lacrosse team but hoping to make varsity next year. She was built like Tug, boxy and strong, tall for a girl. She had his auburn hair, too, hanging in a ponytail from the back of her head. "These little ball things are pretty good," she said, picking another struffoli out of the bowl and popping it into her mouth. "Good thing you brought them. I'm about up to here with the chocolate," she mock sneered at her uncle.

"So, Janie," said her mother, Christa, "you're the friend Tug spent Thanksgiving with."

Mouth full, Janie nodded. *Here it comes,* she thought. She saw Tug shoot Dave a look.

Dave immediately jumped in with, "We went down to Christa's parents' house in Woonsocket for Thanksgiving, so that worked out pretty well," he said quickly. "Ever been to Woonsocket? It's about halfway to Newport. Now I *know* you've been to Newport. All those mansions on the cliff walk. Did you know they only lived in those monstrosities about six weeks a year?"

Dave did his best to keep the conversation blithely impersonal, but he was no match for his wife. Christa chatted Janie up like a new best girlfriend, sliding questions in sideways whenever possible. With every question—"So, how'd that porch come out? You like it?" and "Two kids, that's great. Kids are great, aren't they?" and "Thinking of going back to work? Part-time or full?"—Janie knew she was running a gauntlet. A time-honored, homemade gauntlet constructed of steel-clad love. Her answers seemed satisfactory to Christa, and yet Janie herself wondered if they were good enough. She wanted very much to be good enough for Tug.

At the point where Janie thought she could no longer stand the sound of her own voice, Dave suddenly gave the stand-and-stretch international sign for "we're leaving now." His daughters, who had been intently watching the chess match laid out by their mother, puffed little sighs of disappointment. Janie stopped pinching the back of her hand under the table, and hazarded her first glance at Tug. His face was masked in the studied calm that had grown so familiar to her.

Then everyone was standing and moving toward the front door, tossing incidental thank-yous to Tug for presents, and nice-to-meet-yous to Janie.

"Glad you came over," Dave told her with a smile that was a shade too big. "Have a really merry Christmas." When he was hugged by his brother, he let out a little cough as Tug thumped him hard on the back.

Tug stood on the front step, raising a hand as they pulled out of the driveway. Then he came in and closed the door. "So." He began to clear the table. "Thanks for bringing this . . . what did you call it?"

"Struffoli."

"Is it some sort of family tradition?" he asked.

"In a way," she said. "Actually it's a form of Pology Cake. In my family, when we screw up, we say sorry with baked goods."

"Okay," he said, his face softening slightly.

She held up her unadorned left hand.

"I noticed," he said.

"Sorry it took a while."

"Thirsty?" he asked, and walked into the kitchen. She leaned over the counter and watched him as he filled two glasses from the tap. He seemed to be moving slowly, as if he himself were underwater. He dropped two cubes of ice into one glass. Reached into the freezer. Dropped two cubes into the other. He walked into the living room, set the glasses on a copy of *Architectural Digest* that was lying on the coffee table. Sat down on the russet-colored couch. Janie followed.

"Are you angry?" she asked.

"No," he said. "Though I have spent the last four weeks wondering how I let myself get left out in the cold twice in the course of one year."

"God, Tug, when you put it like that, how could you not be angry?"

"How could I be angry if half of me wants to kiss you so hard you'd need braces by morning?"

"The other half sounds pretty pissed."

"Nah," he said. He took a sip of water. "Just scared, I guess."

Scared? But why wouldn't he be—it was just as much of a risk for him as it was for her. "Exposed to the elements," she commiserated.

He looked at her for a long moment, then nodded. "Yes."

"You know one of the things I did while I was missing you and freaking out about the ring? I went to see the guy who hit Robby."

"You're joking!"

"No, well, it wasn't my idea or anything. His sister wrote to me." She told him about her two visits with Emmett, how Dylan was surprised she hadn't contacted him sooner. How Dylan asked if Robby had said anything.

Tug shook his head. "Amazing," he said. "That kid is something else."

Janie nodded. *Lucky*, she thought, *I am so insanely lucky*.

She reached out with her left hand. The unbanded section of her finger was pressed and pale where the ring had been. She ran her hand down the scar on his right arm, squeezed his hand. "I don't want to make you scared," she said. "I want to be your shelter from the elements."

"I want to be yours."

"Tug, you have been. A thousand times. Times I didn't even know it. Times I fought it," she admitted. "I had to be sure I could give that back to you. It wasn't about the ring, really."

His hands went out and stroked her cheeks like they had when she was feverish. His fingers slipped into her hair and ran gently to the ends of her black curls. "I've wanted to do this for a long time," he said quietly. "Since that day you were up on the roof, throwing gutter muck onto your grass."

"Why then?"

"I don't know. You just looked so sad and angry, sitting up there with your dead husband's work gloves on. I wanted to quiet you down. Make you feel better."

"You cleaned my gutters. And you made me smile with that joke about contractors never calling."

"Least I could do."

Even back then he was thinking of me, she realized. *I was so busy being pissed off, I couldn't see he was trying to lighten my load.*

She leaned forward, into him, and kissed his cheeks, his nose, his eyebrows. She kissed his mouth, her lips parting, flicking her tongue across his teeth, tasting everything. "Man," she whispered, "I have developed such a taste for chocolate."

His fingers, tickling gently up her back, were pulling at the hem of her shirt now, untucking it, sliding his hands along her skin. Briefly, Shelly came to mind. *Good hands*, she thought and kissed him deeper. His fingers moved up under her shirt, sliding over her bra, pulling along the tops of the cups. She kissed him harder, pulled at his hips.

They slid down onto the couch cushions, Janie on her back, Tug alongside her, kissing, groaning when her hand passed across the front of his jeans. He pressed toward her, onto her, rocking slowly against her.

Then his hands slowed and he pushed himself up a little, their hips still pulsing into each other. He looked at her, ran the knuckles of one hand gently down her cheek. "Janie, girl," he whispered.

"I love you," she said.

He closed his eyes, shook his head. Sighed. "I love you so much."

She slid her hand across his shoulder to his back and kneaded the muscles of his neck with her fingertips. They smiled at each other, waiting for the next good thing.

"I don't need any more than this," he said, finally. "But if you want to, we could go upstairs."

She nodded, but they didn't move for a moment. "Um . . . do you have something . . . ?"

"Yeah, I've got that."

"Just in case?" she asked, realizing in the following second that she really didn't want to know if there had been other women here requiring protection or if he had purchased condoms with the assumption that the two of them would be together eventually.

"Left over from before," he said.

"You haven't slept with anyone since Sue?" Another question she really didn't want answered. He raised his eyebrows. "Don't tell me," she said quickly.

"I did a little consolation dating after she told me it was over. I slept with a couple. The last one was Valentine's Day. Not since then. Too depressing."

"Sorry, it's none of my business."

"It is your business. I want it to be."

"Okay. Well I haven't since . . ."

He smiled. "I'd be kind of surprised if you had."

He stood and gave her a hand up. They walked up the stairs, Janie thinking that this was the first First Time she'd had in over a decade. The last First Time, with Robby, she had been . . . well, younger. More confident, less aware of the unforeseeable future, where life could take such sudden turns it could send you to hell for a year. Her way of considering things had changed so much since then. And, come to think of it, so had her body. An image of the "supportive" body stocking flashed across her mind.

The sheets and blankets lay in a twisted heap on his bed. One of the pillows was on the floor. "I thought you were a holiday bed-maker," she said.

"Yeah, I lied about that. On Thanksgiving it was more like 'I'm hoping I'll get a chance to show off my house to this woman I'm totally gone over, so I better straighten the place up.'"

"Looks like you were wrestling alligators."

"I haven't been sleeping that well." He pulled her toward him, wrapped an arm around her waist, with the other hand he brushed the hair away from her face, his fingers raking gently through the ends of her black curls over and over. He studied her face. "Worried about something?"

"I haven't had a first time in a long time."

"We'll take it slow. We don't even have to, you know. I'm just happy to have you with me."

She sighed. "I have stretch marks."

He reached for the hem of her shirt. "Let me see them."

Instinctively she pushed his hand away. "They're not exactly a turn-on."

"Listen," he said, looking her hard in the eye, "I would have given my right arm to be sleeping with a woman with stretch marks all those years."

Yeah, right, she thought. But it was Tug. It was probably true. She pulled her shirt off over her head. He knelt down in front of her and inspected them, running a finger over the puckered lines. His finger trailed to the waistband of her pants. He unbuttoned and unzipped them. Then he was kissing her, his lips traveling up and down the topographical map of her stomach. His hands went to the small of her back and pulled at the edge of her pants. Down they slid along with her underwear.

"God, Tug," she breathed. Gripping his shoulders she lowered herself to her knees, naked now except for her bra. She kissed him hard on the mouth, her hands moving quickly to unbutton his shirt. Behind her back he unbuttoned his cuffs, and unhooked her bra. She pulled at his belt, unbuckled it, unzipped his pants. His hands were running up and down the backs of her thighs, and one hand came around between them, sliding down between her legs, his fingers probing gently. She had worried that she might be too nervous to come, but as the sensation of his touch exploded in her brain, she lost the ability to consider anything that might or might not happen.

His pants and boxers were around his knees and she was strok-
ing him. "Janie," he moaned. "Is this too fast?"

"No," she told him. She felt like she couldn't have him fast
enough.

"I have to get a condom." He pulled away from her, struggled
to his feet, stepped out of the jeans and over to the bedside table.
Janie got up, pushed the hill of blankets off the bed and circled
around behind him as he sat ripping at the little packet. She kissed
his back, raked her fingertips up and down his thighs.

Then he turned and he was on her. "I don't want to go too . . . ,"
he breathed, but she was kissing him and guiding him into her.
And there was that feeling of fullness, of something being there
that hadn't been missed until it arrived. That remembering, "Oh
yes, this was what I was waiting for."

It was different. He didn't smell like Robby or feel like Robby.
He didn't do things in quite the same way. It was new, but somehow also familiar. The newness was exciting and a little scary.
But there was comfort, too, and the safeness of knowing she could
release herself to him and it would turn out okay.

Afterward, they lay there, drawing air into their spent lungs.
"Apparently I was wrong about those stretch marks," she said.

He laughed hard and squeezed her, the muscles of his stomach
bouncing against her hand. "So much for taking it slow."

Her skin cooled and she moved away from him to get a blanket from the floor where she'd tossed them. He caught her wrist.
"Covers," she said, and he let her go.

"You're not leaving, right?"

"My mother is going to flip." She spread the blanket over him
and crawled in beside him. "God knows what Shelly told her when
she got home from Aunt Jude's."

"Call her."

She checked his alarm clock. "It's eleven fifteen."

"Janie."

"Hey," she said. "I'm not leaving. I'm just thinking out loud."

"Hmm," he growled at her.

She rolled onto his stomach and looked down. "Look at us," she whispered. "Look what we have."

He pushed the hair out of her eyes. "I'm not going back," he warned her.

"No," she said. "How could we?" Still, she could sense his worry. "I love you, Tug. I am so grateful for you."

The muscles in his abdomen relaxed, and she felt herself sinking lower into him. She slid down to his side, curling herself to the contour of his body.

"Hey," he whispered against the top of her head. "What's this about apology cake. I get the feeling it's something I'm gonna need to know."

"I'll tell you tomorrow," she yawned.

Drowsiness settled on them and they slept.

A DULL GRAY GLOW was starting to press into the room as she rose to go to the bathroom. When she returned, Tug's eyes were open. His hands were folded behind his head and he was watching the light swell through the window.

"I'm trying to think of the best way to handle this with my mother. And Dylan," she said. "What do you have going today?"

"I gave the crew the day off. I could go over to the Pelham Heights house myself and get some work done." His eyes flicked over to her, catching her. She smiled, almost laughed. "What?" he said.

"I just feel so goddamned good!" And she was on him, laughing, kissing his collarbone, tickling him until he squirmed and wrestled himself on top of her, pinning her arms above her head.

"You KNOW you're not going home, now," he said.

"Oh, please," she whined. "PLEASE don't make love to me. Please let me go home and deal with my MOTHER!"

THEY LAY PRESSED TOGETHER in a heap, and he murmured, "At least let's have dinner together."

She sighed. "That seems a long way off."

"Well, I'll be busy, you know, making mistakes on that big house."

"Don't go to work. Let me go home and face her and then I'll call you."

"I can't sit around here. I'll go crazy waiting."

"Then keep your cell phone on, okay?" She got out of bed quickly, like yanking a Band-Aid off to minimize the duration of pain, got dressed and left.

WHEN SHE ARRIVED HOME, the kids were still sleeping off the excitement of the previous day. Noreen was in the kitchen, her white chenille robe pulled tight around her, sipping black coffee. She watched her daughter, wearing yesterday's clothing, slump into a kitchen chair across the table.

"You're up early," Janie said.

"Seems I get up earlier and earlier these days," said Noreen. "It's age."

Janie rose and poured herself a mug of coffee. "So, how much do you know?" she asked, leaning against the counter, as if sitting would give her a disadvantage.

"Well, that Shelly, she gave me quite an earful."

"*That Shelly*," thought Janie. *This isn't going to be pretty.* "Like what?" she asked, willing herself not to get defensive.

"Like you're in love with a carpenter, the man who built the porch."

"Tug Malinowski. He's a pretty amazing guy."

"I suppose he must be." Noreen sipped again, swallowed self-consciously.

"What's bugging you about this, Mum?"

"Nothing's 'bugging' me, as you put it."

"I spent the night with a guy I'm not married to? Is that it?"

"Don't insult me," said Noreen. "I'm not that much of an anachronism."

"That I didn't tell you about it before? Because, honest, Mum, this was not planned. I was half thinking it was over."

"What, exactly, was over?"

"This thing between me and Tug. He wanted more than I was ready for, and we kind of took a break for about a month."

"So this has been going on some time, now. I had no idea."

"Aunt Jude didn't tell you he came to Thanksgiving?"

"No. And don't think I didn't have some words with her about it."

"So, you called her last night after Shelly left."

"Of course I did! I was worried about you, going off with some man I'd never even heard of!"

"You met him, Mum. He was at Dylan's birthday party."

"Well, I didn't realize that I should pay such close attention— to the carpenter, no less!"

Too busy eyeing the priest, Janie realized. "Okay," she said, taking a breath, forcing herself not to ramp up. "To be honest, I didn't, either. I didn't think much about him, but we became friends over time. He's been very good to me, and he's wonderful with the kids. Dylan adores him."

"Oh, you can believe Jude had plenty to say on that score. Rattling on, as if I don't know my own grandson."

"Mum, for goodness' sake. Aunt Jude is here. You aren't. How can you expect to know as much as she does?"

"Oh! I see now! I always knew it would happen. You're making me pay for wanting a life! I stayed here, trapped in this house for the better part of thirty years, making sure you kids were properly secure in your adulthood before I EVER gave myself ANYTHING! I had admirers, too. I had offers. But I had a DUTY to you and your brother, and sense enough to know I couldn't just start dating around because I felt like it. And now—now I'm cut out like some crazy aunt who lives abroad!"

"Mum, I'm sorry you felt you couldn't date, but honestly I am not making you pay for anything! It's just a fact. Crazy Aunt Jude lives here, and you live over there—which is fine. But you can't have it both ways. You can't expect to know everything as it happens while you live in a foreign country!"

"Don't you get superior with me," Noreen hissed. "You stand there with your wedding ring probably lying in a drawer somewhere, and it hasn't even been a year! Not one year could you wait before you're in another man's bed!"

The bells in Janie's head, ringing ever louder, began to clang furiously, and the heat in her chest boiled up into her neck, and the screaming wrath of childhood disappointments and adolescent hormone surges and a year of being a motherless daughter in hell—these surged into all the empty spaces. "That's it!" she said. "That's what this is all about. You think you gave up everything for me—including LOVE, for godsake—and now I'm supposed to conform to some twisted idea in your head about how it should go. I should get married to a good man, which I did. And then tragedy strikes, and I should protect you from your own nightmares about being a single mother trapped in goddamned Pelham, which I DIDN'T. You ran right back to ITALY so you wouldn't have to sully your delicate sensitivity, and you LEFT me here. ALONE."

Janie slammed the empty mug on the counter, pointed at her. "No, not alone. WITH JUDE, your annoying, dotty sister, who's done nothing but help the BOTH of us all our lives! But THEN, and this is the real kicker, isn't it, Mum? This is where I really let you down. I had the nerve to find ANOTHER good man who adores me within an inch of my life, and God knows why, because I've been so unbelievably bitchy and miserable. And that's the final straw, isn't it, Mum? What's worse than me living your life of unhappiness? Me NOT living it!"

Noreen was on her feet. "That is completely absurd! I . . . I don't have to listen to such venom!" and she left the kitchen. Minutes later she was fully dressed and holding her tightly packed carry-on bag. She went out to the screened porch—Tug's work of art, Janie thought, appreciating the irony—and waited.

Janie knew her mother couldn't go to Aunt Jude's this time. Maybe Uncle Charlie's. Maybe a hotel. Maybe back to Italy, where old women who missed the boat to see the Baby Jesus spend the rest of their lives giving gifts of penance.

JANIE WAS STILL SITTING in the kitchen absorbing the aftershocks of her own tirade, when Uncle Charlie pulled up. A car door opened, then slammed. The Ford Tempo grumbled out of the driveway. In a few minutes, Dylan came down. He drifted slowly, sleepily into her lap, rubbing Nubby's ear across his lips. "Merry day after Christmas," she whispered to him.

"Yeah," he said.

"Did you have fun yesterday?"

"Uh-huh."

"Are you hungry?"

"Not yet."

She breathed in his cozy smell: baby shampoo and slept-in sheets and boy. She rocked him for a few minutes and he snuggled deeper into her lap.

"Dylan?"

"Mmm."

"I really love Tug."

"Me, too."

"I want him to spend a lot of time with us."

"Me, too," said Dylan. "Can he come over today?"

"I think he can. I'll call and see."

23

NEW YEAR'S," TUG SAID to her that night after the kids were in bed. They were sitting on the blue leather couch, nested against each other.

"Cormac's wedding," she answered. "Dylan is the ring bearer—he keeps calling it 'ringmaster,' which kind of fits. The wedding party's so big it's like a circus act."

"And you're in it."

"Yeah, bridesmaid number 247. There's no way I can get out of it."

"I like weddings," he said.

"Too bad my dress wouldn't fit you, you could take my place."

"You don't like weddings?"

She thought about this for a moment. "No, I do. I've just been dreading this one for so long . . . I guess I need to tune up my attitude. Going alone isn't exactly . . ." She looked at Tug.

"Love to," he said. "Thanks for asking."

"God, I'm stupid."

He gave her a squeeze. "Call him."

"Barb will freak. Cormac told me the seating arrangements alone made her cry three times."

"I'll sit at the bar. Call him."

"You seem pretty sure he'll say yes."

"Janie, the guy would give up a kidney for you. Plus, he likes me."

Janie smiled, intrigued. "Oh?"

He shrugged. "Thanksgiving. He kind of gave me the thumbs-up. Not in so many words, but you know . . ."

Janie went into the kitchen to place the call.

"Merry day after Christmas," Cormac said.

"You, too," she said. "How's the countdown going?"

"Barb's been having a glass of wine with dinner. It helps. Wish she started at breakfast."

"Cormac, I need a favor . . ."

"You want to bring Tug to the wedding."

"Yeah, how'd you . . . ?"

"Your mother's staying at my parents'. Cat's out of the bag about your little overnight."

"Oh." Janie felt a little queasy.

"Chickie, come on. Everyone loves Tug. A guy brings lumpy pudding to Thanksgiving dinner, how could you not? I practically invited him to the wedding myself," Cormac chuckled. Despite the pressure of the wedding, he seemed happy, she realized. Content in a way that he hadn't before. "And don't worry about my parents," he said. "They just feel a little sorry for her."

"Why?"

"Oh, you know. Aunt Noreen. The sensitive one."

MIKE ARRIVED ON THE twenty-ninth, as planned, with Alicia. When their rental car pulled into the driveway Janie watched them for a moment from the kitchen window. They removed suitcases and packages from the trunk as if the other person weren't there. Alicia was small and pointy, like the herons that nested by Lake Pequot. She had straight brown hair and was dressed mostly in black: turtleneck sweater, dark pants, long-toed black boots. Mike was in jeans and a gray fleece V-neck over a white T-shirt. His mess of black hair curled onto his shoulders. *Same*, thought

Janie, who'd been expecting something different. A new Mike to go with a new, real relationship, maybe.

"Hey," he said, when Janie met them at the front door. "Nice porch." He put his bags down and went back out to study it further. Alicia remained just inside the living room. She stared at the couch. At least Janie thought she was staring at the couch. Alicia's gray eyes didn't seem to be looking in the same direction at once.

"I'm Janie."

"Alicia." She hadn't put the bags down yet.

"Nice to meet you. I can take those."

"It's okay." Alicia continued to hold onto the bags as if they were ballast and she might levitate uncontrollably if she were to let them go.

Mike came back in from the porch. "That's really something."

"Yeah," said Janie. "My friend Tug built it. You'll meet him later."

"Okay," said Mike. He looked around. "New couch."

She nodded. "I thought I'd put you two up in my room, and I could stay in the back bedroom down here."

Mike's brow furrowed. "Where's Mum?"

"She's staying at Uncle Charlie's. We're not really getting along so well at the moment." She knew he wouldn't think to ask why.

"Well, I'd rather stay down here," he said, and started to move across the living room.

"Mike," Janie said. "There's more room up there. For you and Alicia."

"We don't need more room," he said.

"There's only a twin bed in the back bedroom." Janie hoped she wasn't embarrassing Alicia, but the obvious wasn't always so obvious to Mike.

He looked at Alicia, who nodded. "It's enough," he said, and they went to put their bags away.

"Where's Dylan?" Mike asked when he returned without Alicia. He sat down on the couch, ran his hand back and forth over a pillow, watched how the light changed the color depending on how he brushed the nap of the suede.

"Tug took the kids over to the Confectionary while I was doing some house cleaning. He should be back any minute."

"Who's Tug?"

"The guy who built the porch." Janie sank down onto the couch next to him. "Listen," she said. "Tug's pretty important to me." Mike looked up from the couch pillow. "We're seeing each other," said Janie.

"You're dating?"

"Yeah, I know it's a little shocking. I was pretty surprised myself, to tell you the truth. But we got to know each other while he was building the porch, and he's a really good guy."

Mike went back to brushing his hand across the cushion. "What did Mum say?"

Janie squinted. "She wasn't too happy about it. That's why she went to Uncle Charlie's."

"What about Cormac?"

"He likes Tug. He thinks it's a good thing."

There was a low sound from the back bedroom, a tiny cough, as if a bird were clearing its throat. Mike looked up, listened for a moment. "Alicia's shy," he said. "I think she might be worried you won't like her."

This was new—Mike didn't generally anticipate and interpret other people's feelings. "I'm sure I will once I get to know her," said Janie. "You two seem pretty close."

"Yeah." A slow smile spread across his face. He glanced at Janie, then away. "She gets me."

The air caught in Janie's chest for a moment, and she felt a twinge of emotion pressing behind her eyes. Very few people got Mike. Janie herself didn't always fully understand him. The miracle and surprise of being "gotten" by someone was fresh in her experience. She put her hand on his shoulder, gave it a little shake. "Way to go," she whispered.

He nodded, satisfied.

ON THE NIGHT OF the rehearsal dinner, a certain frenzy blew through the house as Janie tried to get herself and the children appropriately attired. Alicia flicked in and out of the bathroom, and by her silent, panic-faced wardrobe changes, Janie had assessed her to be generally anxious and rather wealthy.

It had been so long since Janie had worn a serious dress and the requisite accessories, she felt at a loss to decide what looked good on her anymore. She found herself asking Dylan, the only member of the household who was available for comment. His opinions, however, tended to run to bright colors and big jewelry, neither of which Janie was sure she could pull off. He sat bouncing on her bed in his little button-down shirt and tie, as she pulled out one outfit after another. Carly climbed off and on the bed, the skirt of her green velour dress slipping up over her tights-covered diaper.

"The purple one!" yelled Dylan, as if he were a game show contestant. "I pick the purple one!"

The dress isn't actually purple, Janie thought, humoring herself, *it's more of an eggplant color.* It was a little more fitted than she felt entirely comfortable with, but it was pretty, and she seemed to remember there was some good silver jewelry that would work.

She was finally dressed and ready just as Tug arrived with his niece Sophie, who had been hired to come with them and play with Carly during the rehearsal at the church. Janie would bring her back to the house to babysit the kids while she went to the dinner afterward.

Tug gave Janie one of his soaking-you-up-like-a-man-sized-sponge looks, and the tension in her neck and shoulders released. She slipped over to him and adjusted his tie. "You look so . . ." She couldn't think of the word. He was handsome to her even in his sawdust-covered work clothes. The formal attire only offered a different view of her attraction to him.

"I am not leaving tonight," he whispered in her ear. "Everyone's just going to have to deal with it. You included."

_____

THE REHEARSAL AT OUR Lady, Comforter of the Afflicted Church went smoothly. Barb's uncle, a Jesuit priest with a passion for liturgical dance, was to preside at the wedding, and he conducted the run-through as if it were an old standard song that required a little extra in the way of choreography. He asked the flower girls, four-year-old twins who were sticky from the lollipops they'd been bribed with, to skip on their tiptoes as they strew their petals. Dylan was supposed to balance the black velvet pillow on one hand and hold the other arm out "inviting the congregation to view the sacred symbols of nuptial consecration." Dylan squinted, confused, at Janie. "Just smile a lot," she whispered.

Janie and Tug stood together watching the show. She leaned toward him to whisper something about Father Guys-and-Dolls, and his arm slipped easily around her waist. She caught a movement from the corner of her eye and saw Father Jake standing in the sacristy doorway behind the altar. He was half in shadow, his black clothing blending in with the darkened room behind him. But she knew he was watching, taking in the man beside her with his hand resting with such familiarity on her hip. Tug's head turned to follow her gaze. The priest closed the door behind him and went out the side door to the rectory.

WHEN THE CURTAIN FELL on the rehearsal at the church, Janie and Tug stopped home to drop off Sophie and the children. Dylan had been shy with Sophie at first, promising Janie he would not "do any trouble" if he were allowed to attend the dinner. But by the end of the rehearsal, he was sick of his tie and button-down shirt, and Sophie had won him over with the physicality of her confidence. Dylan and Janie watched with startled fascination as Sophie stood at the back of the church and threw a happily shrieking Carly into the air over and over. She arm-wrestled Dylan in one of the pews and let him win, but just barely. Back at the house, Sophie was chasing them up the stairs on her hands and knees as Janie called good-bye.

The rehearsal dinner was held at Bradford Country Squire Restaurant, a long brown building with tiny-paned windows and a wood-shingled roof, built in the 1970s to resemble an upscale Colonial home. It was chosen by Barb's parents because they considered it to be the classiest restaurant in Pelham. The food was distinctly unmemorable, but jackets were required. The effect was reduced somewhat by its shared parking lot with the Pelham Ball Field.

"After dinner we'll have batting practice," Janie joked. Tug's face remained blank. "What?" she asked.

"Your mother," he said, and Janie immediately regretted giving him such a detailed account of their quarrel. She had perhaps gotten a little too comfortable telling him everything, forgetting that items involving him directly required a certain amount of discretion. *Relationship 101,* she thought. *I'm rusty.*

Though they had been invited to come to the church, Noreen and Aunt Jude had opted to meet the wedding party at the restaurant. They were standing in the hallway outside the banquet room, waiting for everyone to arrive. Janie saw Aunt Jude lean near her mother to say something as they approached. Noreen stepped away from her and began to look for something—*or nothing,* Janie thought—in her purse. Disgusted, Janie had every intention of walking right past her mother and finding the waitress to order a drink.

"Mrs. Dwyer," she heard Tug say, his voice friendly without being obsequious. "Tug Malinowski. We met at Dylan's birthday party."

"Yes," said Noreen, allowing him to shake her hand.

"It's nice to see you again."

Noreen nodded, looked away. "You did a fine job on that porch," she said. "My son-in-law would be very happy with it."

"I'm glad you think so," said Tug, waiting a moment to catch her eye. "That was my goal." He turned to Aunt Jude and kissed her on the cheek. "Jude, how are you?"

"Oh, Tug, dear. I'm just fine. It's so exciting, don't you think? A wedding? And Cormac seems happier than . . . than . . ." She looked past his shoulder, distracted. "Michael!"

"Hi, Aunt Jude," muttered Mike. He delivered a quick, stilted hug, then another for his mother. "Mum, this is Alicia."

Alicia reached her trembling fingers forward and shook each of their hands with a small, sharp jerk, startling Noreen.

It's a tough day to be sensitive, thought Janie, as she and Tug slipped away toward the banquet room.

AFTERWARD, TUG DROVE SOPHIE home. Janie sat at the kitchen table and waited for him to return. Mike and Alicia went immediately into the back bedroom. Then Janie heard a tinkling sound, like a small bell ringing from far away, and wondered what it could be. It faded but did not stop entirely. Mike came into the kitchen, put a little water in the teakettle, and set it on the burner.

"Is someone crying?" Janie asked.

"Alicia," he answered. "She just needs to, sometimes."

Janie nodded. "I know how that goes."

Mike looked at her for a second, uncomprehending. "Do you have any lemon?"

When he'd left with the cup of hot water and wedge of lemon for Alicia, Janie sat in the silent kitchen, at the table Robby had assembled from a kit. She glanced up at the framed photo that Barb had taken of her and the kids giggling together at Dylan's birthday party. She waited for Tug. The crying stopped in the back bedroom, and then she heard a short, low burst of laughter from Mike.

One surprise after another, she thought.

WHEN THE FRONT DOOR opened, Janie expected that Tug would want to go up to the bedroom right away. She expected a little romance. But he poured himself a glass of water and sat at the table.

"What?" she said.

"What's the deal with Father Jake."

It took Janie a moment to switch gears from anticipating ravishment to having to answer for herself. "There is no deal," she said. "I haven't even talked to him in months." This was not entirely true, she realized. It was only a few days ago that Jake had said, "Body of Christ," and she had said, "Thanks." But did that even count?

"I saw him at the church tonight," said Tug.

"It's his church," she said, sounding defensive even to herself.

Tug crossed his arms. "I saw him come and go all summer."

"Aunt Jude made him come because I wouldn't go to that grief group."

"I was in the yard that morning he skulked out of here barefoot," he said quietly. "Don't bullshit me, Janie."

"Nothing happened!"

The unblinking stare.

So she told him. A version of it anyway, remembering his reaction to the fight she'd had with her mother. She didn't reveal Jake's secret, but she admitted there was some terrible trauma in his past. She didn't tell quite how drawn to Jake she had been, but she did say that she'd felt understood for the first time since Robby's death. She told about the middle-of-the-night e-mails, and what a lifeline they were. She'd felt safe with Jake, and so she'd called him after the home invasion. And he'd empathized so fully, he'd rushed over without thinking to change his clothes or even put on shoes.

"If it was all so wonderful, why did he stop showing up?"

"My mother thought we were getting too close, so she told him to stop coming."

Tug ruminated on this for a moment. "Heck of a spoiler, isn't she."

"If I'm honest with myself," Janie said, "she was probably right about Jake. We were getting too . . . dependent. It could have been a problem. I just hated how she went behind my back."

"So," said Tug. "Nothing I need to worry about, then." This required an answer.

"Not a thing."

"Except your mother."

"She's coming around." Janie smiled. "I think the family is leaning on her to ease up."

He gave a sly grin. "Little bit of pudding goes a long way."

TUESDAY, JANUARY 1

Everyone's still sleeping. Tug doesn't snore, exactly, but his breath makes this funny "fah" sound sometimes, and it was bugging me. I'm drinking my coffee, enjoying the quiet. All year I've hated the quiet. Now I like it again.

The wedding was . . .

(Can't think of a word other than "magical" which is so annoyingly Disney. I hate it when good words go bad.)

Dylan was great as the ringmaster, and only dropped the pillow once. The rings had been tied on with a little thread, so they didn't go rolling under the kneelers, which was a huge relief. When he saw that, he yelled down the aisle to Cormac "Don't worry! I still got 'em!"

Barb looked great, except she cried through the whole service, practically. Cormac just smiled and smiled. He didn't give a shit. He's in love. It makes me sigh like an old lady the way he's in love. My sweet, smart-alecky, gigantic cousin.

Stephanie, my little dressing-room friend, had makeup on and her hair all done up in twists and curls. Beautiful, but I liked it better when her face looked more like who she was, not so grown up, and not so touched-up. More of a candid, less of a formal, portrait. She introduced me to her very pregnant mother, who thanked me for looking after her daughter at such a tricky moment. She commented that as they get older you have to rely more and more on them being able to find pockets of kindness in the world. She pointed to her stomach, all swollen and heavy, and said, "This is as easy as it gets."

Alicia clung to Mike the whole time like one of those birds that rides on the back of a hippo. But once, during the reception, I saw her in the bathroom, and I caught her pinching the back of her hand. And I said, "I do that." And she said, "For goodness' sake, WHY?" which is about the longest sentence I've heard from her. So I told her I don't know, it just distracts me from feeling like my head's going to explode or something. She laughed and the sound was just like when she was crying, like a little silver bell in a rich person's house, only happy.

Tug saw my mother sitting alone at her table, and he asked me if I thought it would be okay if he asked her to dance. I told him, Lay it on, Pudding Man. He gave me his little grin as he got up, and said not to call him that.

Heidi didn't have any plans for New Year's, so at the last minute I had invited her to come to the reception after dinner. She wouldn't even consider it. Then she showed up! Wearing a candy pink satin mini-dress with enough spangles and sparkles to blind you! Apparently she had been forced to wear it as a bridesmaid years ago. It was so awful and so completely unlike her, it was great. I swear, half the guys at the reception (and one or two of the women) couldn't take their eyes off her. Officer Dougie looked completely smitten.

Uncle Charlie swaggered around, grinning like a madman and thumping people a little too hard on the back with those giant paws of his. Just before midnight, when everyone was loose and giggly, Aunt Brigid brought out a curling old photo, the one she's been blackmailing him with since they were young. They'd had a deal for forty years that she could give it to Cormac on his wedding day. It showed Uncle Charlie standing in a hospital waiting room, cradling his newborn son in his arms, sobbing. His face was all twisted up and his mouth hung a little open and his cheeks were shiny with tears. Raw emotion. True *love. The smirk Cormac always wears around his father went away, and he said, "I hope that's me someday, Pop." Uncle Charlie just nodded. I think he couldn't speak, for once.*

After her dance with Tug, Mum came over and saw me looking at the picture. "Have you seen this?" I asked. "I took it," she told me. When I said how amazing it was, she got teary and patted my cheek. A parent's love is the most desperate thing on this earth. She and I both know that.

At midnight everyone kissed and hugged and wished each other every happiness in the new year. Took about half an hour. Aunt Jude got ahold of me and clutched me up against all those necklaces of hers, and said, "I couldn't love you any more if you belonged to me." I told her I do belong to her. It's the truth.

THE FOLLOWING SUNDAY, JANIE and Aunt Jude and the kids went to church at Our Lady's. Janie invited Tug to come, too, as he shoveled pancakes to the kids in the syrupy smell of her kitchen. She wondered if he were still uncomfortable about Jake. "You could see for yourself," she said.

"I don't need to," he said. "But I'll come."

As Father Jake processed down the aisle that morning, Janie noticed that his hair was shorter. And he had new shoes, the leather kind, not the black sport shoes he'd always worn. It was the Feast of the Epiphany, when the three wise men brought gifts to the Holy Family. *La Befana,* thought Janie, her thoughts flitting to her mother, now happily home in Italy. *Maybe this year the old woman will have the sense to tag along.*

"When I am lost and weary, Lord, you make for me a shelter of your love," sang the cantor, the notes trailing sweetly over the congregation. Janie slid her hand along the pew bench to Tug's. *So grateful*, she thought, as their fingers laced together.

Everyone rose when Father Jake read from the Gospel of Matthew:

And on entering the house, the Magi saw the child with Mary, his mother. They prostrated themselves and did him homage. Then they opened their treasures and offered him gifts of gold, frankincense, and myrrh.

When Father Jake closed the book and set it aside, everyone took their seats again and he began his homily. He spoke about the readings and the incalculable impact the birth of this one child had on the course of history. He was somewhat scholarly, but sprinkled in a humorous comment here and there for the purpose of retaining some, though certainly not all, of their attention. He took a breath, and Janie supposed that he would wrap things up and move on to the consecration. But instead he did something his parishioners rarely experienced from him. He began to speak in the first person.

"What I find myself marveling at is that men came from so far away to find a tiny baby. No one else seemed to anticipate this momentous event, except for a mere three people, foreigners from the East. This story would have been shocking to the Jews who were hearing it. The first people to believe in the miracle of Jesus were not Jews! They were not even neighboring Gentiles. They didn't have the same skin color or customs or worldview. They were the most unlikely sources of grace imaginable. Yet grace Him they did, with their gifts and, more importantly, with their faith in him.

"Why is that? What does it mean? And who are their present-day equivalents? Who are the unexpected people who show up from time to time in our lives, bearing rare and valuable gifts? Who goes far out of their way to reach us? Who are those unlikely souls who seem to understand what a miracle each of us is?"

Father Jake stopped for a moment, presumably to allow the congregation to ponder these questions. But Janie sensed that he wasn't really aware of what was before him, people clustered on wooden benches, some listening intently, some politely waiting for Communion, some impatient for the service to be over. He was pondering the questions himself, in the silence of his own solitary world. Then he went on.

"The Magi in my life have always surprised me. They have often been people I initially felt I had nothing in common with. Sometimes I didn't even like them. But they came bearing gifts. Of wisdom, of acceptance. One or two came to give me a kick in the pants."

The congregation, many of whom had tuned in at this unexpectedly personal turn in his comments, chuckled appreciatively.

"And some left as suddenly as they had arrived. They returned to their respective homelands or continued on their own journeys. I miss some of them." He smiled to himself, as if some private memory had interrupted his thoughts. His eyes flicked up, scanned the crowd for a moment, and lit for the briefest possible moment on Janie, then quickly darted away. "But we all have to find our way toward whatever miracles await us. And to perform miracles, when it's in our power to do so.

"Maybe the most important question is: how do I serve as Magi for others? How generously do I give my gifts—and not just to the obvious recipients in my life? How far out of my way do I go to recognize and pay homage to miracles? Not very far some days. But on good days, just far enough."

A FEW DAYS LATER, an idea came to Janie that was so strange she had to push it away for a while. But it returned to her over and over, at odd times, such that it became familiar, if not any less unorthodox.

"Could you take the day off on Monday, the fourteenth?" she asked Tug one night as they unloaded the dishwasher.

"The anniversary of Robby's death."

"Yeah."

"It'd be understandable if you wanted some space," he said.

"I don't want any space. I need your help."

She told him her idea, and it took him a few minutes to digest. Then he shook his head. "Janie, girl," he said. "You are something."

She called Aunt Jude and then Emmett's sister Fran. When they regained their composure, they agreed.

MONDAY, JANUARY 14

It's a lot colder here on the Cape than it was back in November. But it was sunny today, and we were prepared with warm clothes and blankets. It's such a relief not to be in Pelham. Not to be thinking unbearable things like "I was probably sitting in this very chair when it happened."

I'm glad I thought to bring Aunt Jude. Robby's death happened to her almost as much as it happened to me, just by virtue of how much she loves me. And she keeps things from getting too quiet. She has a knack for that.

It was good to be by the ocean. Emmett and I sat next to each other in our beach chairs. He looked at his watch a lot, and I knew what he was doing, but I didn't try to stop him. I'm sure I couldn't have, anyway. Dylan wore his swim goggles. Everyone has their way.

And then Emmett took my hand, and I knew that was the moment, a year ago, when it happened. I squeezed his worn old hand, and we cried.

A million things went through my head. Malcolm and his sister. Uncle Charlie holding his newborn baby. My mother and her quilting squares. Too many memories of Robby to count.

Fran held Emmett's other hand. Carly sat with Aunt Jude and played with her jewelry. Dylan climbed into my lap and we rocked. Tug stoked the fire, but then he went still for a while, gazing out at the ocean.

We're all on loan. The only thing that makes sense is to be together.

A⁺

AUTHOR INSIGHTS, EXTRAS, & MORE...

FROM

JULIETTE FAY

AND

AVON A

Questions for Discussion

1. The theme of shelter, both literal and figurative, arises again and again throughout the course of the story. Who shelters whom? Are all the instances of "sheltering" helpful, or are some misguided?

2. Janie's mother, the person whom she expects can help the most, is unable or unwilling to be there for her. Meanwhile, the people who offer the greatest support are often people Janie doesn't even like at first. Are her instincts just off, or is life sometimes that surprising?

3. To varying degrees, Janie feels abandoned by a number of people in her life: her husband for dying, her mother for staying away, her neighbor Shelly for moving, and Father Jake for discontinuing their relationship. Are these real betrayals? How do they pulsate with the support she experiences from unexpected sources?

4. Janie becomes acquainted with several people who have experienced sexual abuse (Katya in the self-defense course, Father Jake, and Beryl the homeless woman). How do each of these people and their experiences affect Janie? What does Janie get from writing the letters for Malcolm to his dying sister?

5. Did Janie's mother, Noreen, do the right thing by going to Father Jake and asking him to end their relationship? If not, was her action forgivable? What would have happened if she had gone to Janie instead? Did her letter to Janie sufficiently explain her rationale or not? Does Janie ever fully forgive her mother?

6. Janie's husband Robby was the love of her life. How is it, then, that she could fall for two other men within one year of his death? Is it possible to have more than one love of your life? If Father Jake had been willing to leave the priesthood, would they have been happy together?

7. The story has several "travelers": Janie's mother, Beryl the homeless woman, and even Janie's daughter, Carly, seems to

be destined for flight. Beryl claims that Janie is, too. In what ways might that be true or not?

8. How might this story have been different if Janie hadn't had children? What various meanings might Dylan's goggles represent?

9. The skills that Janie learns in the self-defense course end up coming in very handy. Besides self-defense, are there other lessons she uses throughout the story?

10. Janie spends a lot of time both asking for and granting forgiveness. How does this alter the course of her relationships? (And can cake really solve interpersonal strife? Might a massive baking effort be the answer to the world's current morass of aggression and destruction? . . .)

11. What happens next? Do Tug and Janie stay together? If so, which "shelter" do they choose to live in—his or hers?

12. If there were a movie based on this story, how would you cast it?

Q & A with the Author

What inspired you to write a novel? What led you to this particular story?

I never really set out to be a writer, but when I look back, there may have been some early indications. For as long as I can remember, I've told myself stories when I'm bored—during long insufferable car rides with my younger sisters' legs actually *touching* mine, Mr. Todd's mind-numbing geometry class, work meetings bogged in detail, nights when sleep eludes me, etc. Sometimes I was the protagonist (in adolescence aren't we always the lead characters in our own little dramas?), but increasingly since then, these stories are about other people. And I've always been a voracious reader. As a general rule, I don't buy a purse too small to hold a paperback. One of the greatest benefits of being a writer is that reading is now a job requirement! (I really wish I had time to weed the shrubs, but I have to go read now . . .)

During my teens and twenties I was also an avid journal keeper. This, more than anything, helped prepare me to be a storyteller. I learned to express myself to myself, without fear of anyone looking over my shoulder, telling me the punctuation was wrong or the story was inconsistent or that they couldn't quite envision the setting. I took literary license while narrating my own life. An embarrassing story could be made funny, a sad story could be made even sadder, a victorious moment could be exulted—not so much by altering the facts but by consciously choosing which facts and descriptors to highlight and which to set in the background. I learned to please myself before I ever had to please anyone else, and this helped me to develop my own writer's voice.

I was inspired to write a novel, finally, when my friend Amanda was trying to unload some books she'd been given, and handed me a paperback with the words, "It's beach reading, just take it." I was about to go to Cape Cod for a family vacation, so I brought it and read it. It was so unbelievably awful, I couldn't put it down! The plot was absurd, the characters were barely two-dimensional, and the dialogue was hilarious. ("Oh, darling, we mustn't!")

Being on vacation, I had more time than usual to spend thinking about what I would have done differently, and actually starting scribbling down my ideas. I found the story taking off in some very unexpected directions. After I got home, I'd steal an hour or two every day to see what the characters would do next. I was very secretive about it at first, but once I had a hundred or so pages, I admitted to myself that I was writing a novel.

The story of *Shelter Me* has been in my head for a long time, in various forms. I think its first cell-divisions began when I got married. I had never loved anyone the way I loved my new husband, and had never felt so loved. I became quietly, privately terrified of losing him. I wonder if everyone doesn't have these thoughts at some point. You love someone—your spouse, children, best friend, aunt, dog—so much, you know that if anything happens to them, you might not be able to put one foot in front of the other anymore. Nothing would make sense. You'd forget how to do simple things like make toast or swallow.

Then we started having children and I thought, "Okay, now I'm really in trouble." Not only did I worry that something might happen to them, I still had the fear of losing my husband, *and* I now had to worry on my kids' behalf about losing their father. Making up stories about how I would manage was a way for me to process my own fear. But after a while it morphed into a plotline about someone else. I had begun writing by this time, and decided to try and put this new person, who was thankfully no longer me, down on paper and see what I could make of the situation.

What are your writing routines? How do you balance your writing career with the demands of a family with four young children?

I love to read about other writers, what their credos are ("write every single day" or "read the daily paper to pick up new ideas"), what their routines are ("light special incense ordered from Oregon" or "dance to the Talking Heads' *Burning Down the House*—the live version, not the studio one"). I wish I had the luxury of a credo or a routine, but I just don't. If I had a credo, it would be something like "Don't make eye contact with the kids while you're writing unless they can prove they're bleeding from a major artery." My routine is something like "Go to Whole Foods, buy five gallons of milk, remember to put them in the fridge, throw in a load of laundry, eat the leftover toast crusts from breakfast, sit and write."

I'm lucky in that I seem to be able to get in the zone pretty fast. I've written in a lot of noisy, distracting places—Starbucks, hair salons, surrounded by chatting friends on a weekend away, for example. I can't possibly write every day, though it's the ideal to which I strive, but I don't find it too hard to jump back into a story after days or even weeks away. Sometimes I think it's good to take a few days off and let the story float around in my head for a while, picking up details and ideas for plot threads in my travels.

I started writing when my youngest was two, and at first I could only get in an hour or so of writing during nap time or an exceptionally convivial playdate. I would write at night or early in the morning, sneaking it in when I could. To be honest, I just love to do it, and I think if you really love something, you can carve out the time for it somehow. I learned to let things go—let the house stay toy-strewn a little longer, say no to volunteer activities a little more—and I learned to take my writing seriously. I tell the kids, "I'm working, this is my job. Just like you have to do your homework, so do I."

An unexpected bonus is that my kids are excited for me. Occasionally, I'll be talking to a teacher or the mother of one of their friends, and they'll say, "I hear you're a writer." The kids talk about it to people outside the house. Often they'll ask, "Was that your agent? What did she say?" They like to feel that they're a part of it. My teenaged daughter has read some work I've done on adolescent girls, and she's very helpful with whether the dialogue sounds right, or the thought process makes sense. It's great to have in-house editorial staff.

Are you a baker in "real life"? Did the idea of the Pology Cake come from your imagination or does it have true-to-life origins?
I bake, but I'm not particularly great at it. The idea of Pology Cake just popped into my head one day. However, I really like the concept of "restorative justice," which involves performing a service for the

wronged party. Apologizing is such an essential skill, but sometimes words alone aren't enough.

I do believe in the power of baked goods. One day a friend came to me with the idea that we could get the children in our town to make bread and decorate the loaves to give to food pantries and soup kitchens, as a way to get them involved in philanthropy and community service. We planned the kickoff for October of 2001, which happened to follow the 9/11 tragedy, so we decided to give them to police and firefighters, as well. It took off like a rocket, and by now tens of thousands of breads have been given. There are "bread spreaders" in all contiguous forty-eight states and several foreign countries. For more information about Spread the Bread, check out www.spreadthebread.org.

In a story about relationships, why did you choose to give one of your characters Asperger's syndrome, which is often characterized by poor social skills?

Asperger's fascinates me because it's such an interesting brain configuration. Often people with the syndrome have a particular interest or strength, and in the context of this area, they can be near genius. But social interaction can be uncomfortable. Asperger's was a good vehicle to talk a little more about Robby, Janie's dead husband. His ability to connect with Mike contrasts nicely with Janie's own difficulties with her brother. I think in families we get used to people being a certain way, and we adapt to it, but that doesn't necessarily mean we fully understand them. We also don't expect our family members to grow and change. Janie's surprise that Mike had finally found a woman who "gets him" was a way to look at that.

How did you get into the mindset of the women in the self-defense course? Have you ever been attacked yourself?

Years ago I took a self-defense course that was something like the class Janie takes. It left an indelible impression. I have never been physically assaulted myself, but several of the women there had, and watching them learn not only to defend themselves, but also to further process the past was incredibly moving. They were changing right before our very eyes, getting stronger, more confident, and as a result, so were the rest of us. I felt the hum of sorrow with those women, but I also felt hopeful at the same time. I worked for years in the field of child abuse prevention, so I drew on stories I knew to flesh out the characters and their backgrounds.

Are any of your characters based on real people? Where did your ideas for them originate?

None of my characters are specifically based on real people. I feel it's my job to create people, not to copy those I already know. Also, I think the possibility for hurt feelings would be enormous. I do constantly make note of interesting habits, gestures, vocal patterns and the like. But I go out of my way not to assemble a character that someone might confuse with themselves or someone they know. I also like to pick up on interesting phrases people use. My friend Karen is a particularly good source. Her husband was talking to me about a colleague of his who had recently lost a son. He sighed and said, "We're all on loan." I mentioned this to Karen and she told me, "I say that! He got that from me!"

I got the idea for Tug a few years back when we put an addition onto our house, which included a screened-in porch. I got to be friendly with the contractor, who was nothing at all like Tug. I found it funny how spending the day with strange men roaming around your house, talking about their wives, children, sports teams, health problems, you name it, as they tore the back off your house, you could get to know a lot about them. I was also surprised to see how much control the contractor had over the end product, no matter what the plans (or for that matter, I myself standing right there in front of him) said.

Aunt Jude was always a member of the cast, but she changed over the course of writing the story. She started out a lot more abrasive and irritating. I was surprised to find that she was so sweet, if a bit annoying. Shelly came out of nowhere. I started writing and within a couple of pages she was knocking on Janie's front door, fully formed. She came to me just as you see her, impeccably dressed and bossing me around.

Religion, specifically the Catholic Church, plays a pivotal role in the story. Are you a member of a faith community? How did you come up with the character of Father Jake?

I am Catholic, and have known a lot of priests, and have found some of them fascinating in that they have chosen a life that is so different from the way that most of us live. When I began writing *Shelter Me,* we had recently had the clergy abuse scandal that seemed to break first here in the Boston area. The news, the allegations, the depths of deceit, the damaged lives of the victims broke our hearts on a daily basis. I wanted to talk about that, and I used Father Jake as both a priest and a victim. I didn't want him to be a hero. I wanted him to be, as Janie ultimately concludes, "just a guy."

Also, I have always had a secret desire to write homilies. I sit in church, listening to the readings and thinking, *If I were the one up there with the robes on, I'd be talking about such and such.* It was a nice added bonus to finally get my wish.

What are you working on now?

I am working on a story about a divorced woman with an eleven-year-old daughter. The social scene in middle school and issues with body image and self-esteem with which the daughter struggles are not so different from the ones her mother faces in her forties. I think that some human interactions—power struggles, loyalty, peer pressure, being popular, keeping true to oneself—seem to go on in one form or another no matter what your age. It's fun to try and talk about that while devising a plotline that will, with any luck, keep readers turning the pages.

Pology Cake: Bake As You See Fit

No single apology could ever fit the countless circumstances in which we humans seem to find ourselves hurting each other. In fact, the words themselves don't often seem to matter so much as the sincerity of delivery, and conveying the trueness of our feelings is as individual as our thumbprints. Accordingly, no one recipe for Pology Cake could ever suit every situation. It is incumbent upon the Pologizer to determine what kind of baked good best communicates the message. So, bake responsibly, but more importantly, bake sincerely.

Lemon Cream Cake

After hurling invectives at Father Jake for his "secret life of misery," Janie ultimately decided to bake him a Lemon Cream Cake.

"Sweet but not gooey. Self-effacing without being overly self-denigrating. It says I was right, but I had no right to say so."

See if you agree.

> ½ cup vegetable shortening
> 1 cup white sugar
> 3 eggs
> 1 tsp lemon juice
> 2 tsp grated lemon peel
> 2 cups white flour
> 3 ½ tsp baking powder
> 1 tsp salt
> 1 cup sour cream

- Preheat oven to 350 degrees. Grease and lightly flour two 9-inch round cake pans.
- Beat all ingredients together for several minutes until smooth.

- Bake for approximately 20–30 minutes or until a toothpick comes out clean.
- Do not overcook. Cool completely before frosting.

Lemon Buttercream Frosting

   ½ cup butter, softened
   4 cups confectioners' sugar
   4–5 tbsp lemon juice

- Cream the butter and sugar. Add lemon juice one tablespoon at a time until desired consistency is achieved. Add a few drops of yellow food color if you feel like it.

Peanut Butter Blossoms

Peanut butter cookies are a whiff of sugary childhood. Easy to make, fun to embellish, and one of the few cookies that boast that extra bonus of protein. (That makes them healthy, right?) Baking with children is also a great way to find out what's on their minds. As Janie and Dylan make Peanut Butter Blossoms, Dylan suggests that they bring the cookies to Keane. Janie asks why he hasn't been sitting with Keane at camp.

Dylan pressed a cookie too hard and it splayed out over the edge of the baking sheet. "I felt bad to him."

"What did you feel bad about?" Janie picked up the smashed batter and rolled it into a ball again.

"His mom scared you, and you yelled and he cried, and I was very not happy."

Janie studied the wad of dough. "That happens sometimes. People don't always get along."

"So I guess we should just eat the cookies all ourselves."

She sighed. *Pology Cookies,* she thought, *a first.*

   ½ cup white sugar
   ½ cup packed brown sugar
   ½ cup peanut butter
   ¼ cup vegetable shortening

¼ cup butter, softened

1 egg

1 ¼ cups flour

¾ tsp baking soda

½ tsp baking powder

¼ tsp salt

1 bag of chocolate Kisses, unwrapped

- Beat sugars, peanut butter, shortening, and butter together until smooth.
- Mix in remaining ingredients. Cover and refrigerate at least 3 hours.
- Preheat oven to 375 degrees.
- Shape dough into 1-inch balls and place on ungreased cookie sheet.
- Flatten in crisscross pattern with a fork dipped in white sugar.
- Bake until just starting to brown, 8–10 minutes.
- Press a chocolate Kiss into the middle of each cookie.
- Remove from cookie sheet and cool. Makes about 3 dozen cookies.

Struffoli

My little Italian grandmother made struffoli every Christmas. She would yell at us for picking them out of the bowl with our fingers. One year, I led a revolt of the grandchildren and encouraged them all to grab a handful right in front of her. She laughed her head off. Grandma appreciated a certain amount of right-back-atcha.

Unfortunately, I never got her recipe. Actually, I'm quite certain she didn't have one, at least not written down. My aunt and I once tried to get her recipe for tomato sauce, and all the measurements were something akin to "enough salt to fill the lines in the palm of your hand." When we mentioned that our lines might be different from her lines, she just shrugged. Our problem, not hers.

What follows is my best guess about how she made struffoli. It doesn't quite look like hers, but it tastes good, and she would be pleased that I made the effort. Also, she would love the idea that Janie gave them to Tug as an apology. Grandma was tough, but also deeply romantic.

With the bowl of struffoli in her hands, Janie felt like Oliver Twist, begging for gruel.

2 cups flour
1 tsp baking powder
¼ cup white sugar
4 eggs
2 tsp vegetable oil
1 tsp white vinegar
1 tsp vanilla
vegetable oil for frying
½ cup honey, warmed
candy sprinkles

- Mix dry ingredients together in a bowl. Add liquid ingredients except oil for frying and honey.
- Knead well until smooth and pliable. Add more flour if needed.
- Roll pieces of dough into ½ inch ropes. Cut into ½ inch pieces. They'll look like little pillows.
- Pour enough oil into a frying pan to generously cover the bottom. Heat to medium high.
- Place the little pieces of dough in the hot oil, leaving enough room to flip and roll them around.
- In a minute or two they should be golden brown. Remove with a slotted spoon or spatula and place on paper towels to drain off excess oil.
- Place in a bowl and drizzle warmed honey over them, tossing to coat evenly. Add candy sprinkles.
- As an alternative, you can make a mixture of cinnamon and confectioners' sugar to sprinkle over it, however, I must warn you that my grandmother would not approve.

The muscles in his abdomen relaxed, and she felt herself sinking lower into him. She slid down to his side, curling herself to the contour of his body.

"Hey," he whispered against the top of her head. "What's this about apology cake? I get the feeling it's something I'm gonna need to know."

"I'll tell you tomorrow," she yawned.

Drowsiness settled on them and they slept.

Shelter Me Goes Out the Window

My great friend Megan Lucier has been a consistently excellent editor for me since I first began writing. Not only has she peppered me with solid insights, suggestions, questions, and challenges to my drafts, she has also been a terrific cheerleader, demanding that I keep churning out those subsequent chapters so she can find out what happens next. Every writer should have a Megan in their lives.

Which is why it was more than a little surprising when she threw the manuscript for *Shelter Me* out the window.

She would beg to differ, of course. She would say it was sucked out.

I had made many changes to the first draft, and asked her to take a fresh look at it. I printed off the several hundred pages, hole punched them, put them in a nice binder, and even attached a new red pen with a ribbon tied to one of the clasps. She read it over the summer and made countless notes. Well, she said she made countless notes. I never actually saw them.

She and her husband were on their way to a wedding in northern Vermont, driving up I–89 at what could be considered near-felonious speeds. They were late; she said it was his fault, he said it was hers. Again, I wasn't there, I wouldn't know. But since they were barely speaking to each other, Megan figured it was a good opportunity to put in some time on my manuscript.

As she read, a bee dropped out of her hair and onto the page. Quick to respond, she rolled down her window and attempted to toss the bee out, using my manuscript as a kind of shovel. Out went the bee, with the binder following quickly after. She screamed, scaring the heck out of her husband, Mark. He reports that when he glanced in the rearview mirror, it looked like a snowstorm in August, pages fluttering everywhere across the highway. A huge truck burst through the mess seconds later, the driver none too pleased at this bizarre exhibition of apparent road rage. At that speed, there was no way to pull over, of course, and even if they had, no way to pick up the pages without getting themselves killed. Besides, they were still late for the wedding.

She called me immediately from her cell phone, and we alternately laughed and yelled at each other. (Me: "Megan, how could you do this to me!?" Her: "It wasn't my fault! There was a bee! Mark was driving too fast!") I had this strange urge to race up there and rescue my poor orphaned pages, each with my name printed across the bottom, worried that someone might gather them up and use them for nefarious purposes. What those purposes might be I never was able to fully conjure, but I felt worried all the same. A book is like your child; you feel undeniably bound to protect it.

A week later I was traveling up this same road on my way to pick up my daughter from camp. I searched for those pages, having grilled Megan and Mark about the exact spot where it happened. There wasn't a trace, not even a fluttering scrap of white skittering along the breakdown lane to indicate that my poor novel had ever been dismembered there.

At this time I would like to offer my deepest apologies to the Vermont Highway Department. (I have a picture in my mind of a bunch of guys wearing fluorescent orange vests, saying, "Hey I got page 142, who's got 143?") I'm sorry for all the time you obviously spent cleaning up the mess. There's a Pology Cake with your names on it.

Juliette Fay received a bachelor's degree from Boston College and a master's degree from Harvard University. She lives in Massachusetts with her husband and four young children. *Shelter Me* is her first novel.

Juliette Fay